Acknowledgements

First and foremost, I am extremely grateful to you, dear reader!

Next: to my incredible parents, Robert and Noeleen Grace. You are always there for me and I appreciate you both more than I can tell you, every single day.

I Always Knew was inspired by the idea of true 'soul mates' – so thank you, Kevin, for being my muse. Love is not logical, it is of the soul. And the soul knows a thing or two . . .

To my adorable daughters, Grace and Maggie Cassidy, our greatest gifts EVER! We love you girls so, so, so, so much!

And to my extended family: Samantha, Niall, Mia and Zoe. Keith, Cillian, Olivia and Conor. Caroline, John, Jay and Ava. Colin, Angela and Rian and the best present-buying uncles Peadar and Damian. Kathleen Fogg, Linda and Michael and family, David, Marie and Paul Woodcock. Nicola, Nigel, Max and Nell Pawley. Aunt Maureen, Angela and Jimmy Darragh and family.

To Tara, Amy and Honour who take such heartfelt care of Maggie. Thanks to Miss Grant for guiding Grace so brilliantly through Senior Infants and to Julie and Joanna at The Learning Curve for her fantastic after-school care.

Big huge special thanks to Elaine Crowley and all the

wonderful panel of *Midday* women I have the pleasure of working with. I truly laugh so hard every day on the show my jaw aches.

To my fellow Smart Blondes and partners in my other passion, our film and television work – Sorcha Furlong, Sarah Flood and Elaine O'Connor. We are juggling it all, girls, so well done to us. I'm extremely proud of our work.

Extra special thanks to my Sarah Flood for being an early reader of *I Always Knew* and naming the book!

To Ciara Geraghty, Emma Hannigan, Caroline Finnerty and every single Irish author who I have the pleasure of now knowing! What a great bunch of supporters we are for each other.

To Barbara Scully and Fiona Looney . . . for the liquid lunches and great laughs. I feel blessed to have found two fabulous new friends in this . . . my late 20's . . . ;)

To all the brilliant buddies. Marina Rafter, Louise Murphy, Alison Canavan, Samantha Grace-Doyle, Susan Loughnane, Gail Brady, Amy Joyce Hastings, Leontia Ferguson, Claire Guest, Maeve Callan, Amy Conroy, Tara & Paul O'Brien, Maia Dunphy, Ciara O'Connor, Suzanne Kane, Lisa Carey, Karen McGrath, Jenny Barrett, Eimear Ennis Graham, Steve Wilson, Steve Gunn, Michael Scott, Graham Cantwell, Neil Bedford.

Special thanks to my agents MacFarlane Chard.

Thanks so much to all the lads at The Park Studio & Park Pictures who have worked with us on our films. I can't tell you how much we appreciate your expertise, time and effort – yes, I'm talking to you, Kevin Cassidy, Emmet Harte, Paul Power and Erik Clancy!

To Jeanne Baeur at Anu Jewellery in LA for teaching me

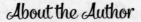

About the Author

Caroline Grace-Cassidy lives in Knocklyon in Dublin with a lovely husband and two beautiful daughters.

She is an actress, a Creative Director of Smart Blondes Productions and a panellist for *Midday* on TV3.

Her first two novels, *When Love Takes Over* and *The Other Side of Wonderful*, are published by Poolbeg. She is delighted to introduce you to her third novel.

Also by Caroline Grace-Cassidy

When Love Takes Over
The Other Side of Wonderful

Published by Poolbeg

about the art of jewellery-making and allowing me to be inspired by your amazing designs.

To Lya Solis who dresses me in her amazing creations whenever I ask!

To all at Poolbeg, huge heartfelt thanks. To Paula Campbell, David & Ailbhe and especially my editor Gaye Shortland who is the Charlie to my inner *Charlie's Angel*.

For my inspiration, Margaret Kilroy. I think about you every single day . . .

READERS!! Once again I reiterate, my biggest thank-you is to every one of you who will read this novel and who bought *When Love Takes Over* and *The Other Side of Wonderful*. Your comments and feedback are so important to me so please do drop me a line through my website www.carolinegracecassidy.com or through the Facebook link www.facebook.com/AuthorCarolineGraceCassidy or Twitter@CGraceCassidy

I hope you enjoy *I Always Knew*.

All my love and thanks

Caroline x

For Kevin Cassidy, for everything

PROLOGUE

Down, down in my bones
Somewhere I'd never have known,
Right at the back of my head
It hit me like a beam of light,
Hit me like a hook of the right
And I could have fell to the floor

'Cause you talk to me and it comes off the wall
You talk to me and it goes over my head
So let's go to bed before you say something real
Let's go to bed before you say how you feel

'Cause it's you,
Oh it's always you
Oh I always knew

'I Always Knew' (The Vaccines)

June 2012, Dublin City

"He's playing with you, Beth!" Alice wagged her bitten fingernail furiously at me before curling it at an incredibly awkward angle to chew some more. (It was probably Alice's only bad habit.) She studied the abused nail, her breath heavy, then dropped her hand onto her lap. "I can't believe you right now." She narrowed her eyes. "What on earth are you playing at? You know only too well what he's like. Honestly, it's like I don't know you at all any more!" She spat the bitten nail now, very discreetly I must add, from the corner of her mouth, in a temper, and then chewed some more.

We were sitting under the huge gleaming window of Bruxelles bar off Grafton Street, staring at our untouched pints of Guinness and Raspberry. The pints sat dead centre of the scuffed oak table on two black-and-white *Guinness is Good for You* beer mats. No bubbles floating merrily to the top. Deadly still – like two anxious soldiers standing to attention. People in dark shades shuttled quickly past the window in the sticky warm Dublin lunch hour.

3

I went on the defensive. I had no other choice.

"So what, Alice? Shut up about it, will you? God, I'm almost sorry I told you. I'm a big girl and I went into all of this with my eyes wide open. Don't . . . just don't lecture me any more, please. I can't take it. I just don't need it from you. I feel bad enough about myself already." I leaned in to pick up my pint, but instead turned to her again. "You don't know the full story so you really shouldn't judge – this is so unlike you!" I flung my hands rather dramatically up in the air through sheer frustration and my bracelet flew across the bar.

I jumped up but Alice pulled me down by my wrist and eased herself out of the well-worn, soft brown-leather seat to retrieve the bracelet for me. She knew it was my favourite. The very first real piece of jewellery I had ever made. It was a charm bracelet. Four sterling-silver charms, slightly tarnished as they were all so old. I had searched all over Dublin for the oldest, most worthless and loneliest charm pieces I could find. Pieces that felt and looked like I did. Pieces that nobody wanted. Broken pieces. I only wanted four pieces so I could space them out. Give them more room on my arm to be even more isolated. They couldn't touch off each other. Zero contact. It had been made with pure heart, through gushing tears, running snot and furious anger, and I wore it every single day. It was a part of me now. We had been through so much together. I whispered thanks to Alice as I slipped my wrist back though the loose silver links. There was never a mark on my skin from where the bracelet had sat. It would never hurt me. It was a bit like Alice to me, an old precious friend who was always there (although I'm not so sure Alice would like the 'old' comparison).

Alice was shaking her head now as she sighed heavily again. I hated it when Alice was upset with me and I knew I'd more than upset her right now. I stared out the window, seeing nothing. The big bright clear-blue sky I always craved was up there but I couldn't even imagine it. It was all too normal. I fiddled with the charms to avoid any more conversation.

The truth was, I didn't really go into it with my eyes wide open. I mean, the truth was, if I could have taken it back and rewound the previous night I would have. At least I thought I would. I knew I should. The truth was, I didn't really know myself. I was so confused. I knew I deserved to feel like this. Yes, I was a complete and utter bitch but I was also a complete and utter naive eejit, a silly romantic fool, and yes, I only had myself to blame. No matter what way I looked at the situation I knew I'd put myself back years.

I reached forward and clasped my fingers around the heavy pint. I lifted it and gently swirled it around, the combination of black meeting red giving me inspiration for a new piece. I was thinking a thick black velvet choker with tight blood-red seed beading. Almost masochistic. Uncomfortable but stunning. I took a long bittersweet mouthful.

But no. I swallowed the liquid down hard. The real truth was this. I just honestly couldn't help my feelings. I was out of control where he was concerned. Always was, always would be. I needed to accept that.

I, Beth Burrows, was a fake.

Chapter One

1 month earlier, a very warm month of May, 2012, Dublin City

Beth

"I can't believe I'm taking pictures of you in an actual wedding dress and we're not even planning one of our crazy Charles Dickens fancy-dress parties!"

I scrolled my index finger speedily across the dozen or so iPhone pictures I'd snapped of my best friend Alice, in the couture Vera Wang frocks.

I was itchy. My Oxfam T-shirt had a bit of a plastic tag still sticking out of it into my neck but I'd scratched three times already and I was likely to be thrown out if I attempted one more scratch. They were watching. There was no sign that read *'Scratching Is Prohibited'* or anything like that but I could read between the lines. I wriggled my neck and shoulders around as I watched the images become a moving film.

I had whispered my Charles Dickens quip to Alice through the rich thick green-velvet dressing-room curtains, from my too-low and very uncomfortable mushroom-shaped footstool, in a respectful hushed tone – the type of tone this showroom expected of one. If you shouted in here someone could die. The tinkling background music was so low it was almost inaudible. I didn't see, or should I say hear, the point. A bit of Billy Idol's 'White Wedding' blaring out would get women much more in the mood to buy.

"This day, four weeks, on June sixteenth, you will be Mrs O'Toole. You will be a missus, Alice, someone's missus. Can you believe that? I still can't. Young fellas can yell at you in the street: '*Here, missus, get's a pack of twenty blues, will ya, alright?*'" I said this last bit in the voice of *Love/Hate's* Nidge. I did a pretty good impression and I shocked myself. She made a chortle sort of sound behind the curtain and I knew she was beaming from ear to ear.

Now don't get me wrong – it's not that Alice was a romantic-chortley-beamy type of girl, you understand (nobody's mad about beamy girls, are they really?) but it is hard not to beam when you're looking at yourself in a Vera Wang creation.

I stared at the row of dresses twirling delicately from bright golden hangers on an even brighter golden rail. Each one like a prima ballerina, in warm-up before the opening night of *Swan Lake* at the Bolshoi Theatre. All expertly crafted. Luxurious and exquisite. Detailed to perfection. Blood, sweat and tears had gone into creating these masterpieces.

Alice stepped out again. I screwed my face up like I had just seen a newborn puppy rubbing wet noses with its mother.

I had just read about this dress in the Vera Wang book on the table. A gorgeous strapless gown this time that fused yards and yards of shadow and Chantilly lace,

8

blossoming into a chrysanthemum organza skirt, with a thick black ribbon under the bust. It was the Naomi Campbell of dresses. Uniquely beautiful.

Obviously there was no way Alice was ever buying one of these insanely expensive dresses but, ever since Vera Wang opened in Dublin years back, every Irish bride felt a compelling desire to go and try them on, just so she could say, "I don't even like any of them!" or "Even if I had the money, I honestly wouldn't buy it!"

Alice made a face as she stared at her reflection, pulled at the black ribbon identifying it to me as the culprit, and stepped back inside the changing area (it wasn't a room – it was an area).

There was a huge sense of relief or indeed barefaced lying involved, depending on what the mirror revealed to you. The sales assistants must drop to their spindly knees and bounce slightly on the thick spongy carpet whenever they hear the magic, rare words: 'It's perfect. I'll take it!' Then, their thin blue-veined arms outstretched and shaking, they must take the precious plastic and cradle its tiny angular shape to their enhanced busts like a newborn baby (giving the plastic just as much care and attention), running their ten-inch nails over the row of little magic numbers, caressing each minute pop-out number individually.

I stared again at the pictures of Alice Callan. She'd been my best friend since we were fourteen years old. She looked stunning. Alice always looked stunning. Alice just simply was stunning. Alice looked stunning that time she had gastroenteritis. Alice always looked stunning with the severest of no-sleep-at-all hangovers. Alice was blessed with that flawless sallow skin that allowed you to look the same with or without make-up, that dark-brown glossy-textured mane (so much of it) and those perfect petite features of hers. Luckily she was my friend or I'd probably have hated her guts.

She was marrying the equally wonderful Dan O'Toole next month and I was her chief bridesmaid. I don't know why she kept calling me her 'chief' bridesmaid though as I was the only one.

And I had not one ounce of jealousy that Alice was getting married (what? honestly!). I must admit I adored her Dan O'Toole almost as much as she did. He was such a man's man, yet kind and sweet, and he completely and utterly adored Alice, as I wanted him to. Dan was the type of guy who everyone just wanted to hang out with. Totally chilled. He was just so easygoing, relaxed and sunny. The best way to sum him up was that Dan just loved life. When in his company the time always flew by. He only saw the good in people. He was really tall, built like a brick shithouse, with red hair and red stubble. He always wore black jeans with sloganned T-shirts, was a truck driver from Cork and told it like it was. Dan also had full custody of his incredible four-year-old daughter Lucy and was an amazing father. Lucy's mother had handed her over to Dan when she was a mere six days old and they had never had any contact with her again. She had simply vanished from their lives. *Poof!* Dan had been Lucy's hands-on primary carer from that day on. When he'd show us photos from Lucy's first year it was enough to break your heart – and, boy oh boy, did he have albums of them! Dan making up the bottles, chaotic countertops, his face covered with formula, three tea towels thrown over one shoulder, multi-coloured baby vests scattered like ice-cream sprinkles all over the place, tired black-bagged eyes – but still, in every photo he was smiling pure love at his daughter. Dan, with Lucy on his chest, asleep on the laundry-piled kitchen floor (taken by his dad in their home in Cobh). If it wasn't for the ginger hair he could easily have been the BabyBjorn-carrier model. Not that I didn't love ginger hair but I'd never seen a ginger-haired model playing the part of a BabyBjorn dad.

The little girl adored her daddy and with very good reason. In all the time Alice had been dating Dan I had never ever seen him lose his temper with Lucy or even say a cross word to her. It helped no doubt that Lucy was the most obedient kid I had ever known. She was simply adorable. It was as though she knew Dan had enough on his plate.

Lucy's mother had suffered from an alcohol problem apparently and Dan wouldn't say a bad word about her. She was "a poor, abused, sick girl" was all he would say on the subject. I was fascinated and wanted to know more about her but he pursed his lips any time I probed further and shook his head slowly. "Nothing more to say, Beth – like, she was a poor, abused, sick girl." Alice knew more about her but Alice was oh so loyal. You told Alice a secret and you knew it went to her grave with her, so I knew better than to ask her. Alice was going to be an amazing mother to Lucy. She had been in their lives for the last eighteen months and was simply besotted with them both. She had become an instant mother to the then two-and-a-half-year-old Lucy – immediately giving up her job as a clothes buyer for a unique online boutique, Rock Fountain, to take care of the little girl full time. "A dream job," Alice called her new role.

Alice had met Dan in the Phoenix Park when she had picked up a soother Lucy had thrown from her pink buggy. It had been a cold dark winter's day. Alice had been struck by how cosy the little girl was in her buggy, wrapped up from head to toe. Coat, hat, mittens, earmuffs. So well looked after. "How cute!" Alice had said as Dan sucked on the soother himself to clean it and then at the same time they had both said: "Snug as a bug in a rug!" They had laughed as Alice bent down and tickled the little girl under the chin and then walked on with her brisk strides. Dan and the buggy quickly followed and fell into step beside her. Then his elbow had rubbed off her arm and Alice said the sun had suddenly come out. I had no reason not to believe her.

But she hadn't changed. She was still Alice. I don't know how she did it. My mother kept telling me "Aah, now that's the end of you and Alice!" *Sniff.* "You'll never see her again." *Sniff.* "She's gone and left you behind now, so no more sharing that – what's it the pair of ye used to share now – oh yeah, The Fear – well, you won't be sharin' yer fear any more either." *Sniff.* "Maybe it's time you thought about marriage and babies too, I won't be this fit forever, you know." *Sniff.*

My relationship with Alice hadn't changed one bit except she was more loving and open to me than ever before. Alice wasn't the kind of girl who changed, you see. She grew constantly, she evolved, but her values never changed.

She was allowing me to wear a *normal* dress, thank God. I wasn't really a dressy-dress kind of girl. I was mostly jeans and T-shirts and maybe a nice suit jacket to smarten it up. (*Blazer*, I hear Alice correct me in my thoughts.) I had good legs (even if I do say so myself) so I usually wore skinny jeans tucked into high-heeled boots if I was going out in the evening (when I say 'high', I mean a bit of a chunky heel or a wedge. Stilettos hated me and I hated them right back, evil bastards). Otherwise I wore everything with Converse runners. I had a huge crush on Converse runners, any colour, any design, any style. Old or new, I wanted them all. Especially the designs for babies. Oh, how I drooled over Baby Converse! If I'm perfectly honest I thought they were cuter than the newborns they looked so damn cute on! I have been known to stare into shop windows at them for a hypnotic amount of time. Don't even get me started on the smell. They warm me up inside.

Okay, so that's me and Converse. What else should I mention? Oh, yes – my stomach area wasn't my best feature. I had let it go over the last couple of years and quite frankly I accepted it was gone forever – let's just say Gwen Stefani would never lose any sleep over me – so loose one-shoulder T-shirts were items I always scoured shops for. I liked the one-bare-shoulder look a lot. I liked the curve of my own shoulder.

So that was my basic wardrobe, and Alice understood I was a basic kind of girl.

I had seen a dress I loved in Brown Thomas already. (This was so unlike me.) It was a soft full-length pale-pink halter-neck in a ruffled material. Very Grace Kelly, I thought. I had tried it on four times and I had stared at myself, delighted. Listen, I was no fool. I was well aware of the flattering oh-so-soft lighting up above (why do you think I tried it on so many times?). I pulled my long wavy strawberry-blonde hair up into a bun and pouted at myself. My green eyes crinkled back at me, not in a cute way but in an you're-getting-old-skin-love type of way, so I stopped the pouting and just stared. My mother was convinced I was born with blue eyes but they turned green when I was in primary school. She always said this in an accusatory manner, as though I was somehow to blame. They could be luminous neon pink for all I cared – it didn't matter to me once I could see. I was pretty enough – I knew that. I wasn't a total ride like Alice by any means but I wasn't unsightly either. I had an oval face and large dimples which I wasn't mad about but which I was always complimented on. To me they looked like two big holes in my face when I smiled. Once, while I sat perfectly still in front of her bedroom mirror, Alice carefully and painstakingly filled them in with green Plasticine, then doubled up laughing. I liked the look as I felt slightly Hulky. "*Don't make me angry. You wouldn't like me when I'm angry!*" I said, turning to her, trying to talk and keep the Plasticine intact, thereby managing to sound unbelievably like Dr David Banner. Alice said she peed. Slightly. A dribble.

Anyway, with the effort put in on a good day, I knew I could look well. It's just that the effort to me was just that: effort.

I'd need feck-off heels of course. Alice was a lover of Jimmy's shoes. Apparently Jimmy's shoes were sky high. Jimmy knew shoes, Alice assured me. She was gobsmacked I didn't know Jimmy. Sure I barely knew any lads. Jimmy was God, she informed me. Good for Jimmy, I said back.

Yes, I could do with losing a pound or two on the ole stummy – who couldn't, though, right? I mean, even women who don't need to lose a pound or two think they do. We are brainwashed by the flat stummy. But the dress was pretty good on me otherwise. I sucked in hard and stood tall on my tippy toes. (I always remembered reading an interview with Joan Collins in the hairdresser's where she said she sucked in her stomach twelve hours a day. That's how she trained her stomach muscles. Surely, Joan, life is simply too short?)

Alice stirred me from my Alexis Carrington shoulder-padded daze. She pulled back the thick velvet drape, dressed now in her navy pencil skirt and cream blouse. The curtain's gold cord was swinging slowly from side to side like a pendulum awaiting a life-changing decision. Alice shook her head, impressively sadly I might add, at the assistant who didn't even look up. She was poring over a glossy magazine, one of those that people paid crazy money for just to look at advertisements. I never got it.

"Even if I had the money I wouldn't buy it!" Alice whispered into my ear, spitting slightly with the excitement of it.

I rubbed my ear and we grabbed our bags and, rather guiltily, softly bounced out of the lemon-zested showroom.

We linked arms as we always do without realising it. Apparently the very first day we walked to secondary school together I linked her arm. We were the exact same height back then. We had met at the pedestrian crossing at the end of our road and smiled at each other. We had never seen one another before that morning. It was an instant connection. I thought she linked my arm but she was adamant it was the other way round, so I just chose to believe her. I usually just chose to believe Alice as she had a way better memory than me. Alice could tell me the type of veil I wore to my Communion from old pictures I'd shown her, Alice knew more about me than I knew about myself.

We headed straight down Grafton Street for River Island and unlinked at the double doors and went our separate ways as we always did. Me to the jeans and T's and her to the dresses and skirts. We never talked about how long we would be or where we would meet up – we were always finished at the same time and just walked into each other – it was amazing. Dan was truly baffled by this any time he came shopping with us.

Believe it or not, Dan enjoyed shopping with us. He'd sit and grin as we rummaged and tried on. "Fascinating environment," he'd tell us afterwards. One evening in the pub he even said, interrupting a conversation about the American Tea Party movement: "Alice, I was thinking, that knee-length mauve dress on the sale rail in Top Shop would be a good buy – you're right. We do have two weddings next year and couldn't you dress it up with maybe those high red shoes ya have, add a pop of vibrant colour?" He rubbed his beard as a top designer might rub his, arty-like. The table fell silent. I stared at the engraved *Bob Loves Noeleen* in the table. Alice smiled at him and said in a low but serious tone: "Dan, I think you're coming shopping with myself and Beth too often – it's simply not right – time to take a back seat, buddy." He pulled at his beard and said, "Duly noted, my love."

I stood back now at a red-signposted sale rail against the back wall of the shop as girls manoeuvred each other out of the way, fierce yet polite. I saw a sleeveless navy T-shirt I liked with a black dragon down the side and swooped in just as a stunning peroxide-blonde-head put her hand on it. I won.

"Oopps!" I smiled at her.

"Is dere ownleeee wan, d'ya tink?" she asked me, dragging every word out oh so slowly in the voice of Darth Vader – with the face of a younger uncut Brigitte Nelson. "Eh, I'm not sure, hun," I replied. I have no idea why I called her 'hun'.

She blinked three times very slowly at me. "Are ya gonna try dat on, den?"

I nodded, palms beginning to sweat as I clutched the plastic hanger too tightly.

"D'ya tinkyer gonna buy dat, den?" she said heavily.

I nodded. "Yeah, probably, it's eh . . . well, eh . . . it's the kind of thing I really like . . ." I stuttered back. I was wishing Dan was there – damn Alice and her shopping embargo – he'd have got a great laugh out of this scene.

"Be hiphoppin' on ya, I'd'magine," she drawled.

It was hard to listen to her, the words left her mouth so slowly.

"Well . . . absolutely . . . thank you . . . so nice to meet you," I managed and I backed away from the oh-so-scary one and headed to the dressing room.

I entered the cruel mirrored box and pulled my Oxfam-bought old red Levi vintage T-shirt over my head.

Suddenly my mouth was dry again and I was feeling out of my own body. I knew why only too well as the image of *him* engulfed my mind's eye. Every day, these last six months, ever since Alice had told me she was getting married, it had preyed on my mind.

John. John. John. John would be home.

17

Her brother John. My ex-boyfriend John – and pretty much the-guy-who-had-danced-all-over-my-heart-and-my-head John.

John had destroyed me. Oh, listen, I had moved on. Of course I had. Sure I'd been going out with Rory for almost a year and a half now.

I couldn't get my head through the neck of the dragon T-shirt. I pulled it back off, agonisingly catching both my ears, and turned it inside out to see the tag: 6. It was a 6. A bloody Size 6. The number of the devil. No wonder it was on the sale rail. It should have come with a warning: "*Beware! Likely to rip the ears off your head and make you feel like a pregnant elephant.*" I flung it over the dressing-room door and pulled my own T-shirt back on. Was there anything worse than trying on clothes that didn't fit? The wasted energy totally exasperated me. It put me right off shopping.

Anyway . . . Rory. Here's something I wrote in an old notebook some months before, God knows why: "*Yes, Rory and I, we have a life together. We have shared days, weeks and months. I pee in front of him. I wipe in front of him. I eat spaghetti bolognese without dabbing my mouth after every single bite in front of him. I occasionally do long loud burps in front of him. I never fart. That's just not me. But I do let Rory see me in a way I'd be mortified if any other person saw me. Bare. We are happy as Larry. As content as Conor. We are as comfortable as two peas in a pod or wherever they live nowadays, in PC organic terms. (I don't like to offend.) Well, we still don't live together but we will, eventually, I'm sure.*"

But John . . . Not only did John Callan dance all over

me but he went to New York to follow his dream. He became an actor. A very successful actor at that. Over there – not over here, thank God. I had to look at him in magazines every now and then though. The Irish media had a small interest in him. He was a bona fide television star in the US. Okay, so I Googled him a lot too. I had to, it was a compulsion. I also checked his agent's website a lot for updates and news on him. To be fair, I did it less and less lately but I was still not normal where John was concerned. Put it this way: if a mother called after her child "*John!*" in the market, my heart leapt out of my chest. If I saw the word *John* in a book I traced my finger lovingly over the four perfect letters. Even the two letters O and N shook me. Have you any idea how many times the word ON appears in any given day? I sometimes just mouthed the shape of the word to myself before I fell asleep.

Alice had been really upset when John and I got together in the first place. "But you are *my* friend!" was her bloody good argument. I had asked him along to my college final Christmas party, as a friend, and we had kissed. To be honest, never in my wildest dreams had I thought he would have any interest in me – I just wanted other people in my year to *think* he had. I was in the final year of my Arts degree. I was older than most of the other girls at twenty-six. I had bummed around working part-time in an Art Supplies shop after school before resitting my Leaving Cert and deciding I needed a degree in something. I was always one of those people who never really knew what they wanted to do. Mind-blowing frustration. Anyway, John Callan was the type of guy that, when growing up, schoolgirls had doodled his name on their journals, on their khaki canvas schoolbags, all day every day. He was the pin-up of the area. I had almost fainted as his perfect hands found my face that night and I smelt the leather from the sleeves on his black biker jacket. He had teased me with his lips inches close and stayed there for an age before moving in, slipping his tongue softly between my lips and parting them, his dark stubble wonderfully painful. It was an incredible kiss as he explored my mouth slowly with his tongue and bit down not so gently on my bottom lip. I actually staggered as we parted but lied after and told him it was because I was so hammered. Cupid's arrow hadn't just found me with a bull's eye, it had pole-axed me. He liked me right back. I sensed it. I suppose I had always sensed it but never in an I-want-to-ride-you-sideways type of way. I made him laugh. He thought I was clever. I didn't even have to try hard. He just got me. He liked my mind. Most likely because never in my wildest dreams had I thought he could ever fancy me so I was just me around him. I was always myself.

John was completely and utterly sexy, totally perfectly gorgeous, smart, witty, clever, funny, kind, generous, charming and dangerous. He drank too much. He ate cigarettes (not literally but you know what I mean). He had dropped out of school at seventeen just ten days before he was due to sit the Leaving Certificate. He painted weird shit and wrote really awfully vulgar poems. He was all about the Art. I completely adored him. He took all sort of strange classes at night and during the day he *observed* people. He would sit outside coffee shops for hours, drinking black coffee and rolling cigarettes and just watching people. He called himself an *observationalist* sometimes. If we were out at a party, or just meeting new people and someone asked John what he did for a living he would say in a very posh voice: "Thank you for asking, my good man," (or 'my good woman' depending). "I am proud to tell you I am in fact an *observationalist*." Then he would stand perfectly still and silent as the other person, confused, digested this and then he'd smile, a little madly, and walk off with a pretend limp. I couldn't really understand this but then again I didn't want to. I didn't need to. I just loved him. Every inch of him. I loved the uncertainty of what he was about. No matter how many times I kissed him it was always like the first time. He charged me with the chemistry. He was fearless. He never really worked, as in earned any money, but he was constantly busy creatively. Of course John had an amazing body, did you really need to ask? He was perfect. Speckles of dark hair on his chest. Same sallow skin as Alice's – caramel skin. John had a natural six-pack and the area from his hip bones down to his . . . well, it was taut and sexy as hell. At six foot he was a clotheshorse. He wore clothes like a Tom Ford model (or indeed like Tom Ford himself). He didn't do gyms but he liked to run. John was super fit. He'd sometimes get up at three o'clock in the morning and run up and down an empty Grafton Street. "At night Grafton Street can be all yours – it can be your street," he used to tell me.

A model scout called Crispin Smart once approached us in the Garden of Remembrance when we were sitting on the grass eating a Leo Burdock's between us, completely drenched in vinegar the way we liked it, and gave John his card to come by and do some test shots. I was more than surprised when John, licking his fingers very slowly, told him he'd be there the next morning first thing. John did indeed go along at ten o'clock wearing his mother's best Sunday outfit – a beige linen dress and beige cardie, red fishnets (they were mine from an old fancy-dress party), a straw hat and orange wedges – smoking a massive cigar. I literally cried laughing outside the pebble-dashed, white-bricked, trendy model office. They threw him out. He stood outside for ages, holding his middle finger up to their window. I went around the corner to Centra and got us two cans of Lilt and a Twix to share while he stood there.

"You look stupid, Mr Smart!" he called out over and over again. "I think you're a really stupid man, Mr Smart!" He kept this up for over half an hour.

I was becoming increasingly uncomfortable and was glad when at last he decided to take my advice and walk away.

He always wore loose, low-hung jeans with the same old vintage brown belt and gold buckle his granddad had left to him, and tight (but not *too* tight) T-shirts. He wore dirty Converse. I once washed them and he lifted me out of it. He had silky floppy jet-black hair that never sat in the same position and dark stubble and the darkest widest eyes I'd ever seen. When he focused those dark brown eyes on you it was as though you were the only person in the world. I had been known to drown in his eyes for long periods of time. His eyebrows were dark and bushy and angry. His skin was so dewy I sometimes licked his face just because I could. Everyone wanted him. Everyone didn't get him. I did. Girls in college would shake their heads as we kissed passionately on the campus outside the little Spar shop. "How did *she* get him?" they would hiss and hitch their skirts a little higher. I openly encouraged all women to do this as this kind of behaviour was typical of the type of women John Callan honestly wasn't attracted to. He liked androgynous women. John always told me I really reminded him of Claire Danes from *My So-Called Life*. His first ever crush. In fairness to Claire she'd moved on since then, won Emmys and Golden Globes for *Temple Grandin* and *Homeland* and the like, but John never watched her in anything else but *My So-Called Life*. He wasn't loyal like that.

To be honest, I don't think most girls could have put up with him. He was fierce moody and had dark days where he just wouldn't speak. He could quite literally cut you in two with a simple comment. I could handle him.

Anyway, why am I telling you all this? It really is old, old news. So he dumped me after five fantastic years, eight electric months, and three tumultuous days. I collapsed. I crumbled. I won't lie. A part of me died a painful death. He went to America. I gave up my latest job as a PA to a theatre director and went back to college to study fine art and jewellery-making. It was, at long last, what I'd finally realised I had always wanted to do. I had sort of figured it out after my Arts degree but I had taken the PA job to pay our rent. I closed our silver hand-painted door on our Temple Bar apartment, got my own apartment in Ranelagh, established a little life for myself and tried to move on. I had finally set up my own jewellery business which I'd christened 'Beth's Bitz'. I was now a full-time jewellery designer and for the first time in my life I loved my work. I was a creative self-employed woman and it suited me. John had always been inspired by his daily use of the Steve Jobs' quote: "*The only way to do great work is to love what you do. If you haven't found it yet keep looking.*

Don't settle. As with all matters of the heart you'll know when you find it. " I had, at long last, found it in my work.

I had never met anyone who I even remotely liked since John until I met Rory. I had been on a few dates that had mainly been set up by Alice and Dan and I had despised every one. "You need a good man, Beth," Dan used to tell me, dragging me into one of his massive bear hugs. "A gorgeous woman like you should be happy in her heart – look at me and Alice – we are blessed." They went on and on and on at me so much that eventually I gave in just to shut the pair of them up for a while.

One date I went on, the guy – don't even ask me his name as I have totally blocked it from my memory – anyway, him with the brown-leather patches on the elbows of his Aran jumper and his thick black woolly Bally socks in his white scuffed slip-on shoes. He who brought a notepad and pencil and did a checklist while we ate our starters. We met in Manty Moo's, a new restaurant on the seafront in Dun Laoghaire.

"No point in going out on a number two if we aren't compatible, wha'?" he snorted as he bit down on his fork way harder then he needed to.

Clink. I winced.

"Have you seen *Moneyball*?" he accused more than asked, I thought, so I said no.

I was wrong. I should have said yes.

He clicked his tongue and looked very disappointed in me. "You have to rent it. In. Cred. A. Bul. It's all about the maths, you see. Life is all about the maths, wha'?"

Clink. The sound of the metal clinking off his teeth made my eyes shut tight. It was involuntary. I pushed my prawns in filo around my plate. I never thought food had a place on dates.

"So, Elizabeth . . ." He licked the lead of the pencil three times, lizard-like.

"It's Beth." I feebly raised my hand to correct him, my charm bracelet rattling.

"I don't do abbreviations, chicky, wha'?" Bite. *Clink*. Rattle of teeth. He put his fork down but not before his index finger had a good rummage in his back molars.

I tightened the cream bobbin in my high ponytail. I pulled it so tight it hurt. It felt good. I had spent ages straightening and styling my pony-tail and now I hated myself for the wasted time.

"First things first: you definitely don't got no sprogs, do you? I know Desperate Dan said no but I have to double-check. I was caught out on this little chestnut before, wha'?" He pointed the wet pencil at me now accusingly.

I shook my head. He nodded. I stared at the brown-leather pads, wondering how the hell Desperate Dan thought this guy was a runner – or even a crawler. As for Alice, she couldn't possibly ever have met him.

He ticked his page. He lifted his fork. I couldn't take it. I hummed loudly. Unfortunately it was the *Jaws* theme tune. He stared hard at me.

"Excuse me?" His fork dangled, prawn hanging on for dear life as the rocket now slowly began to jump to its own imminent death.

I envied the rocket. Understood its pain.

"Just humming." I grabbed my wine and downed it in one go. Could I not just get up and leave? Couldn't I just say: 'Hey, listen, pal, this is a total nightmare for me. I'd rather be in the transatlantic queue for Dublin airport at

JFK on Christmas Eve, surrounded by babies with the winter vomiting bug whose parents are all phlegm-coughers.' Apparently not.

Bite. *Clink*. Rattle. I took a long deep breath.

"You don't have any mentaller-type issues, do you, wha'?"

Okay, time up. I grabbed the passing waiter by the belt-loop on the back of his black well-ironed trousers, almost toppling him over, and ordered a second bottle. Mercifully I don't remember Patchy Boy putting me into a taxi. I guess 'alcoholic' wasn't a requisite on his checklist. Wha'?

Alice took it on the chin for that date (though it turned out I was right and she hadn't actually screened the candidate) and both she and Dan promised to ease off on me.

So back to Rory. Rory had been browsing my jewellery stall in Blackrock market for a birthday present for his mother. He was all wrapped up in a green woolly hat and matching scarf and, with his oversized brown horn-rimmed glasses and green anorak, he looked the typical nerd.

"These are good," he managed to say through the howling winter wind as he picked up a necklace and actually held it up to his own scarf-wearing neck as he peered in my tiny IKEA mirror. (I had so many good mirrors stolen from the stall I just had a box of cheap IKEA ones now. It never ceased to amaze me the things people would steal. Once someone stole my emergency Tampax that I had sellotaped under the table)

"Thanks." I wrapped my navy-leather-gloved hands around my disposable plastic cup filled with hot chocolate from my *It's a Wonderful Life* movie flask. I was becoming immune to the cold.

"What is this made from then?" He sniffed.

26

"That particular piece is made with nickel and beading wire, amethyst beads and briolette interwoven."

I sipped my drink. The market was quiet today and I was looking forward to going home to my apartment, making a toasted ham-and-cheese sambo with thick white doorstep bread (bit of a scallion if I had any left) and opening a freezing cold can of Budweiser. I was also planning on having a cigarette later. I did that. I treated myself to the odd cigarette. That was the problem with running a stall outdoors. Everyone around me smoked. All day long. I loved to smoke but I was curtailing it nowadays. Both for my lungs and for my skin's sake. I have to be honest, what with the cold air, alcohol and wipes instead of cleanser and lack of SPF, my skin wasn't ageing quite as I had hoped. That one cigarette after dinner, before bed, at my open window, watching the late-night antics on the street – that was my downtime.

The horn-rimmed one spoke. "Go on, I'll take it!"

"Great! That's twenty-eight euro, please." I removed my glove from my right hand and pulled off one of my tiny cerise-pink paper bags from its string and popped the necklace inside. I used to wrap everything in wonderful soft tissue paper and bind it with my personalised '*Beth's Bitz*' silver stickers but I couldn't afford them any more.

"It's for my mam's birthday," he offered now.

"Oh cool, I hope she likes it. There's a bracelet to match?" I tried my best Alan Sugar. He shook his head. I didn't push. I was never getting on *The Apprentice*.

"You're Beth Burrows, aren't you?" He narrowed his big blue eyes behind the thick frames.

"Yeah." I nodded at him. "Do I know you?"

"No, but I saw an article on your work in last month's

Hot Press magazine while I was in the queue at The Grafton Barber – well, I go to the one in Jervis Street, it's less busy but it's called The Grafton Barber too, I guess they need to use the name because of its popularity even though – it's not – well, ya know – actually on Grafton Street . . . or . . . em . . ." He pushed his glasses so far up his nose his eyes were squashed behind them.

"Oh really, and you remembered me? You came to check my work out?" I sipped some more and bit gently on the rounded rim of the plastic. I had toyed with the idea of framing that article for the stall but in the end I figured it would be naff. I hated naff.

"Yeah, em, well, no. I didn't until I came in here. I came in to find the guy who sells the bonsai trees – I rather fancy one for my flat." He shuffled from one brown shoe to the other.

"Oh yeah, Big Brown Beanie Boy – he's gone – he decided to go to Thailand for a year with Bookstall Brenda and Saoirse the hand-knitted tea-cosy woman . . . you can get the trees in the Powerscourt Townhouse Centre though . . . well, actually, I have five – Beanie couldn't get rid of them – I'd be happy to give you one or two?" I took a breath.

"Brilliant – how much do you want for two?" he asked.

"They're all yours." I drained my hot chocolate and dumped the cup in my doubled old plastic Superquinn bin bag. It was holding up well. I emptied it into the market's metal bin every day. I missed Superquinn.

"Do you have them here?" he asked, peering over the stall as if I might have the bonsais tucked underneath it.

"No – they're at home. I haven't actually been trying to sell them."

"How can I get them from you?"

"Where do you live?" I moved around the stall and faced him now.

"Rathmines." He moved back an inch.

My spatial awareness with strangers had never been good. I rummaged in my jeans pocket and popped an Airwaves gum in my mouth, just in case.

"I'm only in Ranelagh. I'm opposite the rowing club – do you know it?"

"Yeah." He looked confused. "What, em, like, do you just want me to call in and get it? Get them?" he corrected himself quickly.

I thought about this as I looked at him closely, his blue eyes kind behind his glasses.

"Yeah, I'm sure that will be fine. I'm in all night tonight if you're around later?" I stared at a grass-stain on the white plastic tip of my dark-green Converse. Bastard, I cursed it silently.

"Cool." He needlessly pushed his specs back up his nose again. "What number?"

"Eight." Then I added, "Your mother isn't allergic to nickel, is she?" I never usually asked but I felt compelled to ask him for some reason.

"No, never heard her say that but she's allergic to tomatoes alright and turnip gives her wind," he answered thoughtfully. "I'm Rory by the way. Rory O'Dowd." He took his change and walked off.

So that was that. The start of our love story. No, there wasn't a piercing pain from Cupid's arrow as I fell dramatically to my knees or fireworks that made me gasp and applaud at the wondrous spectacular array of combined colours. There was calmness and an easy smile as I watched him walk away, carefully avoiding puddles, and I wondered if he would call in.

He did. He called for the trees that night just as I was sitting down to reruns of *The West Wing*. He was a freaky fan and began to say the script verbatim with Rob Lowe. I paused it. I hated when people did that. Did they just not get how utterly annoying it was? Rory took this as a sign I wanted to talk and he kicked off the brown numbers and curled his grey stocking feet under him on the couch and stayed chatting that night until two in the morning. When he removed his winter wear he'd revealed his brown closely shaved hair which was surprisingly trendy. He had a warm round face with high cheekbones and full pink lips. His blue puppy-dog eyes were uber-cute. Rory was my height and my build. We could have been related. He drank three of my cans of Budweiser and smoked three of my Silk Cut Blues that night. Like me he was a secret night-time smoker. He was complete and utter easy company. We clicked immediately. As friends, I mean. No sex.

Rory had a mobile-cinema business. It was very successful. Basically it was a large truck fitted with old cinema seats (from the old Stella cinema in Rathmines), a large screen, a popcorn machine and a minibar. He travelled all over the country with it. People hired it for kids' parties mostly but occasionally a porn film or two was shown for a stag party. He understood my pain with John as Martha, his ex, had pretty much performed the original Michael Flatley and Jean Butler Eurovision version of the *Riverdance* on him too. He had answered a call from Martha one evening and overheard the entire lovemaking session between her and his friend Boyler.

Martha had dialled poor Rory's number by accident in her pocket. Rory had sat on the cold metal steps of his mobile cinema and listened for twenty-six long minutes as his girlfriend and best friend roared out each other's names. To make matters worse they had both denied it. So painful.

For the first few weeks it was all we did. Talked about our exes. We were great for each other. It had been over a year since John dumped me and a year and a half since Martha dumped all over Rory so it wasn't a new thing to either of us. None of my friends even let me say the word 'John' any more so it was great to have freedom of speech again with this stranger.

Rory was so nice to be around and we liked the same things. We went to the movies (yes, sometimes in his van but mostly to the Savoy on O'Connell Street), we ate really cheap crisps like Chickatees and Burger Bites and bought kids' sweets like Refreshers and Love Hearts and Dip Dabs, we loved nachos with jalapeños and we drank beer and smoked our sly night-time cigarettes. We went for walks in Herbert Park. We looked at exhibitions of everything. We loved Sunday morning street art. We listened to The Frames and Crowded House and Fleetwood Mac. We helped each other.

We never kissed. We never talked about kissing. I never thought about kissing him. Until one night John's new TV show was premiering on Atlas TV. I was sitting alone at 8.58 p.m. with a bottle of wine (okay, it was a box of wine with a little black tap) and my tall silver ashtray.

The buzzer went. It was Rory with a single red rose and a shy smile.

"Don't do it, Beth," he said. "There's a Seth Rogen comedy on in the IFI – shall we?"

I took a breath. So Rory liked me. In that way. I'd kinda guessed. I took the rose. I pulled him in the door and my red Converse-clad foot with undone laces kicked it closed behind me. I ripped his hat off and then gently folded his glasses away and dropped them on the hall side table. I walked Rory down to my bedroom and had sex. It wasn't John. It was Rory. I was finally ready to move on.

Chapter Two

Rory and I were going out for dinner with my parents. It had to be done.

I did love my parents deeply but my dad could go on a bit about himself and it became very draining. Brian, my dad, was a very famous photographer in his day, so he liked to tell everyone. I mean *everyone* – a taxi driver, a woman walking her dog, the grumpy old lady who worked at the post office, randomers, anyone – anyone Dad came in contact with he would tell them his life story, and everyone and anyone would be deafened by his tales. He had no self-edit button. His ability to talk was astounding. In fairness he was really good, extremely talented and he had photographed some of the most famous Irish personalities over the years. He had captured momentous moments and opulent occasions and I was very proud of him. He was a loving if slightly emotionally distant father. Our house was a picture book of Irish celebrities and dramatic events. Less on the battlefield, more on the pitch. Jack Charlton, the old Republic of

Ireland soccer manager, was one of the faces he had snapped the most. I could never go to the toilet at home in any of our three bathrooms without Big Jack staring at me – those pursed lips above that long chin oh so disapproving as I tried to avoid his eyes while I wiped my bottom. Jack had been in our house on several occasions. He was a larger-than-life dinner guest and I'd loved his stories and his outlook on life. "Ya shauld cam' oaut and meaet ta pleeyaers," Jack offered one evening. I graciously declined.

My mother, Ellen, was a saint, God bless her. She never got a word in. She rarely moaned about this fact unless she'd had too many red wines and then she did. She let loose. In fairness to her, she needed the release. Dad's stories could go on for over half an hour without him pausing for breath. It was very difficult to keep focus at times. Sometimes I just watched his mouth move and I heard nothing.

My brother David (named after David Bailey, the famous photographer) lived in Belfast, but it might as well have been Outer Mongolia for all any of us saw of him. Inappropriately named David worked in banking and banking worked in David. He called regularly and talked about himself, his life and his job, but he wasn't part of the family any more really. He'd decided to leave the commune a long time ago. No arguments, no ill feeling, no hassle – he just wanted to be on his own. I think probably Dad had been too much for him – they were like chalk and cheese. The son my father had so desperately wanted was for all intents and purposes a disappointment to him. David hadn't turned out to be the soccer-rugby-acting-singing-star Dad had hoped for. Dad sort of admitted this to me one New Year's Eve as we stood in the back garden nursing our Irish whiskeys and watching the neighbour's feeble fireworks – well, more listening to his profanities every time a firework sizzled out.

"I thought he'd be more exciting, you know, Beth? More creative?" He'd sipped his whiskey. "He's a bore – hard to say it but he is. I mean most people can't believe he's Brian Burrows' son. Don't get me wrong – I love the bones of him, but I just thought, ya know, well, he'd be more . . . well, I suppose, more *craic*."

I shrugged my freezing shoulders as a blue flare zipped into the air this time but then died away with a slow miserable hiss. The profanities from next door were getting more X-rated.

Although the departure of David from our family had deeply upset my mother, she loved her husband dearly and I knew nothing or no one would ever split them up. David and I had never been particularly close growing up even though he was only two years younger than me. Our interest and hobbies had always been universes apart. I liked watching *Home and Away* and he liked *Blockbuster*s. I liked *Dallas* and he liked *University Challenge*. I liked Wham! Bars, he liked natural yogurts with added raisins.

I had gone up to visit him with Alice when he first moved to Belfast. He had a lovely new apartment overlooking the Hotel Europa.

"I am usually in bed by nine thirty so I'd appreciate it if you guys could be as quiet as possible – I like to read for an hour," he'd informed us in his quiet voice with his monstrosity of a hard-backed novel tucked neatly under his arm.

We had laughed. Very loudly. Then sniggered as we saw his expression.

He had muttered, "So immature" (which we were) but this just brought our sniggering up another level.

Alice was laughing so much she had begun to cross her legs. Never a good sign.

"Come out and have a drink with us?" I'd practically begged him, pulling him by the perfectly creased, cuff-linked navy-shirt-sleeved arm.

He shook his tidy brown hair. "Beth, I don't drink, I don't go out, and I am perfectly content with what I do here in my apartment. I watch the documentaries I want to watch, I read the books I want to read, I eat the food I want to eat and what is best about all of it is this: I am answerable to no one any more about why I don't go out, about why I don't go to football matches, about why I don't fall in drunk, about why I could care less about Katie Taylor. To no one."

He was angry. I knew this because his nostrils were red and pinched.

We had left early the next morning. I left him a note saying sorry and that I thought his apartment was lovely. Then I added: *PS Katie Taylor's achievement was monumental.*

I loved him because he was my brother and for, sadly, no other reason.

It had been a long, warm week at the market and I was dog tired. I could have had a stool at the stall but I didn't. I stood all day. I preferred to be moving around. I pottered around it. I fixed my jewellery, I polished my jewellery and sometimes I even made new jewellery. Occasionally I talked to my jewellery. That was one of the perks of working on a stall rather than a shop: people expected all sorts from stall-owners. My designs were selling slowly. I was ambitious, I won't lie to you. As in I wanted to see Kate Moss wearing my work sort-of-ambitious. Falling asleep every night I pictured the world's most glamorous women in my designs. Hey, if John Callan could be dressed by Stella McCartney why the hell couldn't her skinny pal wear my earrings?

I saw Rory standing under Siam Thai outside Dundrum Town Centre and I smiled a little. He was always there. Always on time. Always in a good mood. Always reliable.

"Hi there, sexy!" I bounded up, breathed hard on his glasses and fogged them up. I laughed.

He took them off and wiped them good-humouredly with his paisley shirt sleeve.

"Let's do this, shall we?" I said.

I linked his arm as he put his glasses back on with his free hand. I knew he wasn't really in the mood but he'd never say. John would have. John used to get to the door of the restaurant where my parents could see him, wave enthusiastically at them and then double over and feign some sort of awful stomach bug, clasp his hand over his mouth, then shout in between gagging, "You stay! Why ruin both our nights? I'll be fine – twenty-four-hour-thing, I'd say!" and run back out the door, hand over mouth. Usually to The Long Haul where he'd sit at the bar and drink Captain Morgan straight and chat to old men. John never called them 'old men' – he always called them 'Lifers'. John was obsessed with 'Lifers' – what they had done, what they believed in, what their memories were, he loved it all. John would without any doubt in my mind prefer the company of a Lifer to that of a Victoria Secret model. That was John Callan.

Anyway he did this getting-out-of-dinner thing many, many times. In the end my parents asked if he was all there.

"Mentally like?" my mother added in a pitying voice, tapping her head with her index finger very slowly by way of explanation.

"I don't know, Mam," I answered. Honestly.

My parents loved Rory. My mother, after a few glasses of the red tongue-loosener, would hug him tightly to her bigger boob (mam had one boob very notably bigger than the other) and tell him he was going to make the best son-in-law ever. I would fish an imaginary eyelash from my eye. Rory would redden and pretend his glasses needed cleaning with the ends of his T-shirt, holding them up to the light this way and that and shaking his head before rubbing the daylights out of them again.

Tonight we were organising their move to Nerja in Spain. They were out of here. Leaving dreary old Dublin for a life of sun, sea and drinking wine during the day without ever being judged. Heaven. They had bought the quaintest two-bed-roomed villa on Burriana Beach with a small swimming pool, barbeque area and views to die for. We had visited Nerja over and over during our summer holidays as kids and they'd always planned to retire there. Almost everything was done for the move. The majority of their 'good' furniture was in storage as they planned on renting out the Dublin house. I had done all the hard work of getting their electricity, water, phone line, wifi and banking stuff together over there but, as a precaution, as my parents were not the best organisers in the world, this evening I had brought along foolscap and a pen for final checks. They would come back   to celebrate Alice's wedding next month and after that pack up the last of their belongings.

We headed up the steel stairs. The smells were incredible and I took it all in slowly through my nose. I loved the smell of food. I still appreciated how much I liked it as I couldn't stomach the smell of food for months after John.

Mam and Dad were seated at the very back at a window table. They jumped up and embraced us.

She wanted to fix my hair but resisted I could tell as we manoeuvred into the round seats and she sat on her hands.

The lads struck up a conversation about some snooker player who had been found with a snooker ball up his anus. Again. It was the again part that got me, funnily enough.

"Hello, Booboo," my mother said. "So are you all set for Alice's wedding?"

"Yeah, we're getting there." I flicked open my white napkin.

I knew what was coming as she now placed her relaxed hands on the table, stuck her chin into her chest and lowered her voice multiple octaves. "Will *he* be there?" Mam, her face stony and sour, sounded like Kenneth Brannagh playing Hamlet at the Barbican where Hamlet has just mistakenly killed Polonius. (I did the book for my Leaving Cert. Leaving Cert Shakespeare just never leaves you, does it?)

"Yes, he'll be there, of course he'll be there – he's

Alice's brother, Mam." I raised my hand to get the attention of the waiter although I hadn't even opened the menu. I waved a little and my charm bracelet danced.

"I met him once, you know, at a snooker tournament in Asia, he was all over me . . ." Dad was off.

"Are you ready to order?" the waiter asked, slightly surprised at our speed.

Rory and I nodded. We gave our orders and I asked for a bottle of the house white Pinot Grigio.

"Oh, hang on!" My mother pulled her glasses with their square gold frames from her smart short grey-haired bob and put them on. She then, with her index finger, did a short jog around the page, her long nails blood-red. Always blood-red. I couldn't remember when I had last seen my mother's original nails. She ordered, and ordered for Dad too. The waiter smiled and left the table. Mam always ordered for Dad. She still sugared his tea for him. And stirred it. She still watched him take that first sip, spoon in mid-air, awaiting his approval on sweetness before she replaced the spoon in the sugar bowl and began drinking her own sugarless tea.

"So are you all excited?" I asked as I pulled my hair into a low pony-tail and pulled out my notepad.

"Yep." Dad poured the waters, tipping all the pieces of lemon into his own glass. "I hear Tom Jones has a place there – I bet he asks us for dinner – I met him a few times, you know?"

"So here's the thing," I interrupted quickly – I honestly didn't have it in me to hear the Tom Jones story again. "Have you decided what to do with the house yet? Like what letting agency you're going to use?" I scribbled furiously on my clean page to get the pen's ink moving.

"Yes," Dad said as the waiter leaned in with the bottle of white wine expertly balanced along his tanned, very hairy forearm.

"Lovely. That looks lovely. Pour away," I said before he offered to let us taste the grape. I wasn't a taster. None of us were tasters. Just drinkers.

"I was telling Jenny my hairdresser all about your jewellery designs this morning." Mam pushed her glasses back up onto her head. "Her daughter works in Penney's, you know. She was admiring my earrings – you should talk to her."

"Thanks, Mam," I accepted the wine from Dad, steadily by the stem of the glass, "but I don't think Penney's are into one-off pieces really."

Mam nodded but didn't look convinced. "It's the most popular shop in Dundrum, you know." She sniffed now and patted her bob.

"So, must be fantastic to think of those warm sandy beaches that are waiting for you in Nerja, Ellen?" Rory helped me out.

"Ah, I am excited but I will miss Beth something fierce." Mam was going to blub.

"No, Mam, stop. You are two and a half hours away. I practically spent every summer of my life in Nerja – it's like second home to me. I will be over and back so much." I put my wine down and rubbed her hand.

Both my parents would be seventy this year. It was hard to believe. I was thirty-five years old. I'd stopped telling people my age recently. It's an age for women where people are just too judgemental. When people ask now how old I am I say I can't remember. I'd prefer to be thick than old. Sometimes.

The food arrived really quickly. Piping hot. De'lish. I had a hot sizzling beef dish with fried rice and extra chillies. I loved chillies. Rory didn't really like spicy food so he always had a dry dish. He had a chicken and broccoli plate. I did spicy so much I even carried a bottle of dried chillies in my bag in case I ever needed them.

We ate and chatted about the move. Rory was taking Mam and Dad to the airport on Sunday morning. I added a lot of soya sauce to my rice and swapped the chopsticks for the fork. Then Brian, my wonderful dad, dropped his bombshell.

"So, Beth, you were asking about the house there earlier. As you know we are thankfully mortgage-free – thank you, Celebrity Pictures!" He laughed, put down his cutlery noisily, clicked his tongue, joined his index fingers with his thumbs and pretended to take a succession of photos with his hands. "So we'd like to invite yourself and Rory to move in. Rent free."

I started to cough. A chilli had gone down the wrong way. I tried to gasp. Three pairs of wide eyes stared hard at me. Rory handed me my water. I noticed he had already drained his.

"You okay, love?" My mother battered me on the back. "Do you need the Hime Neck?"

I drank slowly, gathered myself together and took a deep breath before I croaked, "No, I'm good for the Hime Neck, thank you, Mother." I drank more water.

"So what do you kids say? The house offer?" Dad continued, stabbing at his beef with his fork.

Rory and I avoided eye contact.

Dad chewed for eternity as we all looked at him. Then he swallowed. "We don't need the rent money, you see, and you kids aren't flush, we all know that. These quirky jobs yis come up with. Take it – it's all yours!" He beamed now. He was, and rightfully so, proud of his and Mam's extremely generous offer.

I steadied my voice. "It's unreal, Dad – really, Mam, what an offer – isn't it, Rory? Wow . . . that's such a nice offer, isn't it, Rory? What about that for an offer? Rory?" I served the ball and found the edge of the inside line. Chalk flew.

Rory picked it up. "It's way too much though, really kind of you both though, we'll let you know though . . . before you go. Obviously. Brian . . . com'ere, though, do you really know Tom Jones?"

Rory, with that top spin on the Tom Jones line had hit a forehand winner straight down the line.

Rory and I said goodbye to my parents and headed for the car park. I had driven my trusty old 08 Red Toyota hatchback. We were silent for the walk. A teenager asked me for a cigarette. I asked him for a euro. We did not enter into a contract. We reached the car-park machine and I dug out the card, popped it between my teeth as I searched for change in my bag. The elephant was so heavy on our shoulders we were almost falling down. I watched the machine swallow the card, I put in the change and it spat the card back out at me. We walked to the car. The screech of tyres from parking cars on the surface was enough to drown out our silence.

"What do you think of that then?" Rory asked eventually as we sat into the car and did our seatbelts. Rory had to pull his at least six times before it came loose. His nerves were gone.

The tyres screeched on the noisy surface as I reversed slowly. I pulled out, fed the ticket again and headed for Rathmines.

"I don't know," I said at last, shaking my head.

"Should you really be driving after a glass of wine?" he asked, concerned.

"I barely touched it, Rory, and I ate loads and I drank like six glasses of water. Relax, will you? It's not like I've drunk a bottle of vodka and shot up!" I took a deep breath. Sometimes his straightness bugged me. It choked me. There was not one iota of daredevil in Rory – he refused to even come to Funderland with me because he said it was just too dangerous. "Even the Waltzers?" I'd begged. "Especially not the Waltzers!" he'd said, clearly horrified at my out-of-control, adrenalin-junkie mad streak. "If one of those came loose and spun off it would not only kill you but innocent people walking around eating candy floss and avoiding the dangers!"

I pulled up the handbrake at the red light in Dundrum village and turned my head to look at my boyfriend. He was pale. "What do *you* think?"

"I'm a bit scared, I guess, Beth." He stared straight ahead.

"Yeah, me too." I turned back and stared at the red light.

A young couple were kissing passionately outside a bar and I watched them closely. His hands cupped her backside and hers massaged his head. She was wearing a very short black skirt and barely black tights with ankle biker boots. She looked sexy, I thought. They parted and the guy caught me looking and I jerked my head back to the road ahead.

I wasn't ready for this. I know that sounds ridiculous but I wasn't. It was a step too far. I really, really, really loved Rory but I couldn't imagine ever being hurt again like John hurt me. I knew Rory wouldn't do that to me but if I was being really honest it was because he didn't have that power over me. I didn't think I'd ever let another man have that sort of power over me ever again. To be honest, it wasn't as though it was a conscious decision I had made. I just didn't think that I could ever have the chemistry I had with John with anyone else. It was a one-off.

"Look, why don't we drop in to Alice and Dan?" I said. "It's after eight and Lucy should be in bed. Alice asked me earlier but I forgot to mention it to you." I looked at the side of his shaved head.

"Green." Rory pointed at the light as he pushed his glasses back up his nose. Rory was a back-seat driver in the passenger seat. "The light has turned to green, Beth," he repeated as I put the car into first gear and pressed the pedal down hard. "Yeah, let's do that – that sounds nice."

Rory tugged at his seatbelt as though it was choking him and I headed for Portobello.

Chapter Three

Alice opened the yellow hall door in her yellow pyjamas – with bunny rabbits that appeared to be shagging.

"Strange?" I nodded at them.

"What? Oh yeah, Dan got them in Amsterdam on a long haul last week. He knows how much I love my unusual jim-jams. I don't think he quite looked at the subject matter that hard. Never mind, come in, come in!"

She closed the door very gently behind us with a quiet click.

My heart skipped a beat. She'd avoided eye contact with me. Alice had not looked me in the eye. I stepped further up the hallway, a mute Rory in my wake.

"What?" I stood back and stared at her now, removing my old faded denim jacket slowly. She looked about twelve years old with her long dark glossy hair in a bouncy high pony-tail and make-up free face. Not a broken red vein or a spot in sight. Eyelashes the length of Daddy Longlegs' legs.

"What? What?" She averted her eyes again.

The pyjamas looked like they were tailor-made to fit her. Like something Vivienne Westwood might have designed especially for her.

"'What what' is right – I want to know what's what right now, missy!"

I found the stylish silver peg for my jacket after three attempts, my eyes never leaving hers.

She contorted her face and stared at me before sticking her tongue into her bottom lip and pushing the lip out.

"Attractive," I said. "Now what's going on!" I pinched my nose. Hard.

"*Waaaaait, Beth!*" she hissed at me, then "Would you like a drink, Rory?" she asked my still shell-shocked bespectacled lover.

"Paaaaleasssse . . ." He drew the word out long and hard. He really wasn't able for shocks.

We went into the front room where Dan was seated cross-legged on a cushion in front of the TV. Massive bowl of popcorn by his feet. His presence seemed to occupy the entire space. Apart from that, the room appeared to have jumped straight out of the pages of *Interior Design* weekly. It always gave me house-envy, Alice and Dan's place.

"Howdy, lads!" he greeted us warmly.

I hugged Dan's back. He was on PlayStation and in his defence he did make an effort of sorts to get up. If I had encouraged it at all he would have put his joystick down. I didn't. I patted him back down.

"You good, love?" he asked me. "'Tis great to see you both – get a drink and a bite inside, whatever ye want." He was relieved he didn't have to get up.

Rory took up position beside him on another cushion.

I just wanted to talk to Alice and I wanted to know what she wanted to tell me but was afraid to. You see, I was watching her like a hawk of late. I had her under my suspicious surveillance every second I was with her. We hadn't mentioned John in all the time she'd been engaged, apart from that afternoon at my stall when she and Dan had arrived to announce their engagement after a weekend away in Ballinahinch Castle and she casually mentioned that John would of course be home for the wedding. I knew she was afraid to talk about him. I also knew now she had news on him. What news?

We went into the kitchen and shut the door and she raised the volume on Lucy's monitor. It hissed loudly in the background. Dan had asked her time and time again to pack away the monitor but she said she liked the security of it.

"Sit," she said.

I did.

She opened the fridge and took out an opened bottle of wine. Then she plonked two glasses down on the kitchen table. Her John Rocha ones. The really big ones. My heart started flipping over.

"He's here, isn't he?" My hand flew over my mouth and I whimpered like the predictable victim in a teenage horror movie.

She stared hard and cold at me. "Stop. Just stop it, Beth." She poured. And poured. "It's, well, it's like this . . . take your glass." She handed it to me and she pulled up a seat beside me, her perfect pixie face starting to burn a little. "As you know, Beth, Dan has no brothers and Dan's from Cork . . ."

Where was this going? I rubbed my sweaty palms on my jeans.

48

"And he has a gang-load of close male friends, as they do in Cork . . . em, anyway he's been finding it impossible to pick a best man, so, well, Beth, to avoid offending any of his mates, and as he has no brothers of his own, well . . . he's asked our John." She took a massive swig from her wineglass, her eyes watering as the liquid hit the back of her throat.

I swallowed. My mind raced ahead. The best man linked arms down the aisle with the bridesmaid, didn't he? Were they supposed to dance too? Would I be in his arms again? Would I smell him that close to me again after all this time? Would I feel him hard against me?

"Are you okay with that?"

I could see she was trying to read me. I pulled a Lady Gaga. "So what?" I was as calm as a stoned biker. "Chill, Alice, it ain't no biggy . . . dude."

She looked really worried now and darted her head from side to side. "Sorry, but whose voice was that? Who talks like that?"

Just then Lucy made a noise and Alice jumped.

"Hang on, will you? She'd a bit of a sore throat earlier – I want to keep an eye on her temp – she may need another seven and a half mils of Calpol." She grabbed a thermometer off the table and a small purple bottle and syringe. "Just drink your wine and . . ." She had no words. She just patted the air softly with both hands.

The excitement was starting to make me dizzy. Alice left the kitchen and I put my head between my legs. I stared at the chequered black-and-white squares on the kitchen floor. I spotted a silver stud earring back in between the tiles. It was hard enough knowing I would see him again in a month but now we would definitely have to speak, have to do things together. John and I had to interact. John Callan and Beth Burrows. The rehearsal.

I drained my wine and sucked the droplets from the end of the glass, and then I walked along the wall, looking at pictures of Dan and Alice and Lucy as I headed towards the kitchen mirror. I could hear Alice singing to Lucy on the monitor now, her tones full of love and comfort. Something about a rockidy horse. Didn't sound very safe or soothing to me. Surely that would panic Lucy more than calm her? I still had nightmares about those poor unfortunate three blind mice being chased to their deaths.

I stared in the mirror. What the fuck was wrong with me? I rubbed some grey eyeliner away from under my left eye.

John had never made any effort to contact me over the last two and a half years. He had been home once and I hadn't seen him. Oh, I had tried. I had a crazy beating pulse and dry mouth the entire time. I had gone to all his old local haunts. I had been a regular in the Long Haul for that long weekend, chatting to the 'Lifers' (who actually were so much more interesting than I'd ever imagined). I had called to the house to see Alice's parents, returning an old glass fruit bowl that didn't even belong to them (I'd taken it from my parents' house), my heart in my mouth, but he'd always been out. He was home for some casting with a famous reclusive Irish director and had practically spent the week in the guy's mansion in Killiney getting completely shitfaced. Alice's dad's words, not mine.

When he had dumped me it hadn't been easy for him, I knew that.

"We need to talk, Beth." He sat in front of me in the Globe bar on South Great George's Street.

I smiled at him and grabbed for his hand. He pulled it back. One of his moods, I guessed. I reached for my rosy-tinted Vaseline that was on the table and slathered it onto my lips. He stared hard at me.

"What?" I was completely oblivious to how he was feeling. Completely dumb.

He didn't pause. "I wanna go to New York. I wanna act." He coughed hard into his cupped left hand and sat back hard, his body engulfing the chair. All black leather and denim and sex appeal, his presence, as always, all-consuming.

I digested this. He wanted to act? Well, I had a good job as a PA but it wasn't anything I couldn't leave behind. I didn't particularly enjoy it. It was just a job. Basically just an administration job. I did it for the money. For us.

"Okay." I stared hard at him. "If that's what you want. We'll go." I slid the Vaseline tin behind my pint and reached for his hand and again he declined my advance.

"*Fffffuck!*" He twisted the silver promise ring I had made him on his wedding finger. "*Fffffffffuck!*" he said again and this time he ran his hands through his long dark hair over and over again. His stubble was extra dark, I noted.

"What?" I asked, totally confused now.

"On my own, Beth. I want to go to New York on my own. I'm bored. I'm so fucking bored of being me. You don't get it!" He smashed his fist down hard on the already wobbly table and spilt my pint of Budweiser. The glass lay on its side, unharmed, but the contents were dripping all over my light blue jeans, my Vaseline ice-skating around the table. I watched my jeans turn a darker shade of blue – it was a nicer colour.

51

"You . . . you're bored with me?" I don't know how I got the words out.

Time stood still between us.

"Yes," he admitted eventually, his dark eyes heavy and sad. He dropped his face into his hands now and moaned loudly, moaned angrily, those long fingers covering his entire face.

How I loved those fingers. I tried to swallow. I couldn't. "So then go!" I gasped eventually. "Then just go, John!" The words bravely left my mouth and I imagined how a boxer felt as that killer punch knocked him to the canvas. Slow motion. Playback. Every other person around us in the bar was blurry now, their voices distant and muffled.

He put the palms of his two hands between his open legs and slowly pushed himself up, then he left and I had never seen him since that evening.

Alice had found me in the Globe in a type of semi-coma but still sobbing gently, after I called her and made no sense. I'd drunk six pints of Budweiser, in a complete and utter state, on my own. Eventually, after I'd thrown up in the bathroom, on the strict advice of the barman I had called Alice. She couldn't get too involved. She loved John too. They had a great relationship as brother and sister, honest and loyal. John would do anything for Alice. Alice would do anything for John.

"Let him go – he's too wild, Beth, you always knew that," she said. "You are very different. You really are better off without him. He's not and never will be the settling-down type – I saw this coming . . ." She trailed off.

I literally couldn't breathe.

Alice had to carry me to her double-parked car outside

the Globe with the help of the lovely barman and she spoon-fed me for weeks afterwards. She knew better than anyone how broken I was. She moved into the apartment I had shared with her brother in Temple Bar and minded me. I never went back to work. I never got dressed for weeks. I wouldn't wash my hair or look at myself in a mirror. I missed him so much it was a real aching physical pain. I doubled over sometimes when I thought of him in New York surrounded by other women. Alice brought a doctor around one evening and she prescribed anti-depressants. Alice threw the prescription in the bin. Instead she slowly began coaxing me out for walks with her. Around Temple Bar. Slowly, slowly. She linked me like she always did, but on these walks I was like an old woman. Alice would make idle chit-chat and tell me about her day in work. She would fill me in on the latest fashions and what worked and what didn't. Who wore what to the latest music or movie events. She would look up the joke of the day every day and perform it for me on our rambles.

One evening as we walked (like we always did, same route every time) by the Bad Ass Café, I stopped suddenly and sniffed the air.

"I think I want a pizza?" I said.

Alice did a dance on the spot, the one where it's like a victory dance. She stuck out her backside and rotated it three hundred and sixty degrees whilst waving her hands in the air. We went in and ordered a bottle of house red and a plain Margherita pizza, I drank a glass and ate two slices (I left the crusts). Alice was beside herself with happiness on my behalf. She leaned over the red-and-white-chequered tablecloth, pushed the overly waxed wine bottle hosting the red candlestick to one side and pushed my limp greasy hair behind my ears for me.

"See, it will be okay, Beth. You are a wonderful, beautiful, amazing, talented woman, my best friend in the entire world, and you will be fine. The worst is over. You will get over him and you will move on, and someday, not now, not next month, but someday soon you will forget about him."

I picked up my wineglass and sniffed it. I couldn't say it to her but she was quite wrong. Quite, quite wrong. Never as long as I lived would I forget John Callan. I put the glass to my lips. Nothing tasted of anything. It was as though my palate had been wiped out along with the rest of my senses. Alice asked me if I'd liked the extra chillies. I shook my head. I just wanted to go back home now, curl up under my worn-out duvet and think about John.

My parents were worried sick and I was mortified at how I was handling myself. If I had been an outsider looking in I know only too well I'd have uttered the useless words "Pull yourself together". Although I hadn't been hit with it yet, I knew it was what everyone was beginning to think. I was trying. I was starting to climb up the deep well but it was greasy and slippy and it was a slow agonising process.

And now I was going to see him again. I shook. Literally shook.

"You ready?" Rory was at the kitchen door, looking exhausted. "I've an early start in the morning, a pre-Communion booking in Sherriff Street. I'm running *Give Up Yer Aul Sins*. I have to fill the popcorn machine and get to the wholesaler before I go too. I need bottles of fizzy water and Dip Dabs."

I pulled myself together. "Yeah, of course, let's go, but we'll have to grab a cab on the road, I'm afraid – I necked half a bottle of wine there."

Rory's eyes bulged behind his frames but he said nothing. We took each other's hands.

Alice was no longer singing about the banjaxed horse and I knew she'd passed out beside her little friend. Lucy was a very lucky little girl to have Alice in her life. I was usually very jealous when Alice made new friends (ridiculous, I know, but I couldn't help it) but I was never jealous of Lucy. I adored her.

"You okay?" he asked.

"Yeah, I am. I'm a bit all over the place, Rory . . . with John coming back . . . I can't lie to you . . . and now Alice tells me he's going to be Dan's best man."

Rory nodded. "I know, D just told me. He asked me was I okay with it? Well, I mean, what could I say?" He looked down at the floor.

I loved to see his lovely eyes without the severe dark framing of his glasses. He was adorable first thing in the morning.

"What are we going to do now?" he asked me.

"I don't know," I whispered and squeezed his cold hands tightly.

I couldn't tell him how I really felt. I was sure he felt my damp clammy palms. How could I stand here before him and admit that I was excited beyond belief? I wasn't surprised at my reaction; I always knew it would be like this whenever I saw John again.

"I have to make so many pieces tonight for this new collection and finish Alice's wedding necklace," I said. "I think I just need to focus on my work right now."

It was a brush-off and we both accepted the fact. We stared at each other.

The thing was, I just wanted to be alone with my thoughts and memories of John right now. No one could separate me from them. From him. I wanted to sit in the quiet and rerun our life in my head. I wanted to rerun and pause all our holidays, our fights, all the spine-tingling sex we had shared. I felt like bursting into tears. I wanted to let Rory in and tell him my true feelings but I couldn't do that to him. He looked sad.

"Ye off?" Dan rubbed his slightly bloodshot PlayStation eyes at the kitchen door, his red hair sticking up in the air like a flamethrower. He was barefoot, wearing a Cork football jersey and black baggy tracksuit bottoms. He pulled at the drawstring.

"Yeah, we both have busy days tomorrow and Alice is conked with Lucy," I said.

"Has she the little one in our bed again?" He shook head, amused. "But, sure, she has only a bit of a sore throat!"

"I'm working on Alice's neckpiece for the wedding still – I'm a bit behind and I'm starting to panic," I confided.

"Relax, girl!" Dan put his massive hand on my shoulder. "It won't be the end of the world if it's not ready!"

Men.

"Okay, we're gone."

I opened the door. A car looking for parking reversed way too quickly down the road. I stood on my blue-Conversed tippy toes, kissed Dan on the cheek and pulled Rory out the door behind me.

I sat alone in my scented-candlelit apartment, curled up on the couch, looking at a picture of me and John, the fragrance of Black Coconut surrounding me. Yes, I had saved one picture. Just the one. This well-thumbed one. We were in our old apartment off Temple Bar on the rooftop on a rare, boiling-hot sunny Sunday afternoon in May. Slightly drunk. He was shirtless, tanned, navy shorts, dark heavy stubble and laughing, with a bottle of Heineken in his hand. Me in a sleeveless black cropped top (pre-pints-of-Budweiser-beer-belly days), drinking a bottle of Corona with the lime sticking out.

I stared at his body. It went in and out of focus. Jesus, he could make me feel things Rory could never imagine. His features were so familiar to me. I tried with Rory, I really tried to make the sex just as good as it was with John but the chemistry simply wasn't there. The raw, wild passion just wasn't there. With John I wanted to rip the clothes off his back all the time. I wanted to devour him. I wanted to feel every inch of his body and spend hours naked on top of him. With Rory I wanted to wrap him up and softly cuddle him. I wanted to taste John all over with my tongue. I wanted to plant soft butterfly kisses on Rory's nose. I wanted to get into bed early and snuggle with Rory; I wanted to get into bed late and have sex until the sun came up with John. And I didn't have an explanation for this. It just was what it was. I didn't even have another boyfriend to compare them to.

I dropped the picture onto the round glass coffee table and went into my open-plan kitchen.

I loved this apartment. It was basically one big room, with the small bedroom and bathroom off the living-room-cum-kitchen. All the walls were painted the same pale yellow colour and the floors were sanded back to the original floorboards.

I opened the fridge and pulled out a longneck bottle of cold Budweiser – I had absolutely no appetite. I bent down to unlace my runners. I placed them tidily under my small kitchen table, laces shoved inside. I took out my old bottle-opener and popped the cap with a hiss, then rubbed the top of the bottle with a tea towel (my mother was always convinced rats urinated on every bottle in every cellar all over Ireland). I took my seat on the windowsill before lighting up a cigarette and pushing the old sash window open. Although it was past ten at night it was still very light out. I welcomed the warm breeze.

Was I being fake? Was I really who I appeared to be? Was I being true to Rory? No. I knew I wasn't but I didn't feel it was altogether my fault. I was damaged. As dramatic as that may sound to you, I really was. I did love Rory, very, very much. He was a super boyfriend. That wasn't fake. I wasn't pretending to be in love with him. It was just such a different type of love. I exhaled slowly and watched the smoke billow out onto the Ranelagh evening, its grey tones streaking and polluting the clean clear air. "Pull yourself together, you saggy old tit!" I snapped at myself.

I had to finish Alice's wedding necklace. It was a really intricate piece – it was a three-tier choker of Ernite Swarovski crystals and tiny white pearls. Inspired by Audrey Hepburn. Alice had the most beautiful long neck and I knew it would look incredible on her. I still also had to create a ton of work for the stall. I also had a really important meeting with the owner of Maks, a designer store, with shops in the city centre, Newbridge and Belfast at the end of the week. Paula Mak, the owner, really liked my work and if she took it Maks would be the first proper shop to stock my work. Beth's Bitz was so important to me. It was mine. It couldn't hurt me – well, financially it could cripple me, I knew, but I loved it. I loved jewellery with as much passion as I loved Converse. It was the first thing I noticed on a person (apart from their footwear).

I dropped my half-smoked cigarette into my ashtray, a Volvic water bottle on the window ledge, tied with a piece of string from the neck of the bottle to a nail on the window frame so it never fell.

I headed for my bathroom and scrubbed my hands before locating my workbox in the front room. I opened it carefully. It wasn't unusual for beads and supplies to jump and make a run for it as soon as the lid opened. I understood. They didn't want to be on a market stall any more than I did. They wanted to be in a shop window on a velvet tray with other worthy friends. They wanted to be admired through a crystal-clear massive window. They wanted to be pointed at and oohed and ahhed over. I sniffed the box.

To me creating a piece of jewellery was much like making music. Every bead, every component was similar to a musical note. The blend of all the materials created a feeling. I could put together a design and then switch around the slightest aspect and it would change the feel of the whole creation. Just the way a song reflects the emotions of an artist, my designs were all an expression of my personality, my emotions, what I was thinking or what I was going through. Some vicious, some dainty, some sultry, some rich, some sexy and some robust. In a weird way I had John to thank for this business. He created this artist within me. He made me really feel.

I removed the tiny pearls and laid them on the coffee

table. I draped my measuring tape around my neck like I always did. It was the only place I could ever find it. I unravelled some fine clear wire. I became lost in my work.

I woke up with a banging headache, hanging off the couch. Why did I keep mixing wine and beer? What is it that they say? *Beer and wine fine. Wine and beer queer.* It wasn't true. Or maybe it was just my age. I poured myself off the couch and went into the kitchen. Hand clutching head, I looked up at the clock. Ten past ten. I opened the fridge, took out the carton of orange juice and grabbed a glass from the draining board. I should have been on the stall by now. I hated when I didn't get to work on time. It made me feel lazy and I hated the feeling. I filled the glass to the brim and gulped the entire contents down in one go. It stung my throat. I rinsed the glass.

My iPhone rang and I went to answer it. I couldn't find it. I had it set on three rings for some reason. I had no idea how I did it or how to change it. It drove me mental. I never got to it on time. I hated looking for it even more with all the effort it took with a hangover. It had to be down the back of the couch somewhere, but I just didn't have the energy to lift heavy cushions.

I showered quickly and pulled on last night's jeans and runners and a white T-shirt that had seen better shades of white, before throwing a red cardigan around my shoulders. I didn't bother putting any make-up on. I just ran some eye-make-up remover under last night's panda eyes. My skin felt sore and blotchy and it was calling out for some moisturiser. No time. The car was still packed with the remainder of my stock. I always left stock in the car. Rory used to go mad at me. He was right. It was pure laziness. I just lied to him now, telling him I always cleared the car at night – but sometimes I did and sometimes I didn't.

I would not leave the market today until I had sold a lot.

It was now into countdown in weeks to the wedding. Three weeks. Alice and I were going dress-shopping again that evening, this time to a small French designer on the Naas road. Alice wasn't remotely panicky about not having a dress yet – in fact, I think she had seen 'the one' the very first day we went into Fitzwilliam Square to Lya Solis – but she was just playing the game. I knew my neckpiece would go with whatever she chose as I knew her taste so well.

Her hen party was the following weekend and I hadn't had anything to do with the planning of it. Alice's decision. I was over the moon. If only I didn't have to go at all. But I did. It wasn't that I didn't get on with Alice's other friends, it was just that I hated sitting around a table with large groups of women. I always felt really self-conscious. This usually led to me drinking far too much wine and making a show of myself. Then I had to deal with The Fear when I woke up the morning after. I was getting too old for it all.

The phone rang again and then died completely after two rings. I knew the battery was on red – my iPhone was always on red – I'd never find it now. I didn't care. I just wanted to get to work. Whoever wanted to get me so badly would more than likely know where to find me.

Chapter Four

Louise

Louise sat barefoot and cross-legged in her living room and crocheted the last stitch on the canary-yellow tank top. She pulled the wool from her finger. It ached as she rubbed the wool dents with the thumb and index finger of her left hand. Her headache was starting to ease but she leaned over and grabbed the Solpadeine from her overflowing bag: two more should see her good for a while.

She had to deal with her mother who had been calling and calling – she daren't ignore one more call. She lived at home so her mother paid for this beautiful roof over her head and everything else in her life, although she knew her mother was making money off her too – she had to be. The company was doing really well – it was in all the top magazines and had huge runway shows behind it. She was the designer. She created pieces at home and then the team copied them in bulk. She rarely left the house.

She pulled her thin frame up from the floor and padded barefoot on the cold white marble into the kitchen to get water to plop the tablets into.

The current crisis had arisen because the staff – the workers, as her mother called them – hadn't copied the last pieces she had made exactly. They weren't right. Her mother was behaving as if it was somehow Louise's fault. But it wasn't Louise's job to oversee the process. She never went near the factory. She knew how to crochet and that was it. Her life had been spent on her bed, curled up crocheting, avoiding the outside world.

She twisted the fancy chrome tap and added a small amount of water to the glass. The tablets hissed as they met the liquid. Someone once told her to try snorting them but she'd never do that. Wasn't she bad enough? She watched the roundness of them disappear and then knocked them back. The bitter taste made her squirm. Hated the taste, loved the effect.

"Story of my life," she said aloud in her sweet high-pitched voice as she pulled hard at the oversized shiny red door on her American-style fridge. She blew her blunt fringe up into the air with her bottom lip sticking out. She reached in and pulled out her morning bottle of chilled white Sauvignon Blanc. Taking her wineglass from the freezer she carried both in one hand, and walked over and pushed open the patio doors.

It was a bright beautiful morning and the sound of lawnmowers pierced her brain a little. The heat of the sun warmed her cold bones. The smell of the freshly cut grass made her sneeze. She sat at the garden fountain and poured. The high trees and bushes protected her privacy from the few surrounding houses. She took her first sip of the day. She couldn't say it was enjoyable per se – it was just needed. Like how you felt when you hadn't washed your hair for days – the itch, the darkness of the strands –

but then when the water hit and you scrubbed the scalp, the relief! Drinking felt like that to Louise. Always had. Since she tasted her first glass of wine at her parents' twenty-fifth wedding anniversary when she was fifteen. She could suddenly talk. Her crippling shyness was gone. She felt fresh and clean and alive. She felt pretty and clever. She felt worthwhile. Louise marvelled at the magic of the clear long-necked bottle.

She pulled up her elasticised Nike white track-suit bottoms to let the sun at her legs.

Louise was dark-skinned all over, with jet-black hair. "Where'd we get you at all?" her dad would joke. She was an only child and her parents were so outgoing and successful she had always felt pretty useless. She wasn't academic and failed miserably in her private school. Her mother had been furious. "Is there anything in that head of yours at all?" she had yelled. She had never made any friends there and had dreaded every day. Some of the girls had teased her mercilessly throughout the six long years. 'Dumbo' they had called her. She swallowed the contents of the glass and squinted her dark-grey eyes against the sun as she rubbed her temples. She was a mess. Always a mess. She poured another glass from the bottle.

She thought about him, as she so often did. He had been the only one who had ever stood up for her. She'd met him in Scotland on a buying trip, almost five years ago now. Her mother had been with her. They had pulled into a petrol station to refill the huge BMW rental car and she'd been having trouble working the pump.

Suddenly he was beside her.

"Can I help?"

Her mother rolled down the window and called out:

"She's completely useless, I'm afraid! Honestly, she can do absolutely nothing. I don't know where I got her from – the knackers' yard, her dad says."

"That's a bit harsh – it's not her fault the pump's defective." He'd stood glaring in at her mother who had quickly rolled the window back up. He pulled out the pump and began to fill the tank.

It didn't seem to be defective when he used it.

"Friend?" He nodded at the car window.

"No – mother." She looked down at her pink flats.

"Worse, so!" he laughed and then so did she.

And for some reason when she looked up she was able to look him in the eyes. This almost never happened to her.

After he'd filled the tank they entered the shop together and he'd held the door open for her. The door had opened in but still he'd held it.

She watched him fill his red-and-white flask with coffee as she waited for her change.

"Thank you again," she said as he reached the counter.

"No bother at all. That a Dublin accent yeh have there?"

"Yes, we are just here on business – till Friday." She needed to look down again. She could feel the pinkness creep from her toes to her bum and then race, sprint even, into her face.

"Where are ye staying?" He handed over his credit card and a loyalty card.

"Just over there in the King's Arms." She pointed across the road.

"Ahh, me too – grand spot, isn't it?" He took his coffee and his cards and thanked the girl behind the counter.

"Thanks, Charlene." He winked at her. "See you next week." He'd held the door again. "Good luck then – sure I might see yeh in the bar later if yeer down for a scoop, like?"

She'd smiled and didn't answer but he'd held her eye for a minute and she'd felt at ease.

"And . . . don't let anyone talk to yeh like that, okay?" And he'd gone.

She had met him that night. That fateful night. She had gone back across to the garage and bought a bottle of wine which she'd drunk in the toilet of the hotel after dinner.

"I'm going for a swim – see you in the bar in an hour?" she'd told her mother as she escaped.

Her mother had been lying on the bed in a face pack she didn't want to crack so she had waved her away. Her mother and her face packs. Morning, noon and night. When Louise was a child she had thought her mother had two faces. Ha, she hadn't been too far off the mark.

When she'd arrived in the bar he was talking to her mother at the window table. She steadied herself and took a glass of water from a brown tray.

"Hi!" She was a bit wobbly but neither seemed to notice.

"Sit, darling!" Her mother was enjoying the male attention. "How was your swim?"

"Divine," she'd lied.

"Can I get you a drink?" he asked.

"Oh, just a soda water for now, please."

He obliged.

They had a great laugh and the conversation flowed. He was such a character.

Her mother was well tipsy. "My God, Louise, I must take you away more often – I've never seen you so animated! You're usually as dead as a desert and dressed like a widow. Miss Personality she is not."

He had scowled, shook his head and took a long swallow of his pint.

She had felt okay about herself. She was dressed in a tight maroon dress with black suede ankle-boots, her dark hair pulled back in a low pony-tail and her fringe getting to that length she loved. Just hovering over her eyes. Her security blanket.

"I'm going to the bar, Mam – can I get you one more?" She was suddenly aching for a drink. The effect of the wine was wearing off after that comment of her mother's and she was becoming herself again. No one needed to see that her mother was quite right in her opinion of her dull personality. She ordered a double vodka and soda water for herself and got her mother her whiskey sour but dumped a second shot of whiskey into it.

When her mother excused herself Louise knew she wouldn't be back.

They chatted and laughed and when the shutters came down on the bar she took his hand.

"Are you single?" she whispered as she examined his wedding finger.

"I am, yeah," he'd answered.

"Can we go to your room?"

He sat back in the chair, startled. "Are you sure? We've only just met."

"I don't see what that has to do with anything!" she'd laughed.

"I know – sorry if I sound a bit old-fashioned and

prudish but I'm an old-fashioned type of guy and, if you don't mind me saying, I know you haven't had much but you seem pretty drunk."

"I am not," she'd slurred.

"You are, yeah," he'd slurred back.

"You're pretty drunk too, mister," she'd giggled and then so had he.

"I am, yeah. Doesn't take much for me."

She put her hand on his knee and rubbed it.

"Ah, come on now, Louise!"

He'd sat bolt upright as she'd moved her hand slowly up towards his groin, stopping only briefly to pull her chair in until she was only inches from his face. He'd moaned. "Stop now, that's enough so it is," but his eyes were closing with desire.

She had him. "I want you." She nuzzled his ear and he put his two arms around her waist.

"I don't like to take advantage of women who are tipsy. Tell ya what, let's go up to my room and make two woeful coffees, yeah? Sober ourselves up a wee bit."

She'd stripped naked while he was filling the kettle and he'd dropped the cups on the carpet when he turned around. They'd rolled under the bed.

"Holy shit!" he groaned. "I've no condoms. I'm not prepared for this."

"It's fine, I'm on the pill – and I don't have any diseases – do you?"

"No, but . . ."

She had put her finger on his lips and he hadn't said another word.

They had made love all night and she knew it was a loud cry for help. It wasn't the first time she'd had sex with a stranger whilst very drunk but it was the first time she'd had unprotected sex. He had understood her though and had wanted to help her. They had chatted at length throughout the night. They arranged to meet up in Dublin a couple of weeks later and they had.

They saw each other every other night for three months. He had fallen in love quickly and passionately. She had fallen in love with him but not as much as was enough. She couldn't love herself so how could she love anyone else?

She stared up directly into the sun now, the rays stinging her wet eyes.

In her own way she had loved them both but she was too weak. Much too weak.

Her mother had never understood. She shut her eyes and remembered back.

"You can't have this child," was the first thing her mother had said when Louise had come to her to tell her she was expecting a baby. "You are not well, Louise – it's not possible for you to bring a helpless child into this world and I am too busy with my business to look after a baby. There is no discussion. You have no choice."

She drank another long gulp and put her head in her hands now as she could hear their raised voices from her memories in her head once again. They were shouting downstairs as she tried to sleep it off.

He was shouting louder than her mother which wasn't an easy thing to do. "She will not murder my child!" he was yelling.

"Please, son, keep it down! We have neighbours! They are important people," her father contributed.

"We will not be responsible," her mother shouted.

"Then I will!" he said, his voice deep and full of bellowing anger. "I will be responsible. This is my child we're talking about and I will be a father. Let her have the baby and I will raise it. You have my word. I will sign any documents you want me to."

The voices faded then as she'd passed out, quite contented for some reason, her hand lying gently across her swollen tummy.

Chapter Five

Beth

It was warm and sunny again. The best few weeks of continuous good weather in years, everyone said. The Irish people were elated. Cars happily waved other cars out at junctions. People in supermarkets let people behind them with fewer items go ahead. Bus drivers didn't complain when people rummaged in their purses for the correct change. The words, "Take your time" could be heard all over the country.

The sun hurt my eyes though and I had no sunglasses. I never remembered my sunglasses on hot days, only on rainy ones. I really liked to wear sunglasses as hair bands but Alice told me it was a fashion no-no. I stood in line at the Buttery Bakery waiting for my take-away extra-large low-fat latte and my flaky apple Danish pastry. I still had no appetite but I wanted to make myself eat. I hated feeling like this.

"Oh, fuck you, John Callan!" I muttered to myself, grinding my teeth.

"It's comin'! Right!" The girl with the pierced nose

behind the counter scowled at me, mistaking my personal mutterings for insults directed at her. It wasn't my fault she hated her butter-coloured uniform and butter-coloured hairnet.

"Oh no, I was talking to myself, sorry . . ." I trailed off as she thrust the goods over the too-high glass countertop at me, blowing air out quickly through her pursed lips right at me.

It's one thing I never was. Rude. Ever. I hated rudeness. Okay, once I was exceptionally rude to a clamper but in my defence he was an absolute fucking arsehole. He had clamped me on a Good Friday as the rim of my wheel was in a bus lane. The rim. The barest edge. The street was deserted of cars. He'd actually had to get a ruler out of his repulsive van to measure the tiniest edge of my wheel on the line. I surprised myself at the level of bad language I was able to aim at him.

I sipped carefully through the tiny white hole but the latte was only lukewarm. I liked my lattes hot. Burning hot. I thought about going back but then remembered the mood on the butter-coloured server and decided against it. I beeped the alarm on my car. I had residents' parking discs and I always got the same space outside the Buttery Bakery which was at the end of my road. I slipped the latte into the hole at the side of the driver's seat and took a bite from the Danish. Spat it back into the foil. I couldn't eat. Weight Watchers or Slimming World should get all the women who want to lose weight into a room, send John Callan in to flirt with them and then lay out a table full of fresh creamy chocolaty profiteroles. No one would have the appetite.

I needed to focus on what pieces I was taking to Paula

in Maks on Friday. This was the biggest meeting of my designing career. My work for Maks was at the higher end of the price scale and the materials I used were all incredible. I could ill afford to make pieces that I couldn't sell on. I would put my heart and soul into my work this week. I had a couple of pieces that I was delighted with, but I needed at least three more. I knew the theme of my line – I just needed to complete it. I blasted some Sunshine Radio easy listening and drove to work, sipping my lukewarm latte and not thinking about John Callan.

The market was already busy as I pulled up onto the grass verge. What was it with sunny days in Dublin that also made people want to spend their money? If only we had this weather constantly we might be singing "Recession? Who cares! It's sunny!" as we all grew our own food and dove into the sea at the Forty Foot with our tanned bodies, rejoicing in our take-your-time-no-please-after-you new attitude to life.

I set up my stall and decided to show my most expensive pieces today. I was in a killer mood for selling. Someday I hoped I could just design and someone else could do the sales. I hated it. It was only when I was getting close to being broke again that I could push sales. Barrow Boy Sugar I was not. I laid out my earring tray first. I was going to sell earrings today, and lots of them. I wiped down the black velvet board with my old pink J-cloth. I gently laid my creations out. I always started with my longer pieces on the top of the tray – my fishhooks, my lever backs – and worked my way down to my French backs and push-backs and finally to my babies, my stud creations. My stud earrings were my favourites. The simplest of all the earring family. They could be diamonds, gemstones, pearls and gold or silver balls. Always on a metal rod that sticks through the earlobe, with a small backing to secure them. Always. They didn't change. The starter earrings that everyone gets when they first get their ears pierced. Simple and classic. They never go out of style. When I designed my stud range I always felt they were timeless and could be worn in fifty years' time as vintage. Everlasting. I had studs in today. I slept with these studs in. John had bought them for me at the Dublin Horse Show in the RDS not long after we first started seeing each other. Small sterling silver studs with Omega backs.

I finished setting up, put away my dirty cloth and straightened up. My stall was in a great location – at the entrance to the market. I stepped in front of the stall, ready to sell.

"Hi, would you like to look at some original Beth Burrows designs?" I asked a couple who passed by slowly hand in hand.

She was all boho chic in a cream flowing maxi dress with two gold spaghetti-string straps, decked out in gold bangles and massive gold hoops teamed with massively oversized Aviator shades and towering brown wedges. From Dublin 4, I guessed. Ballsbridge. I'd pigeonholed her already. I always read the book by its cover. It was a habit I'd been trying to break for years. Her long sun-streaked blonde-brown hair was the same colour as her perfect skin. He was slightly on the too-thin-for-a-man side with drainpipe purple jeans and a skin-tight shiny black shirt, his hair greased back like someone's from the 1950's might have been. She smiled at me and shook her head but he pulled her back.

"Take a look, sweetie pie," he urged her. "I want to buy you something."

"I'm fine." She dug her wedges into the grassy edge before my stall.

"Look, she has a whole tray of earrings – you love earrings, Tara! There are even long dangly ones, look! If I can't get you into the city-centre jewellers', at least humour me and take a look here?" He pulled her towards the stall.

I felt like saying 'Piss right off! Stay away from my work, bitch, if that's how you feel!' Then my sleek white-leather wallet appeared to me in a vision, empty and sad. It was a birthday gift last year from Alice, Dan and Lucy. Now that Alice was part of a threesome her presents were even better – this pleased me greatly. I was a sucker for a good pressie.

"Please, just take a look, see if you like anything?" I grovelled.

She approached and her scrawny fingers tipped the edges of my work. Like piano keys. I heard the first few notes of Billy Joel's "Piano Man" in my head. Her nails were simple – polished clear.

Then she paused.

"Oh, Franco, look at that!" She pointed over my red-cardiganed shoulder to my necklace tray which I hadn't displayed prominently, being in earring mode.

"I see you like hoops . . . these are . . . brass, zinc and copper alloy . . . they're a really close-to-gold colour? This material is quite resistant to tarnishing," I lied.

"She likes the necklace – can we see the necklace?" Franco spoke and I listened – his tone was so low you had no way of not giving it one hundred per cent so you could hear him.

Whatever, Franco, you skinny fuck! I screamed in my head. Jeez, I must be due my period. I was really very inwardly angry today. The dreaded inner rage. I turned and lifted the tray gently. "Which piece?" I placed the tray in front of them.

"That one – the glass pendant."

Her accent wasn't D4 after all – it was unplaceable, like American meets Australian on the way to South Africa stopping off at a finishing school somewhere along the way. Switzerland, no doubt.

I loved this piece. It was at the expensive end of my market collection at fifty-five euro – I gently removed the red-topped pins from it and held it out to her. It was simple. Elegant. I had made it one evening after Rory and I had seen an old Vivien Leigh movie – she had inspired me with her incredibly beautiful piercing blue eyes. It was a large circular white glass pendant on a thick quilted pink-ribbon necklace. The pink ribbon was chiffon in the middle with thick darker-pink silk borders. It whispered elegance. It could be worn as loosely or as tightly as you wanted.

Franco took it and she lifted her hair. He tied it tightly around her giraffe-like neck and twisted the barrel clasp shut.

"Do you have a mirror, please?" she asked politely.

Shit. I hadn't even put up my mirror yet. I bent under the stall and removed a fresh IKEA handheld and gave it to her. She removed her massive shades. I made an audible sound. They both stared at me. She was fantastically beautiful. Brown eyes the size of saucers. Like two grossly oversized Malteasers. She reminded me of a cartoon princess – the girl from *Tangled*. The one with the horrible mother. In my day she was Rapunzel – I had forgotten what Hollywood had renamed her. Probably It's-okay-to-have-freakishly-long-hair-just-love-yourself-for-who-you-are.

"I love it – it's perfect, don't you think? I mean I've had this in my mind! I even asked Dallas if he could, you know, make what I was thinking, but he couldn't. I'm like so stoked here!"

Franco leaned in and kissed her perfect rosebuds. I bet her breath never smelled of anything but minty mouthwash. I bet she never grew body hair or found an unexpected hair growing from a mole. Or from her nipple. I bet she was a horny little devil in the bedroom every night in skimpy lace underwear with a writhing body and a filthy imagination she kept solely for her loved one. I bet her period came for one day a month and was a pleasant fragrant light, light flow. I bet she had never got her head stuck in an item of clothing in a dressing room. I bet she had never had her fucking heart broken.

"We'll take it!" Franco removed the piece and laughed as he showed her the price tag.

She replaced her sunglasses. I was glad.

"This is why I love you – never mind low maintenance – no maintenance whatsoever!" he said to her as he handed me a fifty and a twenty. "Keep the change, doll," he smiled at me.

Doll? Did he really just call me doll? I bit the insides of my cheeks until they hurt. I didn't bother giving them a bag. They were really annoying me. I just handed over my precious baby as it was. "Bye bye," I whispered to it. I know this was ridiculous as I was now a businesswoman but after I sold a piece I mourned it for a while. Where would it live? Would they treat it right? I'd created this thing, I had a responsibility. Sometimes I could relate to Geppetto and his puppet.

Mini-Muffin Suzie approached me. I really wasn't in the mood. Her stall was next to mine.

"Here, taste this!"

She was always way too happy and way too full of energy. All the E numbers in those luminous multicoloured muffins, I guessed. She called them 'cupcakes', I called them 'muffins'.

She shoved a greeny substance into my mouth. It tasted like toothpaste.

"Well?" She jumped up and down on her bouncy white hush puppies. "Isn't it?" She kept bouncing and looking at me. "Isn't it just to die for, B?"

I nodded slowly and swallowed hard. I wasn't really one for cake. I was much more a crisp girl, a cheese-and-onion crisp girl. And I hated people calling me 'B'.

"It's good," I managed and leant over my stall for my bottle of flat Diet Coke.

"So, I was . . ."

She was bouncing and talking as I came back up but my brain was freezing, slowly freezing, like water that has just gone into the freezer in ice-cube trays. Wobbly. My brain was typing a message to my eyes. I think it was typing RED ALERT! RED ALERT! RED ALERT! but I couldn't be sure. I was starting to hyperventilate. I panted loudly. My knees turned to jelly. Right there. In front of bouncy Suzie.

"Like O to the M to the G, are you okay, B?" She suddenly stood still, noting my paling face. "Fock! Sweet shitty balls, it's not a reaction to the toothpaste I put in the cupcakes, is it? Tell me asap! You're white as a sheet!"

I felt white. I was dizzy. I felt like I was boiling up all over. You see, I'd just seen John Callan across the market.

Chapter Six

The pure state of me. I had never looked this bad even in all the times I had dragged myself to this market hung-over and exhausted. I always made a bit of an effort to look presentable. Except for this morning. It was an out-of-body experience. I had been almost prepared to meet him – in my BT pink halter-neck dress, hair coloured and Gwyneth-Paltrow straight (John loved my long poker-straight hair – it was why I never changed my hairstyle), high heels, professional make-up, eyelashes, (vodka), on my own terms, not like this.

He was directly in my eye-line as I fell to my knees and crawled around my stall, hissing at Suzie: "Mind my stall!"

Suzie was gaping at me, scratching her head, her pink cropped hair mocking my blushes. "What's that, B?"

"Mind my bloody stall!" I shouted in a hiss now.

"Jesus, B, have I poisoned you? It – it's just like my insurance is there and stuff but like right this second it's . . . well, like . . . complicated . . ."

I crawled away like a baby who'd just spotted Tinky Winky at an unattended milk stand. Jesus, please don't see me, I mantra'd in my head. Jesus, please don't see me! Jesus, please don't see me! I saw my car. Usain Bolt wouldn't have beaten me to it. I leapt in. I turned the key and tore out of the market, grass flying up behind me. I was hyperventilating. It was crazy. My palms were sweating so much they kept slipping off the steering wheel.

I had just seen John. John was in the same air-breathing space as me. John was home. He looked amazing. He looked like he had the day he walked out of The Globe. Out of my life. His hair was longer – it was too long, in fact, over the eyes. I didn't see those eyes. The last picture I had seen of him in a Sunday newspaper glossy-magazine supplement they had slicked his hair back with gel – "*One to Watch in Acting*" or something like that – and dressed him in a pinstriped suit. He looked ridiculous. I loved that he'd looked ridiculous. I had gone around all the shops in town to open the magazine and look at him. I couldn't buy it. Today he'd been wearing black jeans, hands dug deep into his pockets, a tight grey T-shirt and green Converse. I took a lot in for the micro-second I looked at him.

But what the hell was he doing in my market? Was it coincidence? I pulled over and punched the hazards as I tipped my bag upside down on the passenger seat to find my iPhone. "Alice Callan, you are so dead!" I repeated over and over. Lipstick, Airwaves gum, tobacco, McDonald's napkins, used batteries, cinema stubs all over the passenger seat. I'd forgotten the phone. I just remembered. It had rung this morning and I now knew for sure just who that was. Alice. Warning me.

I drove straight to Portobello.

I did not pass GO. I did not collect a single steady breath.

"He's home, Beth." Alice started to speak before she'd fully opened the hall door. She was holding Lucy by the hand and they both had flour all over their faces.

"No SH-one-T, Sherlock!" I barged past them, proud of myself that I hadn't sworn in front of Lucy.

"You look pretty, Ethy," Lucy said, smiling at me.

Never one to ignore a rare enough compliment I took the time to step out of the moment and turned back. "Do I? Ahh, thank you, darling!" I smiled and rubbed her affectionately under her soft chin. "In what way?" I probed. I knew I shouldn't but out of the mouths of babes and all that.

"Your hair is like a bird's nest and you have puwdgy lips."

"Hmm, I really shouldn't have asked." I wiped some flour that was a bit too close to her eye. "Thanks, I think, Luce."

Alice let go of her hand and Lucy skipped ahead of us as we went down the hall into the kitchen.

I couldn't sit. "When did he get back?" I leaned against the open back door.

Nursery-rhyme music filled the hot kitchen. A sailor had gone to sea, sea, sea, and I wished he'd see what he had to see, see, see, and shut up as I wanted it to stop. I couldn't think straight.

"Last night." Alice opened the fridge and took some weird-looking green stuff from a clear plastic bowl and spooned it onto a Minnie Mouse bowl in bright pink.

82

Then she lifted Lucy into a black canvas chair attached to the table. "Eat up now, Bubble." She handed her an orange plastic spoon and kissed her cheek.

So many colours. I had to ask. "What the hell is that?" I made a face, I knew I did, and Alice gave me the eyes.

"It's some beautiful pureed kiwi and lime, Beth. Yummy, isn't it? But you can't have any as it's all for Lucy!" Her face dared me to make another comment. I didn't.

Alice flicked on the TV and Lucy was lost in the magical land of injury-prone Daddy Pig.

We pulled wooden kitchen chairs to the back door. It was such a glorious hot day. "We'll just be sitting on the chairs by the step here, Bubble, okay?" Alice called in but the child was already Peppatosed.

"Last night?" My heart was in my mouth again and I actually felt nauseated.

"Yeah, he called here about five seconds after you guys left by all accounts – borrowed Dad's car and drove over. I was asleep as you know so Dan let him in and they got pissed. Typical John." She sighed.

I tried to move slightly into the shade. Five seconds. I had missed him by five seconds. That was his car I had heard reverse-screeching down the road. He still had parking rage, I noted.

"Why is he home when the wedding's not for another few weeks?" This wasn't how I was planning it. "You're planning it?" I said out loud to myself.

"What?" Alice was on to me like a flash. "What are you planning, Beth?" She shielded her eyes from the sun with her hand. To all intents and purposes it looked like she was saluting me. I liked it.

"At ease, Lieutenant," I laughed.

She didn't. "Beth, what's going on? He's home, so what? You're with Rory now. Please don't tell me you're in any way thinking that something will ever happen romantically again with John?"

I held my face up to the sun now. Cardinal rule of wrinkles broken. Again.

"Beth," she asked gently, flexing her feet back and forward. Alice did that all the time. She was a foot-flexor. Stopped you getting swollen ankles, she told me. Helped you avoid rheumatism in later years.

I pulled a thin grey bobbin from my jeans pocket and scooped my hair into a knot on the top of my head. The warm breeze found my neck. I kept my last-night's-made-up eyes closed. The mascara had come off on my pillow. My eyes without mascara were like a picture without a frame.

"Why don't we ever speak about John, Alice, ever? I know you're always in touch with him – he's mentioned you in magazine interviews and stuff – but you never mention him to me."

"Oh, come on, Beth, don't give me all that now – you know how it was, it is – it's better that way, this way – you weren't able to cope with me talking about him so we just dropped him from our relationship and rightly so. But are you kidding me – you read his interviews? Next you'll be telling me you follow his life over the internet!"

Thank God I was already holding my face up to the hot sun.

"I am only ever looking out for you, Beth, you have to believe that, and I can only do what I think is best." She curled her toes up tight now before saying, "Do you want a drink?" and she got up.

"Wine?" I asked hopefully.

"It's twelve o' clock – you can have a smoothie or pineapple cordial with fizzy water?"

"The pineapple thingy," I muttered. "Was that you calling me this morning to tell me he was home?"

"Yes." She went to get the drinks but more so to check on Lucy, I knew.

Returning with the drinks, she kicked off her orange flip-flops, tugged down her denim shorts slightly, then her knickers discreetly, and sat back into the chair. Her orange toenails matched her flip-flops perfectly.

I couldn't remember the last time I'd painted my toenails. Probably the night before John dumped me in the Globe. I always used to look after my toenails when I was with John. I definitely didn't take as good care of myself as I used to.

"So basically I got up this morning and Dan said –" she put on her best Cork accent here, "'Your brother's home, girl – he called in after Beth and Rory left – I had hardly closed the hall door on their backs. We had a few – a few too many like – and now I can't go to work.'" She coughed as I think the accent hurt the back of her throat. Cate Blanchett she was not. "He was due to drive to Donegal but he will never drive if he's been drinking the night before, he's so good like that . . ."

"Go on with the story!" I had fuck-all interest in Dan's driving habits right now.

She glared at me. "Soooo . . . John just said he got the chance to take some time off – he's shooting a period drama in London for the next six months. He . . ."

I stood up, blocking the sun from her face as she sucked on her red straw. "Did he mention me, Alice? Did he ask about me? Did he?"

"No." She sucked harder now and the green liquid made the straw look brown and the drink very unappetising.

"So why were you calling me? Why was he in my market just now?"

"He was?" she blurted out and dribbled a bit down her chin.

"Yes, this morning. I ran."

She put the drink down and wiped her chin with the back of her hand. "Why would you run, Beth? Why? You'll see him at the wedding, you do know that?"

"I know but look at the state of me! I don't want our first meeting after two and a half years to be when I'm looking like this, Alice – come on!"

After a few seconds she reluctantly nodded her head. She understood.

"I asked, you know," she said. "I asked Dan if he mentioned you."

My mouth was bone dry. I fished under the chair for my pineapple thingy, hands shaky.

She slipped back into her Cork accent. "'No, no, not really,' Dan said. 'I just said that Beth and Rory had just left like and he said ahh that was a pity like and was she still in the market?'"

"So he did mention me! How did he know I was there in the first place, Alice?"

"Oh God, I don't know, Beth – Jesus, I may have mentioned it, you, over the last few years or others may have. Dublin is a small place, you know."

He knows about Rory, I thought. He knows I've moved on. I didn't feel right about him knowing about me and Rory. For whatever reason I didn't want him to think that I had moved on. In all the time he'd been in America there had never been a girlfriend. There was a couple of sightings of him with a girl from a soap – *Spinning Through Days* it was called (STD's, I'd quickly noted) – I bought the box set of the specials online just to see her – but they had both denied any romance. She wasn't unlike me in that she was blonde and around my height and she wore casual clothes. She was obviously much prettier, much richer and much more talented. But I was still John Callan's last steady girlfriend. I knew I clung to that like Demi Moore to her youth.

"I was just calling you to tell you he was back, that's all. I was waiting until after ten when I knew you would be in work. I didn't want to panic you when you were driving." Alice smiled at me now.

I sighed and felt my face burning red.

"Are we still going to look at the dresses in Naas later as planned?" she asked.

"Yeah." I pulled myself together. I had to get out of the sun. "Yes, totally, I can't wait – be so nice – why don't we go for dinner there too – post-fittings obviously!"

Lucy appeared at the door. One plait had unravelled but she hadn't noticed or if she had she didn't care. "Is over, Maman."

My heart melted. My heart was being put through the mill today. I loved how Lucy called Alice 'Maman'. Alice hadn't wanted the little girl to call her 'Mammy' because she wasn't her mammy – but she was more than just Alice. They were finding it difficult to come up with a name. Then the three of them went on holiday, camping in France, and at the camping site Lucy made friends with a little girl called Delphine and her mother – her 'maman'.

And Lucy began to call Alice 'Maman'. Alice loved it instantly.

"Okay, Bubble," said Alice as she fixed the plait. "Let's get our packed lunch together, our hats and sun cream on, and go to St Stephen's Green to feed the ducks, yeah?" She was back in mammy mode.

"*Yippeee!* Dulks!" Lucy raised her hands in the air and ran out into the hallway and back waving them frantically, quacking as she went, her pink flats, pink shorts and *Doc McStuffins* T-shirt all perfectly coordinating.

"Call back to me around half sixish, yeah?" Alice said to me as she gathered up the glasses and I took the chairs back inside.

"What if he's here? Can't I just meet you at the end of the road?"

Alice made a noise that sounded like 'grow up' but I thought it was a cough. "Whatever." She dropped to her knees and planted kisses on the little girl's lips.

"Ethy, you didn't finish your juice?" Lucy shook her head at me.

"I will, pet." I picked it up and knocked it back in one go.

"That is not how we finish our juice, Beth!" Alice wagged a bitten nail at me.

"Bite me, Mommy," I whispered and slipped out.

I sat in the driver's seat with the cold air-con blowing for a few minutes. I pulled down my visor and slid the mirror open. I was a state. I snapped it shut again. I opened the glove compartment and knew what I was fishing for among my CD's. At the very back.

Don't do it! I shouted to myself.

Too late, I told myself.

I opened the case and slid the dusty disc into the CD player. I started the engine. Chris Isaak began to sing "Wicked Game". It was our song.

I headed for my apartment. Even though I knew he was long gone I couldn't face the stall again. I'd ring Suzie and ask her to pack away until tomorrow for me. She'd do anything for me right now – she thought she'd poisoned me. I was going to spend a few hours on Alice's neckpiece. I was feeling inspired.

Chapter Seven

I had cut out nearly twenty-six pictures of Audrey Hepburn. One from almost all of her big movies. Her as Holly Golightly, Eliza Doolittle, and my personal favourite: her with Humphrey Bogart as Sabrina Fairchild in *Sabrina*. I laid them all over the floor now as I found my necessary chemist reading glasses and slid them up my nose. A new addition to my life.

She was so incredibly beautiful. Such a delicate-looking woman. Pure physical perfection. She oozed beauty and talent from every pore. Now, Audrey had the X-Factor. I knew Alice loved her too and I also knew Alice was every bit as beautiful as her. I wanted Alice's neckpiece to be out of this world. To be iconic. I put on some more John music in the background and sat down to work. This time I played "If I Should Fall from Grace with God" by The Pogues. My fingers moving without me having to think, I beaded and beaded. I held the piece up to the window every few minutes. It glittered at me. It worked with me. Every bead obeyed my hand movements.

We were completely in tune. Each tier was beaded on a silver wiring and it would reach from the collar bone to just under the chin, the gaps between the tiers showing a tiny amount of bare skin. It was a total statement piece. I could see Alice's neck as clear as anything and I knew her well enough to know low cleavage wasn't her style so we could do this. Alice loved my work. She always bought it. She always wore it. She always praised it. She told everyone she met about it. She would never take my stuff for free and I knew there was no point in fighting her on it any more. The money would just end up in my purse the next day.

I worked hard and it was only when I started squinting behind my age-appropriate eyewear I realised it was getting too dark to continue. I'd been at it for hours and hours and realised my eyes were very sore and I was bursting to go for a wee.

As I unfolded my two dead legs, I noticed my now charged iPhone was lit up. I'd had it on silent since I called Suzie. I grabbed it and pulled out the charger connection. It was Rory. I immediately was swamped with massive guilt and closed my eyes tight as I listened to his gorgeous gentle voice.

Cop yourself on, Beth, I screamed at myself in my head before I pressed answer. "Hi!" I pulled the phone from its charger and dashed to the loo.

"Hi, is all okay?" he asked worriedly.

"Sorry, Rory – yeah, I'm just here, I'm at home, working on Alice's wedding neckpiece. I'm nearly done."

"Oh brilliant, well done, you! Can I see it?" Always enthusiastic.

"Sure, eh, where are you?"

"Almost at your door," he said as I peed. Loudly. I was never one for sitting towards the front of the toilet seat so my pee trickled silently down. I always sat too far back and made a splash. Rory kept talking and walking. "You wouldn't believe the day I've had. *Give Up Yer Aul Sins* turned into a bare-knuckle fist fight and two ripped Communion suits," he panted. "An unruly popcorn fight then broke out and someone stole my lunchbox."

I wiped.

"I'm not the better of it, Beth, I can tell you that much. Actually, will I cross over the road and grab some beers in the offie first?"

"Yeah, that would be magic, and –"

We both spoke at the same time: "Twenty Silky Blues!" We laughed.

"Any nibbles up there?" he asked.

I shook my head. "Not really, no – I'm shaking my head here." I flushed.

"No bother – should I grab a large bag of cheesy nachos and a jar of jalapeños?" he suggested.

"Lovely," I said. "I have to go meet Alice in an hour to look at dresses in Naas but I won't be late-late – though we did say dinner – so you can chill here and wait for me, okay? I'll bring you back something hot? The nachos will tide you over."

"Eggsellent," my boyfriend said and we both rang off at the same time.

I sighed loudly. I stared at my reflection in the bathroom mirror. "Stop this, Beth," I told myself. I bit my bottom lip so hard it went white. "Stop being a fucking bitch. Rory is your boyfriend, John's gone. Gone! G – O – N – E!" I spat the four letters at the mirror, covering it with my spittle. I wiped my chin, tore some loo roll off and wiped the mirror.

I flushed the loo again – bad habit – and washed my hands in my kill-every-known-germ-dead soap. This was my after-toilet soap. It wasn't girly soap by any means. It was proper old-school carbon soap.

I did a quick tidy-up and placed the neckpiece ever so gently onto my soft black mannequin head and neck. I wished I hadn't drawn that beard on her now in white marker when I was tipsy one evening after watching a box set of *Little Britain*. "She's a lady! She's a layyydeee, don'tya know!" I'd kept shouting as I'd sketched in the beard. Rory had told me I'd regret it in the morning – to put the marker down and step away. I hadn't listened to him. He had, of course, been quite right.

I went back to the bathroom. I filled the sink with warm water, ran the sponge with some shower gel under my arms and put on some Chanel extra-smoky-black eyeliner. I lashed the Vaseline on my lips and let my hair down. I pulled on a clean white T-shirt from my bedroom radiator and cut-off denim shorts and slipped my feet into red strappy Next wedges. "*Wowzers!*" I looked at myself in the mirror on the back of my wardrobe door, shocked. If I'd spent hours trying to achieve this look I couldn't have pulled it off like this. I loved when that happened. What was seldom really was wonderful.

The buzzer went. I threw four Brazil nuts into my mouth from my nut bowl on my bedside table. My mother was always on at me to eat Brazil nuts: "They contain selenium – it helps prevent coronary artery disease and liver cirrhosis." It was the liver-cirrhosis bit that always stuck in my mind. Chewing madly, I went to the buzzer before swallowing. Rory deserved better and tonight I was going to kill every other thought in my sick head and just concentrate on my lovely boyfriend. I closed my eyes and hit myself three times on the head. Hard. It hurt.

"Come and get me, big boy!" I buzzed him in, laughing.

I stood at the top of the stairs, door open, leaning seductively against it, my left leg perched on the door behind me.

It wasn't Rory. It was John.

Chapter Eight

"Howareya, Beth?"

He stood in front of me. In the present.

My mouth dropped to the ground. I could feel it hanging open there like a clown's face at a Crazy Pitch and Putt course, waiting for the ball to roll in.

"John? John? Oh . . . what? I mean hi? Why . . . what are you doing here, John?" I knew my eyes were like saucers. I couldn't blink. My heart was beating faster than a pneumatic drill.

He slouched, then shrugged his incredible shoulders easily. "I dropped by your work this morning but I was told you were off sick so I just decided to drop by, say hi – see how you are – and all that stuff. Dan told me where you were living now – great little place."

He was slightly nervous too, I realised now, as he entered my home and peeled off his leather jacket. He threw it over the back of my couch. He left his grey hoody top on, though he pulled the zip down a few inches. I could see the top of the grey T-shirt from earlier that morning peeking out.

He made his way over to my window, his dark hair flopping around his eyes – he pushed it away with both hands. He turned and smiled at me. The smile I knew so well. Full of cheek. He lit up the darkening room.

"So, how have you been, Beth?"

I swallowed. Fuck me, he was overpowering. I tried to stand still but the wedges were a bit high and I felt wobbly. I leaned against the safety of the door again.

"Well . . . yeah, good. I'm actually great, thanks – thanks for asking." It didn't sound like me. I sounded in control and slightly bored. "It's nice to see you."

"Any chance of a beer?" he drawled.

A beer. Oh Christ, Rory. Rory was on his way up! I had to get John out of here.

"No! No, I mean I'm – I'm – I'm going out – I have no beer – I'm late actually, John, I have to go. It's not – it's well – well, like – it's just not convenient."

I moved to the couch, picked up his leather jacket and handed it to him – stroking it unintentionally as I handed it over. It was the heaviest jacket I had ever lifted. I loved the feel of it.

He was staring at me. He moved towards me, zipping down and removing the grey hoody. He was now in denim jeans, grey T-shirt and old brown boots – distressed boots although I imagined he'd paid a small fortune for someone to distress them that way. Perhaps Jimmy had distressed them? The T-shirt had writing on it but I was too embarrassed to look at his chest to read it. A thin gold chain swung slowly around his neck. He was inches from me now. I could smell his aftershave. Still the same. Joop. It was as though no time had passed between us at all.

"You look so great, Beth . . . well, you always looked great but . . ."

His breath hit my face – Tic Tac mints mixed with wine. When he said my name – *Beth* – it always sounded like 'Bed'.

"Look, can we meet up? Before the wedding, I mean? Chats?"

I wanted to lick him. I wanted so badly to grab his face and lick it. My body was on fire. I wanted him to lift his arms high above his head so I could rip the grey T-shirt up and over and run my hands all over his naked body. I wanted to put my hand hard on his cheek and pull his lips onto mine. Reef that brown belt off and fucking whip him with it (not in a Fifty Shades of Masochistic Muck type of way, just my own little randy quirk).

Instead I simply said, "I'm not sure that's such a good idea, John." Again my voice was giving an Oscar-winning performance. I swallowed hard to coax some saliva back into my mouth. I pulled on my jacket and scooped up my keys from the hall side table.

He pulled the grey hoody back on, grabbed his jacket and followed me. "Can I have your number?" he said.

I opened the door and stepped outside. He followed, pulling on his jacket. I closed the door, locked it behind me and hit the fire escape, his presence beside me like an erupting volcano. I knew Rory would use the lift. Rory thought undesirables took the fire escape. He was probably right. I took them two at a time and pushed the green exit-bar heavily at the bottom door out onto the street. I pulled my hair out from the neck of my denim jacket. John was still following. I hailed a passing taxi and it stopped immediately. God bless the recession. I had walked too far, too late, too many nights and stood for far too long in freezing taxi ranks not to thank the recession every single time I successfully hailed a cab.

I turned to face him. He was bent over, rolling a cigarette on his knee.

"My number never changed, John." I got in and slammed the door.

I sat back and listened to my own heart beat out of my body. Every last nerve was on edge. Pins and needles in the tips of my fingers and toes. My breath was fast and furious. Every sense on tenterhooks. The familiar surroundings out the window suddenly looked unfamiliar. I felt like I was watching myself in a movie scene. I felt like I had just been hit by a double-decker bus.

"Eh, yeah, I'm norra mind-reader?" the oh-so-pleasant driver growled at me.

"Just around the block, please."

"Sorry? You wha'?" he asked, his arm around the seat as he now turned to face me.

"Oh, just around the block," I repeated.

"Ah lookit, I'm not goin' around the block – there was another bird with her hand out behind ya an' she had two fuckin' suitcases, love – yer wasting me bleedin' time!" He spun back around now.

I stared at his bulging eyes in his rear-view mirror. His smiling identification picture was nothing like his expression right now. False advertising.

"Whatever!" I shouted and got out and slammed the door, relieved to leave the stale-smelling cab behind.

"Mind me bleedin' door, ya fuckin' fruitcake, right?"

I caught sight of John's leather jacket turning the corner.

"Hey, Beth?"

"*Arghhhh!*" I screamed, way over the top.

"Jesus, Beth, what's up?" Rory jumped back, shocked, his hands clutching two brown-paper bags and his glasses sliding down his nose. "Where were you going?" He was struggling, trying to balance one bag on his knee and look over his glasses.

"Em, I'm going to help you carry the cheesy nachos." I prised one bag from his hands and pushed his glasses back up for him with my index finger.

"Did you not just get out of that taxi?" He stared after the cab screeching around the corner to catch the suitcase girl.

"No, he was asking for directions." I nodded and pointed into the distance, shaking my finger in the air.

"The taxi man was asking you for directions?" Rory sniffed. "Seriously, though, you'd think they would all have Sat Navs at this stage, wouldn't you? I suppose Google Maps does waste the iPhone battery though."

I nodded weakly in agreement.

"Well, okay, thanks for taking the bag – the beers are so chilled they're ripping the paper bags – it was becoming a bit of an issue for me." He looked at me over the top of his glasses. "Shall we?" He nodded towards the door of my block.

"Yes, of course." I plastered a fake smile onto my face.

Back in the flat, I spilled the nachos into a big white ceramic bowl and Rory twisted the always-too-tight cap from the jalapeños. I guessed he had been working on loosening the jar in the shop before his walk back over here.

"I'm just . . . I'm getting something . . . be back in a second." I headed for my bedroom and closed the door behind me.

I fell onto my bed face down. My heart was still beating too fast. I needed to steady my breathing.

The television butted into my thoughts as Rory turned on *Come Dine with Me*. I bit my clenched fist hard.

"This can't be happening to me again," I whispered between fist and teeth.

"Yer one from yesterday, Alison from Liverpool, got a score of twenty-six – remember we missed the end?" Rory yelled in at me through the closed door. "How'd she manage that? That lamb shank she served was raw and she drank way too much wine! She was the one who went through the other one's knickers-drawer, remember? She found the stained Y-fronts, 'member?"

He loved *Come Dine with Me*. Honestly, I didn't.

"No way!" I called back shakily as I stood up. I tried to steady my breathing. "Rory!" I shouted as I pulled my white T-shirt over my head. "I'm just going to hop into the shower!"

The door opened. "Huh?" He stood there, some nachos in hand, his face-stubble orange from the fallen flavourings. "Oh, just in time for some naked viewing, I see – well, here, while you're undressing it would be rude of me not to do the same."

He grinned at me, popped the nachos in his mouth and dusted off his hands. He approached the bed and sat. He raised his finger to my mouth. "Sorry, I meant to say you have, like, black stuff on your teeth."

I froze. I nearly threw up. I actually retched. "What? What? Oh Jesus, no, please no, say what?" I ran to the mirror and stood in front of it, my mouth clamped shut. I couldn't bring myself to open it. I put my left hand tight over my mouth too.

"What is with you?" Rory fished with his tongue around his mouth, looking for nacho fragments.

I took a long breath in through my nose. My right hand prised my left hand off my mouth. I slowly opened my mouth and there it was. Right in the middle of my two front teeth was a massive black thing. I peered in closer. I couldn't believe this was happening to me. I slowly raised my shaking index finger and placed it over the invader. I slid it down my tooth.

"Are you okay, Beth? You're acting a bit all over the place. Is it Alice's neckpiece? I realise I haven't asked you to show it to me yet but I just thought you were waiting till after *Come Dine with Me*?"

It stuck to my finger like a little map of Italy. I held it right up to my eye. It was the skin from a Brazil nut. John had seen me with the skin from my handful of Brazil nuts stuck in between my teeth.

"I don't really care about the thing in your teeth, Beth – it's not a sex-breaker for me," Rory laughed as he now pulled his green, round-neck woolly jumper up over his head.

I was frozen to the spot. We stared at each other.

"I'm talking about the thing in your teeth, Beth – we all get stuff stuck in our teeth." He laughed heartily now. "It looked like you were missing a front tooth!"

The mood was well and truly lost on me but I couldn't let him down now. I returned to the bed. It served me right.

He leaned in and kissed me softly. I didn't need softly-softly right now – I needed hard and fast. I was so angry with myself. I felt so stupid. There I was thinking I had been looking pretty hot and playing it all pretty cool and all the while I had black teeth. Would he have even realised it was something stuck in my teeth or did he think maybe I'd just really let my dental hygiene go? My head felt like it was going to explode.

"What are you thinking about?" Rory whispered softly and pulled my hair back with his hand.

I looked into his kind eyes and just knew I couldn't do this to him. It was so unfair. He was so kind and treated me so well.

"John Callan," I admitted as the tears started to fall.

Rory sat back. A whiter shade of pale.

"Oh, I see." He stood up now and then sat back down on the edge of the bed. He turned his jumper the right way round and put it back on as I cried hard.

I was crying for a whole load of different reasons. Why had I just admitted that to Rory and hurt him like that? Because I didn't want to lie to him or because I just wanted to say the word 'John' out loud? Because I only wanted to have sex with John right now?

"I'm really sorry, Rory," I sniffed.

"What, is he already home or something? Have you seen him then?" he asked, his mouth clenched now.

"Yes, he came by the market yesterday and I ran and then came by my apartment a while ago and I asked him to leave." I pulled up the edge of the duvet and wiped my nose – it needed changing anyway.

Rory tugged at the sleeves on his jumper as though they were somehow now too short.

"So is this it then? Has he . . ." he shrugged his shoulders, "has he won you back? The wondrous John Callan?" His eyes were glistening.

"No!" I jumped up. "No way, Rory, it's not like that.

I would never, ever take him back! It's just he's been here and it was the first time I'd seen him – spoken to him – in two and a half years – I'm bound to be affected by it."

Rory turned and left the bedroom. I stood looking after him. He came back with some yellow toilet roll for me. I blew my nose hard.

"If it was Martha you'd be the same, you know you would, I know you would." I crumpled the wet tissue up.

He shook his head. "No . . . I really wouldn't, Beth. I really wouldn't feel the way I know you are feeling right now. I love you, Beth. No one else, just you." He shuffled now from one black-spotty-socked foot to the other.

"I love you too, Rory," I said and I meant every single word. I did truly love him. "Please believe me, I really do love you. But I couldn't lie to you . . . please tell me I did the right thing . . . I had to be honest with you. I – I don't know why this is happening to me . . ."

I started to bawl again and he came over and hugged me tight. My body rocked.

"I know you love me, Beth, so let's not mess this up. Don't let him mess this up for us, please? Please don't let him ruin your life all over again? He's not worth it."

As he whispered into my ear, his lips were cold. He was scared. I could feel his heart racing in his chest.

"I won't." I nuzzled into his warm neck and could smell his tea-tree shower-gel.

We stood hugging for a while as my breathing returned to normal.

"Want a faggie?" He rubbed at my obviously smeared eye make-up gently.

"Oh God, yeah." I smiled at him.

We strolled out to the front room area, hand in hand.

"You missed *Come Dine with Me*," I said, nodding at the television which was now showing the news.

"Beth," he turned me in to face him, "I couldn't give a shit about *Come Dine with Me* or anything else. I care about you. I care only about you. I'm not as demonstrative as I'd always like to be but I am what I am and I know we are so good together and I don't want to lose you but I won't be hurt again either. I don't want to be your second fiddle, I won't settle for it. I deserve better." He paused for breath then leaned down and pulled the cigarettes from the brown-paper bag and unravelled the plastic very slowly as I watched. He respected my ritual, taking the middle cigarette out, turning it upside-down and replacing it – something I always did for luck. Then he removed two and gave me one.

I handed him the lighter as I opened the window and we both lit up. He was right. He was a wonderful boyfriend and he'd never hurt me. I didn't want to hurt him ever in any way, shape or form. I was terrified I'd hurt him. He was so right: he didn't deserve it. I took a few minutes to think before I said what I knew I was about to say.

"Rory . . ." I took a long drag and blew out slowly, "I think we should move in together."

Chapter Nine

"I am so, so sorry, Alice – I am just at your house now!" I panted into the phone as I ran around the corner from where I'd found parking in Portobello. I hadn't even tied my laces as I was already so late to collect her for the wedding-dress hunt in Naas. My hair was stuck to the lip gloss I'd hurriedly applied in my wing mirror. The thought flashed into my mind: John hated kissing sticky lips – he always said it made his drink and food taste weird. I banished the thought. My black jeans and black V-neck T-shirt were clean at least.

"Hurry up! I am out the door right now – Dan's up with Lucy!" she hissed at me.

I didn't bother to answer as I shoved the iPhone back into my tiny bag across my chest. Why I'd bought this ridiculously small cream overpriced Frame bag I'd never know. I was a huge fan of the Frame label. I loved the craft of the work and they were all hand-crocheted and exceptionally pretty, but really I was hard pressed to even get my purse in. Every time I put an eyeliner or pen in, it just slipped out through one of the many tiny holes.

I now had a splitting headache. I was also wearing two different-coloured Converse I suddenly noticed as I dropped to one knee to tie the laces. One dark purple, one light. Both Splash. I liked the look. I doubted I'd start a trend or anything but I didn't care.

I reached the driveway and she was standing at the pillar.

"Don't start – I am sorry – it was unavoidable."

I put my hand on my hip so she could link. She did. We fell into step together.

"Where's your car?" She snuggled in to me. She smelled of Jo Malone Figs and some other plants. She was wearing a red shift dress and black pumps. She could have walked straight off a television advert.

"There was no parking on your road as usual." I squeezed her arm.

"So why didn't you just double-park and beep?"

"Oh God, I don't know – I'm a bit all over the place right now, my lovely friend."

"I can see that. You're wearing odd runners. Lucy just coloured in a picture of Iggle Piggle and kept it all in between the lines. I brought it to show you."

"No way!" I was impressed. I had been teaching her for a while so I felt a little stab of pride. "Go, Luce! I told her she could do it. Concentration is all it takes." I beeped the car.

We got in and did our seatbelts. I grabbed for the Chris Isaac CD cover before Alice saw it and shoved it under the driver's seat. She kicked off her pumps as she always did and placed them on her lap. I was immediately reminded of Alice's upcoming hen – I'd have to wear proper shoes.

Alice saw me look at the pumps and instinctively knew what I was thinking. "Don't worry, I have shoes for you to wear for my hen on Saturday night!" she laughed. "But don't forget it like you nearly forgot our date tonight, will you?"

I wished I could have forgotten it. "I hate shoes and I didn't *forget* this evening – I was just delayed." I turned the key and my trusty Fiesta roared to life.

"Do you want me to drive?" Alice asked as she rubbed the foggy window with her hand. It was a pet hate of mine.

"No." I indicated and pulled out.

Alice was also another one of the worst passengers in the world. Apart from John no one else was ever comfortable with me behind the wheel.

"Watch him!" She leaned in and grabbed the dashboard, pumps going flying.

"Alice, I haven't even got to second gear yet – stop now, please. Between you and Rory and my mother! I did pass the national driving test, you do all know that?" I was into second and then third in a flash. "So I'm excited – aren't you? What do you think these *gúnas* will be like then?"

Alice laughed. "Oh stop it, Beth! I'm as sick of wedding dresses as you are. It's all a bit like looking at wallpaper to me at this stage but I'm just enjoying spending the time with you."

I glanced at her.

"*Eyes on the road!*" she screeched back.

"Thanks, Alice, but I want you to have a fabulous dress." I stared straight ahead.

"Oh, I will have – I'm wearing my mother's," she announced matter of factly.

"*What?*" I turned again.

107

"Road!" She pointed now, orange nails flickering madly like tiny traffic cones.

"After all this shopping you're wearing your mother's dress?" I gasped.

"Yeah, of course I am – it's beautiful, it's good luck, all lace and vintage and full of memories and history. Why would I wear anything else?"

It made sense. "So why are we driving all the way to Naas then?"

"Oh no, sorry, we're not. Pull in at the next available old man's pub and we'll just have a few drinks. You can leave the car." She grinned and tapped the orange cones against the glass window on her side.

"Okay." I was relieved. I knew a nice little pub at the end of the road before the roundabout. I could so do with a dirty big pint and a fag. I couldn't have the fag unfortunately as Alice was so anti-smoking she even put me off and I was a sort-of smoker. Every time I lit up she described the lungs of a smoker she had seen in a documentary once. This was my last night out this week though – tomorrow night I'd be up all night finishing pieces for Maks and in a blind panic.

I pulled into the car park and turned off the engine. Alice slid her pumps back on, undid her seatbelt and hopped out. I leaned my head back against the headrest and exhaled slowly. Life was pretty hectic right now.

We sat up at the bar and ordered our usual two pints of Guinness and Raspberry. "Chin-chin!" we clinked when they arrived.

My pint was in a Heineken glass. I hated when barmen did that. I wanted my pint of Guinness in a pint Guinness glass.

Alice had her hair up in a messy bun, very little make-up on and her sallow skin glowed.

"Seriously, what are you putting on your skin this week?" I always asked. It was always something different.

"Lately pure coconut oil." She sipped from the pint. "Ahh, that's Bass!" she said and we giggled.

"You could fry an egg on the sand . . . if you had an egg," I replied and we giggled again. Her face lit up when she laughed. Those perfect straight white teeth lighting up the room like the lights along a runway. "I'm so happy for you," I said, now deadly serious.

She narrowed her eyes. "I know," she nodded. "I'm happy for you too. We are both very happy where we are right now, aren't we, Beth?" Her eyes were still a little too narrowed, as though she wasn't totally sure what my answer was going to be.

"Of course. I just wanted to tell you again that I think Dan's an amazing catch and little Lucy, well, she makes me want to have kids – no other child in the world has ever had that effect on me, not even the little kid with glasses and the cute lispy voice in *Jerry Maguire* and even Rory thought that strange."

"I know – here – look." She opened the silver buckles on her black Mango bag, the one I had bought her for her last birthday, and carefully removed the folded Iggle Piggle drawing.

I took it and opened it, smoothing it out on the bar top. "Oh, you didn't say it was this good!" I pulled the picture up closer to my face and examined it as though it were the Mona Lisa herself. It was bloody great. I had taught young Lucy well. My Jedi.

"Here, I don't want to wreck it, I want to get a frame

for it in the morning." Alice carefully refolded and slid it into her bag.

I peeked in. As always it was the tidiest bag I had ever seen. You could actually see the black material at the bottom. She removed her phone and we spent the next while gazing at adorable pictures of Lucy.

"So will you officially adopt her then once you're married?" I put my half-empty pint beside Alice's almost untouched one.

"It's not that simple really as her mother is still alive as far as we know. Somewhere." She lifted her pint now. It always seemed too big for her delicate hands. She could put them away though. When she wanted. She just didn't want to as often as I did. Never had.

"How could any woman just abandon their child?" I asked again for the hundredth time and she explained again.

"She wasn't well, Beth. God, who are we to judge anyone? I mean, maybe she did the best for Lucy by leaving her, who knows? You know that Dan won't say a bad word about her – says she couldn't help her addiction . . ." She trailed off.

It was very unlike Alice not to finish a sentence.

"What happens then with Lucy?"

"Well, obviously Dan is her legal father so I'd love nothing more than to adopt her as it would establish parental rights for me but, you know, we have talked about this at length. What is it but a word and a piece of paper at the end of the day? She has a natural mother who some day may or may not come back into her life. I will be her stepmother until then . . . if that ever happens. Actually Dan and I hate the word *stepmother* so we are going to use second-mother. If it's something Lucy wants me to do in the future then I will fight tooth and nail to do it but I think we will sit on it for a while. I don't want to push her mother out of her life any more than she already is, if she is around anywhere. Dan feels the same . . . I . . . we both feel the same . . ."

"You should have been a nun, do you know that?" I said.

"Funnily enough, wimples don't suit me, not that they wear them any more – and I simply enjoy sex too much." She grinned and her face lit up again.

I felt it best to change the subject. She and Dan had the healthiest of sex lives, I knew, but Alice kind of kept it private. I liked that.

"Do you think you will ever go back to work?" I asked.

An older man pushed in between us at the bar and we leaned back on our stools. He smelt of dinner. Old-fashioned dinner. Corned beef and cabbage.

"Oh definitely, yeah, when Lucy goes to school. I'd love to get back into fashion again. I miss it. I loved buying." She paused and licked her lips. "Maybe one day we can open our own boutique, Beth? I can do the buying and you can design the jewellery?" She arched her perfectly waxed dark brows.

"Wouldn't that be amazing? Really, though, that's a dream to hold onto, Alice," I enthused.

"Yeah, it really is, isn't it?" she enthused back.

We grinned at each other. Very enthused.

"What are you girls gossipin' 'bout? Diets and boys, I suppose," the older man said, winking rather gratuitously at us as he moved on.

"Random," I said.

"Weirdo," Alice said.

Then she exhaled slowly and I knew it was coming at last.

"So spill the drama then, Beth."

I thought she'd never ask. "I saw him today!" I blurted out.

"I guessed so," Alice returned.

"How did you guess so?" I had done a twelve-week drama Saturday course at Betty Ann Norton's when I was twelve and I rather fancied myself as a bit of an actress.

"Well, you are all over the place and very shiny."

I dragged my hand down my face. "Oh God, am I?"

"Where did you see him?" she heaved.

"He came to my apartment," I heaved back.

"I'll fucking *kill* him!" She banged her hand down hard on the bar.

"Ye all right there, ladies?" the barman asked, flinging the white tea towel over his shoulder. Its landing was with the unexpected grace of a fluttering butterfly – it fluttered high above his head before falling slowly and gracefully, perfectly in line, over his shoulder.

"Oh, grand for a minute – yeah, thanks a million," I replied.

"What did he say to you?" Alice shook her head.

"Ah nothing really, said he just called to say hi, that he'd been looking for me at my work. He asked me for my number. He said it would be good for us to chat before the wedding or something like that. I can't really remember." I drank.

"What's he at? I don't mean to sound cruel but he's just bored, Beth. Don't let him get into your head. Dad said he

112

doesn't know what to be doing with himself. None of his old drinking buddies are alive any more, and the ones his own age all have kids. He's lonely, I guess. The sooner he gets his ass to London the better."

"Yeah," I acknowledged her comments. I drained my pint.

"How did it feel when you saw him?"

"Amazing," I answered her almost before the words left her mouth.

"Oh no, Beth – please, please snap away out of this right now! I'll cut his fucking balls off!" She looked for a nail to bite.

"Can I hold them for you?" I asked meekly and, despite ourselves and the obvious seriousness of my state of mind, we burst out laughing.

"Rory is such a good guy and I think he's a total hottie too," said Alice. "Don't mess anything up there for a one-night stand with my brother."

"I wouldn't, Alice, I really wouldn't, but he has some sort of mysterious power over me – it's like when I'm with him I lose all control. And then something even worse happened. Something so bad . . ." I hung my head, almost hitting it off the bar top. "No! You didn't? Oral?" Her eyes bulged.

Mine bulged back. "Alice Callan. What? No! Wash your mammy mouth out! I had the skin of a Brazil nut or nuts in between my teeth the whole time – and it looked like I had a tooth missing." I shut my eyes tight, the pain still very real. I stared at my charm bracelet and the little silver dog with the one eye looked back at me.

Alice's body started to shake and then she snorted and then she started to laugh so hard.

"It's not one bit funny, Alice," I said, stone-faced, as tears rolled down her cheeks.

"It is a bit funny," she managed to quote *Peppa Pig* as she searched for a napkin on the bar.

I was not amused. Usually when Alice laughed really hard it was so contagious that, even if you didn't know what she was laughing at, you couldn't help but laugh too. She had one of those silent shaky laughs that takes ages to explode. The Brazil-nut skin between my two front teeth was not funny to me in any way, shape or form. It was horrific. I seriously doubted there would ever be a day when I could laugh it off.

Alice found a packet of miniature baby wipes in her bag (as you do) and dried her eyes with one before she composed herself. She took a drink and found her serious face. "Then stay away from him. After the wedding he goes to London and then probably back to New York or LA or wherever his career takes him. Don't get messed up in the tailwind."

"You're so right and that is why . . . drum roll, please, Alice Callan . . ."

She dutifully drummed her lean and now slightly bitten orange-polished fingers on the bar. Although she bit she never, ever bit them to a stage of buttiness.

"Rory and I have decided it's time to move in together!"

"No way!" Her face lit up. "That's absolutely amazing news! Oh my God, you waited until now to tell me that? That's wonderful – I am so happy for you both!" She really was ecstatic. A little bit over the top if you asked me.

I twirled a charm: it was now the broken lady with the cane, a tiny woman with no arms but a beautiful face with tiny thin legs and a cane. I'd had numerous discussions with this small lady over the years. She really was an excellent listener. I purposely didn't give her a name as I wanted to her remain anonymous to me. A stranger I could tell anything to and she couldn't judge. I took a deep breath and exhaled slowly.

"Is he moving into yours then?"

You would think I had just told her we'd invented an anti-wrinkle cream that actually worked, she was that delighted.

"No, we're going to move into my parents' – rent free, if you can believe that. We are talking . . . just talking, so calm down . . . about saving up for a house!"

She rested her pink tongue between her two front teeth. Took her time with the information I had just given her. Then slipped her tongue slowly back into her mouth. "I think it's great, I really do," she said at last. "Why so suddenly, though, is my only question."

"I told Rory about John – well, that he had called and I was a bit all over the place. He was so good and so understanding and told me how much he loved me but that he wouldn't be hurt by me and, Alice, you know, I never want to hurt him."

My lips were suddenly dry so I reached into my bag hanging on the back of the stool for my rosy Vaseline and generously smeared it all over my lips. Alice tipped her own lip to subtly tell me to blend more. I did. Then she smacked her top and bottom lips off one another so I followed her lead.

"What is it you want from him really, Beth? I've never pushed you on your relationship with him before but I think I need to know now."

"I just want for him to be happy and for me to be happy, I guess. I mean, isn't that what you want from your relationship with Dan?"

She shook her head. "To be happy? Well, it is *one* of the many things I want out of my relationship but I also want his friendship, his passion, his heart, his world, his mind, his everything really. Do you want all that with Rory?"

"I suppose," I managed and ran my finger along the froth on the empty pint glass. "You 'suppose'? What does that mean?" Alice tilted her pint glass.

"You don't understand, Alice – John broke my heart – he –"

"For fuck's sake, Beth, I know!" She raised her pint glass high in the air. Just under half full now so there was no danger of spillage. "I know all this but it was almost three years ago and you have to let it go. You have to learn to kill him off – he's gone – he will poison your life if you don't." Her eyes were cloudy.

I clenched my teeth and raised my voice. "It was only two and a half years ago, Alice, and it's hard!"

"It shouldn't be. Not any more, Beth."

She had no sympathy for me now, I realised. I'd worn her out. I'd drained her.

"I'm only trying to help you," she told me.

We sat in silence. I stared at the clock above the bar. Alice tidied her already tidy bag.

"I'm moving in with Rory and that's that," I said at last. "Do you mind if we leave now? I have so much to do and I have my big meeting with Maks in two days."

"I know you do, no worries, let's go." She zipped up her bag and drained her pint.

I asked her if I could drive after the one, though I knew too well what her response would be.

"Are you out of your mind? You've had a pint!"

"But I thought one was okay?"

"No, none is okay – none. Zero alcohol. Dan will tell you that."

"Okay."

We thanked the barman and he muttered something about getting "rich offa you pair".

We opened the heavy oak door and I stuck out my hand and a recession cab magically appeared. We didn't continue the conversation in the cab. Alice talked about my meeting with Paula Mak and I just listened. What pieces she preferred, what way I should display. I wasn't listening any more. I rubbed my spherical mirrored disco-ball charm on my bracelet. I loved the texture of where the stones were missing. It was bitty and sore on my fingers. I liked the feeling.

Alice got out and I kissed her goodbye. I closed my eyes for the rest of the journey home.

Rory was asleep when I got in, the TV still on showing a foreign football match. He was on the couch, glasses hanging off. I stared at him. He was really so handsome. I gently folded his specs and threw the red Laura Ashley fleece rug over him. Then I kicked off my mismatched Converse without opening the laces, padded into the kitchen and took a large bottle of Ballygowan from the fridge. I tugged up my heavy workbox and took it and the water into the bedroom and closed the door.

Tonight I was going to create. Tonight I was going to use every ounce of the pure physical emotional energy

John Callan had instilled in me and I was going to make jewellery. Brilliant jewellery. Beautiful unique pieces. Lone statement pieces. Tonight I was going to make new brooches, rings, necklaces, earrings and bracelets.

It was ironic. I was well aware that jewellery originally had been used for a number of reasons. Functional, as in basically to clasp something closed with pins or buckles. For symbolism, to show membership or status of a religious affiliation. For adornment. As a way to amass wealth. And for protection – as amulets to ward off evil. Now it was doing what it was originally intended to do. It was protecting me from my thoughts about John every time I made a piece. I always started off thinking about him with every movement I made but eventually became so consumed by the work my mind drifted to a place I didn't know where.

I carefully laid out seeded beads, crystals, gemstones and shells. Shove that up your hole, John Callan, I thought as I began my work. I popped open my black box of wire and beading thread. I wanted to make something tight. Something striking. I measured out my wire, adding another good six inches for a sturdy clasp. I draped my measuring tape around my neck. I dug out two crimp beads and clasp and then I searched through my beads. I waded through my supplies – pearl beads, glass beads, crystal beads, seed beads, plastic beads – until finally I saw the right beads for the mood I was in. Metal beads. A thick heavy metal beaded necklace with Tibetan silver.

I dug out my beading board – I always found it beneficial, allowing my designs to be laid out and measured before stringing. I played around with the design for a while until I was satisfied. Then I made the necklace.

I loved it. It made such a strong statement.

When I finished that, I decided on working on a piece of jewellery for myself. I rarely made for myself as all I really wore was my charm bracelet but now, coming up to the wedding, I felt like making something for me. I had bought some rare silk pink material last week that was the exact match of my Brown Thomas bridesmaid dress. I wanted it to be something pretty and soft. I grabbed my pad and sketched it. I wanted a soft decorated bracelet made with this silk fabric. I leaned over and removed twenty-one pale-pink glass-tinted beads from my box and laid them out. I removed the piece of fabric, cut the ends off it and then cut it in half. Perfect size for my wrist. I fed one half of the fabric through a jump ring and tied a knot to hold the beads, then did the same with the other piece of fabric. I attached several jump rings to one of the pieces of fabric I had knotted and a clasp to the other. I loved the mood of this piece. It wasn't angry: it was ladylike and together. Sophisticated. I folded the material in half and cut to make same lengths, then I folded the ribbon lengths in halves again and tied them together forming a loop. I threaded the first glass bead onto the material, immediately tying a knot after it. It was like every glass bead was my head and I was trying to protect it. I tied those knots really tight. I beaded and knotted and beaded and knotted until I had used all twenty-one beads. I wanted a cigarette. I left a couple of centimetres of fabric after the final set of beads, then I tied a double knot to form a loop to end the bead section. I took my time finishing it, lost again in the moment, and when it was done it was perfect. A perfect chief bridesmaid's accessory. A pale silk bracelet adorned with pale-pink glass-tinted beads. Fragile, transparent but original.

I should make one for Lucy too, I thought now, as I rummaged for suitable larger beads and went through my old fabrics for something white. I found it. I was lost again. I didn't think about John. I just kept going: beading, cutting, threading, beading, cutting, threading. I was happy.

Chapter Ten

I woke early and Rory was beside me. I snuggled in to him and he stirred. His skin was warm as toast. He rubbed his foot along the inside of my leg.

"Sorry, love, I fell asleep on the couch," he said. "I drank all those cans . . . I didn't realise I was drinking so much . . . I need to take a few weeks off it." He turned to face me, his shaved head bristly as I ran my hands over it. "Did you work late? I got in beside you around six."

"Yeah, until around five this morning but it was so worth it. You had four cans of Bud, Rory – you're not exactly Oliver Reed. I'm delighted with what I made – I even made some bits for myself and Lucy for the wedding – will I show you?" I knew now every time I mentioned the wedding we would both be tense.

"Please." He rubbed his eyes and leaned over for his glasses.

"I took your glasses off for you last night – hang on – I'll get them." I pulled the sheets back, jogged out and grabbed his glasses from the arm of the couch. Padding back into my room, I picked up the work on my dressing table. I was wearing his grey Penguin bargain-bucket T-shirt (it had a tiny hole under the left armpit – the only reason it was in the bargain bucket – I'd fixed it in two seconds) and my pink knickers. Old knickers, really old knickers. The material had even come away slightly on the elastic around the top so a bit of the pink fabric hung down. I needed to make more of an effort in the bedroom. Alice had an underwear drawer that I almost considered pornographic. The flimsy things she called knickers! She wasn't a thong girl by any means, but all these red and black silky, lacy numbers were amazing to me. Alice had low rise, high rise, boy shorts, girl shorts – she had the whole range. I had knickers: they came tightly rolled in a pack of six and they covered my arse.

I gently placed the items I'd made last night onto the bed and handed him his glasses. He sat up and picked up the pieces I had made through the night, one by one, examining each piece for lengthy periods of time. He held the thin silver bangle with the leather trim for an age.

"Is this for men and women?" he asked.

"Maybe," I answered. It was a bit butch.

"Can I have one?" He rubbed his thumb across the brown leather.

"Sure – you really like it?" I scratched my hair. It badly needed a wash.

"I love it." He pulled his wrist through and it was good on him. Manly. Not like One Direction type jewellery but more like a Johnny Depp piece.

He admired the fabric bracelets and necklaces. He held up the brass hoops with the small brass ball slipped through and the silver dangling five-chains-entwined piece

I loved. It was ultra-long and came down to the navel. I had also made some backless jewellery to go with backless dresses. I loved women's backs. John had always loved my back. As we lay naked in bed he would spend hours tracing his fingers down my spine. Vertebra by vertebra. He gave the best back massages. He would warm the baby oil in his hands for ages and then smooth it all over my skin, rubbing gently at first, so gentle sometimes I wasn't quite sure he was touching me at all. Then it would get harder and the muscles in my back would drop and relax. He spent ages on me. He never wanted to stop. It was never a chore. He seemed to enjoy it just as much as I did. Funnily enough he didn't like being massaged himself. "It makes me itchy," he'd say every time I tried and he'd turn over and pull me down on top of him. My body always felt so desirable after his touch, so soft and relaxed. It was some of the best foreplay we had: a simple massage.

"You are so talented, Beth," Rory said, breaking into my despicable daydream. "These are incredible – Paula's going to love them, I know she will. Well done!"

He kissed me hard on the mouth. I could taste cheesy nachos. I kissed him back. "I'm going to have to run," he said. "I have to be in Salthill by midday. I've a hen's booked, believe it or not – *Dirty Dancing* followed by *Shame* – go figure." He kissed my nose and left my bed.

I gathered the pieces and laid them all out on the dressing table. I needed to put final touches to the earrings and other bits. I'd run out of plastic backs and I never used metal ones – so I'd need to pop into my suppliers in town and get a bag of backs. I did a quick stock-take: I also needed bicones, bead-aligners, jump rings, split rings and cotton waxed cord if I was to work again tonight. I jotted these things down on my notepad. Almost as important, I also needed something to wear to the meeting, so I needed to raid Alice's wardrobe.

"Do you fancy an omelette?" I called in through the bathroom door as Rory showered and sang "Bitter Sweet Symphony" at the top of his voice.

"What?" he shouted.

"Omelette!" I shouted.

"Great!" he shouted.

"Great!" I shouted back.

The kitchen was a mess. Rory was not tidy. John had been immaculate. All his dishes were in the sink all right – he just hadn't washed them. His place was worse. Entering Rory's flat was like returning home to a crime-scene re-enactment from a vicious robbery on *Garda Patrol* (because his wallpaper was that old!).

I opened the fridge and removed the egg box. There was little else in the fridge apart from a bit of cheese and half a packet of processed cheap ham. "Cham" John used to call it. I really needed to do a healthy shop. "Please do not be empty!" I implored the egg box and it wasn't, joy, it was hatching four eggs.

I don't check dates. I once ate a sandwich late at night at a music festival when a scruffy-looking dude sporting the longest dreadlocks I had ever seen knelt down beside me in his flip-flops, very obviously stoned. "Word of warning, sugartits – management got me to change all the best-before dates on the sambos so avoid the prawns, yeah?" He winked at me before tugging on his reefer and slowly walking into the moonlight. John had burst into spontaneous applause. He thought the guy was great for some reason. When I pushed him on it, he said, "He called you 'sugartits' – how funny is that?" I hadn't laughed. John had run after the guy and spent ages talking to him. Then he brought him over to the burger stand and bought him a double cheeseburger with fried onions and chips. "Fascinating dude," he informed me as he flopped beside me on the grass an hour later.

Anyway I never checked dates. Things were always out of date. I hadn't died yet.

I cracked the eggs into my large brown mixing bowl – it had been a joke gift from John when we got the Temple Bar place. "So as you can bake 'n' shit," he'd laughed, his left hand holding the bowl and his right hand mock-mixing. "Next year I'm getting you a pinny and some oven gloves," he added, dead pan. I'd loved the bowl and I'd wanted to bake for him, as pathetic as that now sounds. I'd even taken a few classes. I'd made bread-and-butter pudding and crap flaky apple tarts. John ate them all.

I mixed the eggs and grabbed some hard cheese and the two last slices of equally hard ham and chopped them in. I heated the pan and my creation came to life, the eggs bubbling together like the bittersweet symphony Rory was still singing. Rory spent way too long in the shower.

"It's ready!" I called as I heard him emerge.

"Smells fab – I'm Starvin' Marvin – all's I had last night was another bag of nachos. I didn't know if you were bringing me home a dinner so I didn't bother cooking."

"Shit, sorry, I did say that, didn't I? Listen, I'll cook for us tonight . . . a nice spag bol and a bottle of red? How's that sound? I want an early night before my Maks meeting."

I handed him his plate and he took it to the table. I plated mine.

"Would you, Beth? I'd love that. I imagine this is going to be a mad day . . . these hens are from Liverpool and sound like some party animals – they want me for lunch time! I've told them I have to be on the road by six so I will be back around eight. Will I come straight here?" He added salt and then brown sauce to his omelette. YR never HP. John was HP never YR.

We tucked in. It was nice but here's my problem with omelettes – no pizzazz! Always the same – grand, bit bland. A bit of Tabasco sauce was what I needed. There was no point in getting up: I knew I didn't have any Tabasco sauce.

John and I used to steal Tabasco sauces from restaurants whenever we saw them on tables. Once Rory and I had been in County Clare at his cousin Nora's wedding and we went to O'Looney's on the pier for lunch the day after and I put the Tabasco sauce into my bag. He was horrified.

"Put that back, Beth! What on earth are you doing?"

"It's only a sauce!" I blushed scarlet.

"It's stealing is what it is! Imagine if every person just went around taking sauces off the tables – the owners would be bankrupt!"

I put it back. I felt like a total eejit. He was right of course. It was stealing. John had never looked at it like that so I hadn't either. John reckoned, what with all the mark-ups on the food and drink we had paid for, the Tabasco should be covered – sure, as he said one night, what if we'd just used the whole bottle during one sitting?

Right now I wished I was one of those people who did

a proper weekly shop. I just got what I needed on a daily basis. But that was the problem. I didn't know I was going to be making an omelette this morning so therefore how could I be prepared?

Rory finished in seconds and got up. He went and grabbed his keys from the hall table. I could hear them rattle. He was like a prison warden there were so many keys on that bunch.

"Shit, sorry!" He ran back and cleared his plate away. "In the sink, right?" he asked, pleased with himself.

"Yeah, thanks." I smiled at my Domestic God boyfriend as he clattered the dishes, unrinsed, into the ceramic sink.

He kissed me again and was gone.

My apartment was quiet. I liked it. I washed up and then showered and washed my hair. With my hair in a towel and my fluffy robe on, I sat on my couch. Things had gone from ever so quiet, plodding along on the market stall, watching movies with Rory, to this: massive opportunity work wise, moving in with Rory, and John's return. I lay my head back on the soft beige cushions and rubbed some wonderfully expensive wonder-cream all over my face. I knew it wouldn't make me look ten years younger, I knew it wouldn't reduce the appearance of fine lines and wrinkles, and I knew eighty-nine per cent of women didn't think it would either – it just felt nice to pretend to believe it. I couldn't quite gauge how I felt. I let the cold cream soak into my pores and my skin drank it up.

But I knew one thing was wrong. Very wrong. I was about to have a cigarette . . . in the morning. That could mean only one thing. I was officially all over the shop once again. My devil-may-care attitude had come back to visit.

I had to get a cab to collect my car and then I drove straight to Portobello. Alice took down her impressive variety of teas, read the back of a few boxes and made me a green tea.

"Here, sip this," she said.

Alice Callan. Medicine Woman.

"Lucy, will you help Auntie Ethy and me choose some clothes for her big important meeting?" she asked the little girl.

"Yes, please," she said and Alice smiled that goofy grin she sported basically every time words left Lucy's tiny mouth.

Lucy looked adorable this morning, dressed in denim dungarees and a beige top with black tights and beige mini Uggs (they weren't real Uggs but they were the exact same to me and especially to Lucy). Her blonde hair was in two plaits and she was cuddling Loopy Loo, her favourite doll. Her mother had bought her the doll from the hospital shop in the six days they'd spent together, and had christened the doll Loopy Loo, Dan told me. Said a lot about her mother, I thought – though I never said.

The three of us made our way up the stairs.

Alice's room was like somewhere you could easily find Kevin McCloud wandering around enthusing into the camera about its design, speaking softly about how everything in the room just fit. It was perfect. Perfectly girly and perfectly tidy and perfectly spacious. Perfectly perfect. Just like Alice. Her King-size double bed was neatly made in black-and-white satin sheets with matching duvet cover and she had all those tiny, fluffy

128

extra pillows scattered over it in matching pillowcases. There were two small white lockers with black handles on either side of the bed with matching silver lamps on top (no plugs or wires – you simply clapped your hands). Nothing scattered on the tables. Perfectly tidy. Soft cream thick carpet massaged your feet. A small chrome bookshelf was handmade to fit by a design student at the Dun Laoghaire College of Art & Design and ran under the window. It sported books about Childcare and Healthy Eating and The Secret. The glass-mirrored sliding wardrobes were open. I couldn't imagine ever being able to leave my wardrobe open . . . surely all that shit piled up would fall out? Alice had no shit piled up. It was row upon row of hangers. Shoes and boots sat matching and spooning each other in a weird plastic contraption. It was all very futuristic.

Lucy climbed up on the bed and settled there happily, Loopy Loo on her lap.

"Okay." Alice plopped down beside the little girl. "I thought something suity, rather official, but something you can add your own touches to with your jewellery . . . so I thought this . . ." She was up again. She leaned into the wardrobe.

I had to close my eyes, partially blinded by the white shirt she pulled out on its padded hanger. "So a nice white shirt and this . . ." She leaned in again and removed a black trouser suit on a cream-velvet padded hanger.

Where would one buy padded hangers, I wondered?

"I love this suit – I got it in London, in Soho, when I was on a buying trip years ago. Now I think the waist will need to be let out a little and you'll need to check the leg-length." She draped herself across the bed now and pulled

129

out a tiny drawer in her bedside locker. She didn't have to tug at it, it just glided open. She removed a card. "This is the alteration company I always use. You should go over there now and see if it can be done this afternoon. This is the perfect outfit for Paula Mak. Trust me, Beth."

I did trust her.

She plopped back beside Lucy, picked up Loopy Loo and made her do a little dance across the bed. Lucy loved it.

I did trust her. One hundred per cent.

"I can't wreck your suit though," I said.

"You can. You can alter it and keep it. I don't need it, you do. It's too important for you not to make the right first impression. But, Beth, I'd like you to keep it well – you know, use it, mix it up with different vest tops under – it's a staple piece for your wardrobe. With a bit of tweaking it will be perfect on you."

I was holding the white shirt under my chin in the mirrored wardrobe. "So basically that all means you don't think my style is acceptable?" I looked back at her.

"I mean, dear friend, you can't go to the biggest meeting of your life in Converse and old Levi jeans." She made a funny face.

"Funny face, Maman!" Lucy laughed and proceeded to convert Alice's face into different looks. Some good. Some not so good.

"As if!" I turned back to the mirror and widened my eyes. Now it was my turn to make a face – that had been exactly what I'd been planning to wear before Alice suggested this 'Maks Clothes Meeting'. "Okay – thanks."

"Now what I suggest is you get a white vest top – just go to Penney's or Dunnes – and put it under the shirt.

Leave the shirt buttoned way down so that you can really see your necklaces – wear a few – rock your style. I love that long thick silver chain with the smaller chains intertwined and the diamante silver cross at the bottom. You are your creations, Beth."

I nodded. I felt sick. I picked up the green tea I'd brought upstairs with me. I sipped the foul browny health drink. My God but it was gross. I sipped again. A cup of tea was supposed to make you relax not retch.

"We have a wedding meeting with the hotel tonight so I will be out . . . don't panic . . . get to bed early . . . leave in plenty of time in the morning . . . do not smoke in the car on the way there – I cannot stress that point strongly enough . . ."

I knew now I'd definitely smoke in the car – it was in my head now and I wouldn't be able to think about anything else. I must remember to buy an Impulse and spray myself clean of all smells after.

"And most important of all, Beth, just be yourself. Your work is amazing and I know she will love it."

Pep talk over.

Cuddles.

I left to get the suit altered, to buy a vest top, to pick up supplies and to buy my ingredients for my romantic dinner.

Chapter Eleven

The white shirt, white vest top and black suit hung from the shower rail. I left them there and closed the bathroom door. I tugged it harder. It never closed properly. I didn't want the clothes to smell of spaghetti bolognese and smoke. I had opened the bathroom window out on the street – the room was full of condensation.

I returned to stir my Nigella masterpiece. I wished I liked my own food like Nigella did hers. I suppose that made me a bit weird. I wasn't really all that mad about food I had to make myself, I realised. Maybe because I picked. I kept picking so by the time I sat down to the meal I was full.

John used to make me paella. "Here, try this!" He'd hold the spoon out and I would open my mouth and he would feed me. It was always so hot my mouth would hurt.

One time when we were on holidays in Nerja John asked the chef of Cyril's (plain name for a traditional Spanish restaurant, I acknowledge) if he could shadow him while he made the day's massive pot of paella. John, who was really tanned by now, was wearing black shorts, white boot Converse unlaced and no socks . . . and more importantly no top. Even Carlos the chef looked twice at him and I bet Carlos had never really looked at a man's body before in his entire life.

"Eees all in zee sauce, Johaan." Carlos spooned some paella into John's open mouth and John groaned.

"Inzeed it is, Carlos, my good man, inzeed it is." He winked at me.

I was sitting on the high-backed wooden stool, my bare bronzed legs swinging. I laughed. I always laughed when I was with John – sometimes when I didn't feel like laughing at all, other times when I found things so hilarious I almost peed my pants. I watched Carlos shell prawns, chop chorizo, red peppers, scallions, coriander, dice chicken and pork and all sorts of multicoloured ingredients that I hadn't a clue of the names of. Then he added the saffron and the magic happened. The colours changed. The smells were incredible.

I wondered now whatever happened to that light-blue halter-neck top I wore that day? I stirred my pathetic bolognese. Tinned tomatoes and a jar of Uncle Ben's. Nigella wouldn't taste this. I did chop and add the eight mushrooms and the two onions I had bought in Get Fresh.

"'Tis only me!" The door banged. "How are ya? Something smells bloody good!" Rory removed his glasses and rubbed his eyes. "Hens! Honest to God, the things ye women get up to when no men are around! It's truly frightening." He smiled now and sniffed the air as he unravelled his extra-long black-and-white scarf.

He reminded me of Pepé Le Pew. I didn't tell him this.

"Hope you're hungry?" I ignored his last remark because I knew only too well how true it was. It was one of the reasons I hated hen parties so much. This licence to be a crazy woman. I didn't need the licence for one hen party a year. I could go crazy any time I wanted. I just didn't want to. I flicked on the stereo and played some Beatles – "The Long and Winding Road". Rory loved this track.

"A glass, sir?" I offered.

"Red would be lovely. This is great – I could get used to this." He ran his hands several times over his closely shaven head. He'd been to The Grafton Barber on Saturday. The one in Jervis Street.

I stirred and turned off the gas. I loved the smell of gas. Ahh, I know gas doesn't smell – so I loved whatever it was they added to the gas to make it smell. I poured us two very full glasses of red wine (I didn't do units, I did glasses) and carried them to the set table.

"Wow, easy – you have a big, big day ahead of you tomorrow." He took the glass steadily from me with both hands as though it was so full and so heavy he needed two hands to hold it.

"It's just one glass of red wine with dinner, Rory." Suddenly I was in a bad mood. Just like that. His comment had really bugged me.

I turned my back and went back to the cooker. I spooned out the bolognese and drained the spaghetti. I piled the plates. I added parmesan.

Rory obviously felt the silence kick him in the balls. "No, I know, I'm not saying that," he said at last. "God, I'm not saying that at all, Beth – I'm just saying we should be mindful of your meeting in the morning and don't you need to finish the leather trim on the bi-bracelet?" As we had now christened it.

Rory was never argumentative. John and I would scream and shout each other down. I needed a bit of an argument sometimes just to vent.

"Yeah, I know." I sat.

We tucked in. I had no appetite as I thought about John sitting opposite me feeding me the bolognese and refilling my wineglass at every available opportunity.

"Mmmmm – gorgeous," said Rory. "You really should cook more, you're so good at it. When we move into Parkside we should definitely home-cook as often as we can." He swallowed. Sipped. Scooped. "How about one of us cooks night on, night off, and then we alternate the cooking every other weekend? In fact, wouldn't it be a great idea to take a cookery course together? They do them in the Iona community centre."

It was already too complicated for me. Too domesticated.

He continued: "Another thing we should look at is home freezing. Say you made an extra batch of this – we could just take it out of the freezer before we go to work in the morning and, hey presto, a readymade," he raised his index finger in the air here, pushing home this point, "yet freshly made tea."

I shoved another spoonful in and shoved it down my neck with a huge gulp of red wine. The CD ended and the living room fell silent. We both put down our cutlery.

Rory leaned across my table and took my hands. "I can sense how nervous you are. Don't be. You are wildly talented. You are the most talented, hardworking, funny, clever woman I have ever met. Don't think for one second I don't count my lucky stars every day you choose to spend your life with me, because I do. I love you so much, Beth. I pinch myself sometime that you chose me."

My mobile rang. I coughed. My heart started to race. It couldn't be John, could it? I had taken his name out of my phone but I still knew his number off by heart.

"You better get it?" Rory said as he lifted his fork again.

I found it just on the third ring on top of the microwave. It was Paula Mak.

"Beth?"

"Hi, Paula." I breathed heavily.

"Listen, I'm so sorry to do this to you at such short notice but I have to cancel tomorrow . . . something has come up."

My heart hit the kitchen tiles. "Eh . . . oh . . . okay . . . sure no worries." I shut my eyes tight and waved frantically at Rory who was leaning over his plate and twirling the pasta around his fork and sucking it up at a ferocious speed.

"It can't be helped, I'm afraid . . . it's a very personal matter . . ."

I jumped in. "No, absolutely, don't you worry – that's okay, Paula, I completely understand."

Now Rory looked up, a saucey chin on him.

"I love your designs, Beth, you know that. Can we reschedule? I'm looking at my diary here . . . I am flat out this month . . . let's see . . . oh, here's a rare window . . . say June sixteenth at noon?"

The wedding. The day of Alice and Dan's wedding. "Oh, I can't, Paula, that's the day of my best friend's

136

wedding – I'm her bridesmaid – chief bridesmaid."

Silence for a moment. "Damn, I am away the next week and in China the week after . . . and then . . . okay, leave it with me for now and I'll get back to you."

"No!" I almost shouted. "No . . . I mean . . . sorry, pardon me, I just . . . can we not settle a date now so we both have it in our diaries, please?" I groaned loudly into the phone.

Rory jumped up. He shook his head at me so hard his glasses almost fell off. "What the hell? Calm down!" he mouthed wildly.

"I'm afraid not, Beth. Speak soon." Paula Mak from Maks hung up.

"*Fuck!*" I bounced the phone off the floor and it shattered. "*Fucking hell!*" I screamed and fell to my knees. "All that fucking work! *Arghhh!*" I screamed again. "*Fffffuuckkk her!*"

Rory stayed silent. He knew me better than to give me the old there-there-it-will-be-grand-so-it-will-so-it-will line. He did what any decent loving boyfriend would do and refilled my wineglass, put it on the floor beside me and left the kitchen.

I cradled the glass, sitting on the floor, until it got kind of dark in there. I was mourning this lost opportunity like it was the end of the world. Beth's Bitz had saved me. Beth's Bitz had given me back my life. I owed it so much. I had worked damn hard on getting Paula to see me. I had called and called, emailed and emailed, handwritten letters, facebooked her, tweeted her and dropped in to see her when I knew she was in the store. She didn't suffer fools gladly. She could make a label. She had taken in Frame, a label of knitwear from an Irish designer and made it a national and now international label. That was the label of the tiny crochet bag I had. The designer behind Frame was never seen. She was fragile apparently. I knew it was just a clever marketing ploy by Paula to raise interest in her profile. Frame now employed hundreds of people and was a huge success. All because of Paula Mak.

I dragged myself up to the kitchen table and sat. The dinners were cold and unfinished, grease film slowly covering the top of the uneaten unlean mince.

Rory was in the bedroom. Poor Rory, I didn't deserve him. He certainly didn't deserve me. I scooped my hair up and tied it with the black skinny elastic from my wrist. I let out a slow breath before refilling my wineglass. I just needed to hold it all together until after the wedding. He would be gone again. I could get back to normal. Sit by the phone and wait for Paula to ring. I would use the time to design and create even better pieces. Build up my stock. Sure this time next year Frame and Beth's Bitz could host a joint buyer's party in LA maybe? I gulped and the strong liquid eased my anxiety.

"You okay?" Rory sidled into the seat opposite me.

"Yeah, sorry, bit of a Meryl Streep moment there, huh? She cancelled on me."

"I know." He sat perfectly still. "Sorry," he offered now.

Rory hated this type of rally. But sometimes life knocked them back to you hard and you had to hit the ball with your best instinctive lob or lose the point.

"Why?" he almost whispered.

"Some family problem or another, I dunno . . . then she wanted to reschedule –"

"On Alice's wedding day."

138

"Yeah," I sighed.

"She will get back to you, Beth, I know she will." He twisted the unfinished plate round and round in front of him. Round and round.

We were going round and round and we both knew it. I knew Rory hadn't been ready to move in with me either when Dad had offered but the fear of losing me to John had pushed him to agree so fast.

"I'm going to bed, Rory." I stood.

I needed to be alone with my thoughts again. This was happening all too frequently. I should be sharing all these innermost thoughts with my boyfriend. But how? How could I share when all I wanted to really think about was John?

Chapter Twelve

I removed my cerise-pink hard hat with '*Alice's Hen Extravaganza*' on it, excused myself from the choking confines of the party dinner table and slipped away for a quiet smoke. I couldn't think of another thing to say on the subject of *Britain's Got Talent*. I didn't watch it. I knew nothing of the immensely talented dog from a few years ago.

"Yer joking, aren't ya?" Angela had screamed in my face. Orange face, severe bun and too much purple eye shadow for my liking. She sprayed perfume on herself at the table, oh, every fifteen minutes or so and it was all I could do not to throw up.

"How could you never have heard of Pudsey?" She shook her head at every other girl at the table, dragging them onto her side whether they agreed or not.

If this was a tug-of-war I was being pulled very quickly to the white line.

They all shook back. Alice stifled a laugh in her napkin. I glared at her.

"I really can't answer that, Angela – it's just another one of life's mysteries, I guess," I'd said deadpan before I'd pushed back my chair and muttered "Loo".

John was obsessed with life's mysteries. He could never understand whose cruel idea it was for the word 'lisp' to have an 's' in it or why 'abbreviation' was such a long word. I smiled to myself now as I squeezed through the crowd. I laughed at John's favourite mystery of the world: why Tarzan never had a beard.

"The smokin' area's full." A bouncer blocked my way like a policeman at the scene of a violent murder, his two arms lifted high by his sides. I imagined him saying, 'There's nothing to see here . . . go back to your houses, folks, please!' Instead he merely said, "Take a seat and I'll call you when there is space." He pointed to a black leather low-slung three-seater.

A queue to smoke. I'd seen it all now. I sat. The bar was heaving. The couch jerked me forward as someone threw themselves on it. I turned to see who'd flopped beside me. I immediately lost a breath.

It was a very, very drunk John Callan.

I bit my tongue hard. It hurt. I felt my brain perform a waltz with my eyes before it twirled them back into my sockets, bowed in thanks and got back to work. I shook my thoughts straight as he spoke.

"Heyalo there, Beth Burrows," he slurred at me as he pulled a bottle of rum from the inside pocket of his leather jacket and twisted off the cap.

I stared at the silver buttons on the pockets of the jacket and the small silver zips on the sleeves.

"Ya want some?" He thrust the bottle under my nose as the bouncer turned his back again. Had he followed me here? He must have known the hen party was here. Was he here to see me? No, surely not? I curled my toes up tight in Alice's black kitten-heeled ankle boots. I felt slightly lightheaded at the unexpectedness of it all.

"Go on then," I heard myself saying in a relatively normal tone. Those Betty Ann Norton drama classes had really paid off. I took the bottle, drank a long drink and then shuddered as it scalded my mouth. His elbow rubbed off mine, the electricity startling.

"You always loved your Captain Morgan, Beth." He slugged now, replaced the cap and put the bottle back inside his jacket. The music was loud. He put his hand on the back of my head to pull me in close so he could speak into my ear. "I like Goldfish now," he said.

I pulled back and stared into his dark drunken eyes. He was so close. It was almost surreal. The smell of his hot skin so familiar. Like a dream.

"Shut up, John."

He could lip-read that. He gave half a smile. He pulled my head in again, his hand warm on my cold hair.

"I wouldn't eat a whole one though."

Now it was my turn. I entwined my fingers into his long hair and pulled his head, rather too harshly, and spoke into his ear.

"We haven't talked in over two and a half years and this is what you choose to say to me?" I could feel his breath on my face. We were inches from each other, our noses almost touching.

He pulled his hair back from his eyes with his left hand. I was mesmerised by his closeness. "Here is the thing . . ." He fidgeted then coughed and reached inside his jacket again for the bottle.

"John? John Callan!" A very thin tall blonde in a red halter-neck, cut-off denims and cowboy boots shouted over the music. "Oh my Gaawwddddd, it *is* you! Well, howl at the moon and grow me some freakin' *Twilight*-like fangs! Amy! Gail! Quick! Here, look – it's John Callan! We were just in New York, shopping like, and we watched your show *Bleak*, and it's amazing! You are incredible, totes amazeballs! What are you doing here? Yo, hold this!" She thrust her glass into my hand and reached into her skin-tight back pocket for her iPhone – how she fitted anything into those pockets was a mystery.

I looked at John. He was sort of loving it. He was smirking at her in his *'I love myself too'* kind of a way. "Yo, cool, yeah," he said and slowly stood up.

"Can we get a photo with you?"

"Absolutely," John said.

"Here, chick, can you take it?" She thrust her phone at me now, in its all-pink sparkly Playboy cover. Why on earth any woman would want her phone in a Playboy cover was completely beyond me.

"You need me to wipe you too?" I asked as I now stood up, her glass in one hand and her phone in the other.

She made a face at me. It didn't suit her.

I snapped a few pictures of the girly sticks with the manly tree and handed back her dirty iPhone and her smelly Red Bull drink. I walked away. I wanted to walk out so badly – I just wanted to walk out and leave him there behind me but he was drunk and I knew he was going to talk to me and it was all too much for me. I couldn't leave when he was this near to me. I wiped my sweaty palms on my long-sleeved black-lace dress. Okay, I wiped my sweaty palms on Alice's long-sleeved black-lace dress.

I stood at the bar now and watched him. For all he knew I'd already returned to the hen dinner or indeed walked down the stairs and was in a cab. He was still talking. He didn't care. Go back inside to the table! I shouted at myself. You stupid cow, what are you doing? Have some self-respect! What about Rory? My self-esteem was already crawling back into the old gaping-open black hole.

But I was once again under the John Callan spell. He had worked his magic on me. Every sense in my body was heightened. I felt alive. I felt like I always did when I was with him: that sleep was a waste of time, that the world was so big and we had so little time to see it all. That every second was for living. Wildly. I felt like there was so much I wanted to see and do. I was never tired. I was never lacking energy. It was like he was my charger.

I breathed the air into my lungs more deeply and held it there for a few seconds before exhaling slowly. I loved how he made me feel. Jesus, I loved how I could just want him with every inch of my body. It was thrilling. Completely exhilarating. His smell still lingered under my nostrils.

One of the sticks was now feeling his biceps and he was slowly becoming uncomfortable. I could sense it. John was never tactile with people he didn't know. He didn't even like shaking hands. Then the other stick pulled up his T-shirt to check out his abs. Bad move, bitch. I narrowed my eyes. If there was one thing John hated it was people who invaded his space. He started shaking his head slowly at first and then he leaned in really close to the one who had pulled up his shirt. I had no idea what he was saying but the expression on her face was priceless: big beaming smile to wrinkled-up frown and ugly mouth.

She was at a loss for words, I could tell, as John swaggered off.

Was he looking for me? I was standing behind the big white pillar at the bar. He walked around once. Then he saw me.

"Hide and seek?" he shouted. "Great! My go?" He skipped off and stood behind the other big white pillar at the other end of the bar.

I started to laugh. I couldn't help it. I beckoned to him and he returned to me, took off his leather jacket and threw it on the bar top.

"Cool! I haven't played that in ages. It's such a good game – we really should play it more often."

His shoulder was touching mine. He had said '*we*'.

"Drink?"

"Vodka," I said.

"So I hear you have a serious boyfriend now." He was turned, facing the bar and waving a fifty-euro note wildly in the air.

I couldn't take my eyes off his arms in the tight black T-shirt. "Yeah, I do." I turned and leaned on the bar counter now too, putting my two elbows in a pool of spilt beer. Neither of us making eye contact.

"D'ya love him?" Waving. Waving. Waving.

"Can I help you?" the irritated barman asked.

John was very irritating.

"Two double vodkas, please, sir, with a dash of your finest tap water please if you please."

"I don't want a double . . ." I trailed off as the barman was already gone.

"So do ya?" He turned now and pushed his hair back from his eyes.

I took a long slow deep breath. "He's great, yeah," I answered truthfully.

"Do you love him? Do you fucking love him? Do you love fucking him?" His dark thunderous eyes poured into mine.

"Jesus, John, stop! That's so rude and – and inappropriate." I was shocked. It did sound horrible.

He put his face inches from mine now. "Does he fuck you like I fucked you?"

He was drunker than I had thought.

The vodkas arrived.

"I'm not continuing this conversation, John." I put the little black straw into my mouth and sucked for dear life.

"I'm back for a while." He rocked and steadied himself against the counter top. He ran his hands over his stubble. "I've stuff, important stuff I need to sort out."

Ask him! the voice inside my head shouted at me. Ask him now why he left you – he won't remember any of this in the morning – ask him. Find out all you can – this could be your only chance to try and understand. Closure. I scratched my head. Do it, said the voice. It wouldn't let me relax. I could no longer hear Rihanna singing out about her rude boy and wondering if he was big enough. The club became silent in my ears.

"Why did you leave me?" I shut my eyes tight.

His response was instant. "Because I loved you too much."

We looked at each other for the seconds that followed. Silent. Our breaths synchronised. Our eyes not blinking. It was not what I'd expected to hear. It was confusing and thrilling.

He opened his mouth again and I wanted to pull the words out with a tweezers. "Because I felt that you –"

146

"Beth! There you are! Come on! She's just going to open the hen gifts and the chocolate willies are melting with the heat in there! I mean, where'd you go? I've searched the vile, stinky smoking area for you – I thought you must be doing a poo or something?"

Angela had found me. I'd never really liked Angela to be honest – she was way too nosy for my liking, she interrupted all the time, was incapable of listening and the spraying of perfume at dinner was a complete nightmare for me. I mean, I didn't really hate many people but right now, right this second, I almost, almost wished her dead.

She pulled at my beer-drenched elbow. "Urgh, you're soaked – what's that? Oh hi, John!" She smiled madly at him now, blinking the purple eye shadow. Her eyes looked like two small ballroom dancers. "I forgot you guys dated moons ago. Save a dance for me at the wedding, won't you?" she guffawed.

"Yeah, go," said John. "Go eat your cocks. I should split . . . I have to see a man about a Boney M CD." He threw the straw out and downed the drink, liquid spilling onto his chin, then banged the glass too hard on the counter. He grabbed his leather jacket and stuck it under his arm.

"Why?" Angela asked. I knew not to.

"Why what?" He rocked.

"Why do you have to go and see a man about a Boney M CD?" She looked confused and it was not a good look. Her top lip curled and her nose bent down to meet it.

"Well, why on earth not? See ya at the wedding so, ladies!" He pretended to remove an imaginary hat and tip it at us, replaced it and staggered out.

I now hated hen parties even more than I ever thought possible. I was raging. He'd said he'd loved me too much?

I hadn't got to finish the conversation. He'd been going to spill it all, I could feel it. I'd waited two and a half long years to have it and I was interrupted. I was beyond angry. I knew it was Alice's hen and not my night so I returned with a forced pained smile and took my seat beside Alice at the table, which had still not been cleared. *He'd said he'd loved me too much*. Another pet hate. I can't stand looking at dirty dinner dishes. *He'd said he'd loved me too much*. Dirty dishes made me want to pee.

"Where were you?" Alice asked me.

She looked quite frankly absolutely ridiculous (remember when I said she never looked bad not even when she'd had gastroenteritis? Well, I take it back). She was draped in green, orange and pink fluffy feather boas, she had a large inflatable rubber penis-shaped hat on her head. She was wearing penis glasses and there was a huge sign taped on her back in the shape of a penis that said . . . wait for it . . . VIRGIN. Ha ha ha. I know, hysterical, right? All the women at this hen party were annoying me, except Mrs Callan. These women who wanted it to be their own hen party. I was never ever having a hen party.

"Your brother was here," I whispered into her ear.

"What? Why?" She always asked very good questions.

"He was very drunk and I think he knew I'd be here." I stacked a half-eaten Chicken alla Diavola on top of a half-eaten Mushroom Risotto. Women never finished meals any more.

"Are you serious? What is he at? Will you tell Rory he was here?"

"Yes, I dunno, and yes." I nodded as the penis-shaped cake arrived with penis candles, no doubt tasting like a penis (sorry). I passed on it.

148

"*Are you watching your weight, Beth?*" Angela screamed at me through an open mouthful of penis cake.

I wanted to stab her in the eye with her own creamy pink fork.

The rest of the evening dragged by and all I could do was think about John. I tried to participate in the conversations but I was only half there. What had he meant he loved me too much? I was bursting to tell Alice this but I knew I couldn't. Rory was collecting me at two o'clock – he was always so good like that. The table was scattered with wine bottles. I picked up various bottles, turned them upside down but all were empty. I'd still have to pay for the lot them even though I'd drunk only about a glass and a half. Alice was drinking a very strange-looking bright-blue cocktail and I doubted she was enjoying it.

"Are you looking for more wine, Beth, ya alco?" Angela was sitting beside me, her perfume engulfing my nostrils. "Isn't it a brilliant night for Alice? She looks absolutely freekin' hilarballs, doesn't she?"

Before I could answer there was a tip on my shoulder.

"Excuse me, ladies, sorry to interrupt."

I was facing Alice's cousins and friends on the opposite side of the table and as each jaw dropped with over-glossed lips I knew it was John back even before the voice registered over the noisy restaurant.

"Howdy, sis."

I turned around.

"May I have a quiet word in your shell-like, Beth?"

"John!" Alice pushed back her chair back and tried to stand but the weight of all the penises pushed her straight back down.

"You look like a dick, sis. Literally." He held out his

hand to me. He seemed more sober.

I pushed back my chair and stood. "I'll be right back." I put my hand on Alice's shoulder.

She threw her eyes to heaven and returned to the blue cocktail. I knew she now hated every second of this. I had tried to warn her.

"Hello, my lovely handsome son!" Mrs Callan swayed on her chair – she was on the Baileys' coffee now and enjoying herself a bit more. The alcohol was numbing her pain.

"Mother, dearest." John pecked her on the cheek and dragged me behind him.

"*What are you two up to at all at all? Haven't you a serious boyfriend, Beth Burrows, you diiiiirrrrty girl?*" Angela yelled at our backs.

He pushed me further through the heaving club into the corner by the cloakroom.

"I want you to come to my hotel for an hour – I'm at The Shelbourne," he said. "I want to talk to you."

I pulled my hand away. "I can't, John. Rory, my boyfriend, is collecting me at two." He pulled his phone out of his back pocket and it illuminated his chiselled face. The heavy black stubble was almost a beard. "It's only midnight, Cinders. I will have you back."

Why did he have a hotel room? I thought he was staying at home?

"It's not appropriate, John." God, I loved being able to say his name out loud.

He burst out laughing. "Ah Jesus, Beth, please don't tell me you've become . . ." he swallowed hard, "appropriate!"

He made me feel small.

"No . . . well, yeah, I don't mean appropriate." I pulled the pins from my up-do and my hair fell around my shoulders, caked in hairspray. I knew it wasn't straight enough for John but I was rebelling.

"Come on – one joint."

Aha! *That* was why he had the hotel room.

"I am not smoking joints!" I pulled my hair between the palms of my hands to try and straighten it.

"Oh, I guess that isn't appropriate then either, Beth? Smoking joints and being late for your boyfriend's pick-up . . . neither are appropriate, right?"

He thrust his hands deep into his jeans pockets and that's when I saw it. His belt. His vintage gold-buckled belt. I loved that belt. He'd had it forever. His granddad had left it to him. I had been holding strong until that square gold buckle looked up at me through its denim confines.

"Oh, come on so! One hour!" I was fuming with myself.

We left the gastro pub and club off Kildare Street and walked inches apart the very short five minutes to The Shelbourne. I loved The Shelbourne. It was pure old Dublin. It was still a very special place. We entered through the swinging door and headed for the lift. We hadn't spoken a word. I was now trailing behind him. His perfect bum in his perfect faded denims. His swagger. I was in a sort of daze.

The lift doors opened and we got in. Alone. Alone in this tiny space. The two of us. Just the two of us. How many times since he had walked out on me had I imagined this scenario? He smiled at me. I melted into the lift floor. I could smell coffee now off his breath. He had tried to sober up. Why? For me?

151

He stopped smiling. "I'm so horny for you."

My jaw dropped. I swallowed. I swallowed again, my mouth now bone dry. I tried to lick my lips. I couldn't get the moisture back into them – they were sticking to my gums. I shook my head. My heart was beating at a dangerous pace.

Words left my mouth of their own free will. "No way, John, are you for real? You walk out on me over two years ago with no real reason and never contact me. You broke my heart. You destroyed me, John. Do you have any idea what I went through? You think you can just reappear and fuck me?" My lip started to quiver and my eyes filled up.

I stood in front of him. I didn't cower. He didn't flinch. I steadied my breathing. I smelled the leather from his jacket.

The lift doors opened.

"Let's just talk then, Beth. I have a lot to say to you, if you'll listen?"

He pointed to the left and I got out and sniffed back my snot. Then I stopped. An image of Rory standing in my doorway with that red rose was painted behind my eyes. I turned on my heel and just as the lift doors closed I squeezed in and hit the sixth-floor button twenty times in a row. *Bang bang bang bang bang bang bang bang bang bang bang bang bang bang bang bang bang bang bang bang.* I jabbed the button over and over.

The doors closed. I knew he'd take the stairs so there was no point in going to reception as he'd cut me off there. I stared at myself in the lift mirror. I looked an absolute fright. This upset me even more. My hair was indescribable. As though I was an extra in a feature film about the living dead. It was a shock to me that a bird had not yet nested in it. Make-up down my face from the heat of the restaurant, nose as red as a poppy. I went to the sixth floor and hid behind a green-leather couch on the corridor. I couldn't quite believe he was making me hide behind a couch like this, I thought, as I squashed myself up into a tiny ball. How had this happened? I stayed there crouched for what felt like an hour before I unfolded my dead legs and took the stairs down. I was in agony and bursting for a pee. He was nowhere to be seen in the lobby and the clock at reception told me it was eight p.m. in New York and one a.m. in Dublin. Great. I hadn't missed Rory.

I didn't have my phone. On a night like a hen-party night for my best friend, I had reckoned it wasn't a good idea to carry it – I always lost things when I'd had a few. However, I regretted it now. I was stone cold sober and I just wanted to go home. I decided to do just that.

I nipped into the toilets and I peed for what seemed like half an hour. I actually heard stifled giggles from the two girls in cubicles either side. I didn't mind. I'd been that giggler before. Really long loud pees were extremely funny. I washed my hands quickly and splashed some water on my face and left the warm hotel. Rory would be up watching the TV at mine – he wouldn't need to leave to collect me for another half hour at least.

I jogged to the street now and hailed a cab. I sat back as I gave my destination and stared out the window. There was a talk show on the radio and some man was giving out about horse meat being found in burgers. Get a life.

What had just happened? Jesus, but John was nothing but drama.

"Always was," I said out loud.

"Always was, pet, yer dead right, ya hit the nail on the head there, always was shite in burgers," the driver answered me. "It's why this country's in the state it's in . . ."

Oh, dear Lord, no, not the state-of-the-country lecture – anything but that. I closed my tired eyes.

Rory was ironing when I got in. My clothes.

"What's the story?" he asked and paused *Modern Family* (it was our favourite programme so he was watching an old episode – he'd never go ahead without me).

"John showed up," I admitted and then sort of lied. "So I just left."

Rory placed the iron carefully on the yellow-and-green-dotted ironing-board cover and smiled at me. "That's great, Beth . . . you are a . . . great girl for leaving . . . well done. Are you okay?" He approached me. "I made a pizza and left you half. Will I heat it and make you a cup of Barry's?"

"No, thanks." I knew before the words left my mouth I should have said 'Yes, please'.

He frowned. "No appetite?"

I thought quickly. "Rory, I've just eaten a five-course meal!" (Lie. I ate half my lukewarm carbonara and nothing else.)

He bought it. Glasses pushed up nose. "Sorry, of course you did."

My head was spinning. "I'm slightly drunk, Rory – do you mind if I crash?" (Lie. I was stone-cold sober.)

"No, go ahead. I'll finish up here and sure I may as well finish the pizza. I'm still a bit peckish."

I kissed him on the cheek and knocked off his glasses. Our symmetry was askew. I never did that. I closed the door of the bedroom and, fully dressed, crawled into my double bed. I pulled the fresh duvet up over my head. I sobbed heartily but silently.

Chapter Thirteen

Louise

Louise felt her concentration slipping as she bent over her work. She was tired – how many hours had she been crocheting? She didn't know. Her back ached and her eyes blurred. She needed a break . . . but, most of all, she needed another drink. It had not been a good day, not a productive day. It had been one of those days when the past preyed on her mind. When Dan preyed on her mind – Dan and the baby.

Dan hadn't kept his word – he hadn't done what he'd said in his letter – he hadn't brought Lucy to see her.

After she'd given birth and held her baby daughter for those first few minutes, it hadn't felt awkward and unnatural as she'd expected. But she had felt pure terror at the fact that this beautiful tiny girl had to rely on her. She couldn't be a good mother, she wasn't good at anything. She literally shook.

Dan was standing beside her. He gooed and gaaed over the baby. "Isn't she the most beautiful little thing you have ever seen in your entire life?"

Her parents hadn't come to the hospital to see them. She tried to smile but the pain from her ripped body was agonising. She had suffered an anal fissure in delivery. She hadn't felt pain in so long. She'd been self-medicating since she could remember.

The baby cried and it wasn't a nice noise. It was too loud and too piercing. It meant the baby needed her. She swallowed the bile that was rising in her throat.

Dan knelt beside her. "She's hungry, love – would you like to try and feed her?"

Louise had shaken her head, her throbbing head. The baby kept crying. Louise was starting to get heart palpitations.

"Can you pick her up, please? I can't move," she said and she winced with the pain as she tried to pull her body up in the bed.

He oh so carefully picked up his precious daughter. He rocked her and made loving, soothing noises and she immediately stopped crying.

It must be amazing to be loved like that by a parent, she thought. She didn't think she was capable of such love, the same way her mother wasn't able to love her. There was no way she could be. Her mother. Her mother. Her mother. How had her mother reacted after she was born? Had she nestled her to her breast or held her bottle gently and bonded immediately or had she felt just like Louise did now. Nothing. Empty. Shattered. Sore. Changed. Old. Scared. Alone. Confused. Unworthy. Maybe she could finally understand her mother. Her mother. Visions of Paula Mak floated before her eyes: the constant criticising, the constant put-downs, the mocking laughter at her and never with her. The way her mother would look her up and down, scorn her clothes, sneer at her hair, rip apart her life with one dirty look.

Her baby didn't like her, she realised now with a jolt back to reality. She should have guessed as much. Why would she like her? What was there to like about Louise Mak?

Dan rubbed his fingers from his spare hand across hers, trying to warm them up. "So what do you think? What are you feeling?" he whispered softy. "Please tell me, love . . . what's on your mind?"

She'd stared into his kind eyes. "Can I really tell you?" She breathed hard and heavy at him. "Can I be totally honest, Dan?"

"Of course you can, you can tell me anything, I'm here for you, Lou Lou."

It had been so long since he used that pet name for her. She had felt him tighten his grip on her hands.

"Can you get me a drink, Dan? Anything – wine, vodka, anything – just hurry. Leave it . . . the baby . . . in the . . . the basket thing . . . I will watch it . . . just go!"

He had stared at her and she saw the disappointment in his eyes . . . or was that contempt?

Then he walked to the door, clutching the baby tightly to his chest. "I'll take her down to the nurses in the nursery – I'll be back in after your tea," he'd said as he closed the door.

He hadn't brought the alcohol.

She'd asked a woman who delivered her tea – a ham salad – that evening to get her a bottle of vodka, told her it was a gift for the doctor, and the woman had obliged and brought it in the next evening. She'd drunk the entire bottle straight, and had to be pumped out. On her request, no one had come to visit her afterwards. She had sent a message to Dan, asking him to give her time alone, saying that she wasn't coping. The hospital staff acceded to her request to be left alone, agreeing that she needed the time to recover. Meanwhile, the baby could be discharged but not Louise who was being seen by the hospital psychiatrists. Louise had signed some forms needed to register the birth and also a declaration that Dan was the baby's father. She never knew who had actually gone to register the birth and she didn't care.

Neither Dan nor her daughter had ever come back. She was told that Dan had purchased eight cases of ready-to-use made-up bottles from the hospital shop and had taken the baby home to Cork. "Your baby girl is in very good hands," the nurses told her. "You just concentrate on you for now."

She had stayed in the hospital for a week as counsellors and therapists came to talk to her. She didn't have post-natal depression – she had been like this all her miserable life.

Dan had sent her a letter to her parents' house and it was there the day she'd arrived home in a taxi. The house had been empty. Her mother and father had taken a last-minute cruise around the Gulf of Mexico. She had stood on the letter and it had stuck to the bottom of her wet runner. When she peeled it off she saw his name and address on the back in his perfect, neat handwriting.

She had taken baby steps into the kitchen, as she was still so raw when walking. She'd sat at the table and opened the envelope slowly. He asked how she was feeling after the hard birth and being pumped out, and she was mortified. He told her that it was all for the best and that when she got better, soon, he'd bring their daughter – "*I've called her Lucy,*" he'd scribbled – to visit her. "*You also know where to find us anytime you want to see us,*" he had written and had signed off with three kisses.

He had never come and she had never gone to them. She had waited in the beginning by the large living-room bay window but they had never come for her so she had drunk herself into a delightful oblivion. She used to read and read his letter over and over, looking for signs in the words that she might have missed before but then one night, in a drunken temper and rage, she'd ripped the letter into tiny pieces and dumped the pieces in the bin. He had been the only person who had ever really loved her and she had lost him. No, that wasn't true – she hadn't lost him – she had pushed him away and that was even worse.

No, he never came back . . . not in the flesh . . . but he came back to haunt her all the time. She couldn't free herself from him.

Chapter Fourteen

Beth

The last two weeks leading up to the wedding were manic. I had little time to think about anything. As planned, Rory and I moved into Mam and Dad's house, into Parkside in the leafy suburbs of Rathfarnham, and I said goodbye to Ranelagh and my little flat. I felt older. I said goodbye to the Beth Burrows I had been and embraced this new Beth Burrows. Oldish Beth. Should-know-better Beth. Forget-about-John-Callan-for-good Beth. Grow-up Beth. It was the right move, I knew that. I hadn't heard another word from John since the hen party and I tried not to check my phone every six minutes. He could get my number easily, I also knew that. I knew in my heart Alice had been on to him and had warned him off. I hated her for this. I loved her for this. I had turned up to my stall every day looking like I was about to be photographed for a daily newspaper.

And now it was the morning before the morning before her big day. She wanted a two-day preparation. "So as absolutely nothing can go wrong. *Fail to prepare, prepare to fail*," she told me. I would be heading to Alice's to stay overnight as soon as I got up, with a bottle of Jo Malone for her – Grapefruit, her favourite – and a handmade handwritten card – but most importantly of all with her neckpiece.

It was only seven in the morning and I'd been lying awake since five, watching Rory sleep, trying not to think about John and fretting about the wedding. I was so nervous for Alice. I don't know why because she wasn't the slightest bit nervous.

I'd been around the previous night. Dan was in Cork for the next few nights (ever the traditionalist) and would be coming up with his parents the morning of the wedding and straight to the church. Before he left he'd called me. "You are a wonderful friend and a brilliant aunt to Lucy, so I wanted to say a private thank-you to you, Beth my girl. I'm honoured to call you my friend." He'd made me cry. I'd never considered myself an auntie before. The evening before, he had taken Alice and Lucy to the exact spot they had all first met in the Phoenix Park and he had presented them each with a single white rose. "My girls will always be this perfect in my eyes," he had told them. He had made a picnic for them of baked honey-glazed ham sandwiches and apples and strawberries. Alice had cried. Lucy hadn't understood a word.

When I'd got to the house Alice had been relaxed and pure happy. She and Lucy had face packs on (well, Lucy's was just some natural yogurt) when I'd called and they were sitting on Alice's bed painting their nails. They made the cutest picture for my saved contact of Alice's number on my iPhone.

"Do you want a drink?" I asked her and she shook her head.

"No, thanks, I'm just happy in my own natural buzz. I want to savour this calmness I feel. It's a great feeling not to need a drink!"

"I'm sleeping in the bed with Maman because Daddy's in Cork!" Lucy clapped her hands.

I stared at her bare feet. They were just too cute.

"We're going to go to bed early but we'll watch a movie, won't we, Bubble? *Toy Story*, maybe?" Alice said before grabbing the towel and catching a creamy dollop of yogurt as it fell from Lucy's chin.

"*Toy Story* is the best film ever I just love flying Buzz! To Infinity and beyond!" Lucy screeched.

"Dan's calling at ten and then we won't speak until the wedding morning at the church," Alice told me.

"Is he nervous?" I asked.

"Not a bit – he's just really excited – he said he can't wait to be my husband but I know that he's also looking forward to a really good party with all his family and friends. You know what he's like – he likes nothing more than a good party."

I'd gone. Left them to this special time together. I did cry a little on the drive home and I'm not sure why. I couldn't pinpoint the emotion. I wasn't due my period for another two weeks so I couldn't pin it on the poor unfortunate scapegoats that were my hormones.

"You awake?" Rory groaned. "What time is it?"

"Only seven, I'm just hyper," I said as I stared at my pink flowing number in its plastic bag on the back of the door. I still couldn't get used to sleeping in my parents' old

163

bedroom. I couldn't put my finger on it but something in me wasn't quite right. I wasn't settling, I realised. I kept wondering when I was going home. I missed my own place.

"What time you heading over to Alice for the pre-wedding preps?" He laughed at our analness and stretched and slid his arm under me. He wanted sex – that was his sign. Arm under = Sex.

I was about as much in the mood for sex right then as a woman who'd just naturally delivered a twelve-pound baby in a corridor on a hospital trolley. I hopped up. "Now! I have to get over there now!"

"At seven o'clock in the morning?" He reached for his glasses under his pillow.

"I've a lot to do, Rory! I'm the chief bridesmaid. Now first, rasher sambo?"

He nodded and lay his head back down on the pillow. Disappointed, no doubt. I headed for the kitchen.

I really had nothing much to do for Prep Day for myself. I had a hair appointment at eleven on the wedding morning (hairdresser was coming to Alice's house) and make-up appointment at twelve (make-up artist was coming to Alice's house). So, to be honest, I had little or nothing to organise.

I wondered was John up? I poured too much olive oil into the pan. "Shit!" I said out loud. Why did they make the hole so big? There really was no need. A small hole would suffice. The wedding day would be the last day I'd have to see him. The day after that he'd be gone. *He loved me too much*. I couldn't think about it. The words were banged out in black-and-white typewriter keys before my eyes every time I closed them. My stomach lurched again.

I hadn't heard from Paula Mak and I was bitterly disappointed. I could feel it slipping away. It was back to the market with me next week. Back to my normal life. My new normal life. I needed to make money. I peeled out each exceptionally skinny rasher, popped them in the pan and they began to sizzle. I hated the texture of uncooked rashers. I loved the taste of the cooked rasher.

"There's some big movie premiere followed by a sound and vision awards show on here soon in the Convention Conference Centre," Rory called in, obviously checking his emails on his iPhone. "Loads of Hollywood A-Listers coming over and they want my mobile cinema for outside – gimmicky thing but great money!"

"Cool!" I called back.

We ate our rashers on toast (bit too crispy) and then I pulled on a vest top, my grey Dunnes track suit and light orange Converse. I carefully packed away the neckpiece, grabbed my keys and pecked Rory on the cheek.

It was another glorious sunny morning and the sound of early-morning lawnmowers assaulted my ears. I stared at the sun until I sneezed. I tugged off the track-suit top and threw it into the back seat. Before I sat into the driver's seat I looked around. Suburbia. I was suburban. Ten tidy houses looked back at me. Ten tidy lawns and ten shiny cars in the driveways. It was pretty enough on this beautiful morning but what would Suburbia be like in the depths of January? It was never where I'd wanted to live. I liked being able to walk to the shops for milk. To walk for a pint. To walk past strangers in the street and see what they were wearing. A bird fluttered down and landed on the wall of my parents' house. My house. I looked at him. All brown and tiny and pecky. So fragile.

At least he could escape from here in the winter, I thought, as I slid into the driver's seat and shut the door.

I drove on the empty Saturday-morning roads towards Portobello to prepare my best friend for getting married. I felt sad.

"Good morning!" Alice opened the door with Lucy in her arms.

"Morning, my beautiful bride-to-be!" I hugged them both tightly. They were like one package.

"So come on, come on, I cannot wait a nano-second longer to see it!"

She was in three-quarter-length jeans with a coral-blue sleeveless T-shirt and her hair was loose around her beautiful face. She was in her bare feet. I followed them through to the kitchen and told Alice to sit and close her eyes. She did. Lucy sat up on her knee.

I carefully laid my creation out on pink soft tissue paper on the kitchen table and took a deep breath.

"Open," I whispered as I exhaled.

Alice opened her gorgeous eyes very slowly. One at a time. Her hand flew to her mouth. She gasped then. She stood up, gently putting Lucy down. She touched the neckpiece ever so gently.

Lucy, now bored as there was nothing for her, wandered off into the TV room.

"My God, Beth, it's absolutely breathtaking . . . I . . . it's just perfect!" Tears fell slowly. First hers. Then mine.

I lifted it gently and she held up her hair. I tightened it into position and we both moved to the mirror. It was simply incredible on her neck. The beads and crystals tiered her neck and made it look twice as long if that was possible.

She fingered the beads carefully. "How long did this take?"

"A while."

We both sniffed.

"I couldn't have imagined I'd love it this much and I knew I'd bloody love it. You are the best friend I could ever ask for," Alice blubbed, letting it all out now.

"Stop it, will you! So are you! I don't know what I'd do without you . . . what I'd have done without you when my life was such a mess. I'm so happy for you, love."

We hugged.

"Beth, I know I'm not always sympathetic about John but it's only because I truly . . . I honestly, on all I hold dear, believe you are better off without him and that's really hard for me to say sometimes because I love him to death, warts and all!" She pulled a clean folded tissue from her jeans pocket and blew her nose.

"I know you do," I sniffed back. I never had a tissue.

"It's just that you are so different but you never saw it, you never see it – it's like you live vicariously through him when to me it's like you are living a lie. I don't think he was ever marriage material for you. I only ever wanted to protect you. I only said what I said to him to protect you." She blew again.

"I understand," I sniffed. Although I absolutely did not. What on earth did she mean? What did she say to him?

"Rory is great for you – he's the one for you. If I didn't have Dan, Rory is exactly the type of guy I'd go for. He's safe and reliable and he won't ever let you down. I could never say that about John. You know, Beth, if I thought John could have been that guy for you I would have been over the moon, but it's just not in him."

"Yes," I sniffed again. What did she mean? I couldn't ask, I knew that much – this was not my day. "But, listen, this day isn't about me and my baggage – it's all about you. You are getting married in two more mornings, my girl! Two more mornings!" We stared at each other for a while then we screamed.

Lucy ran in. "What wong, Maman?" she asked.

"Oh, we're just excited, Bubble!" Alice dropped to her knees. "We are so excited!" She hugged Lucy tight and blew onto her cheek, making a not-so-attractive noise. "Look, Lucy, do you like what Auntie Beth made for me?" She caressed the piece.

"Is pretty," Lucy yawned.

I removed the neckpiece and Alice gently took it upstairs. No doubt it had a seat somewhere, numbered and colour-coded to be in its right place at the right time for the morning. We spent a glorious lazy best-friends' day together. After we painstakingly went through every item on Alice's typed-out checklist, she made the most amazing prawn and chorizo risotto for lunch and we opened a bottle of real pink lemonade that she had made herself. We sat in the back garden (plastered in Lucy's Factor 50 just in case) and laughed and laughed. We reminisced. It took moments like this for me to wonder why we didn't reminisce more often. It was so much fun. We talked about school and old friends and nights out. Old clothes we wore, old hair styles we'd sported. Alice even mentioned John and we remembered double dates we'd gone on with the various guys she had gone out with.

"They all hated John," she sniggered now. "Remember the guy, Eoin, who called me a frigid cunt after I refused

168

to go home with him after Club M that Paddy's weekend?"

I bit my lip. How could I forget? John had overheard. He had gone head to head with Eoin and told him to apologise. Eoin had refused. Before we knew it John had him on the ground and the two were rolling around. Two guys we didn't know had pulled them apart, John perfect, Eoin bloodied lip and swollen eye.

"Apologise to my sister now or I swear to fuck I won't rest until I find you!" John tried to pull free from the heavy-set guy who held him back.

Eoin wiped the blood from his lip. "Sorry," he mumbled as he limped away.

"Just defending your honour, sis," John told us as we both shouted at him in the street that he was a fool.

The sun engulfed us as Lucy paddled in a tiny Dora paddling pool and Alice watched her with the biggest grin on her face. She had the poor child plastered in a green factor and in a sun-protection full-length body suit with a cap and sunglasses. How did we all ever survive as children, I wondered?

"My God, you completely love that little thing, don't you?" I sipped my sweet lemonade. It was like old-fashioned soda stream. It even tasted pink.

"Little *thing*?" she laughed.

"You know what I mean!" I poked her.

"I do. I really do. She's my whole world now. I can't remember who I was before her, you know? She makes me a better person. Not in a corny Hollywood you-complete-me-Tom-Cruise way but in a health way. I look after me so much better. My head is happier. I eat better, I sleep better, I plan better. I look at the world differently.

169

Sometimes I sneak into her room at night and when I look at her I . . . I really feel like she's my daughter." She paused now and I didn't interrupt. "I'm not her real mother and I know that, but I didn't go looking for her . . . you know, she was, well . . . you're going to cringe . . . but I think she was sent to me, I really do."

I remained silent.

"Go on, cringe, scoff, yer only dyin' to scoff!" Alice jabbed at me, curling her hair behind her ears.

I waited a few moments before I answered. "I'm not. Not one bit. I think you are probably right. Sometimes people are just meant for each other. It's as simple as that."

She lifted her chin now and caught my eye. I looked away. We both knew exactly what I meant.

The day flew by and by ten o'clock I was ready for bed. I was shattered – the sun always took it out of me. Alice had asked me to spend the night.

"Where's your dress, Beth?" Alice looked around the kitchen now, her white bulging folder of wedding plans under her arm. "I want to hang everything up so there is not one iota of panic on the morning."

"Dress?" I felt bemused.

"Your dress? Your bridesmaid dress?"

"Oh fuck!" My eyes opened wide.

"What's a fuck?" Lucy asked before Alice's hands found her ears.

"Beth!" she snorted at me.

"Sorry! I left without the dress, I thought I could bring it over tomorrow . . ."

"But I want to press it again, Beth – I'm going to press everything again tonight, I told you that!"

So she was starting to get jittery – it was all over her face now. I defused the anxiety.

"Okay, relax, it's no big deal – I can pop home and get it. I'll take Rory some of that leftover dinner, will I? He loves chorizo. I'll be back in half an hour . . . make me one of those hot-chocolate things you're making for Lucy when I come back, will you?" I grabbed my keys from the fresh-fruit bowl.

"Honestly, Beth . . ." was all I heard her say as I ran back out the door into the darkening night.

"Honestly, Alice," I whispered to myself. "Your wedding's not for two days. Chillax."

As I put my key in the door I sensed the house was quiet. Was Rory out? He wasn't expecting me home but he'd usually text me if he was going out. I stuffed the plate into the microwave, found a pen and wrote him a note. I ran in and grabbed the dress, my shoes and my bag from the back of the bedroom door. I also spotted my bracelet that I'd forgotten about! Alice was right – I did need to have everything ready to go in her house. I pulled the new underwear from my open overflowing drawers. I never usually left them open. I really needed to tidy out my wardrobe and drawers after the wedding. It always helped clear out my mind.

I loaded the car and just as I was about to hop in I noticed the small projector light on in the mobile-cinema van. Aha, he was in there!

I pulled open the door fast.

"I forgot the –" I froze.

"What the . . .?" Rory jumped.

I gagged.

"Beth . . ."

I put my hands up. "Wow . . . why . . . what the . . .? Wha . . . wha . . . why are you . . . ?" I couldn't find the words.

He muted the porn. I guess he tried to turn it off but hit the wrong button. A video camera buzzed in the background. He was filming himself too. I couldn't take my eyes off him. He was frozen to the spot.

So was I. It wasn't the porn. As bad as that was. It was how he was dressed. In my old matching Peaches & Cream polka-dot pink push-up bra and panties.

"It's not . . . oh Jesus, it isn't . . ." he said.

I swallowed bile and slammed the door behind me.

"Wait, Beth! It's not what you think!" I heard Rory yell after me, his voice breaking from the loudness of his pitch. "*Wait!*" A pitch I had never, ever heard him reach.

I knew he couldn't follow me. Not dressed like that.

I drove at one hundred miles an hour down Scholarstown Road and over Templeogue Bridge without my lights on. Cars flashed me. I flicked the lights on.

"What the fuck?" I leaned over the steering wheel while driving. My phone rang in my bag. "Oh God, what is it with me? How do I do this to myself?" What was he? Was he a cross-dresser? A transvestite? Was he gay? I had no clue what to think but one thing I knew for sure: I was not into what I had just witnessed. Not by a long shot. I blasted the cold air and the plastic covering on my dress made a loud rattling noise as the wind sucked it towards the window.

The phone kept ringing. I knew it was Rory calling me over and over again. I ignored it.

I had to tell Alice. I just had to. But on the eve of the

eve of her wedding? No, that just wouldn't be fair. I'd have to sit on it until it was appropriate. I pulled over. I stared at the dark road, my hazards turning it red now and then.

A light bulb went on in my head. It was shining so bright I couldn't be thinking straight. I knew it must be blinding my thoughts because I knew exactly where I was running to.

I took my phone out and texted Alice that I was too tired to drive back and I'd bring the dress over in the morning. It was as though I'd just been handed a free pass. It was why I hadn't let Rory explain, I realised. In some weird way I'd been willing a moment like this to happen. To let me off the hook. I was going to The Shelbourne. He might or might not be there. I slammed off the hazards, indicated and I drove like a bat out of hell into town and parked on the road across from the hotel. I had no change. I'd gladly pay the clamping fee.

I popped the boot and shoved my dress inside – it was going to be re-pressed anyway, wasn't it? Slamming the boot shut I jogged across the road, dodging the cars.

I pushed the revolving door. I was in the lobby. I knew the room. I headed for the lift and pressed the little golden button. My golden ticket. I had a golden sunrise in my eyes. I stared at my flushed reflection in the lift mirror. I tried to push all thoughts out of my head. I was fed up of thinking. I was fed up of pleasing other people. I was fed up of trying to live a life I quite frankly wasn't happy with. I was fed up of pressing thoughts of John to the back of my head on an hourly basis after all this time. I was fed up of being fed up. I was simply fed up of being me.

The doors opened and I strode down that soft carpeted

corridor and knocked three times on the door. He was in. I could hear Damien Dempsey's harsh Dublin tones belting out anger and frustration from behind the door.

He opened it. "Beth!" He looked behind me as if to see Alice or someone else he knew. Some explanation as to why I was at his door at almost eleven o'clock at night.

"John, can I come in, please?"

He stood back and I stepped in, kicking the door closed behind me. Cool, confident woman.

"Cool Converse."

He was looking at my feet. I'd added some crystals to them myself.

I wasn't wasting any time. "You said you loved me too much. What did that mean?" I spat as I leaned my full body weight against the sturdy hotel door.

"Oooookay, it's like this is it, serious chats? Umm . . . drink?" He moved to the minibar that was already swinging open.

"No."

"Smoke?"

"No."

"How about sex?"

"Yes."

His breath went against him. "Yyyes?" His eyes widened in surprise and he smirked slightly.

"Yes." I spoke the word as though it was the answer to a proposal of marriage. Definite.

"What about yer man, the dude, the predictable life?"

"Oh, listen, John, I'm after sex because I want it. Forget what I just said . . . I don't want to talk to you any more. Is that clear?"

"Understood, my lady." He was barefoot and wearing

174

black tracksuit bottoms and a black Rolling Stones T-shirt – an original from the 1960's. We'd bought it in a market in Amsterdam from a guy who was a roadie with them. I had my doubts. John was convinced. "That man is telling the truth, Beth," he had told me that weekend over and over again. "I bet he's seen things on the road we could never imagine." He had spoiled me rotten that weekend on money he had got from selling a painting to an art gallery in Bray. Anything I'd liked or admired he'd gone off and bought for me the following day.

Then I did what I'd been dreaming about doing for the last two long years and all those months and days. I walked slowly over to him. He was so still. Feet planted firmly on the ground. His smell engulfed me again. I allowed myself to lose control. I reefed that Rolling Stones T-shirt up over his head and I devoured him. I was like an animal. I kissed his lips, face, neck, ears, nipples, the whole lot. I kissed him everywhere. He kissed me right back. I inhaled him. I drank him all up. I ran my fingers roughly through his hair. He moaned and called my name over and over. I dug my nails into the wideness of his upper arms. I pushed him onto the bed and he stripped me naked of my grey track suit as only he could. I felt like I was home. I felt like me again. I was totally out of control. I lay on top of him in my bra and pants and he pulled my hair back and we stared into each other's eyes. We spoke to each other through our eyes only. I writhed and wriggled on top of him. He writhed and wriggled beneath me. Strong and hard. He kissed me slowly then tenderly and his tongue nipped in and out. I tried to catch it to hold it in my mouth. I stroked his perfect face. I tugged down his bottoms and he was naked underneath them. Slowly he pulled down my pants, unclipped my bra and slipped me underneath him. We breathed heavily into one another's faces. Then he entered me. We had wild sex. Hard sex. Vicious sex. Pure undiluted passion. Wild and free and I loved every last second of it. I held him so tight I know I hurt him. I moaned and groaned with zero shame and said his name over and over again.

"John. John. John. John. John. John. John. John. JohnJohnJohnJohnJohnJohnJohnJohnJohnJohnJohnJohn JohnJohnJohnJohnJohnJohn.Johnnnnnnnnnnnnnnnnnnn nnn!"

I dragged my nails down his taut back. He didn't use a condom and I could have cared less. Another reason to hate myself – it could join the queue. It was the greatest sex of my entire life. Afterwards as we lay side by side, damp, holding hands, our hearts racing and breaths panting, he said one word. Only one word. And it was the word I had been aching to hear for the last long painful two and a half years.

"Sorry."

He put his free hand on my cheek and held it tightly on my face, pressing me into his chest. I just knew he meant it. What I didn't know was if it was an apology for his wrongdoing or if he wanted me back. I barely thought about Rory, as awful as that sounds. Whatever he was into, it was time for him to move out. I suppose it was a relief of sorts. An excuse. A horrible but realistic way out for me. I slept that night alongside John Callan like a baby and not like the unfaithful, unsupportive, pathetic fake bitch that I was.

When I woke the sun was streaming in through the massive window and I stretched in the bed, the top-notch cool linen sheets massaging my body. I imagined a thread count that must be off the Richter scale. John's hair was messy on his pillow. I stared at him. He was a perfect sleeper. Like he was posing for a pretend sleeping shot, his darkness and heavy stubble breathtaking against the starched whiteness of the pillowcase. I crept out of bed and moved over to the window. I didn't have an ounce of embarrassment about my body – he knew me too well.

The reflection of the light on the marble floor bounced light onto the ceiling, and the room was warm and golden. St Stephen's Green looked straight back at me, its beauty still undeniably marvellous no matter how many times I looked at this park. It was so historic. Michael Collins had stood on that little bridge (O'Connell Bridge – I'd missed that question once in a pub quiz) in the park and passed political notes of humongous national importance. Life and death situations. A rebel. Brave beyond belief. Sometimes when I thought of Michael Collins I got a shiver down my spine. He was definitely always one of my "If you could have ten people to dinner dead or alive" guests. The sheer bravery gave me goose bumps. He'd never given up on what he believed in.

I grabbed my phone from my bag on the floor and texted Alice. She was getting married tomorrow. Tomorrow. It was hard to believe. We had talked about our wedding days so many times over the years. Hers always girly and romantic and sweet. Mine always abroad. Away on a beach somewhere hot. She was getting the wedding of her dreams. When we were younger she always had a recurring dream of getting married on white fluffy clouds.

I knew she was getting her semi-permanent eyelashes

on in Brown Sugar at twelve.

"Sorry didn't get over with dress yet. Have it in car. Meet me Bruxelles eleven thirty? Want to buy u last pint of Guinness and Red as a single woman. Oh and I have something big to tell u so u better come."

I slid into the bed beside him again and just looked at him. I traced my fingers inches above his face all around his features. I knew it was creepy but I couldn't help it. He stirred. I lay down quickly. He reached his arm across and draped it over my body. "Morning," he muttered and then fell fast asleep again.

I had to get up. I showered (with the supplied shower cap), dressed and found my charm bracelet under the bed before I very quietly snuck out. I didn't leave a note. As I waited for the lift the old lady charm looked at me and I shrugged my shoulders back at her. I didn't know what would happen from here but I knew one thing for sure: I had to speak to Rory. I had to change my life all over again, with or without John. How had I not seen that side to Rory? How long had he been dressing up in my underwear? How should I break up with him, because I knew that was what I had to do? Had he been lying all along when he said he loved me? Was I just a mask, a cover-up for his real life? I really didn't know how strong I was – that is why I had to tell Alice. I just had to. I needed her help.

I jogged across the road and, to my utter astonishment, I wasn't clamped! I fed the meter for a few hours, with change I'd taken from John's dressing table, before I headed down Grafton Street.

As I sat in the window seat of Bruxelles I watched her come through the doors. Glowing and radiant. That was about to change, I knew, but I simply had to tell her.

She wasn't impressed as my story tumbled out. Her face clouded over and she stared hard at me.

"He's just playing with you, Beth!" She wagged her bitten fingernail furiously at me before curling it at an incredible angle to chew some more. She was disgusted with me.

It wasn't fair on her and I tried to make light of it by the end. "I don't want anything more from John," I protested.

"What about Rory, Beth? How could you do that to him?"

I hadn't told her how I'd found Rory. All of a sudden I realised I couldn't do that to him. My guilt was galloping in at a momentous rate. No matter what, I had cheated on him.

"I will tell him as soon as I see him," I promised her.

"God, don't tell him today or tomorrow, Beth – it's my wedding! The last thing I need is John and Rory having a bust-up in my church!"

"I won't," I assured her.

I needed to talk to Rory so badly but I just couldn't cope with it right now, so the promise suited me. I'd go back to Alice's today and stay there tonight also as planned. Rory wasn't the type of guy to cause a scene. He'd wait. Whatever happened between us I knew that Rory loved Alice and Dan and that they would always be close friends.

Alice hugged me tightly as she left Bruxelles

"It will all work out," she said wisely as I watched her go.

Chapter Fifteen

I pulled up around the corner from Alice's house and parked on the road. Best to leave the spaces near the house as free as possible for the florist delivery later. I pulled the perfect pink dress out from the boot, grabbed the underwear, shoes, jewellery and bag and went in with them. Tomorrow was about my best friend and for once in my bloody shallow existence I would not think about my bloody miserable self!

I let myself in as the door was on the latch and made myself busy. I was chief bridesmaid after all. I did have responsibilities.

We had a relaxing night and I was very quiet.

"Are you sure you're okay?" Alice asked for the umpteenth time.

"I'm fine," I told her. "I'm just relaxed."

After Alice put Lucy in her bed she returned in her white fluffy robe and slippers and her face smothered in goat-milk face cream. She curled up beside me and went through her folder. She removed pages from the plastic holder as she carefully double-checked them.

"They're almost done, Beth, so let's have the last final check," she smiled.

"What's that on your teeth?" I stared hard.

"Oh, it's like a gum-shield but I've got whitening stuff in it. I need to leave it in for an hour so can we order a takeaway then?"

"Sure – I'm not hungry yet anyway."

For the next forty minutes I helped her by holding a page here and there as she ticked and shaded and coloured various pages and boxes. She could rule the world this way.

"I don't think I've left any stone unturned," she said at last. "If this day doesn't run smoothly, I will eat my hat."

She removed the gooey gum-shield now and we ordered an Indian from Bombay Pantry and while we waited I opened a bottle of wine. She had half a glass – mine was full to the very top.

"Do you think Dan will call or not?" she asked as I rummaged in their DVD collection for something appropriate to watch.

"Of course he will!" I laughed.

"I do hope he doesn't go on the piss tonight . . . okay, I heard myself, strike that."

"What about a comedy?" I could only find Dan's films – Robert De Niro films – everywhere.

"Yeah, that'd be great and then we'll head up – don't want to be up too late."

God, I hoped she'd enjoy this day as much as she thought she was going to.

Her phone rang and she grabbed it from her dressing-gown pocket. "Dan!" she enthused into the phone like she hadn't heard from the man in years.

I excused myself to give them some privacy. As I sat in the kitchen a car pulled right into the driveway. My heart plummeted and I broke into a sudden sweat. Was it John? Was it Rory? No, it was the Indian. I was so up my own arse. I opened the door, paid the guy plus tip and took the food into the kitchen to plate it up. I poured another large glass of chilled white wine. "Don't think about it, don't think about it," I muttered. "Think about Alice, think about Alice," and that's all I tried to do. I could still hear Alice's hushed tones coming from the front room.

She'd ordered a chole, which was just a chickpea curry (Alice was taking no chance on meats or shellfish or garlic) and she had a side of bhatooras. I'd ordered my old favourite – Chicken Tikka Masala and naan bread. I opened my plastic container. The smell was wonderful. My marinated pieces of grilled chicken were covered in the thick creamy gravy. I dipped a finger in and licked it. Unfortunately they needed the microwave. We had one portion of basmati rice between us. I plated up and popped my plate into the microwave. Alice was still talking. She wouldn't mind if I ate and, to be honest, I knew that after two spoonfuls I'd think about John Callan standing beside me tomorrow and I'd be full – so I might as well throw the plate in the bin right now. The ping sounded and I removed my food. I jabbed a fork into it and tasted the chicken. It stuck in my throat. I swallowed it down with wine and tried again. Same thing. I stood and dumped half the plate in the bin just before Alice opened the door.

She noticed my plate. "Oh sorry, love! Ahh, you must have been famished – so sorry!" She put her fork in hers, tasted and made a noise of gratitude. "Come on!" She picked up her plate.

"Is it hot enough?" I was amazed.

"I hate microwaving food, Beth, you know that. It's fine as it is, it's warm enough."

We sat on the couch again, close to each other.

"So how is he?" I played around with my food.

"He's great. He's amazing, Beth, he really is. I'm a very lucky girl. I don't know what I'd do without him."

I patted her bare perfect leg and pressed play. I'd found *As Good As It Gets* with Jack Nicholson and Helen Hunt and I thought it fitting. We watched but I knew she was miles away and when I saw her carefully checking the clock on her iPhone I feigned tiredness.

"Sorry, Alice, but I'm wrecked . . . do you mind if I head up?"

She had the TV off and the light turned out before I had a chance to take my legs from underneath me.

We crept up the stairs.

"Night, Beth."

"Night, Alice."

"I love you, Beth."

"I love you, Alice."

"You could fry an egg on the sand, if you had an egg," we both said at the exact same time and then we giggled like teenagers as we closed our bedroom doors behind us.

Ready for the next phase in our lives.

I was up early and I made a massive pot of raspberry-leaf tea and laid out the cups on saucers with teaspoons. Mrs Callan was on her way and Alice was soaking with Lucy in a nice lukewarm bath that I had run for them. The door was open and women I had never seen before came and went with colourful bags and boxes and bits and bobs. I just smiled at them all. They seemed to know exactly what they were doing. I found a *Best of Crowded House* CD and stuck it on.

It was the perfect wedding morning. The house was filled with fresh air billowing in through all the windows, the crisp white curtains fluttering in the breeze.

I sat at the table and waited for the florist. It was a calm household just as Alice wanted it to be. No panic. Alice hated panic.

Whenever anyone asked me for tea I made it. I made another hot pot of the raspberry tea and brought it up to Alice in the bath. I brought Lucy some pineapple cordial in her beaker.

After I cleared away the remains of the earlier raspberry tea and washed the cups, I wandered around Alice's house in a bit of a daze.

"No one's pregnant, are they?" one of the girls who was sitting at the table had asked earlier. "Because this stuff is highly dangerous during pregnancy."

I hadn't been introduced to her and had no idea who she was or why she was here at my best friend's wedding.

I laughed. Everyone looked at me.

"Are you with child, Beth?" Mrs Callan poked me hard in the side. Not the cleverest thing to do if you even suspected someone was with child.

"Ouch! No . . . no . . . I'm just laughing . . . it used to be hard liquor and fags you had to avoid, now it's tea . . . not even caffeine tea but herbal stuff! Raspberry tea is dangerous . . . I just found that a bit funny, that's all." All eyes were still on me. "It's just, well, all a little bit over the top if you ask me, all the things you can and can't do in pregnancy now, isn't it?"

No one answered me as more people shuffled over and poured their own tea.

"Okay, you're chief bridesmaid, right?" the girl who held the information on the imminent dangers of raspberry tea accused more than asked me.

"Yes – yes, I am – that is me," I nodded.

"Come with me, please." She lifted her cup with saucer and walked out. I followed.

When we reached the top of the stairs we passed Alice and Lucy on the landing, all fresh after their warm baths.

"Did you put the fry on, Beth?" said Alice. "It's just I can't smell anything?"

I bit my lip hard. I was such a tit.

"You forgot to put on the fry, didn't you?" She wasn't mad, she was very calm.

"I forgot." I bowed my head. I really was useless but, in my defence, when she had said, "Beth, you okay with the fry?" she'd been on the phone to the hairdresser so I'd presumed it was some type of fancy blow-dry she wanted me to have but I didn't dare to ask.

"Don't worry – it was just for my mam really and my Auntie Pauline – they can have cereal like Lucy and me."

"I'll run down and get the fry together now if you like?" I offered.

"You will run nowhere except up to the basin chief," I was told.

People were coming and going as I sat to get my hair done. Busy women. Women with jobs to do. Wedding women. I didn't really fit in. I felt I stuck out like a sore thumb.

"Poker straight!" I told the poor girl for the tenth time since I'd sat down on the side of the bath.

"I know," she grinned at me but I felt she was grinning through gritted teeth.

There was one feeling in my brain that I couldn't shake off. I didn't like the way I was thinking but I couldn't lie to myself. I was free to break up with Rory. It was over. I was now free for John. Free to have sex with him again at any rate.

I fell to my knees and threw my hair over the side of the bath. She scrubbed the living daylights out of my scalp and it felt great.

"Conditioner?" she asked.

"Please," I replied upside-down. Why would you say no to conditioner? I must ask that question someday.

Was I actually happy that Rory and I were over? Would I even let him explain? I had no sexual quirks. I couldn't stomach what I'd seen. Well, that wasn't entirely true. John was my sexual quirk. Dressing up and dildos and butt-plugs would never be something that I could do. I found it all quite sad. And sick.

There was one question I was not allowing myself to answer. What if I'd caught John like that? I shoved it back out of my mind as quickly as it popped in.

Rory had called me eleven times and left eleven voice messages but I hadn't listened to one of them. He had texted then: **"Will I still come?"**

Typical Rory to use such a wrong turn of phrase at a time like this.

I sat on the loo now as the hairdresser towelled the excess water from my hair so I had time to think about my reply. Hair-towelling hurt though.

She moved (well, more like marched) me into the bedroom in front of Alice's wardrobe to dry me off. I grabbed my phone from the confines of the soft fabric-softener-smelling duvet on the bed.

"**Of course,**" I tapped in my reply to Rory and pressed send. I watched the green bar fill to the end and eventually fade.

I sat in a trance as my hair was dried. I closed my eyes until I felt a tap on my knees. Alice stood in front of me in her thick fluffy white robe and hair in curlers, her make-up already done.

"Oh, fab face, my love!" I said. Her make-up was wonderful. Subtle and understated. Her eyes popped and her skin glowed. Dewy.

"I think I need a drink." She suddenly paled under the creamy dewy goo.

"Yeah, of course – of course you do – let me get it, that's my job." I raised my hand. "Can you turn that off for a minute?" I shouted at the hairdresser as I stood. "Sorry but I'm needed. I am the chief bridesmaid, you know."

The hairdresser was starting to hate me.

Alice and I padded downstairs in our bare feet. In the kitchen I went to my bag and pulled out a bottle of Moët. "I would have put it in the fridge but there literally wasn't any room." How Alice had so much food in her fridge I'd never know. Fresh food. Food in Tupperwares. Yogurt pots of all descriptions. Zero crap.

"No worries, it will do as it is – there's ice in the freezer, Beth." She sat.

"Your hair?" The hairdresser was standing in the doorway, multicoloured pins and clips falling from her hairy black cardigan.

"Sorry, give me ten seconds!"

She glared at me and left.

187

I popped the bottle, got ice from the freezer and poured us a glass each. "You okay?"

Alice drank fast. "Yeah. Nerves hit me there for a second, but that's all I need – you go, go!"

"No, it's fine, they can wait – it's only hair – you are more important – can't she start on someone else?" I sipped.

"It's not Dan at all – it's just the thought of everyone looking at me as I go up the aisle, or what if I trip or what if I –"

I stopped her there. "Alice Callan, I doubt you have ever tripped and fallen over in your entire life. Now if you were worried about me falling over then I'd understand. Nothing will go wrong. You will be the perfect bride and have the perfect wedding day. I want you to relax now and enjoy it. You have put so much work and preparation into this day . . . and remember the most important thing, Alice . . . you are marrying Dan, wonderful, perfect Dan, and he adores you and you have Lucy too." I took her glass from her cold hands and put it on the table. I warmed her hands in mine. "You are my inspiration. I hope one day I can find what you have and embrace every second of it."

"Now, please." The hairdresser was back. The hairbrush she was waving looked to me like it had spanked before and would do it again, so I ran back like Charlie Chaplin.

I sat and let her do her job and what an incredible job she did. My hair was so straight it looked like a head full of rulers.

"Perfect!" I kissed her. I wasn't sure how appropriate that kiss was but that's how much I appreciated her art.

She smiled despite herself. "Mrs Callan!" she shouted into the air now. "Time, ladies, we need to watch the time! I still have three of you to do!"

I turned on the bed to face the make-up girl. She was wearing the tightest PVC black leggings I had ever seen. It must have taken her hours to get them up.

"What do you want?" She stared at me.

"Eh, you are doing my make-up?" I stared back.

"Yeah, but what look do you want?" she drawled, her eyes darker than shopping in Hollister. It was hard to see the actual eyeball. Her bright green hair stood on end here and there and a sharp fringe crossed her forehead on a mission to somewhere. "Oh. Right." I nodded my understanding. "Okay . . . em . . . just like Alice's . . . is that possible?"

"I'll do my best," she sighed heavily. The PVC must have been taking its toll. She stood back and looked at me. Moved in closer and looked at me. Then she tilted her head from side to side and made a guttural noise as though she was diagnosing a symptom. She removed a small black box from within a large black box and propped it up on her table. She took her index finger and dragged it slowly down the side of my face, her nails as colourful as the cast of *Sesame Street*, each fingertip a different colour and bejewelled style. She grabbed me under my chin and turned my face to the window, turning and twisting and analysing me. She dropped to her knees and stared hard into my face.

Jesus, it was only a bit of eye liner I was after, not a face lift!

"Okay, let's do this!" She whipped a bottle from her back pocket. "Primer," she informed me like I supposed to know what that was and she was off. She painted and coloured and poked and barked: "Open" – "Close" – "Look down" – "Look up" – "Look sideways" – "Smile".

It was seriously hard work.

"Full lashes?" she asked the other make-up girl who came to stare at me.

"Oh, defo," she replied and blew a large pink bubble. It popped. She moved away.

"Is there any way I could ask you to get me a glass of champagne from the kitchen?" I begged her.

She pretended not to hear me.

"Almost done, hun," said my make-up artist through a mouthful of tiny brushes.

Thank God. I was stiff as a poker.

"Lucy for hair, please!" I heard the hairdresser yell.

The make-up girl pulled the last brush from her mouth, poked it into my eye socket and then stood back. I doubt Picasso had ever worked so hard.

"Have a look. I can change anything you don't like."

I walked to the wardrobe mirror and looked. Who was that? Well, flipping Nora Batty, that was me! I opened my mouth but no words came out. I honestly didn't recognise myself. I looked incredible. The girl was a miracle worker.

"Okay, hun?" She was behind me.

"It's . . . I look amazing."

"Yeah, you've great skin and a great face, really easy to work on."

God help the poor unfortunates she thought were hard to work on, that's all I could think.

My eyes were done in dark browns and greys and the lashes made them look twice as wide. The black kohl liquid eye liner made them look like tiger's eyes in my opinion. She had been soft on the creamy foundation and pink blush highlighted my cheekbones as I'd never seen them before. My lips were highly glossed in a sheer nude. The poker-straight hair suited the dark look. I looked like I should be on a red carpet. Well, I would be soon but not that type of carpet.

"Thanks a million!" I said and hugged her.

"Mind yer face!" she shouted at me.

I retreated to the bed to get my toenails painted. Mrs Callan was on toenail duty. Mrs Callan was never without fabulously painted fingernails so we trusted her. We made small talk but never mentioned John. As my nails dried I sat there and watched the madness that is women getting ready together.

Time to slip on the frock. I took it into the bathroom. I removed the plastic. The smell from the dress was wonderful. Fresh shop-floor-fabric smell. I imagined how nervous I would be right now if I hadn't broken the ice with John before the church today. I would be in absolute bits which would have been so unfair on Alice. This was her big day and I wanted to be the best friend and the best chief bridesmaid that I possibly could be. I would not think about what was happening in my life today. I would not be that selfish. I took off my robe and struggled with the Spanx. Once I managed to get into the underwear I placed my nipple daisies over my poor cowering nipples. I was not looking forward to peeling them off later. There was no way I could wear a bra with this dress. I was lucky my boobs were still pretty pert and small so I could get away with the pretty little daisies. I stepped into my BT gown. It glided on easily. I tied the halter loosely around my neck in a long bow. I had made a gold belt. I wasn't sure why – the dress was perfect as it was but I think I wanted to add my own touch to it. The belt was made up of tiny metal gold hoops on a thin gold chain. I draped it around my waist and it sat on my hip bones as I clasped it shut. I slipped in my gold studs and added my new silk bracelet and then I stepped into the sky-high pink shoes and I was done. Ready to meet Alice at the bottom of the red carpet and walk ahead of her up the aisle.

I opened the bathroom door and about ten pairs of eyes glared at me.

"What?" I looked down to see if I had toilet roll attached to my shoe.

"You are stunning, Beth!" Alice stood in her white Gossard underwear set. She reminded me of their out-of-this-world lingerie model, Elle Liberachi. Absolute perfection.

"Ahh, thanks, love, any champers left there?" I hated people complimenting me. I was embarrassed. Someone handed me a glass. I imagined I was the same colour as the dress. "Let's get this show on the road," I muttered as I sank onto the bed and watched Alice slip into Mrs Callan's wedding dress as big fat tears rolled down my face. I'd need to be retouched by Hun.

I got up and went to get the neckpiece. I lifted it and gently placed it on her neck. I did the catches at the back. It glittered in the mirror. Alice glittered in the mirror.

Chapter Sixteen

Louise

Louise finished the dribble from the second bottle, holding it upside down as she sucked hard. Then she tried to stand up. Her feet buckled beneath her and she landed on the warm burnt grass in her perfect back garden. The bottle rolled away down the grassy verge. She sobbed, the fringe from her dark bob falling into her eyes. She pulled herself up by the ledge of the fountain, wiping her wet hands on her tracksuit bottoms.

She had read about his upcoming nuptials at the back of *The Irish Times*. She, this Alice Callan, had taken out an ad. Louise had cut it out and stuck it on her bedroom wall. Her mother had seen it and ripped it down.

"What is this nonsense? Move on. That's all in the past – it's over, Louise!"

They would be a proper family soon. It was time. She poured the last glass of the bottle. Loopy Lou would finally be coming home.

She needed to see him before he made the biggest mistake of his life. She needed to grow up and be an adult.

She'd thought about him all day yesterday until she passed out. She'd awoken early this morning and started drinking as soon as. She wouldn't drink again though – that was her last bottle. He'd never take her back if he thought she was still drinking. She needed to stop this wedding. She had memorised the address of the church from the *Irish Times* before her mother eventually ripped the cutting down. The wedding was at two. She imagined that the groom had to be there by one though. Knowing Dan, he'd be early.

She hiccupped and stumbled and fell again. "Silly milly moo," she stammered to herself. She got up again.

If she left now she'd be at the church by one thirty. She'd catch Dan in time.

And Lucy. She would see her daughter after all this time. Her own flesh and blood.

It was time now, time to fix it all. She wondered why she'd never thought about this before. Her car keys were in the drawer in the hall. She never used them much. In fact, she couldn't remember the last time she had left the house. She really hoped there was petrol in the car as she had no cash or cards. She never had money. Her Valium pillbox was sticking out of her bag so she popped it open and downed the magic tablet dry. Then, wobbling from side to side down her cool spacious white hallway, she left the house.

She got into her silver convertible BMW. She turned the key and the car purred hello. She squinted against the sun. It was so hard to see. She had a fair idea where the church was. It was half twelve so she had loads of time. She pushed in a CD of Bruce Springsteen and revved the accelerator. She reversed out of her house and onto the main road.

He'd never really tried to contact her since she'd delivered the baby. Oh, he'd been there every step of the way during the pregnancy. Begging her night after night to stop drinking because it was bad for the baby. What about her? Did he not care that it was bad for her too? She couldn't stop drinking, he knew that. He'd paid for her to go to the Rutland Centre and she'd gone. She'd listened in the meetings and the second she got out she'd walked the five minutes up the road to Delaney's pub and ordered a double vodka and Ballygowan. She'd sat at the bar and drank herself into delicious oblivion. She'd no idea how Dan had arrived to get her but she did remember the barman saying "She ain't welcome back here, buddy, okay?" to Dan as she blacked out. "The baby! Think of the baby!" was all he'd shouted at her the next day as her head felt like it was going to explode.

She merged into the traffic as someone honked their horn way too long at her. She drove onto the M50 and was beeped at again as she changed lanes. She raised her hand in apology and then she spotted him.

Dan O'Toole. In the next lane. Just like that. Parallel worlds.

She made several jerks of her head to look out her window and then swung her eyes back to the road. They were all laughing. Mr and Mrs O'Toole in the back and Dan driving. In his wedding suit. Suited and booted to move on. There was a woman in the passenger seat she didn't recognise. In an enormous cerise-pink hat. But no Lucy. Her baby girl wasn't there.

She pressed her foot down hard to the floor to pass them so she could get a better look in her rear-view mirror.

195

Chapter Seventeen

It was boiling hot in the church. "We should have got fans!" I said to no one in particular. I had to go up to the top but I strolled up and down, smiling at people. John was at the top of the church. I couldn't see Dan. He must be in the loo. I'd wait. I wasn't going to get into any type of discussion with John today. On anything. Or Rory. On anything. This was Alice and Dan's day. Obviously I was starting to sweat with guilt but I had to push it out of my mind for twenty-four hours. Rory had shocked me into having sex with John, hadn't he? My armpits were dampening. Thank God my dress was halter. This was all Alice's idea – that I should get to the church before her and greet the guests. Hand out the little books. I had thought she'd said "Will you hand out the missiles?" and when I repeated it she stared at me so long and hard that I just laughed. "Joke," I'd murmured. She was coming in the car with her parents and both her parents were walking her up the aisle. Where was Dan?

I tipped Mr Greene in the last aisle, Alice's godfather

and all-round party animal. I asked him the time and his whiskey breath nearly knocked me over. One time at John's thirtieth in our flat he asked me up to dance. He'd spun me around the tiny kitchen to "Money, Money, Money" so fast that I threw up. Slightly. Just in my mouth. I had to swallow it as there was really no alternative.

"Save a dance for me later, Barbara," he said now, grinning a yellow-toothed grin at me.

He'd always called me Barbara. It never bothered me.

What did bother me, however, was his answer to my question. Which was: "It's just gone a quarter to two."

Alice had no intention of being one minute late.

"A quarter to two?" I whispered to myself as I saw John strut down the aisle as though it were a Parisian catwalk during Fashion Week. Hats turned to gaze as he swaggered. Black tux. Pink tie to match my dress. Alice had matched the colours exactly.

"Beth," he smiled wickedly at me.

I pulled myself up tall. Poker-straight hair. "John," I copied his forename-only conversation.

"Where is Dan the man, Beth?" he asked, fixing his tie. John hated ties.

I felt odd as I answered, "I don't know. I presumed he was in the toilet? Is he not?"

I couldn't tell if John was pulling my leg.

"Nah. I haven't seen him and I got here at one. I dragged myself from The Bleeding Horse to be here early – think he's taking the piss a bit now, don't you?" He pulled up his shiny white shirtsleeve through the dark material of his jacket and glared at his watch.

My eyes did a jig in my head. Up and down and round

and round. I patted my body for a phone I knew wasn't there. "Can I have your phone?" I asked him.

"I don't have one." He patted himself now too.

"Shit!" I hissed.

We locked eyes.

"*Fffffuucckkk!*" John exclaimed.

"Please, John, not in the house of our Lord!" Mrs Greene pursed her bright red lips. Her lipstick had bled a lot and the pursing of the lips made it look like she'd been stabbed in the mouth as the colour ran into the lines around her mouth.

"Sorry, Mrs Greene." John blessed his tie. "*Shhhiiiitt!*" he said very loudly now again and patted Mrs Greene's gold sparkly jacket-shoulder before she could respond.

He took me by the elbow and led me quickly out of the church. People were gathered smoking cigarettes in the church grounds, chatting and laughing, the summer breeze warm and rose-scented.

"What do we do?" He looked panicked. "Not about us now, I mean about Dan?"

Only on two occasions had I ever seen John Callan panic. Once when I forgot to take my pill and we had sex three times the night before and the other when he saw his first wrinkle at the side of his eye.

"I get that much, John – of course it's about fucking Dan, you asshole!" I hissed at him.

I couldn't quite believe this. There must be an excellent explanation, I knew that much. Dan would never, ever leave Alice and Lucy stranded at the altar. His parents weren't there either so they must be delayed. I needed a phone. I didn't know Dan's number off by heart. Rachel, his really good friend and Lucy's godmother, whom I'd met at the hen party, was smoking Vogue menthol under a huge old oak tree.

"Come on," I said to John and we went over. "Hey, Rachel, I was hoping you had Dan's number handy?"

She was wearing a black knee-length Rah-Rah dress and her red hair was covered in a huge black feathered hat. "Everything okay?" She stood the white butt into the grass. Women were always on red alert at weddings.

"I hope so, yeah, I'm sure it's just . . . it's almost after ten to two and Dan's still not here." I tried to sound breezy.

Her expression said it all and she fell to her knees on the grass and threw tissue upon tissue and a bag of confetti out of her bag until she pulled out her phone. "Here, it's under Tiddle Time – do not ever ask."

I flipped open her phone cover, pushed Contacts hard and called Tiddle Time. It rang. And rang. And my heart started to race and I stared to sweat. Voice mail. I dialled again. And again. And again. And again. And again. All went to voicemail.

"No answer," I whispered to Rachel and John.

John swore mercilessly under his breath and Rachel just whispered, "Bollox."

"Can I hang onto your phone?" I asked her. "I need to call Alice."

Chapter Eighteen

"Hey, Beth . . . what?" Alice's voice dropped dramatically.

There really was no sugar-coating this information. "Dan's not arrived here yet, Alice. I can't get him on his phone – it's almost five to two – have you left the house yet?" There was silence from Alice as I heard the driver chatting to her dad in the front and Lucy singing.

"Alice?" I said.

No reply.

I eased the words out slowly: "Alice, put your mam on the phone, please."

I heard Mrs Callan say "Who is it, love?" before she took the phone. "Hello? Hello?" I heard her concerned voice now.

"You have to drive around, Mrs Callan. Dan's not here yet. Keep the phone on your lap, will you, and I'll call you back in five minutes. Do you understand?"

"Yes . . . but . . ."

"Okay." I hung up.

John was dragging his hands through his hair. "I'll

fucking kill that Cork prick!"

I grabbed him by the wrist. "Please shut up – Dan would never do this, ever! Something's wrong, very wrong."

I dialled Dan's number again. Voicemail. Again. Voicemail. Again. Voicemail.

And then I saw it. It was far in the distance. It was as though in a very surreal way I had been looking out for it. I stared at it as it got closer and closer. I focused on the thick bright luminous yellow strip around the white of the car. The two blue lights on top. Rachel was talking to me but I heard nothing. The car was at the lights. It had stopped. I could see the thick blue lettering on the nose of the car now. Maybe it would turn right away from the church but I knew in my heart of hearts that it wouldn't. It was as though a magnetic force was pulling it here. All the way here. Every painful inch of road taken up by it. Right up into the church grounds where no cars except the bridal car were permitted to go. And Garda cars.

"It's the cops." John stated the frighteningly obvious fact as the car slowly manoeuvred through the gates and into the grounds.

I approached it. Two guards. A male and a female. She got out first, putting on her hat as she stood out.

"I'm looking for Alice Callan, the bride?" she said to me gently, her plain navy uniform a jolt into reality amongst all the vibrant colours and hats here today.

"She's not here . . . she's driving around . . . what is wrong? Is it Dan?"

John put his arm around me. I could feel the heat from each tense finger.

"I'm afraid I really need to speak to Miss Callan

herself first." Her eyes told me everything. They were full of sympathy.

John squeezed me harder. He'd seen those eyes too.

"I can call her . . . she's waiting on my call . . . they're just driving . . . around."

John peeled the phone from my freezing blue hands. I watched him dial his mother's number in slow motion. The beep from each button sounding like a siren.

"Mam, it's me, John. You need to come to the church. Now. Something's happened, Mam . . . the cops . . . guards . . . the guards are here . . . Just come, I don't know any more."

He hung up and looked at me, his dark eyes full of worry and sadness.

"This cannot be good, can it? Me poor sister," he whispered as he dropped his head.

"Come on, we don't know what's happened . . . it might not be . . ."

The big white bridal car pulled into the grounds, its red ribbon trailing behind like a symbol of God knew what right now. I saw Alice's ashen face pressed against the window with Lucy now on her lap, Lucy's tiny smiling face in stark contrast to the faces of the other occupants in the car.

"Is that his little girl?" the male Garda asked. "Is there a relative nearby now, please, folks?" he almost barked.

Rachel stepped forward. "I'm her godmother – I will take her inside." Her voice crackled.

The car stopped. No one got out. No one wanted to. The female Garda opened Alice's back door. Rachel took Lucy out as I stood beside her.

"Hi, Ethy! I have my pedals to spwinkle, see?" She

showed me her little basket filled with red petals. She was in a cream full-length satin dress with white pearls sewn throughout and white flowers in her hair. Her feet were clad in soft cream ballet shoes. I stared at the bracelet on her tiny wrist that I had made for her. She looked like an angel.

"Beautiful, Bubble." I swallowed hard and smiled wide. "Go on inside with Rachel and scatter a few, yeah?"

"'Kay. Bye bye, Ethy. I need to spwinkle them now before they blowed way on me." She put a tiny protective hand over her little basket and I wished I could do the same to her life.

Alice got out. I'd never seen skin the colour of hers before in my life despite the make-up. She was shallow-breathing as her parents got out. They stood on either side of their daughter. The church and its grounds were silent, the only sounds coming from voices of the people gathered inside the church. The air was heavy.

The female Garda took Alice's hands in hers. "I'm afraid I have some very bad news to tell you, Miss Callan. Mr Dan O'Toole was killed in a traffic accident this afternoon, on the M50 shortly before one o' clock. He was taken to St Vincent's Hospital but I'm afraid he was pronounced dead in the ambulance. I'm so very sorry." The Garda tried to control her own tears.

Alice made a noise that was so unfamiliar it shook me. It seemed to come from her stomach and just spurt right out her mouth. Then she fell to her knees, screaming and sobbing, and then she threw up. John got down on his knees beside her but didn't touch her. No one spoke. The silence surrounding Alice's grief was horrendous.

"We are going to need Alice to come with us," the male Garda told me.

Mr Callan had walked away. Over to the old oak tree. He had one arm outstretched, holding onto the tree, and his head was dropped. Mrs Callan stood, hand gripped over her mouth but otherwise motionless.

I couldn't cry. I was completely and utterly in shock. My hands were still blue as I looked down. I desperately needed to go to the toilet, I suddenly realised. Alice needed me but I had no words. I couldn't help her. I wasn't there. It was all so surreal. Her beautiful dress all covered in pink vomit and grass stains. The pink must be from the raspberry tea, I thought for some bizarre reason.

Jesus, Dan was dead. Dan was dead. I couldn't believe it. This couldn't be happening? This was supposed to be a perfect day. The best day of Alice's life.

I watched John now take her into his arms and rock her back and forth like a baby. Like Lucy. Jesus, poor Lucy. What would happen to her? I needed to help. I needed to pull my fucking self together. I was Alice's chief bridesmaid. That meant something.

So I turned and walked up the steps to the church. Hundreds of people were huddled at the big wooden doors now, aware of the drama unfolding outside, and I ushered them back in. I made eye contact with Rachel who scooped Lucy up and took her out the back into the toilet. I made the long walk up the red carpet and trod on Lucy's red petals as I went. I reached the top and stood in front of the microphone, hundreds of eyes staring at me.

"Hi, everyone . . ." I spoke but the mike wasn't on. I pushed up a little black button and spoke again. It hissed and squealed now so I just stood in front of it and raised my voice. "Hi, everyone, I'm . . . I have some awful news . . . I'm afraid there's been a terrible accident and there will be no wedding today. I'm sorry I can't give you any further information but it's . . . it's all I can say right now." I snorted then. A loud obnoxious snort. The tears followed. I dropped my head into my hands. The tears streamed out of me like a dam had just burst. God, poor Alice, poor Lucy and poor wonderful, life-loving Dan O'Toole. My friend. He had been wiped out in the blink of an eye.

When I looked up I saw Rory stand out of his seat and make his way up to me. I sniffed and blinked hard as the liquid liner stung my eyes and the church remained silent.

"I have her." John put his hand up and stopped Rory in his tracks as he passed him out on the red carpet. "It's grand, mate, thanks." And with that Rory turned on his heel and John wrapped me up in his arms and guided me off the altar and down the church out the door into the bright sunshine. I knew now, looking at Alice, that none of it mattered. Romance was all so trivial in the face of death. Everything that I was worrying about – John, Beth's Bitz, my parents, Rory – none of it really meant a shite. Life was what mattered and now Dan's life was gone. Alice's life was ruined. Lucy was basically an orphan. I had been living in a self-pitying pathetic bubble and I hit earth now with a clatter of reality that gave me an instant migraine.

Alice was sitting in the passenger seat of the Garda car, holding a paper coffee cup. I should have thought of that. I approached her but she didn't look up. People filed out of the church in silence and no one stopped to talk to her. Her head hung low, the paper cup under her dripping nose. No one knew what to say. Least of all me.

Chapter Nineteen

At Vincent's Hospital social services were already waiting. The police had been swift in contacting the right people and they had to talk immediately about Lucy, we were informed. They were privy to information about her birth mother and they needed to act on it. It was now a matter for the courts to decide.

"Please, don't take her away! Please! I need to talk to her first – please give me five minutes – please no!" Alice sobbed loudly as a kindly woman with a bright blue bandana on her grey hair lifted Lucy into her arms. It was so unlike Alice to cause a scene in front of Lucy but this was no ordinary day.

Lucy bawled crying. "Maman, I want my maman! Where's my daddy and the booloons? "

"Will you come with us, please, Miss Callan?" a doctor asked as he stood in front of us now. "Dan's parents are both asking for you. They escaped but both have extreme breaks and cuts and bruises . . . but Mrs O'Toole's sister, Frances, also perished in the accident. I am so sorry."

Alice didn't look up at him. "Please let her stay with me just for a little while – it's for her sake, not mine!"

She 'pleased' again and this time the social worker smiled.

"Shush, Alice, it's okay, Lucy is fine here for now. Of course you can see her, of course you can, but later is better – this isn't the place for her right now, don't you agree? I'm going to take her to the canteen for a lemonade and you come up after, okay? She doesn't understand anything . . . that's all up to you, my dear. I have a whole pile of puzzles and jigsaws in my bag we can play, okay?"

Alice sniffed. "Okay, thank you."

"That sounds like fun, Lucy, doesn't it, sweetheart?" the lady said now as Lucy was looking in the bag. She handed Lucy a beige teddy bear, and then made her way across the hospital floor with her, singing "The Wheels on the Bus" as she went.

"Miss Callan, can you come now please?" the doctor asked again.

I took Alice by the hand for the first time since the news. "Will I come with you?" My voice was a mere croak.

"Beth?" She looked at me as though she hadn't seen me in over twenty years. "Beth . . . oh Beth, can you believe this?" She looked down at her dress. "Can you take this in? I can't, I can't, I can't!"

"Hush," I said, my neckpiece mocking me as I put my arms around her and we both stood in the embrace.

"Miss Callan, if you would follow me, please?"

We followed the doctor towards a silver-doored lift. He pressed the buttons. It was cold inside. We followed him out again.

On a cold corridor I immediately saw a red-haired man in a wheelchair at the bed of a woman, the bed pressed up against the hospital wall. Privacy denied. He had his leg out in front of him on a stool and had his back to us but I could see her face. It was horrific. She was so badly cut and bruised. Her nose was all the way over towards her left ear, her mouth so swollen and split that she didn't really look human.

"Oh God! Victoria – Michael!" Alice ran to the bed.

I stayed at the lift and let the three people combine their united grief over a wonderful man they had all adored and now lost.

After a while they stopped crying.

"I need to go and see him." Michael looked up at Alice. "Do you want to see him? Victoria doesn't. I need to tell you, they told me . . . told us . . . he's in a bad way . . . he doesn't look like him any more, you know . . . he's . . . he's, well . . . Ya know, he got out, Alice, he pulled us out, he tried to give Frances mouth to mouth then he just collapsed. I remember looking at him and thinking who is this man? His face . . . it was . . . all those cuts from that glass . . ." He stopped and put his hand over his mouth.

I couldn't look at him any more. I dropped my head. I saw a penny on the floor beside my feet and wanted to pick it up. We needed all the luck we could get right now but I didn't move, it didn't seem the right thing to do. It was too normal an action and this was the most abnormal situation I'd ever been in, in my entire life.

"Internal bleeding, they told us – I mean he was covered in blood and all but we all were – I knew Frances was gone – she wouldn't put the seat belt across her as she was concerned about it creasing her dress . . ."

"I want to see him!" Alice almost shouted now.

I approached now. "I'm so, so sorry, Mr and Mrs O'Toole, I have no words to say how sorry I am . . . but, Alice, are you sure this is the right thing? Think of Dan – would Dan not prefer you to remember him as he was? I –"

"I have to say goodbye to him, Beth, I have to, I want him to see my dress . . ." She started rubbing at the stains on the dress.

The doctor walked softly towards us then. "Are you ready to see him? The Guards you met earlier are here also – they are ready if you are?"

Michael and Alice nodded. The doctor gently removed Michael's leg from the stool, then began to push the wheelchair, with Alice's hand gripping Michael's.

"Stay with Victoria, could you?" Michael whispered to me as tears rolled over his cuts.

I stood by the bed. It was hard to tell if her eyes were opened or closed.

"I saw her," she managed.

"Saw who?" I leaned in closer.

She swallowed and winced. "Louise."

She must be high on medication, I thought, so I just shushed her and gently took her blood-soaked hard hair and pulled it gently back with my fingers. "Rest now, Mrs O'Toole, just try and get some rest." I held her hand tightly as I waited for them to return, closed my eyes and said a decade of the rosary.

Chapter Twenty

We all sat around Alice's kitchen table. I had bathed her and now she took a seat at the top of the table in her yellow PJ's – the ones she had on last week, the bunny ones. They had given her a pretty strong sedative at the hospital and she was calmer and unfocused for now. I'd gently taken off the neckpiece and removed her dress and shoes. I'd put her in a warm bath with lavender and washed her gently in Dove foam soap and shampooed her hair in Lucy's Johnson's Baby Shampoo after I took every last clip out.

I just made tea. I didn't think alcohol was a good idea for anyone. There were so many people in the house. The front door was open and people came and went. Dan's parents were still in the hospital. His dad had a broken ankle and also fractured ribs. His mother only had the facial wounds and a broken nose but she was in an acute and intense state of shock and the doctors wanted to monitor her. They would be released tomorrow to fly down to Cork with Frances' body. Dan would be laid to rest in Dublin. They told us they would be back up for the day for his funeral and then return to see Lucy in a week or two. I told them I would go down and collect them and drive them up but they said they would manage.

Alice had managed to hold on to Lucy.

"For tonight, pet, and then we have to meet, okay?" the social worker, Fiona, had said as Alice and Michael signed some papers.

Michael had spoken sternly to the woman. "For good – that child stays with her for good! I am her grandfather, and that is what me and her grandmother want and my dead son – that is what my poor dead son would have wanted."

Fiona gathered her pages into a pile, put them in her black briefcase and clicked the gold clasps shut. "I wish it was that simple, sir. I can see just how much Alice loves her but it's a matter for the courts, I'm afraid, as her birth mother is still alive." She wearily put her hand on his shoulder and squeezed it before walking away.

I had put the exhausted little girl to bed, in Alice's bed, and stayed with her until she'd fallen asleep. She still didn't know what was going on. I'd bamboozled her with sweets and crisps and ice cream and read her books.

"I can't lose Lucy," Alice now said, slurring her words as the table fell silent.

"You won't." John stood up. He'd found drink somewhere I could tell. He had changed. He was wearing a tight black high-necked hoody zipped right up to his neck with black jeans and black Converse. He had the hood pulled up tight over his head. "They can't do that to ya, Al, they just can't."

She smiled weakly at him. "Where is Rory?" She looked at me now.

"I'm here, Alice," his low voice came from the sitting room. I hadn't known he was in there. He stood at the kitchen door now. Practically a stranger at this close-knit table.

"Ah, thanks for being here, Rory," she said.

He approached her, knelt down beside her and whispered in her ear. She nodded. He went back inside. I knew I should follow him. I looked over at John. He was staring at me. I stayed where I was.

"I want to go up to Lucy, Beth," Alice leaned over and said to me. Her lips were so cracked they were bleeding and I needed to put Vaseline on them.

"Of course, come on. I'll put the monitor on so you can shout if you need anything."

"Thanks."

I linked her up the stairs. She sat heavily on the bed and I removed her multicoloured slipper-socks. I grabbed some Vaseline from her design table and smeared it generously on her poor lips.

Lucy was snoring lightly, her blonde hair splayed all over her Barbie pillow which she'd taken into the big double bed.

The room was dim, the only light coming from the landing light getting in through the door which was slightly ajar.

"He's never coming back, Beth, can you believe that?"

"I can't, Alice, no," I answered honestly. I didn't see the point in saying it would be alright – it wouldn't be.

I eased her shoulders down into the bed, then lifted her legs in and pulled the soft covers up under her chin.

The packed suitcases in the corner for Disneyland Florida were a sign of another lifetime. Piled on top of one another. I shuddered at the thought of the accident.

"What would we have been doing now?" she asked me.

I looked at the time on her bedside alarm clock. Eight o'clock. "We would be just finished the meal, I'd say, setting up for the band."

She nodded. "I wonder what he was going to say in his speech? He'd told me he'd have difficulty getting through it without crying – what do you think he was going to say?"

I rubbed my thumb across her hand. "I don't know," I whispered.

"Do you think he was happy to be marrying me?"

"Oh God, Alice, I can answer that, I can one hundred per cent answer that. He was so happy to be marrying you. Dan adored you, Alice – he loved you with every inch of his body."

Lucy stirred and we fell silent.

Alice lay deadly still in the bed.

"The band actually . . ." she said at last. "The hotel, the presents . . . the honeymoon . . . Beth, I'd better get up." She shook.

"It's all taken care of, Alice. John and I went to the hotel while you were in with the doctor after you saw Dan – we explained everything. We have all the gifts and I will return them all next week . . . please don't worry about those kinds of things . . . everyone understands. I will take care of everything."

"It wasn't him, Beth, it wasn't Dan. He was so bloated and weird-looking – I'm sure he had –"

"I don't want you to think about that image, Alice, please. Think about him walking out the door on

Wednesday and smiling back at you and –"

She cut me off. "We were trying for a baby. I didn't tell you, I didn't tell anyone, I was afraid to jinx it."

I was at a loss for words.

"I need to worry about Lucy, don't I?"

"Yes," I whispered the truth.

"What will they do?"

"I don't know – we have to wait and see if Dan had a will . . . the social worker woman, Fiona, said –"

"He didn't," she cut me off, sniffing now as tears flowed from her exhausted, reddened eyes again. "We were going in to do them this week before we went to Disneyland."

I wiped her eyes with a soft tissue from the pink box on her bedside locker. "Alice, Lucy should be with you, everyone will see that, so let's just get tonight over with and see what tomorrow brings, okay? You really need to sleep. Will I wait here until you do?"

"No, please go down . . . I'm so drowsy . . . but you need to listen for Luce in case I don't hear her and she needs me in the middle of the night, will you? I will just sleep . . ." She trailed off and her eyes shut.

God bless sedatives.

Rory was at the bottom of the stairs as I padded down in my bare feet.

"Can I talk to you for a minute, Beth?"

"Sure." I rubbed my temples.

I followed him down the hallway and out the front door to the bottom of the pathway. The night air was still warm but the ground cold under my feet. I could smell the chips from Silvio's chipper down the road.

"It's just unbelievable, isn't it?" he said.

"I know, I know, I am still in shock, I can't take it in." I stubbed my bare foot on a stone in the grass now. I had changed into one of Alice's track suits but my feet were so cut from wearing the bridesmaid high-heeled shoes all day I couldn't put anything on them.

"Beth, I know this isn't a good time . . . I can't believe what has happened to Dan . . . but I really have to explain to you . . . especially now . . . it's . . . it was . . . you see, we were all making a DVD for Dan . . . there were supposed to be beers in his room before the wedding, just one or two, ya'know, to give him a proper send-off . . . we were going to play the DVD for him. It was a joke, about how men turn into pussies after they marry – hence the notion we all dress up in women's underwear."

My mouth went dry as my brain slowly unwrapped his words.

He continued. "It was John Callan's idea obviously. All the guys were given a line from The Stunning's song "Brewing Up a Storm" to sing while wearing their girlfriend's or wife's underwear . . . it was . . ." He threw his hands up in the air now. "Ah, what does it matter? You didn't want me to explain, did you? You couldn't wait to run back to him. How long did it take you? Three seconds after you slammed the door shut on me? You're pathetic, Beth."

I froze. I was mortified. I had never, ever, even imagined there was any reasonable explanation for him being dressed in my bra and panties and now I had no way back. I had made my bed.

"But you were watching porn?" I tried feebly to defend myself. I watched his face contort as he listened to my excuse.

215

Did I want a way back? What if John didn't want me? If Alice was right and he was just playing with me? Did I still want Rory then? I was utterly confused. I felt so guilty and horrible and worthless.

"Are you actually serious?" he hissed at me.

"Well, yeah, Rory – what about the porn, those girls?" I struggled to attack now.

"It was supposed to be a joke – you know, porn running in the background. I never watch porn, Beth, you know that – I have to see enough of it in the van for stags – but I wanted to fit in with all the lads. I – I wanted John Callan to laugh at my bit, dumb eejit that I am!" He removed his glasses and pinched his eyes with his index finger and his thumb. "Are we over, Beth? Because I sure as hell am not waiting around here for Mr Callan to decide if he still wants you or not."

He knew. He had my sad pathetic mind pegged. I had no choice. I owed it to him to come clean. How could I have treated him like this? I looked up.

"You are right. You deserve so much better than me, Rory – you always have. I never wanted to hurt you but here's the truth." My breath was fast and staggered as I continued, afraid I'd lose my honest tongue. "Of course I should have let you explain but . . . but I've never stopped thinking about John since the day we got together. I think about him all the time, I fantasise about him when we have sex, I keep an old picture of him that I look at every time I'm alone in the apartment, I wish daily he'd never dumped me. I can't help it, Rory, it's the truth. I wanted it to work with you so, so much. I want to be normal and have a normal relationship. I love you, I really do, but I don't love you enough. I have tried to love you the same

216

but it's not in me. I think you're the greatest guy I have ever met but I'm a fake, Rory. If he hadn't come back then we would have been okay, but I guess one day he would have come back and this was always going to happen. It's why I didn't want to move in with you and I think why you didn't want to move in with me. Deep down, we both knew. Of course I ran to him. Of course I couldn't wait to have sex with him again – that's how pathetic I truly am. I hate myself. I am shallow and I am a fake horrible bitch. I want you to stay in the house and I will move in here for however long and be with Alice. I'm so sorry, Rory."

He said nothing.

"And of course you're right, of course John won't stay with me, of course he's using me . . . I think, I don't know . . . but all I do know, Rory, is I can't lie to you any more. You don't deserve it."

His hands came up so fast and unexpectedly that I was struck dumb. Rory grabbed me by both shoulders and shook me hard, his anger completely taking over his normally impeccably behaved mind. I didn't scream and I didn't react.

But John did.

"What the fuck!" He came charging from the hallway where he'd obviously been spying on us. He lunged at Rory, sending his glasses flying, and the two threw punches at each other while rolling around on the road outside Alice's house. They didn't shout, either one of them. It was a silent fight but it was vicious. I didn't want to scream for help so I tried to pull them apart. I couldn't. They had rolled quite a distance down the road now. I followed.

"Stop! Stop it, please!" I hissed loudly at them.

John had Rory in a headlock and I couldn't see Rory's face.

"Hit her often, do ya? Ya fucking boring dickhead! I'm gonna fucking kill you!" John's voice was raised now.

"Stop, John! He's never raised a hand to me before – he just shook me – please let him go! Please!" I tugged at the hood on John's top so hard I ripped it. "John!" I reefed him with all my strength, almost choking him with the hood and managed to make him release his grip.

Rory spluttered and scrambled back, wheezing, on his hands and knees.

"Please stop, this isn't the time or the place! Think of Alice!" I was holding back the tears now and they were tears for Rory, I suddenly realised. His nose was bleeding, his glasses gone and he looked so vulnerable and sad. And I, Beth Burrows, had done that to him. "Are you okay, Rory?" I ran to him while John decided to light a fag and lean against a Jeep as though he was in some high-end advertising campaign.

"Sorry, Beth," Rory cried now. "That was a terrible thing to do to you – I'm so sorry!"

I fell on my knees in front of him and wiped his tears. "Don't be sorry – I deserved it and it was nothing. Please come back to the house – we'll find your glasses and clean you up – and maybe we all need a drink?" I stood up and hissed at John: "Apologise to Rory now!"

"I will like fuck! He attacked you, Beth!" John exhaled loudly.

"He never attacked me, John! He shook me because I fucking deserved to be shaken!" I tried to keep my voice as low as possible,

"Can I have a fag, John?" Rory got to his feet and

slowly walked over to the Jeep.

John stared at him before digging deep into his jeans pocket and pulling out a Marlboro Red box. "Here."

He offered it and Rory took a cigarette and perched it between his lips. John fished again and found his lighter.

"I can't compete with you, mate," said Rory. "I tried. I tried long and hard. I can't. You win, I lose. I deserved that punch. I should never have put my hands on her. To be honest, I didn't think I had that in me. I'm a fucking animal."

"You are not!" I protested and grabbed the cigarettes from John.

The three of us stood puffing.

"You hit a woman once, you'll do it again," John piped up.

"Please, John, just drop it! He didn't hit me – he shook me and I deserved it!"

"No, you didn't, Beth," Rory said now. "Just don't break her heart all over again, John."

"What business is it of yours what I do, mate?" John blew smoke directly into his face like a twelve-year-old boy in a playground.

"Because she's . . . she's my friend," Rory managed. "Because she's one of the best friends I have ever had."

I loved him. I knew right there and then that Rory O'Dowd would be in my life forever and it was a bigger relief than I had ever imagined.

Chapter Twenty-one

The weather took a turn for the worst and we buried Dan in heavy sleeting rain on Tuesday morning. David came down from Belfast for it. Lucy stood holding Alice's hand before being taken away to live, for now, with her birth mother and birth grandparents.

In an incredible twisted turn of fate it turned out that Louise, Lucy's mum, had also been involved in the crash on the M50 that day. So Mrs O'Toole had been right – she had seen her. The traffic camera on site had been vandalised so no one really could piece together exactly what had happened. Other cars had taken Louise's registration though so the police had looked her up. Louise had said she couldn't be sure what had happened, it had all been so fast, but that she had been too afraid to stop for fear of causing another accident. She'd pulled into a hotel but hadn't called the police as she didn't realise she should, since she wasn't in the actual collision. She had got a shock, though, so had sat and drunk a couple of cups of coffee before she drove on. Unaware of the tragic twist of fate.

We had met her on Sunday in a hotel near the airport with her solicitor. She wanted full custody of Lucy and there was a court case pending but for now the judge had ruled that Lucy should live with her biological mother. Alice had been inconsolable. She'd taken to the tablets again which I wasn't too happy about, but what could I do? They were helping somewhat.

We had a meeting in the morning to see a solicitor for Alice and see what we could do. Victoria and Michael were one hundred per cent behind Alice bringing their little granddaughter up.

We were sitting in Lucy's room now, Alice on the bed clutching Loopy Lou. Lucy hadn't wanted to take any of her toys. She wanted them left exactly where they were for when she came back. "Don't dis'urb them, Maman – they're all asleep." Alice had choked up.

"Tell me something about you – anything," Alice slurred. "I want the distraction. Rory texted me today to ask how I was . . . how is he?"

"He's okay." I stood up and opened the window.

"Have you left him then?" she asked. The medication made her speak in a kind of monotone. It was as though Alice had been taken over by it. Her lights were out.

"Yeah, it's over." I nodded and closed the window again.

"Did you tell him you slept with John?"

"I did, yeah."

"John's gone, you know, Beth."

I immediately started to shake. "Wwwha'?" I asked, staring down at the key charm with the missing lock.

"He's gone, he came to say goodbye to me last night while you went to collect your clothes from your parents' house. He's gone to London to shoot his period drama. Didn't he even bother to say goodbye to you then?"

For some reason I felt she was pleased to be telling me this. "I don't care where John is, Alice," I snapped, really unfairly.

"Like hell you don't." She ran her hands though her greasy hair.

"I need to pee."

I shut the bathroom door and sat on the loo seat. I couldn't handle this any more. He was gone again. Just like that. I had a friend who needed me more than ever and I couldn't breathe because John was gone again. He hadn't told me. I hadn't spoken to him since he'd walked away the night of the row with Rory. Only days ago. I presumed he'd be around this weekend. Or had I? I hadn't really thought about him. I had been only thinking about Alice and Lucy.

When I'd gone to my parents' to collect some stuff Rory had been in. We had a chat and he told me he was thinking of moving to Galway. He got so many bookings in Galway it would suit him to live there.

"Maybe in a few months when my heart starts to mend," he had told me.

Once again I felt so, so bad.

"Have you talked to John?" he'd asked as he poured me a cup of tea.

"No, not since the rumble in the jungle, since I saw him with you last."

He handed me the cup. "God, Beth, I can't believe you would do this to yourself all over again."

He sipped. I sipped.

"I rang Martha, you know."

My eyes widened.

"No, not like that, just to say hi to her and ask how she was. Told her I was in a really happy relationship and hoped she still was too. She said that she was and she was thrilled to hear from me. She told me to keep in touch. I felt nothing, Beth, imagine that, nothing. So it's comforting to me that I know, soon, somehow, someday, I will feel the same way about you. I think the first heartbreak is always the worst. I don't think I can ever feel as bad as that again. You were right, you know – as much as I thought we were perfect together I was always holding back. I just don't think relationships are for me any more – I'm out of the race."

"Don't say that, Rory!" I was horrified. "You are the most incredible boyfriend in the world!"

He didn't respond, just shrugged his shoulders.

God, I hated myself. I sipped my tea and walked around my parents' house. Their flight had been delayed the morning of the wedding and when they rang to say they wouldn't get out of Malaga until three o'clock I told them the news. They didn't come. I wouldn't tell them about myself and Rory until Christmas.

"Are you okay, Beth?" Alice was banging at the bathroom door.

I copped myself on. "Sorry, yeah, massive eyelash in my eye." I opened the door, holding a tissue over my left eye.

Alice suddenly looked alive. "We can go visit her! I just got a text from Louise's mother. Let's go!"

We pulled up outside a massive red-bricked detached house in Malahide with a huge black wrought-iron gate.

"This is it." Alice checked the piece of paper in her

223

hand with the address again.

I turned off the engine. Alice nodded. The medication was wearing off and I was glad. She needed to be present in her life right now as hard as it was, because she had Lucy to think about.

I announced our presence to a male voice through an intercom, saying we were invited guests. The gates opened slowly and mechanically. I drove up to the house.

We crunched over the gravel and rang the bell. A man in a dark grey suit opened the big black door.

"My wife is not here but is expected back soon," he said. "My daughter will be with you in a moment."

He moved away from the door and we walked in. It was like walking onto the set of *Dynasty*. White marble everywhere and white wooden banisters that went up to heaven with steps covered with dazzling thick white carpet.

Mr Mak disappeared.

"Hi there!" Louise swayed out into the hallway in her flip-flops, wineglass in hand, splashing droplets over the side as she went. "Don't mind Dad – he's not a talkative person, he just keeps himself to himself. Always has. Are ye staying long? Like, do ye want a drink of something? See, you might have to go across to the off licence for me as I'm almost out and they don't serve me and Mam's on her way here now and she's like stop and I'm like 'Fuck off, Mam, really like fuck off!' and she wants me to give her back to you . . . she's going to take her away from me again . . ." She gulped from the glass.

I stared at Alice but she couldn't take her eyes off Louise.

"Louise, listen to me, where is Lucy?" she demanded.

"Why?" Louise looked towards the stairs.

"Lucy?" Alice raised her voice. "Where is my daughter?"

My heart skipped a beat when Alice said that.

"That's not your daughter up there – she is *my* daughter – I gave birth to her with Dan right beside me." She pointed to me now. "What is she doing here?"

"What?" Alice asked.

Then we heard the back door bang and out she came.

The woman I'd been pinning my hopes and aspirations on for the last three years. Paula Mak. The one and only. Draped in a white fur jacket, tight black-leather trousers and dark shades, there was still no mistaking her.

"Louise Mak!" she yelled. "Get in the kitchen now! Ladies, you are very early – follow me, please."

She sashayed into the open-plan kitchen with an American-style fridge and through the sliding doors I could see a water fountain in the massive back garden.

I wondered if she would recognise me. Although I'd dropped samples into the shop on various occasions she had really never paid me too much attention. On the few occasions I had seen her when I was dropping samples in she had been looking at herself in a huge ceiling-to-floor mirror, twisting a scarf one way or just standing there staring at herself, lost in her own world.

"Girls, Louise is really ill, really ill, I do not have the time for this . . . for this child . . . for this meeting even. She went behind my back and got her own solicitor. I told Dan this years ago . . . he should have had a will in place. Which one of you was to be his wife?"

Alice was in some kind of shock again.

"She was." I pointed to Alice.

"Well, it's like this: Louise wants her but Louise can't have her. I do not want her here. I can barely take care of Louise as it is, so I suggest you take her away with you. We will sign all the papers you need, so I suggest you get a good lawyer and come back tomorrow but take the child with you now. Sorry for your troubles." She opened the fridge and grabbed a bottle of wine. She leaned over the sink and poured what little was left straight down it. "I need to ask for your confidentiality in this matter. Louise is a very successful designer and her company is growing by the day. I have her in control most days but I cannot be responsible for her trying to take care of a child too. She simply is not capable."

"So I can take her now?" Alice gushed.

"Yes, yes, yes, take her – take her away!"

Louise appeared at the door now, flushed. "No, Mam – please don't let them take her away again. I just got her back. I won't let you do this. I am her mother – I love her!" She slid down the wall and hit the floor with a bump, the flip-flops flying off. I noticed how dirty her feet were. Black soles on bare feet.

Alice ran out of the kitchen and up the stairs. "*Lucy! Luce!*" she yelled at the top of her lungs.

I went over to Louise. "Would you like a glass of water?"

Paula Mak opened the fridge again and took out a can of Coke. "Here, give her this." It hissed loudly as I opened it and I handed it to her.

"Don't take my bbbbaby!" Her frail hand grabbed mine. "Don't, I want her, I need her. I will get well. I will stop drinking, I won't drink again ever if you leave her here with me."

"Grow up, you stupid girl – you can't stop drinking for one bloody morning, can you? Not even after causing that fucking traffic pile-up last week –" She stopped and her head twisted a bit too quickly for my liking to see if I'd heard what she'd just said.

I did a double take. "What? You didn't cause the accident, did you, Louise?" I asked.

"Yeah, I did." She kept nodding her head up and down, picking at her toenails now – the sound was horrendous.

Then I remembered Mrs O'Toole's words. She'd said she'd seen Louise. Now it struck me for the first time that she must have been close enough to see her clearly.

"Not caused it, I mean – got involved in it – saw it, so to speak." Paula tried to cover up again. "Wrong place at the wrong time. Story of her life."

"I know you were in one of the cars on the M50 the day of the accident but were you drunk driving, Louise?" I couldn't believe this.

"Thank you, Miss Nosey Parker, that's about enough!" Paula Mak yelled and wrapped her fur jacket dramatically across herself again. She had watched *One Hundred and One Dalmatians* too many times.

"No, it's not," I said now. "Was she drunk driving that morning on the M50? Because I'm going to the Guards!"

"Oh, don't be so silly – sure the police would have charged her if that were the case."

"But I rang you, Mam, and you said go, drive on, drive on, drive on, drive to the nearest hotel and you would meet me there. You plied me with coffee and Red Bull!" Louise pulled herself up on her knees now by the long thin gold handle of the kitchen door. "No, you're right, I don't know what happened but I think I killed two people, Mam." Her voice rose to a scream. "I killed Dan and I killed his Aunt Frances! I didn't want to do that – I wanted to tell him I loved him, I wanted to get to him before he married her, I wanted us to be a family!"

"Shut up! Don't listen to one word that flows from her drunken lips! She's a drama queen! She'd love that to be the case so she could get more attention. As the Guards said, the traffic camera had been shattered by vandals and there is no verdict on the crash yet – we have to wait and pray they find the cause." Paula pulled out a high-backed stool. "Unless of course there is any way I can make you forget what you just heard . . ." She pulled herself up on the stool. "Name a price and I will see what I can do."

I just wanted to get out of there, get Lucy and Alice out too, and then I would go to the police. I felt sorry for Louise and yet I didn't really know why. Dan had been right all along: Louise really was a poor abused sick girl. I was getting out of here for Dan because it's what he would have wanted us to do – I just felt it in my bones.

"Let's go!" I turned to Alice and Lucy who stood huddled in the doorway now.

"Did you ever even get his letters?" Alice's broken voice floated on the tense air.

"I got one letter." Louise suddenly seemed a lot more sober and she pulled herself to her feet.

"A letter? Just the one?" Alice, gripping Lucy tightly, approached Louise.

"Now, really, we are not going over old ground again!" Paula butted in.

"There was only one," Louise said, her lip quivering. "I got it the day I returned home from the hospital. Mam and Dad were away on that cruise. He said he'd come back with her but he never did, never so much as a picture of her . . ." She started to cry.

"He did write, Louise – he sent you lots and lots of letters and photos and their new address when he got his own place in Dublin – but you never answered."

"He never did – he was lying to you!" she sobbed.

"No. Dan didn't lie, Louise. That's one thing I know for sure. Dan did not lie. You must have got them. I mean your address has never changed – you have always lived here, haven't you?"

The penny had dropped with Alice even as she asked that question, I now realised, as she lifted her head and stared Paula Mak in the face.

"You hid them, didn't you?" she said. "You hid Dan's letters to Louise? What sort of person are you?"

"Mam?" Louise beseeched her mother to deny it.

"Oh, for God's sake, he was a nothing! A bloody penniless truck driver! Yes, I burnt every stupid, soppy, overly emotional letter to protect my daughter. Louise is ill – do I have to keep saying this to everyone I meet? She can't function in the real world – why does no one get this? Why am I always made out to be the bitch? If it wasn't for me this young lady would be standing here dead. I've gone above and beyond being a mother. I'm a carer and a stupid idiot – I still have her living with me for crying out loud! What about me? I wanted to move, live in LA, but I can't! *I'm stuck here in the tiny wiped-out shitty city with an impotent husband and a fuck-up for a daughter!*" Paula was screaming now – screeching would be a better way to describe it, her perfectly made-up face ugly and bitter.

"What did they say? The letters?" Louise whimpered and moved her body up and down the wall.

I wasn't sure if she was unable to stand through drink or through heartache.

"Oh nothing – all crap – he wasn't ever going to let you see the kid until you had sobered up. They were threats – look what you are missing out on – pictures of him and her in a tatty old flat and a tatty old park. Let's face it, Louise, where were you going to fit in there? I did the three of you a favour." She tried to regain her composure and took a huge breath in through her crooked nose. Funny how I'd never noticed how crooked her nose was before.

"Let's go." I stepped backwards and pulled Alice by the sleeve.

She picked Lucy up and we went out into the hall.

"Hold on one minute, Miss Burrows." Paula Mak had followed us out, Louise behind her. I must have looked startled because she added, "Yes, I know who you are."

I didn't say a thing.

"I can make you one of the most successful jewellery designers in Europe. You are incredibly gifted and we can make Beth's Bitz into a massively successful organisation, just like I did with the brand of Frame, maybe even do a joint venture with the two brands."

Alice shifted Lucy in her arms again and the little girl dropped her head onto Alice's shoulder.

"All this garbage about going to the police," Paula went on. "Think about it. It's not as though I'm asking you to do something Dan would have disapproved of. Dan loved Louise in his own weird way. Even if she had caused the accident which I know she did not, he'd never have wanted her to go to prison – he wanted her to get well. That's all I am trying to do. I will send her to Arizona and see if they can't sort her out once and for all. I will step back from Frame for a few months – it's soaring – and I can put all my expertise into marketing Beth's Bitz. What do you say?"

Louise was sobbing loudly now, interspersed with hiccups.

Paula was a crazy lady. She was making my skin crawl. All her apparent success and knowledge of the business melted away before my very eyes. She was a total fake.

"Let's go, guys!" I pulled my keys from my bag and Alice trotted behind me.

"Think about it, Beth!" I heard Paula call as I closed the hall door behind us.

"What's going on, Beth?" asked Alice. "I'm all over the place."

I popped the boot and got my child seat out.

"Was Louise the cause of the accident?" Alice asked as she strapped Lucy in.

"I don't know – I mean, the police already know about her being there and they haven't arrested her – but I'm going to tell them the suspicion I have of her being drunk, just in case. If Louise caused that accident, she's a danger to society and to herself, and she can never be allowed see Lucy while she is this ill."

"So that was her mother?" Alice whispered darkly into my ear now so Lucy couldn't hear her. "Wow, what a cunt – sorry – I don't think I have ever used that word in my entire life but it's the only word ugly and vicious enough to describe her." She got in beside Lucy and clicked her own belt.

I looked back and Louise's pale face was pressed against the huge living-room window. She raised her hand to me and I raised mine back. With a sigh I sat into the driver's seat.

"Can you believe that was the famed Paula Mak?" I said, pulling my own seat belt on.

Alice was quiet for a while, as if absorbing that information. I drove off.

"So what about what Paula just said there?" she said then. "She said you can show your designs in all her stores – you're made for life, Beth . . ."

"Are you serious, Alice? Do you think I'd ever want anything to do with that woman? Never in a million years, but let's not tell her that just yet – let's get Louise out of her obviously dangerous clutches and send her somewhere, wherever that may be, and get her well. That's what Dan would have wanted us to do, yeah?"

Alice nodded back. "I just had to ask you. I mean I knew the answer but I had to ask. I cannot believe she never got all those letters and photos Dan sent her – it's so, so sad."

I nodded. "How come you never told me he'd tried to contact her?" I was curious.

"He asked me not to," she said simply. "Yeah, Dan would have wanted that," she said now to no one in particular.

Chapter Twenty-two

I stood at the market stall, drank my latte and tried to stuff a sausage roll into my mouth. I had lost a lot of weight over the last two weeks and it didn't suit me. My nose looked too big and my dimples looked like the Grand Canyon. Also the skin on my face was saggy and I looked a lot older.

"Would you like to take a look at some Beth Burrows originals?" I managed in a weak voice. No one did.

I was stony broke. Thank goodness I had no rent to pay or I would have been truly screwed. I was now living with Alice, and Rory was still at my parents' although he was in Alice's every night. It was so lovely having him around. He really was a fantastic guy. So kind and loving and, luckily for me, forgiving. He made it the easiest break-up for me by understanding and maintaining a friendship with me. He never judged me. "*If it's meant for you it won't go past you,*" was his new motto. I think he was relieved that he hadn't lost this new family I'd introduced him to and so was I. He was brilliant with

Lucy and Alice adored him too.

I had asked Alice to please not mention John. "Not one word. Do not breathe his name around me. Ever again." And she hadn't.

The court case for Lucy was in four days' time and we were all worried. Paula Mak had indeed sent Louise to Arizona to dry out. I had reported my suspicions to the Guards and they wanted to talk to Louise on her return. 'Help them with their enquiries' type of chat. They had no reason to arrest her yet as the final report into the cause of the accident was still pending – it was still under investigation.

We had met Louise at the airport with Lucy before she'd left.

Paula had smiled broadly at me through gritted teeth as Louise gave Lucy a crocheted outfit for Loopy Lou. It was fantastic. A tiny crocheted white puffed-up miniskirt with a white cardigan, a white tank top, white leg warmers and a white hat.

I swallowed the words I wanted to say to Paula. "Good luck, Louise." I took her hands. "I really hope that you get well – you deserve to be happy."

The tannoy announcer sounded around us, telling us about unattended baggage being moved, as Louise pulled me aside. She leaned close to my ear and whispered, "You know, I think I caused Dan's death, and Frances' death but I can't be sure. You were right – I was drunk, pissed drunk. You need to do the right thing. Let me try and get sober and then do my time and hopefully you and Alice can bring Lucy to see me and then one day, one fine day, I will be a part of the human race again."

I had squeezed her hand tight. "I have already reported what you told me, Louise, about the drunk driving. The Guards will be in touch and will want to see you on your return. I told them you had already gone." The announcement finished and then I raised my voice. "A summons will be sent out for you to check into your local station on your return."

Paula Mak's face went fifty shades of green. "You will regret this!" she hissed at me and turned on her heel, not even saying goodbye to her daughter, her steel-capped shoes disturbingly noisy on the ground of Terminal 1.

A group of young girls set upon my stall now, all talking over one another. I had to watch them like a hawk. I was very mistrusting of people since I had started working on my stall.

They were all dressed the exact same: big backcombed hair, thick black tights, denim shorts, brown Uggs and white T-shirts. Not an ounce of individuality between them all.

"How much are these?" one asked, holding up a simple beaded necklace.

"Take it for free," I offered. "Take it and be a little different to the others."

"Oh, can I have one? Can I have one?" they all shouted at me.

"No, because there is only one. Beth's Bitz do only one-off pieces, because jewellery should say something about who you are. It should make a statement about *you*."

They all stared at me with their perfectly straight white braced teeth and unlined faces. They looked at me as though I had just disclosed to them the meaning of life.

"Now shoo!" I ushered them away.

Mini Muffin Suzie was packing up already.

"It's only three!" I shouted over to her.

She made her way slowly over to my stall. "I know it is but I'm shattered! I was on an all-night bender and the smell of my cakes is killing me. I drank like six vodkas last night, I kid you not! You know me, B, I barely ever drink . . ."

I'd forgotten about simple problems. How great they were. Hangovers, feeling pukey but still having to work. Having The Fear all the next day. Worrying about your stomach not being flat or cellulite on your thighs. My problems were so adult and sad and all-consumingly devastating now. Alice wasn't the old Alice any more – she never would be again, I knew that. I mourned her. Rory was gone as my lover and life partner. Gone was the hope of Beth's Bitz ever being in stores. And John – John was responsible for killing another part of me all over again. There wasn't much left for him to aim at.

I pulled up my bag and took out my cigarettes. I lit up.

"Oh no, Beth, are you smoking again?" Suzie asked.

"I am, Suzie, a lot." I exhaled high above her head.

"It's just soooo gross, Beth," she coughed and batted the air above her.

"Then move away, Suzie, it's a big wide world." My patience wasn't the best today. I was feeling angry. Wanting-to-go-and-cut-all-my-hair-off type of angry.

Rory was in Alice's, helping her prepare for the court case. I didn't want to go back there just yet.

I must have PMT today, I thought. My PMT was getting worse every month.

I hadn't heard a word from John. Not a word. I didn't even feel stupid or used really, I just felt deflated. I had oh so foolishly thought he still loved me. I'd never have slept with him again if, when I asked him why he'd left me, he had said 'I didn't love you any more' – but he hadn't said that, he had said the opposite, and he had given me hope. How was I such a twat? I didn't want to know myself sometimes. Wasn't that what Alice had said to me in Bruxelles the day before the wedding when I'd told her I'd slept with John? "Honestly, it's like I don't know you at all any more."

I stood on the barely smoked cigarette and Converse-crushed it deep into the green grass. It wasn't warm today. It hadn't been warm since Dan died. Two weeks ago. It felt like a lifetime already.

I opened a bottle of Diet Coke and let some fizz escape, twisting the cap a tiny amount each time.

Alice was doing okay. She was taking a sleeping tablet at night but no more mood-stabilizers during the day since Lucy had come back.

It had been beyond awful telling Lucy about Dan. I was there. We took her to the Phoenix Park. We sat her down on the grass and we told her daddy had gone to heaven. Alice had been incredible. With a big bright smile on her face the whole time she told Lucy that he had forgotten about the call from Holy God because they were so busy with the wedding and he'd left it too late to tell them he was going up to heaven, but that he did call Alice quickly to say goodbye to her and Lucy and to tell her from Daddy that he loved her more than anything in the entire world and that he would see her way down the line when she came to heaven to meet him. Alice and I had pressed the two white roses Dan had given them and mounted them in two white frames with *Love from Daddy* and *Love from Dan* printed in red lettering on the top. We had mounted them on the kitchen wall alongside all the other happy pictures.

Lucy had licked her Strawberry Chuppa Chup lollipop. "Why can't I see him now?" she had asked.

Alice had smiled again and told her: "You know the way Daddy is always so kind and so sweet and caring? Well, there are lots more people who need him now and sure we are grand together, aren't we? Daddy will be watching over us. Every Sunday we will go to God's Holy House and we will light a candle for Daddy and say a prayer for him and then we will go out to his big garden in Deansgrange and bring him a can of Guinness and some white roses? Won't that be fun?" Alice blinked away the heavy tears, her eyes swamped by them.

Lucy had laughed at that. "But I won't go to the skinny lady's big house again?" She held the lollipop inches from her mouth.

"No, Bubble, never again. We might, however, look for a nice little apartment for the two of us with a lift and a roof garden?" Alice swallowed hard.

"Yay!" Lucy jumped up. "Can I go running now, Maman?"

Alice was fighting her emotions, smile still spray-painted on.

"I'll take you on, Luce!" I jumped up. "Marks – get set – go!" I set off in pursuit of a squealing Lucy and left Alice to recover. It was utterly heartbreaking.

I was shaken out of these painful thoughts when an older lady approached the stall and began to peruse my display of earrings.

"How much are they?" she asked, pointing to a leaf-encrusted brass pair.

"Twenty-five euro." I smiled at her. She looked worn out. Old. Tired. I wondered what her life had been like. Had she found her true love? Had she been a mother? How had life treated her? She had a tight wedding band on, her skin exploding out around it.

"Pretty." She picked one up and held it up to the light, her old skin transparent and her blue veins like rivers on a map. "I'll take them!"

She looked all around her before opening her tiny purse. She pulled out a tightly folded fifty-euro note.

I put the earrings in a paper bag and gave her the twenty-five euro change.

"How old are you?" I asked before I could hold the words back. "Sorry! That's so inappropriate!"

She laughed. "Quite all right. The unfortunate thing is the older you get – like, well over sixty-five older – you begin to become proud of your age again. I am eighty-five this birthday."

She smiled and I guessed they must be false teeth. Too straight and perfect. Someone should really invent crooked false teeth. A no-brainer really.

"Are you sad about something, dear?" She stood perfectly still.

"I am. My friend was killed in a traffic accident a few weeks ago, on his wedding day . . ."

She made the Sign of the Cross. "I'm very sorry."

"Thanks," I nodded.

She linked her slightly bent fingers together and dropped them in front of her chest. "Life is tough, dear. There is no guarantee for a tomorrow – the only guarantee is that none of us will last forever – we are all equals in that realm. It all goes by so quickly. Your friend, I bet he lived his life well –

that was his life – so live yours. Don't be too sad for him for too long – celebrate his life. Life is simply too short. Don't be a lot of things, dear, but my most important piece of advice is this, don't have regrets." She raised her eyes to heaven and then slowly moved away from me.

"Regrets," I whispered to myself. If I were to die tomorrow what regrets did I have? I perched on the edge of my stall and lit another cigarette. I wasn't married, I didn't have children, my business never took off but the one thing that came shooting into my mind was that I took another chance on John. If I were to die tomorrow at least I didn't have that regret. I'd tried. I'd given it my best. I gave Rory up for the chance of John and me ever making it work. I inhaled hard. I felt a sort of peace at this. If regrets were the worst thing, well, I didn't regret sleeping with him one last time. I didn't regret feeling him inside me again and smelling him and touching him and being one with him. How could I? I loved him too much. Of course I regretted that I had hurt Rory but I had to move on. He had forgiven me – he had told me this over and over again. It was time to forgive myself.

My throat was starting to hurt from the awful nicotine. I stood on another fag and started to tidy up a bit. I pulled up a big box of my pieces and looked in. There was the neckpiece. I had just cleared it out of Alice's room when I cleared the dress and the veil.

"Just get rid them, Beth, get rid of everything," she'd said. "I never want to lay eyes on them ever again."

"But it's your mother's wedding dress?"

"Get them out of my sight, Beth!" she had yelled at me and thrown her hairbrush at the bedroom wall.

I'd thrown everything into this big flower box. I

couldn't bring myself to throw the dress out. I held the neckpiece up and looked at it. It was still beautiful but what would I do with it now? Alice wouldn't want me to throw it away, I knew that much. I'd sell it. I went in behind my stall and made room for it at the back between the bracelets and the chains.

"Hey there!"

I looked up.

Princess Tangled was back. What was her name again?

"Hey," I said.

"I was here a few weeks back – I got the most beautiful necklace from you. Do you sell online by any chance?"

Tara. That was her name. Tara.

"I don't yet but I am going to soon. Do you want me to take your number and give you a shout?"

She was shaking her head. "I can't really, I'm not supposed to . . . but, okay, sure . . . oh wow . . . oh wow . . . can I see that? That's so super-cool!" She was pointing at Alice's neckpiece.

"Sure." I took it down again and handed it to her.

She had no make-up on today but she was still as beautiful as I remembered her. She reminded me of someone, apart from the girl from *Tangled* . . . someone else.

A car horn beeped loudly and she glanced over at a taxi waiting nearby.

"This is phenomenal! I have to have it! But shoot, I've got no cash, no money on me – neither of us have – you see, my flight leaves in like an hour and I just got the taxi cab to stop over there so I could grab your card . . . do you have a card? Oh nuts, I adore this, it's just . . . just . . . ."

"Just what you were looking for?"

She laughed. If those teeth were any whiter I'd need

blackout blinds as shades just to talk to her. She shook her head. "Oh drat, but . . ." She laid it down on the stall regretfully.

No regrets, I heard the old woman say in my head. I'd regret it if this piece wasted away. I'd regret it if Alice ever saw it on the stall. It should go to another country and start a new life. It should emigrate.

"No, I don't have any cards yet – I mean I have ordered some, just haven't got around to picking them up. I've been kinda busy. Here, take it." I didn't bother trying to shove it into one of my little bags – it wouldn't fit.

"Excuse me?" The big brown saucers were out. No shades on today.

"Take it, it's fine. Next time you pass by, pay me then. I don't even have a price for it – it's priceless, you see."

A car horn beeped out loudly again.

"That's Franco getting anxious – we have to catch our flight. Are you sure?"

"Yeah, go ahead, enjoy. Tell your other fairytale friends – like the snoozy one, Snow White and Cinders – all about me."

"Huh?" She held the neckpiece in her two tiny hands. Pink talons today. "My who?"

Beeeeeep!

"I gotta go – what's your name, please?" She was backing away.

"Beth." I reached for my Diet Coke.

"Beth – what's the name of your designs? Your company, I mean?"

"Beth's Bitz. Bits with an Z, like Glitz, ya'know. Now go! Franco is giving me a headache."

She skipped away to the beeps of the horn.

242

Chapter Twenty-three

We set out to celebrate Alice getting custody of Lucy in Captain America's Burger Bar on Grafton Street. Alice, Rory, Lucy and I.

Paula Mak had turned up late to court with a letter from Louise and various doctors' reports which the judge read and folded away. They would not be contesting Alice's application for custody, on the grounds of poor mental and physical health.

Victoria and Michael had returned home straight after the court case. They had been amazing in court, giving their full backing and promising constant support services to Alice. Victoria was still completely heartbroken over her only son and only sister and still very frightened and fragile, and Michael wanted to get her home as quickly as possible. His ribs had mended but his ankle wasn't healing very fast so they'd had a neighbour drive them up. We promised we would be down to see them the following weekend. They had hugged Lucy tightly and I knew they would be the best of grandparents to her and I knew Alice would do all in her power to let them see Lucy as much as she could.

As I walked up the stairs, with Rory by my side, the smell of sizzling burgers and onions greeted me. None of us had had any appetite in weeks but suddenly I felt slightly hungry. Nothing like the smell of fried onions to open my taste buds. Classy chick.

"I'm slightly hungry," Alice said from behind us.

"I'm a starfin, Maman," Lucy said.

"Good, pet, let's eat so. You can have your miniburgers and chippies, yeah?"

"With ketchup?" Lucy stopped midstep, her pink soft shoe mid-air.

"Careful on the stairs, remember – keep going." Alice grabbed her hand. "Yes, lots of ketchup, Bubble."

We were seated in a booth and, as we looked at the menus, I suddenly remembered a night here with John. Not long before we'd broken up. Funny how I'd never thought of it before. It came back to me now, playing out in my head in wide-screen HD.

"Why do we always come here?" he'd asked me as we sat opposite each other in the same booth I sat in now, some red plastic from the seat peeling off under my bum.

"Because we like the burgers," I answered him, sipping through my red straw from my massive Pepsi Max cup.

"But why don't we try somewhere else? Something new? Something different?" he'd probed.

"Like where, John? Like a Michelin-star restaurant perhaps? Fancy some foie gras, do you, love?" It was meant to be a joke but he went on the attack.

"What the fuck is that supposed to mean?" He exhaled

very slowly, his breath catching his hair, and strands blew up in the air.

"It's a joke!" I reached for his hand.

"Comedy isn't your forte, Beth," he said dryly and pulled his hand away.

I was embarrassed and annoyed so I hit back. "You don't have any actual money! I pay for it all, remember. This is as good as it gets, John!"

Then he'd got into a mood and ruined the night.

"Sulking!" I spat at him, my mouth full of beef.

"No. Depressed." He'd pushed his untouched eight-euro burger into the middle of the table, knocking over the yellow plastic mustard bottle.

"I don't have money to throw away, John."

"I didn't want to come here – you did!" he hissed.

"What the fuck do you want then? It's okay for you – you have been sitting on your arse all day while I run around after actors who can't remember my name and keep calling me 'dahling'! Assholes the whole bloody lot of them!" I shoved a vinegar-soaked wedge into my gob.

He pulled his seat in so far the table nearly cut him in half. "Why are they assholes, Beth?" he asked and waited for my answer, his lips pursed, breathing in and out through his nose at a ferocious pace all of a sudden.

"Because they are." I dipped now into the mayo and covered the wedge completely.

"Because they want to act?" he said. "Because they chose Art instead of industry jobs? Because they don't want to be fucking lawyers or doctors or pen-pushers? Does that make them arseholes to you? Is that your real opinion of the people you deal with every day? Just because you sit behind a desk and they aren't like you?"

He was starting to lose it, his dark eyes darting in his head and blazing at me. He was twisting the promise ring I had given him round and round.

"Calm down – I mean, well, come on, John, it's hardly a real job is it now, acting? I mean, of course it's a job but it's not a job as we know jobs to be. What I'm trying to say, I suppose, is that so few people make any money out of it. It's not secure . . ."

"So that's what life is to Beth, is it? Making money, living and existing just to make money. To be banal and uninterested in your daily life because you hate your job but, hey, you're making money? To pass that mantra of life on to your own children? Work, be unhappy, die." He had looked at me as though I was repulsive to him right then. "Wow, I never saw that in you before, I thought we got one another." He pinched the bridge of his nose.

"You can't live without money, John – you can't live on artistic fresh air!" He was really annoying me now and I just wanted to go home. He was picking me up all wrong. I sucked hard through my red straw.

He just stared at me. Through me.

"What?" I asked. Now he was making me really uncomfortable and not for the first time. John could always manage to make me feel like I had just said the most incredibly stupid thing he had ever heard in his entire life. I tried to make amends. "I'm not saying actors aren't hard workers, John. I'm saying the reality of an actor's life is that they are broke most of the time."

"Oh no, that's not what you're saying, Beth," he whispered across the table to me. "That's not what you're saying at all. What you're saying is that money makes the world go round, right? I can't believe you think like that.

I'm sorry but it's a shock to me, a real shock. I thought you were somebody different. I think . . . I think we need . . ."

I hadn't let him finish. "Grow up!" I flung my napkin over my mostly uneaten burger and stormed over to the till to pay.

"Are you ready to order, Beth?" Alice poked me hard in the ribs.

"Sorry, what? Oh, the smoky bacon cheeseburger and fries, please, and a pitcher of Budweiser."

"I'm not drinking, " Alice said.

"Neither am I," Rory said.

"No. It's not for you. I ordered it for me. Is that okay? Am I allowed to do that, guys? Will you indulge my horrific alcoholic tendencies for this evening?"

"What are dendisies, Ethy?" Lucy looked up from colouring a rainbow on the back of her children's menu.

"Oh nothing, Luce, just adult words – great work keeping that red in between the lines!"

The little girl dropped her head again and I stared at Alice.

"Go for it," Alice said and we ordered.

Rory and Alice started to talk about the 'Month's Mind' Mass they were organising for Dan. We were holding it in the house and it was going to be a real celebration of his life. Rory was putting together a projector and photo images for it.

I smiled at the waiter minutes later in his Budweiser braces as my frozen pitcher arrived along with my frozen pint glass and he poured.

How had I forgotten that night with John? I remembered now we had a few weeks in between that night and him dumping me and he had been off – really off with me. I hadn't worried too much as he had been really off with me many times over the years. He hadn't recovered from that conversation, I realised now. He had wanted, dreamed of being an actor, but hadn't been able to tell me. And here I was now, a jewellery designer. An artist. I hadn't meant what I'd said that night but he had been annoying me. He had taken it out of context and put words in my mouth. I had felt the financial pressure but I shouldn't ever, ever had said that to him. It wasn't fair. He'd never asked to be brought anywhere. He hated taking money from me, I knew that. It embarrassed him and made him uncomfortable. He had always had some income: he sold paintings, he wrote freelance articles for magazines and newspapers, he took odd jobs here and there and by 'odd' I mean strange. He'd paint the scenery and sets for the local school plays, he painted murals in the old people's home and, most strangely, he had one of those beeping things and he went around the beaches finding treasures, or shit as it mainly was.

He had seen me in another light. A fake light. That wasn't me at all though. Maybe I had been jealous that I was stuck behind a desk, only working on admin when I wanted to be more creative. Maybe I was jealous that I was surrounded by creative people all day who were doing exactly what they wanted to do with their lives regardless of money, maybe I was jealous that John did exactly what it was he wanted to do. I just never knew back then exactly what it was I wanted to do.

I drank large fizzy mouthfuls of my beer.

Rory tipped my shoulder. "That premiere and sound and vision awards show are on in The Convention Centre this weekend. Remember I was telling you they wanted my mobile cinema as a gimmicky thing outside on the red carpet? E! News are covering it and they want to interview the stars in the mobile."

"Oh yeah?" I shook out my hair and tried to concentrate on my friends.

"All the stars are coming over, big, big Hollywood stars. It's being filmed live for RTÉ so watch out for me."

He was doing okay really. He was happy to be around us all the time. He had loved me, I had no doubt about that, but he had also been so hurt in the past that his heart was slightly closed. No one would hurt him again like Martha had. I understood that.

"Want to share this garlic bread with cheese – it's huge?" Alice asked him as our food arrived and he nodded.

Rory adored garlic bread with cheese. I hated garlic bread with or without cheese. I'd never seen Alice order it before.

"So cheers, everyone!" I raised my pint and Alice looked at me funny. "Cheers because Lucy is sitting here with us – Dan would have raised his pint glass to this moment."

Alice smiled, sort of. Her smile didn't seem to reach where it once had. It was more a wry smile than her old beaming wide grin. She was so incredibly sad and said she felt very lost. All their plans and ambitions and world together were gone. Just like that.

The hotel had been so supportive and had only used her deposit and not charged her more. Myself and Rory had returned what presents had already been sent, mostly cash to be honest, and we had written a little note to every guest on Alice pre-bought Thank You cards. There had been a blank front where she had planned to stick photos of the wedding.

Alice was stuck in the moment – she was miles away but the slight smile remained and she suddenly looked a lot like her old self again. She was awfully thin and terribly pale but the little smile was glorious. I missed her. I missed Dan too. I really missed him. His presence had been so large and so safe.

As soon as Alice took a bite she pushed the plate away, excused herself and went to the toilet. I didn't say anything as we didn't want to upset Lucy – so any time it was all too much for Alice she excused herself to the toilet and I made up a story for Lucy. I was running out of stories.

"Where is Uncle John?" she asked completely out of the blue now.

Rory coughed. Poor Rory.

"I don't know, Luce." I stabbed at three chips with my fork and dunked them in her ketchup.

"He's a very nice man, Ethy. He told me a story that a man got broken and that you had to fix him back together."

I stared at her. "Tell me the story, Lucy," I said, raising my voice.

"Beth!" Rory turned to me.

"Tell me the story Uncle John told you, Lucy." I was starting to lose control of my breathing and a chip went down the wrong way. I coughed and coughed and Rory handed me a glass of water.

"I don't remember, Ethy." Lucy stuck the yellow crayon hard onto the rainbow and I sat back.

"Jesus, Beth, you need help." Rory pushed his glasses up his nose.

"I know, I know, Rory, I know I do."

"How did you hide these feelings from me for so long? I must be a complete blind eejit. I mean, I knew you still had feelings but I had no idea they were still so raw and deep." He picked up his water glass and swirled the ice around in it.

"I don't know, Rory. There's something very wrong with me obviously."

Alice returned from the toilet and ordered a sparkling water. "I'm fine," she mouthed to me.

We discussed the Month's Mind and the video and what food we would make and it kept Alice occupied. I drank my pitcher very quickly and felt drunk. It was good, I liked it. I excused myself to go and have a cigarette at the door. I stood looking at the passersby on Grafton Street and lit up. There were only four months left in this year. Another annus horribilis. I exhaled. I had been so positive about this year what with meetings for Maks lined up and my relationship with Rory. How quickly things changed.

I knew what I wanted to do – it had been on my mind constantly for the last few days. After Dan's month's mind I was going out to Nerja to spend some time with my parents. If anything could make me value my independence it was living with them again, even for just two weeks. I wasn't making a penny at the market and I needed to rethink my life. I needed to tell them Rory and I had broken up and they should give the house over to a letting agency. I was going to go and see if my old flat was still on the market. I doubted it but you never knew. I'd check. I knew the landlord had a few properties around the area. It would be great to move back in for the winter. Alice and Lucy needed to begin their new life together.

Just the two of them.

And that's when it hit me.

I don't know how I held my tongue as Rory drove us home at ten miles an hour.

"Oh, come on, Rory, the lights have just gone orange!" I put my hands on the back of his headrest and squeezed the two thin metal poles as he braked again.

"I am a safe driver, Beth, you know that. If you don't like it, get out and get a taxi."

I hated taxis more than I hated Rory's ridiculously painful slow driving. Lucy was falling asleep in her car chair (it was the seat from Dan's car which he had taken out to make room for his parents and which Rory had now fitted in his car) and I held her head up as it was bobbing.

"Beth, you need a holiday," Alice chipped in.

"Well, as a matter of fact I was just planning to go and visit my parents in Nerja – after Dan's Mass, of course – I wouldn't miss that."

The car fell silent as Dan's name hung heavy in the air.

Alice turned around in her seat. "You have been so good, Beth. I couldn't have got through this without you – or you, Rory. I, we, are so lucky to have such good friends."

Rory moved into first like a tortoise who was dying. We were off up Dawson Street with the horses and carriages passing us out. Old grannies pushing those strange canvas granny-trollies in gingham passed us out.

Alice turned and looked straight ahead. "When will you go?"

"Probably the last two weeks in August."

"Be unbearably hot," she offered.

"I like unbearably hot, the hotter the better for me." I hated being in the back. "Remember you and John used to come back so brown I didn't recognise ye one night in Slattery's?"

She'd said 'John'. I'd asked her not to say his name. Now both she and Lucy had said John in the space of a few hours.

Then Alice started to laugh. It sounded weird and as though she was choking. "I said to John, 'Wow, you two look like ye've been dipped in chocolate!'" She was starting to really laugh now. "The pair of ye looked so ridiculous, him in the orange vest top à la Andrew Ridgley and you in the all-in-one white shorts combo with Spice Girls massive wedged runners and it was bleedin' freezing out!"

Rory started to laugh now and said, "Oh, I'd say he loved himself even more with a tan even then!" never taking his eyes off the road.

"Excuse me, we were fashionable then – that was what people wore!"

I was pleased Alice was laughing. I was pleased Rory was laughing.

Alice said, "John put a face on him and said 'You're only jealous because Beth takes me to Nerja now and not you!'"

Rory turned towards Portobello, thank God.

"That's not true – we asked you to come."

"You did, to be fair." She'd stopped laughing now. "I shouldn't have been so stubborn, I should have gone."

"Go with her in August," Rory suggested as he pulled up outside Alice's house. "I won't come in. I have to get

253

the montage edited for Dan's Mass and then get the van set up for this big award ceremony."

Alice leaned over and pecked his cheek. "Thanks again. I'm going to do a big roast-chicken dinner for us all after the Mass – Dan's favourite. So I'll have a chat with you then."

I got out and gently opened Lucy's door, unclicked her belt and carried her out. "Straight up," Alice whispered as she eased the key into the hall door.

We walked up the stairs.

Alice took off Lucy's shoes and socks and laid Loopy Lou beside her. She pulled the duvet up and kissed her on the forehead. We crept out and left the landing light on. "Cuppa cha? Wine?" she asked as we turned on the kitchen light and closed the door. She hissed the monitor to life.

"There's no more beer, sure there's not? Okay, wine please."

I kicked off my runners and tucked my feet up under me at the kitchen table. My head was still spinning. As though I'd been hit by a plank on the back of the head outside Captain America's earlier.

"I'm going to explode, Alice, help me out here. Am I right in thinking what I am thinking?"

She spun around, wine spilling over the edge of the glass. Just the one glass. "What?"

She moved to the seat beside me. "I don't know if I am . . . for sure." The words tumbled out of her mouth.

I inhaled sharply. "Holy shit!" I whispered, grabbing the wine out of her hand.

"I have it, in the drawer." She was so pale and looked terrified.

"Get it."

She didn't move.

"Get it now, Alice, come on."

I took a long drink and then we both got up and she opened the kitchen drawer ever so slowly until I saw it. Sitting there like a time bomb amongst the napkins and spare keys. Blue and white and pink. The pregnancy test.

I'd guessed suddenly in Captain America's. It was the combination of the way she looked so distant and then had run to the bathroom after her first bite . . . and she was off alcohol. Her words had come back to me: "We had been trying for a baby."

"I don't think I can do the test, Beth." She sniffed hard and wiped her nose on the back of her sleeve.

I'd never seen Alice do that in my entire life. Alice of the Tissues.

"It's the one thing that has been keeping me going – well, apart from Lucy of course – the fact I could be carrying his child, a little piece of Dan could be growing inside me. I need to hang on to the hope."

"How late are you?"

"I'm not exactly sure. I remember I was due my period the week before the wedding because I was saying to Dan 'Typical! I'll get it the morning of the wedding'. I've been off the pill for three months now, you see. Then I forgot about it obviously and the last few days I've been feeling really nauseated and my breasts are really sore to touch and the smell of green tea is enough to make me vomit."

Well, I thought that and I wasn't pregnant so I didn't rate the green tea one as a symptom. "Okay, let's have a cup of normal tea."

Alice blew out her cheeks.

I said. "Okay – water?"

She nodded. I opened the fridge and poured her a pint glass of sparkling water. She was staring at the wall, at pictures of her and Dan, then she moved to look at the pressed white roses.

"I miss him so much already, Beth, and he's only gone a month. I'd give anything to be pregnant with his child – anything. I can't tell you what it would mean to me. I'd have some of him back. I could hold him again and kiss him and love him, in another way, in another form – his son or his daughter, our child, a sibling for Lucy."

I held her hand. "It's just so unfair what happened to him, Alice, it really is."

I wasn't good with words. John would have had magical things to say to Alice right now. John would have told her that time would heal and that she had a life ahead of her and that she was more lucky to have loved and lost than to never have loved at all.

"What did John say to you when he knelt down beside you in the church grounds that morning?" I asked softly.

She sipped her water and paused before answering thoughtfully. "That Dan had no regrets." She looked up at me. "Nice thing to say, wasn't it? He's not the worst, my brother."

"No. He's not," I agreed.

"Can you believe this – we're sitting here talking about John again. John?" Alice shook her head.

"Okay, let's do it, I'm going out of my mind," I said. "Drink all the water – you need a good pee." I held the glass up to her mouth.

"Don't break my teeth, Beth!" She pulled it away.

"Sorry, I'm nervous," I muttered.

I drained the wineglass and put it in the dishwasher. She grabbed the test from the open drawer and we quietly walked the long way up the creaky stairs to the bathroom on the landing. I pushed open the white door and we went in. I closed the door behind us and Alice pulled down her tights and knickers. She sat. I pulled open the box and pulled the blue lid off the test.

I heard a trickle come out. "Wait!" I hissed at her.

"I can't help it – I'm bursting to pee!"

I handed her the stick and she took it in her right hand and shoved it between her legs. Nothing happened.

I sat on the edge of the bath. "Piss," I said. "Piss, Alice!"

"I can't." She gritted her teeth at me. "It's not coming now." She looked in pain – her face was puce.

Shit. "Oh listen, I heard this one before – this should help the flow." I ran the tap. "Running water." I pointed to the taps by way of explanation. "It's supposed to help you go."

She was off. She really was bursting.

I turned off the taps.

"Look in on Lucy there, will you?" she asked as she continued to pee.

I did. I snuck out and snuck back in. She was just wiping when I returned. I prayed I would see no red on that tissue. She placed the test ever so delicately on the side of the bath and washed her hands. "Two minutes." She dried them on her skirt. Again a first.

"Alice, if it's not and you're not, you still have Lucy and you have me and, well, it seems you have Rory whether you like it or not . . ."

"Give me a hug, Beth."

She moved into my arms and I held her tight, her thin body cold and shaking. I loved her so much, right this moment I'd have given my own life for her to be pregnant with Dan's child. We were both facing the bathroom mirror, the all-too-present test behind us. I stroked her hair, pulling it tight into a pony-tail and then letting it loose again.

"Do you want me to look?" I asked after minutes had passed. Probably four minutes. "No. I will." She let go and I shut my eyes tight.

I heard her rattle the test off the ceramic of the bath as she picked it up. She said nothing. I turned and opened my eyes. My best friend stood before me, her hand raised high in the air, the white stick standing upright. A victory salute.

"We did it!" she gushed through tears of joy. "Dan and I are going to have a baby!"

Chapter Twenty-four

Louise

Louise Mak took an evening walk in Arizona around the desert grounds of The Meadows. She recalled reading in the brochure that according to local legend the clear, dry air of the Sonoran Desert had the power to heal. That would do for her. She took a long slow breath. For the last thirty-five years, The Meadows treatment centre had been doing just that, helping people recover, heal, and maintain their wellness. She kicked the hard orange sand beneath her bare feet, the warm grains sticking between her toes. The clinic or centre, as they preferred to call it, was spread across a fourteen-acre campus just fifty miles northwest of Phoenix, Arizona. It was considered one of America's leading centres for the treatment of trauma and addictions. It was licensed by the state of Arizona, and it was also a fully accredited psychiatric treatment centre. She knew it would save her life.

So far they were treating her for all phases of her alcohol addiction, from her detoxification to their primary treatment programme which built foundations for long-term abstinence and sobriety. She understood the programme she was on. The Meadows made sense to her. They got it through to her. Things were so much clearer. Her alcoholism was causing her both physical and intellectual chaos and it influenced every aspect of life. She understood that now. She drank to exist daily. To move out of her own head and into a world that had no feelings and no meaning. Emotionless. Before now it was a way for her to exist. It was the only way she could function. Now it was as though a light had been switched on in her mind. Like someone had pulled one of those hanging strings that turn on light bulbs in dark basements. *Click*.

Overcoming her alcohol obsession required making changes in the way she lived. Louise now had to face her problems, and relate to others. The workshops she attended here spelled out clearly to her that when she drank to excess her body became dependent on alcohol and experienced withdrawal symptoms if it was removed without warning. She knew these signs only too well. Every waking day she had all the basic signs of alcohol withdrawal, had for years now. Her daily morning throbbing headache, her hand tremors, her excess sweating, her racing heart rate, her high blood pressure, her upset stomach, her increased anxiety, her impatience, her stomach pain and her loose stools. She always had difficulty sleeping and trouble focusing and when she'd had to go to the toilet she'd really had to go. Everything seemed to flood out of her – there was never solid waste.

But still – she smiled wryly now to herself – but still she had never considered herself an alcoholic. The way she looked at it was that she chose to drink to get her through the day. Not any more. What was most interesting to her, though, was that there was a variety of mental-health problems that could also be caused by long-term alcohol abuse.

An eagle soared above her head and she stood watching him for some time. The bird was majestic and hypnotic. The sky was so big and so orange. She had never known a peace like this. It wasn't just the fact that she hadn't touched a drop in three weeks. It was more than that. It was this life. This space. No traffic. No noise. No Paula Mak. Warm air. Wilderness. It suited her so well. She loved all the staff here. Brad in particular had been amazing. He had once been a New York Wall Street banker living the high life. His dad had been a New York banker and his grandfather before him had been a New York banker. Brad was a reformed alcoholic who had lost his job but after he sobered up he had gone back to get this degree and now he taught here. "I recovered here but I also left a part of me here," he drawled, "and I always knew I wanted to return to the 'me' who I found here, if that makes any sense to you?" She'd nodded. She understood.

He always dressed the same. It was his uniform, he told her. Black shorts, black flip-flops, white T-shirt and a bright green plaid waistcoat. Brad must have been mid-forties but looked older. He was handsome if somewhat ragged. Alcohol, he told her, had robbed not only his mind but also his looks.

They had talked for hours the previous night over pots and pots of strong black coffee in his office and he got her to tell him things she didn't even know she thought. That her parents were toxic in her life. The company was all for her mother – she had zero interest in it. She loved to crochet as it helped relax her mind but the business, with its overpriced designer crocheted jumpers and cardigans and hats and scarves, was never her idea – she was never comfortable with that. When Paula had forced designer anonymity upon her it had troubled her greatly. She felt like such a fake. She couldn't understand why her mother wouldn't want to show her off. Why couldn't she say, "Look what my amazingly talented daughter can do!"? She couldn't understand why her mother never tried to help her. She had gone along with Frame, done it all, to try and please her mother. To try and make her proud. Paula Mak had never been proud of Louise Mak – not ever. Not when she was a baby, not when she was a child, not when she was a teenager and certainly not when she had become an adult.

"Why do you so badly want her to love you?" Brad had asked.

"Because doesn't everyone want their mother to love them?" She'd shaken her head angrily at what she considered to be a completely stupid question.

"I guess children do and I guess teenagers do to a degree but I guess when you grow to adulthood you have to accept people for who they are. You are now a grown woman, Louise, and you still haven't learnt that you cannot change your mother. No one can, only her. You have to make peace with who she is and, yes, mourn the fact she wasn't capable of loving you. But you can't let this one part of your life destroy you. You have to grow up, Louise. Move on." He'd sat back; black flip-flops aligned together, hands clasped on his tanned knees.

"But she made me give up my baby!" Tears had streamed down Louise's face and she couldn't stop them.

"She didn't, Louise, she never had that power. You did that. You gave Lucy up because deep down you knew the truth – that you couldn't raise her. And I think you did the right thing." He was handing her tissue after tissue. "You told me in these words . . ." He recorded all their meetings and transcribed them for her files. He flipped back some pages on his yellow notepad and read her own words back to her. "'*The first second I set eyes on her, this perfect little girl in my arms, my heart soared with love. I didn't know the feeling – this overwhelming feeling. She was so perfect, so small, so delicate. It was alien to me, this feeling. How could I deserve to love this little girl? I wasn't lovable . . . she'd never be able to love me back. I would only poison her, like my mother always said. I was useless, I was good for nothing. I couldn't breathe then, I wanted to love her so much, and that's when I knew I needed to drink so badly, I needed to escape my head, and I knew Dan could take care of her. I just couldn't let myself kiss her or smell her because I couldn't protect her. I loved her, Brad, I truly loved her, but I didn't love myself. I felt so scared and sore and strange and hurt and old and yet I felt the exact same. A nothing. After I'd delivered this beautiful baby I was still nothing. I'd never be anything. They were both better off without me. That's why I asked him for the alcohol, so I could remove myself yet again from my feelings. God, poor Dan!*'"*

Louise had dropped her head into her thin hands and cradled it. Brad had slowly closed the notepad and clasped his hands together but said nothing. She'd grieved the loss of her baby and let the tears flow. She'd cried and cried and cried. But this time they weren't removed drunken tears, they were real honest raw emotive tears.

She knew Brad was right of course. She could have run away from her mother and kept her baby. She had been an adult. She and Dan did talk about it one night when she was about eight months pregnant but Dan, being Dan, had told her that she couldn't run away from her problems. It still hurt like a knife in her heart when she thought of Dan. He'd been so kind to her – he had loved her and she had known that deep down but she couldn't let herself truly believe it.

"I killed Dan, I killed Frances!" she'd sobbed, her chest heaving with the lack of breath.

Brad had stood and pulled her up and opened his mouth to speak. His eyes had told her this was information that was substantial. "I have news on that. I was going to tell you after this session. I just got an email. As you know we have been in touch with the police in Dublin because we have a one-hundred-per-cent law-abiding system here. It appears that the car in which Dan was driving had a blow-out. That was the finding of the enquiry. Dan's car caused the pile-up."

Her soaking wet eyes had popped out of her head. She'd tried to catch her breath. Her voice came in stops and starts. "No, no . . . no, Brad. I must have . . . it must have been my fault. I remember that . . . I think . . . I mean, I saw Dan's car and then . . . well, then I really . . ." She couldn't picture it any more.

"You don't remember, Louise. You were drunk. How can you believe any of your memories? It's a miracle you didn't cause the accident but you didn't."

Brad had walked to the coffee machine, pressed a black button and a white plastic cup fell. She'd heard the whirr and watched as the brown liquid hit the white plastic. The steam rose. She knew this information wouldn't bring Dan or Frances back, she knew she'd never be able to apologise to Dan now, but she felt a massive weight being lifted off her shoulders. She doubted she could live with the guilt of killing two people, doubted she was strong enough to survive prison but now that she had been released from that guilt she owed it to Dan to try and move on. Not to waste another precious life. Dan had only ever wanted her to be well, to be happy. Dan had been the greatest gift ever sent to her but she had been too ill to embrace it. How ironic that she had seen him dressed in his wedding suit seconds before his life was wiped out. That must mean something surely? She had to take it as a sign. Brad was right. She really had no idea what had happened that day. Her brain remembered seeing Dan. Dan was so near her she wondered now had he seen her? Had she been the last person Dan had laid eyes on? She shivered.

Brad was right. Why and how her life had turned out the way it did was irrelevant to her. Now she had to turn a new page.

Brad left the room and came back with two huge slices of warm chocolate cake and two plastic forks. "Let's take a break," he'd said, smiling at her, and they ate in comfortable silence.

It was the first time in years she had actually tasted chocolate and, boy oh boy, was it magnificent!

"Most individuals addicted to alcohol suffer from some form of severe psychiatric chaos marked by increased anxiety, feelings of hopelessness, alcohol-induced psychosis, panic disorders, and other symptoms. Alcohol abuse is considered the second-leading cause of dementia, as it relates to ten per cent of diagnosed cases. Extreme alcohol use can cause harm to brain functioning, which, if not treated, can be permanent. Recovery from alcohol addiction may not seem possible, but it is. It so is. If a person admits to having a problem, he or she has already started down the path of recovery. Many clients trust us here at The Meadows' alcohol-treatment programme to help them begin their journey toward sobriety."

It was her last day. Brad had seven new people in the room today and he was only focused on them. She was already on the road. On her road to recovery. She planned to leave tomorrow evening and when she got home she would go to the Guards. She would give a statement regardless. Clear her conscience and take whatever, if any, punishment they might give her for driving in that state. It would be humiliating and so embarrassing to admit she had been driving a vehicle drunk, but she would do it.

She had been keeping in touch with the wonderful Alice Callan and she was going to visit Lucy at Alice's house. She and Alice had been emailing each other through Brad. She was happy that Lucy was so well looked after and that Alice had agreed that Louise could and should always be a part of her life. Loopy Lou had a place in her daughter's life at last. It was the right place, she knew.

She was going to see her parents and then she was packing her case and coming straight back to The Meadows.

She was going to begin on the treatment programme for depression. Brad and she both believed that she suffered from depression, that she had done so for many years. She had hidden her prolonged depression though her drinking. She'd answered yes to each of Brad's questions during the stay. "Are you irritated for no reason most of the time?" Yes. "Do you lack the motivation to get out of bed, finding it more and more difficult to start your day?" Yes. "Do you find yourself increasingly alone, Louise – and look at the bigger picture here – as you isolate from loved ones and trusted friends?" Yes. She had no loved ones, not one friend in the world, she told him. Her dad had sort of loved her, she remembered, but he'd never had the courage to stand up for her. Her dad lived inside his own head and just did whatever her mother told him to do. He had never stood up to Paula in Louise's entire life.

"Do you find little or no pleasure in the hobbies or activities you used to enjoy?" Yes. That's what her crocheting had been, a little hobby. It had been the one thing she had enjoyed. The one thing she was good at. Paula had stolen that from her too. Now she hated it. Deep down she knew she'd been depressed for many years but The Meadows had been the first place she had ever attended that made her admit this out loud.

"Some catch, aren't I?" she'd said through a running nose and tears to a silent Brad. She was finally beginning to get it. To admit and understand her problems. Yes, maybe if she'd had a wonderful, loving, supportive family around her she wouldn't have turned out like this, but then again she may have. Who knew?

Louise sat now in her cut-off denims and white cotton shirt, her hair in a high pony-tail, barefoot as the sun went down – her body tanned and healthy, her head clear, her

267

breathing steady and focused. She had wasted so many years. Made so many awful mistakes. But she had been ill for so many years. Now, here she had finally learned that she couldn't blame anyone or anything else. She couldn't blame her parents for her drinking or her depression or her pregnancy. She was sick. But she was now on the right road to getting better and, by God, when she got well she would be a better person. She stood up and shook the sand from her hands and her feet. Louise Mak would make a difference in people's lives – she'd help others just like her.

She'd never try to take Lucy away from Alice again. They belonged to each other – she had seen it in the house that day even through her drunken eyes. But she would be someone Lucy could come to, and someone Lucy could be proud of, and if one day Lucy wanted to come and stay with her in Arizona during her holidays, well, then, that would be just be perfect.

Chapter Twenty-five

We told no one Alice was pregnant. We made a pact.

"Not until I'm so big I can't hide it any more. I couldn't risk telling people and then something happening – imagine telling Michael and Victoria now and –"

"Shush!" I stopped her mid-sentence. "Nothing is going to happen but, yeah, I agree we keep this to ourselves for a few months. You need to go and see the doctor today though, and start taking folic acid."

"I've been taking folic acid for months, Beth."

I found that slightly upsetting. She and Dan had had a life I wasn't a part of. I knew it was ridiculous to feel left out but I did.

She had gone to see the doctor and her pregnancy was indeed confirmed. Her baby, their baby, was expected on January 21st. We had the Mass for Dan and it was even more special. Rory had done an amazing job of putting together old photographs and videos and had compiled them in such a way he had us laughing most of the time. It was very bittersweet. We lit hundreds of small white candles. Alice sat in the front of the living room on one of the rows of chairs and only I would have noticed her surreptitiously rubbing her belly every few minutes. Michael and Victoria had come up from Cork and Lucy sat on her granddad's lap and held a covered candle for her dad. It was all very moving. After, we went to visit Dan's grave and Alice led us in a decade of the rosary. We returned home to a huge roast-chicken dinner with stuffing, roast potatoes, carrots and broccoli in homemade gravy which was eaten mostly in silence. But it was nice. It was appropriate. A Last Supper type of feeling. All my thoughts as we ate around the table were of Dan.

Alice was very together, cooking and making herself as busy as possible.

I caught her in a moment alone pulling a heavy black wheelie bin out for the morning's collection.

"Alice, you shouldn't be pulling the bins!" I whispered.

"I have to, it's fine, and the baby will be fine." She smiled at me and I noticed the tension seemed to have left her face. "I got a sense today at the grave – I can't explain it – that everything would be okay. It was sort of a relaxing feeling as though my shoulders were being pushed down . . . it was weird but so comforting. I'm not going to spend the next seven months in a blind panic. The baby will be fine. I have to do the bins, simple as." She pulled down her gold cardigan and then asked me out of the blue, "Aren't you designing at all lately, Beth?"

I stood back. "Why?"

"Why? Because you're an amazing designer and, well, because it's your job!"

She was right. I hadn't made a thing in weeks.

"Maybe tomorrow night? We've all had a long, strenuous and emotional day," I said.

"Why not tonight? I need to just lie on the couch and do nothing. Everyone will be leaving shortly. I can't sleep with this heartburn so I could sit up with you and watch you work."

"If that's what you want."

"Actually, Beth, there was one other thing . . . I wanted to ask you . . . if you . . . would you be my birthing partner?"

"Of course I will!" I was delighted she'd asked.

When everyone left we blew out all the candles and put them in a box. Lucy blew out the last one. We put her to bed after we'd bathed her and powdered her from head to toe in Johnson's baby powder.

I took my designing box downstairs. It had been gathering dust. We stayed up late chatting about nothing – the news, bands, clothes and old friends: basically we bitched a lot about older singers and actresses wearing clothes for teenagers and about older men getting younger women. I drank three glasses of wine, she drank a carton of organic apple juice. I made some indie-type pieces as we chatted. A long draping necklace from mother-of-pearl and three pairs of hoop earrings with tiny crystal balls hanging from the middle. Alice loved those and bought a pair straight away. I also made chunky bracelets from rubber and plastic in a whole range of different colours.

I wanted to design a piece in Dan's memory. I was thinking something in red – a chain with tiny red fire symbols clipped on. I started to sketch it on the back of Lucy's colouring book.

"Did I tell you I got another email from Louise? She

wants to come and see Lucy," Alice told me. We knew Louise was planning a trip back to Dublin.

"That's okay, isn't it?" I sketched the flames.

"Yeah," she said, still reading her new emails on her phone. "But here she says she's now decided to go straight back to Arizona – she says she wants to start a new life there."

"Good for her but I wonder why?" I finished the sketch and twisted some wire into a V-shape.

"She seems way better. She suggests opening up a private Facebook page for her and Lucy to communicate through. She wants to start it now – she'll be posting daily to Lucy and adding pictures and drawings, like a daily social media diary. What do you think of that?"

I looked up at her. "I think it's great. You can monitor it and they can be in each other's lives."

Alice yawned.

"Go on up – you're knackered," I said.

"I am," she said. "I conk out immediately but then I wake in the middle of the night . . . it's those minutes lying there in the dark that I hate so much. I just see him when I close my eyes – in one way I like it but in another way I don't . . . I guess I'm afraid one night I will close my eyes and he just won't be there . . ."

"I can only imagine, love."

She pulled herself up and put her hand on my shoulder. "Keep at it – they are fantastic." She paused, and then said, "I'm sorry we ruined your chances with Paula Mak, Beth. Whoever would have believed the circle of events?" She twisted one ankle anticlockwise and then the other.

"Oh, seriously, Alice, don't think about it for one second. I don't. She's a total witch. Could you imagine working with her? No way! How the designer of Frame puts up with her I'll never know."

"I know but, still, you would have your collections in all her stores now if it wasn't for us." She moved to the door.

"There are many things more important in life than earrings, Alice."

She halted at the door. "I worry about you, Beth." She twisted the doorknob left and right.

"Why?"

"Because I want you to find happiness and you can't, can you?" She twisted the knob some more before adding, "Without him, I mean." She looked down at the carpet.

I thought for a moment. "You know, a month ago I'd probably have agreed but now I see I need to move on. I have no choice. I can be truthful though and tell you that, yes, I love him with all my heart and he's the best thing that ever, ever happened to me. He can't help it if he doesn't feel the same. It's my problem. If I never meet anyone else, then . . ." I raised my shoulders, "I always have you and Alice and Bumpy, don't I?"

"Always. I'm so happy to hear you say that. Onwards and upwards, soldier!" She smiled at me and blew me a kiss as she closed the door softly behind her.

I wouldn't have much to do as Alice's birthing partner until around twenty-four weeks, she'd informed me. Her bible – *What to Expect When You're Expecting* – had been re-covered with a Cheryl Cole picture (I have no idea why she chose this to be a suitable cover for her reading material – she had no interest in the world in Cheryl Cole or Cheryl Tweedy or just Cheryl whatever). Then we were going to start Lamaze classes. I didn't ask what that was just yet. I didn't want to know. She was already watching *Birthing Diaries* on one of those channels and I had to cover my face and hum loudly every time a baby was on the way out. It was barbaric. How on earth was I going to stay standing? Women mooing like cows. I'd be squealing like a pig.

At this stage Alice was sick as a dog though. She could literally smell nothing of the food chain without wanting to puke. All she could eat was pasta. Plain pasta. But she never once moaned. She was incredible.

I'd booked my trip to Nerja and had my head down on the stall the last few weeks trying to get money in to keep me in paella and *las cervezas* for two weeks. I would leave in two days.

I drove to the market from Portobello where I was still living with Alice and Lucy. The weather had picked up again. Typical – always when I was going on holiday Dublin's weather shone. I drove through Rathmines and suddenly I pulled in. I reversed. The space was tiny but I did it. Three grown men in white stained overalls stood to watch. Why were men so fascinated with seeing if women could park? I smiled at them as I fed the greedy glutton of a parking meter.

I pushed open the door to Peter Mark hairdressing salon.

"Can I help you?" the pretty blonde in front of the desk asked. She was dressed in a short black dress, red tights and red skyscraper heels. How did she stand in them all day?

"Yes, well, I don't have an appointment but I want a haircut," I divulged.

"Okay. Let me check the book." She slipped in behind the desk as Glen Hansard sang out on CD. I loved his voice. "Shirley can take you in, like, ten minutes?"

"Shirley – yep, great."

"Take a seat and she will be with you for a consultation. Can I get you a tea or a coffee?"

"Coffee would be great, thanks – milk, no sugar."

I sat on the black-and-silver leather seat by the window and picked up a *Vogue*. The weight of all those ads. I put it back down and picked up an *OK!*. I never bought these celebrity magazines. My coffee arrived and I opened the first page and there he was. The love of my life. Done up like a fucking dog's dinner. He looked like something from a production of *Oliver Twist* that the local drama society put on. Knee-length beige breeches, orphan rags of a top and a brown tweed cap. What on earth? I pulled the pages closer to my eyes. "*John Callan Stars in* Dulberry Place *This Winter on BBC1*." *Dulberry Place*. Who'd want to live in Dulberry Place? I shook my head and I didn't read the rest.

I flicked the page. I actually turned the page. Now I'm not saying I wouldn't have gone back but just then Shirley trotted over. On wedges – not so bad.

"Hi," she said, showing me her tongue-ring. "So what are you thinking?" She hovered beside me.

"Short. I want to go short. Like this short." I opened the *OK!* again and showed her a picture of Anne Hathaway's short do.

Shirley wasn't happy. Shirley had wanted to trim it. Shirley had wanted me to say "Just tidy it up". Hairdressers love that. I could understand this, though, as even though they did exactly what the client asked, when the client didn't turn out like Cameron Diaz in the mirror, even though she had the exact same haircut, the shit hit the hairdryer.

"Are you sure?" Shirley grabbed the magazine out of my hands.

"Yes." I wasn't standing down. "If you won't do it I will go into the Swan Centre and get it done in there, Shirley."

"Why do you want to cut that beautiful hair off? You're the spit of yer one Claire Danes offa *Homeland*." She twirled a piece of my hair between her index finger and thumb.

"I don't want to look like Claire Danes any more. I want to look like Beth Burrows."

"Oh my God! Are you Beth Burrows? The jewellery woman?" She grabbed my arm.

"Yeah, how did you know that?"

"Oh, Beth Burrows, my little sister Gail got one of your necklaces – 'The Individual' it's called. She has a really popular blog – so she posted all about the necklace on her Facebook page and her whole school is going mad for one. It's like the latest craze – everyone's trying to get on to get your stuff but your website is inundated by buyers apparently and it's down!"

I stared at her. "Me? Beth Burrows?"

"Yes!" She was exasperated with me now. "You sell at Blackrock market when you want to reach out to real people, don't you?"

"I suppose I do," I answered, trying not to laugh.

"Word of warning – get your website back up – there are hundreds of girls in Loretto College wanting to buy your stuff."

"Wow, thanks, Shirley, I'll do just that."

"Okay, come with me."

She sat me in front of the mirror and boosted my chair up higher with her left leg. She pulled my hair back into a tight pony-tail and we both stared at my face. "Actually, Beth, it's quite good – you can pull this off, you have the face for it. Here's what I was thinking: more Emma Watson – you know, the *Harry Potter* girl? – I mean, since she cut her hair."

I didn't know her but I nodded. I'd never seen or read *Harry Potter* so I'd no idea who she was. I'd never been that into wizards.

"I was thinking Mia Farrow's famous Vidal Sassoon's short cut?" I said.

"No pressure then," Shirley laughed then added, "Okay, so we're thinking short but sleek. What about with a modern twist? A sharp sweeping fringe and some sharp locks down each side?"

"Do it," I agreed.

"Yeah? Okay, I will take you down to the basin and Gavin will get you washed and I'll see you in a few minutes."

As Gavin scrubbed the tea-tree daylights out of my scalp, I thought about those schoolgirls loving my jewellery. I knew it was that group I had given the piece to a few weeks ago. They had christened it The Individual. I liked it. I had a website of sorts, a free Word Press thingy I had set up myself with Rory but it never came up in search engines for whatever reason. I couldn't sell on there anyway. I needed a proper one. I knew one person who never stopped going on at me about my website: Rory.

Gavin was massaging my head now. It was glorious.

Then he wrapped my head in a turban towel and delivered me back to Shirley. She had magazines in front of her. Pictures pinned up.

"Can I send a quick text?" I asked her as she set up her equipment.

"Of course."

I sent Rory a text asking him if he had the time to set up my website – I knew he'd make the time though I knew it wouldn't be immediately as he had his big awards movie tonight. He was a whizz at websites. He understood hosting companies and the like and his cousin Finbar ran a top website business.

"Done!" he texted back with a smiley face.

Fantastic!

"Oh will we call it bethsbitz.com or something else?" he texted again.

"Bethsbitz please."

Rory would make some girl a wonderful husband some day. He had it all.

"Ready?" Shirley was opening and closing her scissors.

I blew out excess air. "Cut!" I ordered and she began.

Hair fell like small wigs being dropped to the floor, my dark wet hair disappearing before my very eyes. It felt great. I couldn't give a shit what I looked like after – I just wanted to change me. To change how I looked and therefore change how I felt. I was sick of keeping the hair poker-straight because John loved it that way. I was doing this because I knew he didn't like short hair on women – he used to call Halle Berry 'Harry Berry'. So I could be Ben Burrows now. Fuck him was what. I sipped the cold coffee. I would get my website up and start doing the twitters and the Facebooks and get my finger out of my

278

hole. I might not get my designs into Maks wonder world but I could still sure as hell sell them. They were great designs. People wanted to wear them. I wasn't giving enough people the chance to see them. How had I been so blind? Rory had always been at me to get the website up and running but I could never see how it would sell my work. I was so caught up on Maks taking it. I had been so narrow-minded.

"One door shuts," I whispered to myself.

Glen Hansard was singing "Fake" now and I listened to his lyrics and sympathised with him. *"You're telling me I will regret you – and so – you're talking like I should expect to – but you'll never know . . ."*

"Do you want to look now or wait until I've dried it?"

I was tapping away on my phone to Rory again. "I'll wait." He was after colours for the page. I told him I liked yellow. A yellow website. Bright. Cheerful. A sunrise. We could add pictures later. He had taken all the text off the old Word Press.

Shirley was standing in front of me now, flicking her brush this way and that, and the hairdryer burnt my head.

"We are on it!" Rory texted back. **"Don't forget to look out for me later at the awards show. DO NOT touch the Sky + in Alice's. I have it set to record. I have to go now but Finbar's on the case!"**

Christ, but he was bloody hyper about this ridiculous awards show.

"Will do and thanks so much!"

When someone used an exclamation mark to me in a text I always felt I should use one back. To show I'm in just as good a mood as they are.

The hairdryer fell silent. Shirley pulled a piece of hair

back and then smiled.

"Okay, here you go!" She stood away.

I looked at my reflection. "Wowzers!" I said as I leaned right in close. It was fantastic. I looked about five years younger but I looked like me still. A fresher me. A new and improved up-to-date me. It was like Mia Farrow's old cut, (Shirley had stuck a picture of her on the mirror) but it was edgier. It was cut tight into my head but with a sharp fringe that swept across my forehead, as promised, and some sharp hair at either side. It looked darker in colour as it was so short but I liked it. It was so stylish and so current.

"That is to die for." Gavin put his manicured hand on my shoulder. "Shirley, you are a genius with that cutter!" He sashayed away in his designer flip-flops.

"You happy with it?" Shirley was waiting for the backlash.

"I love it, it's perfect, thank you so much."

She removed my black gown and shook the masses of remaining hair onto the ground.

"Would you mind if I took a picture, for when you are all famous like?" She went a bit red and then so did I.

"Course not, but I warn you I'm a horrible poser."

She removed her phone from a black bag housing huge grips and snapped a few shots.

I paid Debbie and gave a generous tip to Shirley and Gavin, and I drove to work feeling quite okay about myself.

When I pulled in I saw a group of young girls chatting to Suzie. I strolled over and started to set up.

"That's not her!" I heard Suzie say. "She's years older than that girl."

"It is," one of the girls said and they ran for me, all talking at the same time.

"Beth! Beth! Do you have others of The Individuals?"

I laughed. Suzie waved over, embarrassed.

"Hang on, which one did I give you?"

"This." The chosen one put her hand down her One Direction T-shirt and brought up the necklace.

They gasped.

I felt like I was Frodo from *The Hobbit*.

"Okay, how many of you want one?" Six arms flew into the air. "Okay, I will make six more tonight – come by tomorrow afternoon and get them. Now, they will be twenty euro each, okay? I can't give them all away for free."

"Hump, she's just totally like a heroin dealer," the tallest skinniest one at the back said. She was in a Niall Horan T-shirt.

"What?" I said.

"Nothing!" The tall one dropped her head. "Okay, we'll be here tomorrow at lunchtime. If a group of girls in The Wanted T-shirts come by, you didn't see us, hokay?"

"Hokay," I promised.

They linked arms and shuffled off. Hobbitlike.

I was chuffed. I couldn't wait to get home tonight and make my six pre-ordered pieces. It felt really good. My first real made-to-wear orders.

Suzie came over.

"Holy crapper, Beth, I didn't recognise you!" She was eating a stick. It looked like a stick and I didn't ask. "You look stunning, I mean you look so young with that hair, not that you looked old per se but like you easily look five years younger, defo." Suzie had no idea what age I was.

"So I look about forty-five?" I dropped my jaw in delight and she looked confused.

But then she did the maths and looked relieved. "Yeah! Oh, absolutely, you do." Great. Suzie thought I was fifty. Way to ruin my buzz, Suzie.

"There's a real buzz around the market 'bout your stuff. It's like an early Orla Kiley buzz – can I buy something?"

"Sure." She had never looked at my designs before.

"Oh, that's super – that leather-bound bracelet. I'll have that. Do I get the market ten-per-cent discount?"

"Yes, of course." I put it in a bag and then Barry the bric-à-brac guy approached.

"I want to get something for my girlfriend – can you pick a piece out for her?"

Barry had a girlfriend? I would have put my entire collection on Barry being gay.

The stall was busy all day. The Wanted posse came by just as I was closing up and they ordered The Individual too, so now I had eleven Individuals to make tonight. The irony was not lost on me.

When I arrived back to Portobello that evening my car was laden down with new supplies. I was refreshing the lot. I splashed out on a new wire-cutting pliers, flat-billed pliers, a pickle tank, a torch for soldering. I stocked up on flux, bezel wire, a few new cabochon cut gems and lots of acrylic, Czech glass, gemstone, glass, promo, shell, wood and nut beads. I bought everything. I also snapped up a deal at my suppliers on Swarovski Rhinestones, Components and Pearls. I was taking all this to Nerja and I would design like my life depended on it.

I left them in the boot for now as I nervously prepared to unveil my new hair. I hoped Alice would like it – it was important to me that she did. I also hoped it might cheer her up a little.

It hadn't been long since we had got the results of the accident. A blowout in the front left-hand tyre of Dan's car had been the cause. Alice had been absolutely stunned as Dan took such great care of his car. He was so road-safety conscious. But then she had remembered something.

As she placed a mug of tea before the investigator who was sitting at the kitchen table, she had suddenly said, "I just remembered – the day before he left for Cork to collect his parents and his aunt he drove to Rathmines to fill the car up with petrol. It was a penny cheaper or something like that!" She'd half laughed and continued, holding onto the back of a chair now. "When he came home he was complaining about the state of our roads and why we paid all that road tax. I wasn't really paying any attention – he was always complaining about the state of our roads. He'd hit a pothole on the Lower Rathmines Road and he'd told me it was so deep his head had hit the roof of the car – he said he'd have to get that tyre looked at when we got back from our honeymoon."

The investigator nodded. "That could have easily have been it. I mean, every time you drive up a kerb, park with your tyres pressing into a kerb, hit a pothole, and don't get the tyre pressure checked, it can happen."

"But Dan was such an experienced driver – he knew all about blowouts – surely he would have known how to cope? He'd even told me about it before – he'd told me if it ever happened not to fight it, to hold the wheel firmly and let the car slow by itself – he said my immediate reaction would be to brake but not to do that. What happened that he didn't do that? He knew what to do. He was a trucker for crying out loud!" Alice's voice was shaking now.

"It's all great advice, Miss, but most of the time the reality is, travelling at that speed on a motorway it all happens so fast there really is nothing you can do. It was a front tyre so the rim immediately dropped to the road and the rubber of the tyre pulled the car into the other lane. He was actually under the speed limit of 100kmh but an eye witness from behind said he just flew across the lanes, clipping other cars and weaving uncontrollably before ploughing into the wall."

I stood up and coughed. I thought the word *ploughing* wasn't a great choice.

Alice pulled out the chair and sat now. The investigator slurped his tea and reached over for one of the Chocolate Hobnobs that Alice had put on a white plate. He dunked.

The investigator left Alice a large green folder with the findings inside. Alice had emailed The Meadows straight away to tell Louise. A Brad Collins had replied, saying he would pass the information on as soon as he had finished a session with Louise that evening.

Alice had been disturbed by the verdict. The thought that Dan might have saved his life and Frances' if he had got the tyre checked was hard to cope with.

I got a shock as I entered the kitchen and saw Louise was sitting at the kitchen table. I knew she was arriving back but I'd presumed we wouldn't see her until much later that night – though I assumed Paula Mak would have eaten her up first.

"Hi, Louise!" I lifted my hand in greeting.

"Hi, Beth!"

"You got your hair cut," Alice observed immediately and correctly. She was pureeing something orange. Her hands were all orange. She rubbed them in some white kitchen towel. That turned orange too. She ran the hot tap on them. "It's short, Beth, really short – turn around."

I didn't know why I had to turn around but I just did it.

"Your hair's gone, Ethy." Lucy padded past me. "It grow back, no worry."

"It's great on you." Alice dried her hands, moved over and rubbed the back of my hair. "You look sexy as hell – oh wow, do you look sexy! Beth, it's beautiful. Totally different but really, honestly beautiful."

I was relieved I had Alice's approval.

"What made you do it?" she asked now.

"I just decided I wasn't waiting around on the old me any more. I had to move on – and you know what they say: a change is as good as a rest."

I decided to stay for a minute before going back out to my car for my handbag and supplies. "Great to see you, Louise, have you been here long?" I said, leaning over and hugging her now.

She hugged me back. "No," she smiled at me.

"Ethy, how you 'member L'eez?" Lucy was mixing the Rice Krispies into the chocolate (white and no doubt organic).

"I met her with you, remember, Bubble – in the big house?"

"No. I no 'member."

"*Leave it . . . just leave it there . . . don't want to upset*

285

her!" Alice sang out in a strange eerie tune.

I looked at her and immediately and for the first time saw a little bump.

I sat and stared at Louise now as she watched Lucy. She looked so much better. She had colour in her cheeks, clean hair and she had put on weight. Even though her skin had always been creamy it had been an unhealthy creamy. She was dressed in a plaid shirt and faded denims with beige cowboy boots. Her fringe needed a cut as it was hanging over her eyes but now and then she brushed it to the side and it suited her.

"So how was it out there?" I asked her, running my hands through my short locks.

"Hard. Amazing. Life-changing. I was just saying to Alice before you came in – The Meadows will save me, I think." She crossed her thin legs and dunked her tea bag on a string up and down.

"Tea?" Alice asked.

"Please," I answered, "but no string."

"L'eez is taking me to see the zoo, Ethy!" Lucy licked the wooden spoon, covering her face in tiny white Rice Krispies.

She looked to me like a tiny zombie. I made no reference to this though. I turned to Alice.

"I've ordered a taxi and it's collecting them at nine in the morning – remember I told you Louise is going back to Arizona? She's leaving tomorrow evening." Alice took the corner of her pale-blue-and-white tea towel and wiped Lucy's face, much to the annoyance of the little girl.

"Why are you going back there so soon?" I asked Louise.

"It's okay, Beth, I know what you're thinking: if she

has to go back tomorrow she must still be a basket case. And I am, well, sort of. I need to work on my depression now to help me stay sober. We think the depression started the drinking. How's about that, Beth? I'm a depressed alco? Jealous much?"

I burst out laughing and so did she. Her face lit up the kitchen.

"But Lucy and I are going to be special friends, I can feel it, and we have opened this – here, take a look." She turned the laptop to face me and my heart skipped a beat. She had set up a LouiseLovesLucy account and their Facebook page was heartbreaking. Louise had uploaded pictures of herself pregnant! Dan was in them – he looked so young and happy and worry-free. There were various scans of the baby and pictures of Louise holding the scans and then they stopped. As though almost four years had been wiped out and they had.

"I'm going to upload lots of pictures for Louise and Lucy of us all here at home too," said Alice.

God, but she was a saint. I guessed she wasn't going to mention her pregnancy and I thought that the best thing too. "That's great."

Alice handed me a tea. No string. Praise be.

"I signed all the papers Alice sent to the centre and have them here." Louise lifted her straw bag and removed a clear plastic folder. "I plan on living in Arizona, Beth. I went to the Garda station today. As I wasn't 'drink driving caught at the scene' there is nothing to be done. I'm relieved in a terribly selfish way I didn't cause the crash but I can't live here any more. It doesn't suit me – there is too much misery here. I want to stay in Lucy's life as much as Alice will let me. I need to close my company too so my mother can't make money off my good name."

Louise placed the folder on the table and Alice grabbed for it – a little too eagerly, I thought.

"I'll just put this somewhere safe!" She tripped over the words as she opened a drawer and safely locked the folder away.

"You have a company?" I asked as I blew into my hot tea and leaned over for the bikkies.

"Wait for this, Beth." Alice sat. Like a pregnant woman sits. I'd need to speak to her about that.

"Frame. I am the designer behind Frame."

"*Fuuckk right off!*" I shouted, banging my teacup down hard.

"*Beth!*" Alice shouted at me, really annoyed.

"Sorry! I'm so sorry. That was a very bad word, Lucy. Ethy said a very bad word!"

"I no mind," she mumbled from inside a bowl. She had basically licked the ceramic clean.

"That is you? Oh my God, your stuff is amazing, Louise! I have one of the minibags and I got a Frame scarf from Rory as an out-of-the-blue gift a few weeks ago. I wear it on my stall – the heat it keeps in is unreal." I was gobsmacked.

"Thanks, I use really good quality wool – it costs a lot – that's why the stuff is so expensive." She smiled now. "But it was only ever a hobby for me. She . . . Paula, my mam, took my designs and mass-marketed them. She would never let me give interviews or let me meet people. Maybe if she had I might have tried to sort myself out a long time ago."

"Why?" I couldn't understand it.

"Because, I think, she was jealous. Yes, she has all the

288

shops and the respected businesswoman profile but deep down she wanted to be creative. She tried to design her own collection of winter dresses years back and she was slated by the fashion industry and then she wore one of my home-made crocheted dresses to a big event and she was praised for her high fashion sense, for taking fashion risks with wool. So she jumped on me, bought me my drink, let me continue to live with her and Dad and I had a lot of privacy in my wing of the house. She looked after me every day, gave me the convertible BMW – but she just wanted me to design. See, Alice, that was how she got all my letters. I was always so hungover I never surfaced until long after the postman had been. I never questioned why no one wrote to me. Why would they? I had no bills. I wasn't existing in the real world. She wanted me to be a prisoner, her prisoner. If she came by on a Monday and I hadn't new pieces ready she would pour my wine down the sink and not give me any cash. She wouldn't tell people who the designer was but you all heard the rumours, I presume?"

Alice shook her head. "No, what rumours?" she asked, enthralled.

I had heard them. Over and over again. I'd seen it speculated in magazines and newspapers. "That Paula Mak was actually the designer behind Frame," I said. "That she was deliberately creating a mystique about the designer as a sales ploy."

"Exactly. She enjoyed that, of course."

"It beggars belief how a mother can be like that, doesn't it?" Alice said but no one answered her.

I changed the subject. "Do you not want to design any more then?" I asked.

"Not for a while but I'm going to keep the name Frame and buy her share of the business. I feel awful that people will lose their jobs but it's not in my control. I have enough guilt in my life and I can't take that on board as well. I never wanted to be a designer. But eventually if I want I can reopen the business and start all over. Keep the goodwill."

I was truly shocked that Louise was the creative genius behind Frame. "Well, that's the best idea. You are so talented. I cannot believe you created all those pieces."

"I hear you are pretty nifty yourself?" she laughed. "Alice was telling me all about Beth's Bitz. She showed me some pieces she has herself. It's beautiful work, Beth."

"Yeah, it's going okay – nothing near the level of Frame though but I do have a new following in a load of teenagers – I got eleven orders today!" I laughed.

"Did you? That is brilliant." Alice jumped up as the house phone rang out. She couldn't find the handset so she missed the call. Lucy was forever hiding the handset.

The doorbell went. "My taxi," said Louise. "I'd better go, I have an AA meeting in town off Dorset Street at seven that Brad has set up for me and then it's over to Mother Dearest and then I need to pack more bits."

She stood and put her cup in the sink.

"See you in the morning then, Lucy." She hugged her daughter tightly. "Thanks, Alice." There were tears glistening in her eyes.

"Go 'way outta that! See you in the morning. Why don't you come around eight so we can have a coffee and a natter? I can make us an omelette before the taxi arrives if you like?"

"Great, that sounds wonderful."

"I'll walk you out," I said. "I left my bag and supplies in the boot."

She got into the taxi and I wished her well. She'd had such a hard time of it. She was trying to move on and in my own way I could understand her.

"I wish I'd had a friend like you," she said as she rolled down the window while the driver reversed slowly.

"You do now!" I poked her playfully.

She laughed, a real good laugh, and pulled up the window as they moved off.

I went and popped the boot on my car. The smell of roses in Alice's garden took me back to the church, standing in front of all those guests that tragic morning.

"*Beth!*" Alice screamed as I closed the boot. "*Beth! Be-eth!*"

I dropped my bag and my supplies scattered all over the driveway with a prolonged rattle. I ran, whacking the front door off the wall as I pegged it to the kitchen.

"What? Is it the baby? What's wrong? Alice?"

Alice was on her knees in front of the TV.

"*What's wrong, Alice?*" I screamed at her "*Tell me!*"

"Fuck, Beth!" she gasped.

"Maman, now you said the bad word!" Lucy was on the couch sucking her fingers – she popped them back in and rubbed her lemon blanky off her nose with the other hand.

"What the hell is going on? Why are you screaming for me? Alice?"

Alice had her mobile phone in her hand and I could hear a miniature male voice still shouting out of it. She was pointing to the television.

Giuliana Rancic, the American TV presenter from E!,

was interviewing someone. Her pretty, if scarily thin, expressive face filled the screen. *"So how are you enjoying Ireland and how excited are you guys to release the movie here? We know it just premièred this evening. I understand you filmed a lot of it in the County of Kerry and right here in Dublin?"*

New camera shot. Then I saw her. It was Tangled. Tara Tangled.

"Beth, look!" Alice pointed and I looked again.

Tara Tangled was all dressed in a blinding white skin-tight satin man's suit, opened down to the navel with expert tit-tape in place, and black velvet stilettos.

But she was also wearing my neckpiece. Alice's wedding neckpiece.

"Who is she again?" I whispered.

"She's Tara Tomelay the actress – she's incredible, she won an Oscar last year for *Baking in Brooklyn*, remember? How the hell is she wearing my neckpiece? This is unreal. That's Rory on the phone – he called you like fifty times."

"My bag was in the boot . . ." I trailed off.

"Shush! Shush! Listen!" She moved onto her bum now.

"And this necklace is just amazeballs – who is this by?"

My heart literally leapt out of my chest, ran around the room ten times, somersaulted over the couch and crept back in through my nose.

"This is by my favourite jewellery designer right now – her pieces are truly incredible – so eclectic – and I am addicted. It's from an amazing Irish company called Beth's Bitz."

"*Beth's Bitz,*" G repeated ever so slowly. I loved G.

"Okay, Bill, I know you are watching with baby Duke. Hi, Dukey! I want everything from Beth's Bitz, everything! I'm looking her up right now. This neckpiece is stunning."

Alice let out a sound like an orgasm. A bit like an orgasm. I'd never heard Alice having an orgasm, thank God, but if I had I'd imagine it was just like the sound I'd heard.

"*Well, good luck tonight, Tara. I know you are nominated for an Academy Award for best actress for* A Quiet Woman *which as I said just premièred here in Dublin and can I say I saw it last week and it is flawless – another Oscar perhaps?*" Giuliana winked at her and the two super-skinny women laughed out loud.

"*I won't comment on that one but, thank you, and I'd just like to say thank you to the designer of this jewellery,*" Tara put her award-winning hand on the neckpiece now, "*Beth Burrows herself, who has been awesome to me on my trips to Ireland – I have been flying in and out of Ireland so much lately I feel half Irish!.*" She ran her hand down the neckpiece. The camera stayed on it for seconds. A lifetime on TV.

I didn't know how she remembered my full name.

"*Okay, back up to you, Kelly, who have you got?*"

The camera panned to Kelly Osbourne. "*Sorry, G, I'm just still gobsmacked by that amazing neckpiece. Beth's Bitz, was it? Love! Love! Love!*" She turned then to interview Brendan Gleeson.

I adored Brendan Gleeson and for a possible second I was lost in his interview.

"Hello? Hello?" Alice was on the phone to Rory. "Beth, he's running home to get the website live."

"Huh?" I couldn't speak.

My mobile rang out from outside the hall door.

"Get your bags in! Hurry, come on, what are you standing there for?"

I went to get them. I had to gather up all the bits I'd spilled and it took forever. Multicoloured beads decorated the driveway. Looking through the hall door at them was like looking into a kaleidoscope.

I had eleven Individuals to make.

When I got back in, Alice was furiously tapping away at her laptop, back on the phone to Rory. It was the first time I think I'd really seen her with her mind on something else since Dan's accident.

"No . . . nothing coming up . . . I did type BethsBitz.com . . . I'm not stupid, Rory, I can spell . . . sorry, I'm sorry, you're right . . . I absolutely will calm down." She sat further forward on the seat now, her face almost in the screen. For all intents and purposes you would swear it was her jewellery website. "Oh, all lower case! Well, you didn't say that a minute ago . . . but surely people would put a capital B . . . okay, I'm doing it bethsbitz.com all in lowercase . . . hang on, my 'e' sticks . . ."

I watched her press her 'e' hard and type. Then she hit return. The screen lit up. A perfect shade of yellow. Like the midday sun. A very happy colour. Beth's Bitz was emblazoned across the top of the page in a wonderful stylish font. Not too Celticky, not too Oirish. Eclectic.

"He's on analytics." She overemphasised the words as she covered the mouthpiece. I didn't know why or what analytics were for that matter.

Lucy padded over to me in her slippers and cotton lilac nightie. "Want to watch Doc McStuffins with me, Ethy? She's making all Frosty's ouches go way."

"Maybe later, Bubble. There's something very exciting happening for me right now – it's a bit hard to explain but it's about the necklaces and things I put together." I leaned forward to give her a kiss.

"Like how you can fix bwoken Uncle John cos he . . . cos he . . . bweaked?"

I pulled my face back and stared into hers. "What does that mean, Lucy? What did Uncle John say to you, pet?"

"He say to me . . . he say to me . . . it's hard to 'splain but I told him I know because I fixed Loopy Lou when she teared her arm. 'Member, Maman sewed her?"

"Sweet Lord!" Alice hopped up. "Beth, he said the analytics are off the radar – *everyone* is on your site. This is unbelievable! But how did Tara Tomelay get my neckpiece – did you send it to her? How clever are you, you marketing genius!"

I couldn't believe she could think I would have done that. After all that had happened?

"I did in my eyeball! Are you serious, Alice? Do you really think that I would have had the energy and interest to do that recently? I gave it to her, for free if you don't mind! I couldn't throw it away . . . so I brought it to the stall . . . she wanted it . . . she's bought from me before."

"Woh – woh – wow – wow – you what?" Alice stuttered. "Tara T has bought pieces from you before and you never thought to tell me? Are you for real, Beth?"

"I didn't know who she was! You know I avoid magazines in case John is in them, and, sorry, but did you just say Tara T?"

"Yeah, that's what the press call her." Alice waved me away as my phone rang again.

It was my mother. She couldn't know – they were in

Nerja. News took weeks to hit the sleepy town.

"I just heard your jewellery won an award!" She was drunk. The sounds of castanets clattered in the background and I knew instantly they were in La Casita watching a show. "Oh, I'm so proud of you, my sweet baby! What did you wear? Did you have to make a speech? Oh, I bet Rory is so proud. I miss you both so much!"

"It runs in the family, them awards!" Dad shouted into the mouthpiece. "I can't tell you how many I have!"

"Bring it with you when you come out, will you? I am dying to see it. I want to show everyone. Mary Smurfit who runs the second-hand designer shop Once Great Now Good, well, her son Ryan has just been signed by Blackpool Football Club and she never stops going on and on about it. I told her about you and about David, proud I am of the pair of you, but it would be nice to stick that award in her face just the same. How are my geraniums doing by the way? Are you picking the dead leaves off them? I hope you're not drowning them all?" She at last took a breath.

Shit, I hoped Rory had remembered to water the bloody plants in their house. I suddenly didn't want to go into all the details about the neckpiece and Tara and everything, I don't know why, so I just said, "Yep, Mam, all fine and I'll bring it with me for sure."

"It's a shame Rory can't come with you, isn't it? How is poor darling Alice? Tell her I'm praying for her – David said she looked very gaunt at the funeral. I have a little letter I wrote her – I will hand-deliver it when we come back in a few weeks. She was insistent when we spoke on the phone that we didn't come back for the funeral, so insistent that I didn't want to upset her any more by coming back. Coming, Brian – okay, goodnight, petal!" She rang off.

"Bring what?" Alice asked.

"My award," I told her.

"What award?" she asked, tap-tapping away. That 'e' was giving her terrible trouble. "I dunno but my mother wants me to bring one to Nerja next week."

"Take my Irish Dancing trophy to show her but make sure you bring it back – I love that trophy – only thing I ever won in my life."

I needed a drink.

"Okay, let's check your emails," she said. "Rory says that the contact form is beeping every three seconds. Rory's on his way round now, I'd better slip a pizza on for him – he must be starving – he's been outdoors at that awards all day." She stretched now. She was always thinking of others. She'd have made an amazing wife.

"Here, let me put it on – I want to get a drink."

I went to the fridge and found a can of Heineken at the very back. I didn't check the date. I just opened it. I opened the freezer and found a mozzarella and basil pizza. It was homemade and had Lucy's stickers all over the cling film. They'd obviously made it together.

"Nearly bedtime, Bubble, okay, pet?" Alice was returning to mammyhood mode.

Lucy did look tired.

I pulled up a chair beside Alice and logged into my Gmail account with my laptop on my lap. I had seven hundred and sixteen emails and the counter was clicking up every minute. I'd never had more than three at the one time. Ever. And usually one of them was for penis enlargements. I only ever checked my emails once a week.

Alice leaned over and took control of my cursor.

"Look, here's the fashion editor for the *Sunday Times* – they want to interview you . . . look . . . the *Late Late Show* want you on. Anna bloody Wintour! The editor of *Vogue*, Anna Wintour, has just emailed you just to say she loved the piece Tara wore!"

I looked at them all from the website contact form and I listened to Alice read out one after another after another. Old school friends I hadn't heard from or seen in twenty years. Old bosses. Cousins, aunties and uncles I'd forgotten even existed. People who didn't know me but knew someone I had met once at the supermarket. All because a movie star had worn my jewellery.

"Oh, I just have to open this one from Paula Mak!" Alice held her hand on her neck – the heartburn was really playing havoc with her. She grunted and double-clicked, then read out loud even though I was more than capable of reading it myself. "*Dearest Beth, I hope we can now move on with our already formed working relationship. I am happy to tell you that my beloved daughter Louise is now regaining her health every day and I have you and Alice to thank. I will never forget your kindness. I would love to get your first collection into my Dublin store by the end of the week (as discussed). Come in tomorrow and I can take you for lunch and plan? As I'm such a fan of your work (and have been for years as you well know) I'm happy to give you the counter space at the front of my stores where our flag label Frame used to show. Please invite Alice and my granddaughter as I would adore seeing them both. I have a few bits (if you pardon the pun!) I have been collecting for them. The hard times are behind us. Thanks, darling, Paula (Mak) xoxoxo.'"*

Unbelievable. Or maybe all too believable from what we knew of the woman.

"Can you believe her?" Alice gasped. "Can you believe she sat and wrote that email? She is delusional!" She whacked delete with her index finger. I was glad. "What a piece of work! How could she use the word 'granddaughter' about Lucy? The woman couldn't bear the sight of her so-called granddaughter."

"I know, Alice – it's beyond grotesque."

"We won't get through all these tonight, will we?" Alice was back in work mode. "Everything will change for you now, Beth. Will you let me help you? I want to work, I need to work now. Dan left us comfortable with his life insurance and thank God we'd sorted that before . . ." She touched the edge of the wooden table with both hands. "But I need to work. I will have two children to support and, yes, I could get another job but I really . . . I just want to be a part of this . . . I think that maybe Beth's Bitz can save me . . . somehow . . ."

"I wouldn't have it any other way," I told her.

She bit her bottom lip. "Okay, we'd need to see a solicitor to get advice and stuff as soon as possible, wouldn't we? Like Beth's Bitz is a registered company, isn't it?"

"Yeah." I wasn't that thick.

"Oh, Dan would have been so, so happy for you!" She grabbed a pen and a page from her printer. "There's so much to do. Are you okay? Are you in shock?"

I took a moment. "No, I'm okay. And I still have to make the eleven chains for the girls." I drank directly from the can. I knew Alice desperately wanted me to get a glass but she held it back.

"You're still going to make them?" Alice grinned.

"Of course I am. And what's more I'm going to number them now as they may have some value if things go the way they are looking." I stared hard at the emails again, the number of them going up and up and up.

There was only one I really wanted to open. I had quickly scrolled up before Alice had seen it. Then we had shrunk the font tiny and it just remained unopened and hidden. It had been blinding me from the moment I logged onto my emails. It simply read **JCallan** and subject line **US**. I suddenly wanted Alice and Lucy to leave the room so I could read it. Or did I?

I sat on the couch beside Lucy and pulled her cosy feet onto my lap. I rubbed her little toes as I thought about it. What could it possibly say that was going to help me? Nothing. I should just delete it. Now wouldn't that be closure?

"So here's what I am thinking," said Alice. "We need to carefully select who you give interviews to, I mean the mail from Anna Wintour just said congratulations on a magnificent creation – she's not looking to interview you for *Vogue* . . . yet. We need to make a proper PR plan. In fact, I think I will call that PR guru Caroline Kennedy and ask her advice. What do you think? It is bloody amazing!"

"Sure is."

"Beth, you aren't acting the way I'd imagined you would! What is it? Is it your hair? Do you think you look like that girl from *Harry Potter* who cut off all her hair in a wild cry for more media attention?" Alice stared too pityingly at my hair for my liking.

"I thought you loved it?" I felt it.

"I do, I think it's fab! But what's wrong then?" Alice

swallowed the heartburn again.

"There's an email from John there, on the laptop," I confessed. "I scrolled up a bit so you wouldn't see it." I pointed to the desk like a child might point to an imaginary scary dragon behind the curtain.

Alice said nothing for a few minutes. Then she exhaled really loudly. Like one might expend a core breath in a yoga class.

"Bubble, beddybyboo time!" She stood now and lifted a shattered Lucy. "I will be back in fifteen minutes, Beth – there are a few cans of Heineken left out in the shed if you want them?"

I nodded and kissed Lucy.

After they left, the room was so still, so silent and I could still feel Dan's huge presence in it . . . his PlayStation still under the TV.

I walked to the window, pulled the cream drapes to one side and peered out. The road was quiet. I ran my hands through my hair and actually jumped with fright when my fingers slipped into thin air. I'd forgotten about my new haircut. This made me laugh. Slightly.

I walked over to the laptop and sat down. Emails still poured in. It wasn't pleasing to me, somehow, the way the world now worked. Just because Tara T wore my jewellery I was now going to be a successful businesswoman. Really, she had made Beth's Bitz. It didn't matter that I had striven to get there on my own, worked my lonely ass off creating my designs, stood in that market every day in the hail, rain, sun and snow – what it took nowadays was to be endorsed by someone who was born blessed. That was as far as I saw it. She could act, I guessed there was no doubt about that, but so could thousands of other women, probably even better, but who didn't have the looks or the body or the good fortune to be in the right place at the right time. The world worked for Tara T because she had a talent and was aesthetically pleasing.

I stared at John's email. I sat with my fingers hovering over it. I should be over the moon right now, thrilled, hopping up and down. But too many things had happened for it all to mean that much to me any more. Dan's death, cheating on Rory, hurting Rory and losing John all over again.

"So what did he say?" Alice stepped in behind me and put her hands on my shoulders.

"I haven't opened it yet."

She looked down. "It was sent three days ago."

"I know." I blew some imaginary dust off the keyboard.

"What do you want it to say, Beth? That he loves you, that he wants to marry you and for you guys to have babies and get a house in the country with horses and Basset Hounds . . . what?"

I didn't answer her. She edged me over and sat on half the chair.

"It has to stop, Beth, it has to end, you have to end this. He makes you miserable. I can't help you any more but all I can say is here's a new phase in your life – your business is going to soar – you deserve that – you are an amazing jewellery designer. Are you going to be stuck in this headspace about John for another five years because, if so, Beth, I really think you need to go and talk to someone. A professional."

Her words stung and my face burned.

302

"You think I need to see a shrink?" I couldn't believe she would think that.

"Yeah, I do. I think if he said now, in that mail, come with me to the outback and we can see big red baboon-arses, you'd leave this business and go, and I think that's someone who isn't in her right mind."

The clock ticked loudly on the mantelpiece and it was like the cogs in my brain turning. Was she right? If he asked me to leave now with him, would I? I dropped my head into my hands. I physically couldn't think about him any more.

"Delete it." I breathed the words through my splayed fingers.

"Are you sure?" she asked.

"Just do it, Alice." I squeezed my hands tightly across my face as I felt her lean across me.

Click. Then another *click*.

"He's gone," she said.

If only it were that easy.

Chapter Twenty-six

The day after the awards was crazy. I couldn't keep up with the demand to buy my designs. Lots of my stuff was already on eBay for ridiculous prices. I saw Mini Muffin Susie had hers up and in the blurb quoted us as "BFF's". Rory had come and we photographed all my stuff on Alice's perfect bed and we got the website linked to PayPal and all major credit cards. Rory had done it all. I had a bank meeting, I got a lawyer and a solicitor and I hired Alice. I also hired a young designer, Leontia Brophy, from Cavan who I found in the college of Arts and Design I'd attended, as my assistant. She was amazing. I'd help her in a few years to go out on her own.

"Do not cancel your trip," said Alice who was now, believe it or not, wearing one of those ears-pieces you talked into from your mobile. She pulled it to one side now as she spoke to me. "We can cope."

"What about my stall?"

"Stall's over, Beth."

I was sad. I'd been through a lot of cold days with that stall.

"But I thought," said Alice, "when we get our office, we can use it as my desk?"

I liked that idea.

Rory took me to the airport the next morning. Pulling up at departures, he got my case out and carried it over to the door for me, his blue jumper tucked into his cords.

"Here's your parents' house key." He pulled it off his Donor Card key-ring. He was basically living with Alice and Lucy now.

I took it and pushed it deep into the pocket of my faded jeans.

"I'm so sorry about everything, Rory." My lip started to quiver.

"You can't help how you feel, Beth. If I learned one thing in life I've learned that. To tell the truth, I'm glad you were honest with me, I deserve more than to be with someone who doesn't love me totally." He slid his glasses up and held his index finger there.

"You do . . . you really do."

He removed his finger and pulled himself up tall. "Right now I'm looking out for my friend Dan. I'm making sure Alice and Lucy and his unborn child are all well looked after, that they are okay, because he deserves me to do that. He was a great guy. He was a true friend to me, you know, Beth, and I won't let him down."

I nodded. So Alice had told Rory she was pregnant. I was glad. "I miss him too," I said as I took his hand.

"We all do," he replied. "Go have fun, say hi to Brian and your mam and enjoy that sun. Be way too hot for me, see." He gave a wry smile.

I pecked him on the cheek and let him go. He was

right. I'd never loved him enough. God knows I'd wanted to. I'd tried to. But I couldn't.

I entered the airport and as I had checked in online I went straight to my gate. I sat alone. It was the first time since Dan had passed that I'd been on my own. So much had happened and I had so much to think about. I took out my sketch pad and sketched some designs. I planned to do a lot of that over the next two weeks – sitting alone on the beach (Mam and Dad didn't do sand), staring out at the big blue still sea and then up at that cloudless perfect still blue sky. Heat inspired me. I loved how my skin felt and how my bones were truly warm. I was never really warm enough.

I went over to the kiosk and joined the one-hundred-person queue to buy a cold overpriced coffee. I didn't buy cigarettes. I was going to give them up. Rory had stopped but mainly because he was at Alice's so often.

They called my flight just as I reached the top.

"Can you take the coffee on board?" I asked the guy.

"I duunooo, do I?" he told me helpfully.

I bought it. They wouldn't let me take it on.

Please don't let me get a seat putter-backer, I mantra'd in my brain. Seat putter-backers gave me plane rage. Unbelievable plane rage. John used to find it hysterical. Whenever someone whacked their seat back on me I'd see red. Pure fury. "Oh no! Here we go!" he'd roar, laughing as my table-top hit me. I hated it. Why did they have the option? The space was not big enough!

I squashed myself in between two older men and pulled out my book. I'd picked it up in Oxfam – it was for the daddy really: *What to Expect When She's Expecting*. It was a most frightening read. *The Blair Witch Project* had nothing on this.

When we landed in Malaga the blue greeted me. "Good day, Beth!" it said, waving its royal blueness through the tiny plane window as I doubled over the window-seat man to see it. "Good day to you too, Blue," I said out loud and the two men turned to look at me from either side. I put my head down, pretending to tie my lace. I stayed down until my skin stopped burning.

Dad was at arrivals. "Hello, my little sparrow! Welcome to our humble abode!" They didn't live in the airport, or in Malaga for that matter. He had bought a white, sleek sports car. Way too young for him but I liked it.

We made chit-chat on the forty-five-minute drive and, as we pulled up to the big spraying water fountain at the Parador in Nerja, I felt my shoulders drop and my mind and body relax. This was the start of the new me. I had filled Dad in on the Tara T stuff. He said he knew her. He didn't. I was staying in an apartment in the Balcón, the main area for tourists, but it was never busy or too loud and I loved it. It had a small square with a beautiful white church and boasted the most amazing sea views. I could have stayed with Mam and Dad but I wanted space. Head space. I wanted to heal once and for all. I also wanted to work. I arranged to meet them at eight o'clock for dinner in Pepe's.

After I checked in and unpacked my basics I threw open my balcony doors. I inhaled deeply the warm salty smells. I stared into the blue sky and closed my eyes for a few seconds, then I slipped on my green bikini under my full-length sarong and headed straight for the beach. I almost ran down, dangerously looking up at the sun as I ran, to check it wasn't leaving me. I bought a beach sun lounger for four euro for the day and creamed myself up and then I slid onto the hot blue soft plastic-coated sponge of the bed. I let out a long slow breath as I drank in the views of the sea. The smell of coconut sun oil permeated the air. My pupils dilated as I stared at the blue sky. I blinked a lot.

"What did that email say?" I whispered to myself on the wonderfully refreshing warm breeze. I'd never know.

I was so proud of myself, though, that I'd taken that brave step. I was also so proud that Alice had witnessed it. I always felt like a bit of a wimp where she was concerned in relation to John. I had balls after all. Big balls. I thought about Alice now and the new baby and Lucy and Louise and my new company, marvelling at the fact I was an 'overnight' successful moneymaking jewellery designer with so many orders I'd had to employ another person and start to mass-produce.

"Dreenk?"

I bought a freezing cold can of Diet Coke from the woman selling along the beach. I would have given anything for a cigarette to go with it but I had none. I could only smoke Silk Cut Blue – that's how I always knew I wasn't a smoker-smoker (if you know what I mean) – they didn't sell my Silk Cut Blue in Nerja so I couldn't smoke. I opened the can carefully in case she'd been shaking it about. I watched families play sandcastles and chasing and couples kiss and read. I held the can to my mouth. Dad never noticed my hair, I thought, as I drank it all in five gulps and then I lay back watching the motions of the coral-blue sea and fell asleep under the shade of the umbrella.

That night I dressed in denim shorts and beige sandals and a sleeveless white T-shirt. I was already a little less pale.

"Oh, your beautiful hair!" my mother gasped in horror. "Are you sick, Beth?" She jumped up now, panic-stricken, knocking her wineglass over in the process.

"Ah, here now, Ellen, would ya watch where yer jumping! I just bought that!" Dad said, ever mindful of his wallet.

"No, Mam, I just cut it off – you look great too, though, thanks." I sat down.

She did look great. Healthy and happy. It was how I hoped I'd look at fifty, never mind seventy.

Dad furiously mopped up the red with a huge roll of blue paper towels that the waiter had presented him with. "*Señoritas*!" he laughed with the amused waiter.

I ordered another bottle of red and tapas, lots and lots of tapas. I was starving. The sun always gave me an appetite. I hadn't been starving in so long. It felt great to taste food again and flavours.

"So where is the award then?" my mother asked, still looking at me as though I'd cut off my own ear.

I had the time and energy now to tell her the full story. "The is no award, Mam, but it's something even better: a really famous, sexy Oscar-winning Hollywood actress, whom you might know as Tara T wore some of my jewellery to her film premiere and an awards ceremony and now everyone wants to buy it."

She took her glasses off her head and pushed them on her face. "So no award?" She pursed her lips.

"No, no award, but a really famous . . ."

She raised her hand. "So what do you expect me to say to Madam Smurfit when she wants to see it? The whole of Blackpool is wearing her son's face on their T-shirts apparently."

I couldn't believe I was even having this conversation. I picked up my glass and swirled. "Tell her I couldn't get it through customs because it was in the shape of a gun." I sipped and smiled.

The first week flew by and it was perfect. Perfect weather. Perfect food. Perfect company, as I only saw my parents at night for dinner and then I left them to their own devices, so I was just with me. I went to bars on my own and drank cheap wine and watched the Spanish dancers in La Casita and during the day I designed and got browner and browner and blonder and blonder. I was making great work and I knew it. It was an inspired collection because it was free, it was relatively happy, it was a new me.

I thought about John every day, of course I did, but I accepted it now – it was a part of who I was and I didn't fight it any more. I fantasised about him every night before I went to bed and it was comforting. I was free to fantasise about him and about whoever I liked. I sat out on my warm balcony until all hours of the morning making pieces. I didn't turn my phone on once. I was healing and I knew it. I ate mint choc-chip ice cream during the siesta and trawled little jewellery shops for inspiration. I caught sight of myself in a mirror one warm afternoon while I was eating a Pil Pil Prawns in a local eatery, ripping the warm crusty bread to shreds with my bare hands. I didn't look like me any more. My short blonde (really bleached by the sun) hair had a silver clip in it. I had come up with a great range of hair jewellery to add to clips and bobbins – I thought the schoolgirls would love those and after all they were still my bread and butter. I smiled at my reflection and my dimples popped out. I looked hard into the mirror.

I didn't want to be alone for long. I wanted so badly to fall in love again and I wanted to have a family, I acknowledged. Maybe it was me after all. Maybe I was doing something wrong? Baby steps, I said in my head as I dipped another prawn in the sizzling garlic sauce . . . every cloud, I thought – I couldn't stuff this into me all day if I had to kiss anyone. The thought of meeting someone else was alien but I knew maybe someday, in some place somewhere, I might meet another John. Yes, I was lying to myself but at least it was a start. I was slowly putting on some weight but not where I wanted it. Why did it never go where you wanted it? My face was still drawn but my belly was getting bigger by the day. Spongier, my mother had said last night as I tucked into a bowl of linguine mussels. "Your tummy is looking spongier, love – that's good." I wasn't convinced a spongy tummy was ever that good.

Tonight I was meeting my parents at Cyril's. It still had so many memories of John making the paella there with Carlos – "Eees all in the sauce, Johaan!" I laughed now. Maybe I was starting to enjoy the memories. God, wouldn't that be fantastic?

I strolled back towards the Balcón and collected my towel and green bikini from my apartment. I changed in the spotless beach changing cubicles and walked on the hot golden sand for a while. Then I swam in the warm blue sea before heading home to get ready to eat again.

My apartment was cool and fresh and I felt like I was really moving on. I flicked on my iPod and played some music as I put on my make-up and dressed in a short red cotton dress which I'd bought for four euro in the market up in the hot hills of Capistrano. I was brown all over. I tied up my red wedges. My hair dried in seconds – it was magic.

Before I left for dinner I used the phone in reception to call Alice. I wanted to check in with her on how she was doing and ask about Beth's Bitz. Even though she'd warned me not to, I felt I should at least call once. It rang out. I grabbed my white clutch and strolled down the winding streets in the wonderful evening heat to Cyril's. I stopped and looked at every piece of jewellery along the way. The street sellers and the shops were my research. I checked out the jewellery of every person that passed me but I did this at home too.

When I arrived at Cyril's it looked closed. The big white double doors were closed. I looked around. No sign of Mam and Dad, so I waited. Someone had been smoking a cigarette seconds before and I could still smell the tobacco in the air. I was like a tobacco bloodhound. Then I knocked on the door. They had a back garden eatery – maybe everyone was out there. But why was the door shut? I knocked again and it opened.

The blinds were down and it was dark as I stepped in. I couldn't see anyone there. Who had opened the door?

"Cyril? Carlos?"

I took safe baby-steps on the cobbled floor out to the back. The outer garden was lit up in white fairy lights and candles burned brightly on the one table set up in the centre of the garden. It had a blue-and-white chequered tablecloth and sparking silver cutlery. I looked around. There were vases upon vases of yellow sunflowers all around the edges and candles burned brightly behind each vase.

"What's going on?" I called out and then stopped.

"*Hola*, Beth!" John Callan stepped out from the kitchen. "You're very welcome. Can I take your coat? You're not wearing a coat. Okay . . . can I take your bag?"

"John! How? What? What's going on?" I whimpered, my heart flying again. "John, what are you doing here? Why are you here? Where are my parents?" *Oh my God, I reek of garlic!*

"Sit, please." He pulled out my chair and held his hand up. "Your parents are eating elsewhere this evening, Beth. Give me ten seconds." He darted back into the kitchen and I heard a cork pop and then buttons being pressed. He pushed those strings that served as doors out of his way and they clattered as he reappeared with a bottle of red. Faustino V – my favourite.

Then the CD kicked in. "*You're telling me I should forget you* . . ." Glen Hansard's melodic lyrics from "Fake" filled the air and I had goose bumps all over my body as John Callan sat and poured me a massive glass of red wine.

I had no words. I was fighting back the tears like crazy.

"Love your hair." He held up his glass and sat down.

"How are you here?" I managed eventually.

"I came to Alice's – she told me you were here. She told me you never read my email. She told me a lot of things, Beth, did our Alice."

"No, I didn't read it." It felt great to say that.

I immediately saw the panic in his eyes. Only the third time ever. Only the third time John had ever panicked in front of me anyway.

"Do you want to know what it said?" he whispered to me now.

I couldn't believe he was sitting in front of me, here, now. I didn't delay too long. "Yes."

He ran his hand slowly over his stubble. My heart was racing. Eventually words left his perfect mouth.

"I love you, Beth Burrows, I've always loved you. I've been a prick, a fucking foolish prick, but I needed to get away, Beth – I needed not to feel like you were doing it all for us. As fucked up as this may sound I needed to stand on my own two feet. I'd been leaning on you for so many years. I needed to make us different. I wanted to be something, someone – someone different – someone you respected, but I didn't want to upset us. That night in Captain America's when you seemed to have lost your edge and conformed, I got so angry because I blamed myself. I'd turned you into that person. You took those jobs so we could be together and have some kind of steady income. To pay our way. I never wanted that, I always wanted us to be whoever we wanted to be. That night I could see it creeping in – the resentment – you were starting to resent me being me. You, the only person who had ever truly got me. I ran scared, Beth. I thought that at least if I never gave you the chance to say you didn't love me any more, then I'd never have to hear it. So I ran like the fucking clappers, Beth. The minute I got to New York I knew I'd made the biggest mistake of my life. Jesus, I never stopped loving you but I didn't know how to come back then. I tried to get Alice's advice but she was brutal with me. She basically told me to stay away, that you deserved better than me and that I should leave you the fuck alone."

I interrupted now. "Tell me you're joking? She'd never do that to me – she knew how devastated I was!" I was furious and my fists clenched without me telling them to.

"She was right, Beth." He pulled my fingers loose. Electricity shot through my body.

That was what she was talking about before the wedding when she'd said "I did what I did for your happiness"? She knew he had wanted me back and she hadn't told me. His words ran a marathon around my head.

"My sister isn't stupid, you know – she believes in true love – if you love somebody set them free and all that – that's what she told me. She told me to go find myself and grow up and to come back if and when I was ready to make a commitment to you."

Where was this going? Did he want me back?

"I liked what I did, what I do . . . but I know you . . . I know you probably think it's pathetic."

"John, why on earth would I think being a successful actor is pathetic?" I was truly incredulous now.

"Because I know you think I get by a lot on my looks." He sniffed and then squeezed out his packet of cigarettes from his jeans front pocket and put them on the table.

I saw the belt and the gold buckle. "You have real talent."

He laughed as he struck his Zippo, hands shielding the flame from the wind even though there was no need. "Do I?" He exhaled slowly and his mouth made the tiniest hole to let the smoke escape. "It's not what I want – acting, you

315

know – it never was. I want to direct, I want to write, I want to tell stories but I don't want to be the pawn, I want to be the king. I always felt, though, to be a really good director you need to have been on the other side of the camera too."

I couldn't stop myself: I reached for his cigarettes and lit one. Silk Cut Blue could go whistle. I inhaled the Marlboro Red deeply.

"Well, then do it – you can do anything, you know that – you are the most inspiring person I've ever met in my entire life. Why do you think it took me so long to get over you?"

"So are you?" His dark eyes darted in his head.

"What?" I tipped the ash with my index finger even though there was no need.

"Are you over me?"

Spain engulfed us with its heat and its scents.

"I want to be," I answered truthfully as I looked into his dark eyes, his hair long now and pulled back behind his ears.

"I don't want you to be," he whispered and leaned over and took my hand. "I can't tell you how much I really do not want you to be."

"What do you want from me, John? Really? Please . . . I'm so tired of the heart pangs and the pain and I just really want the truth."

"It's simple really, Beth." He stubbed out his cigarette and then, just like that, John Callan dropped to one knee. On the warm sandy garden in Cyril's restaurant. He produced a little blue box. "I love you, Beth. I want you to be with me forever."

He held back his tears and I exploded with emotions I

never knew I had. I fell off the chair and I didn't care. I fell to the ground beside him and I roared my head off.

Carlos looked out from behind the beads. "Now zee time, Johaan?" He looked confused.

"Yeah, Carlos, thanks, mate! *Gracias*!" John removed the ring. It was a beauty. It looked vintage and was timeless.

I knew I'd Alice to thank for this. I just knew that much. She had been right all along. It had to be all or nothing with him – he wasn't able for the in-between stuff. In the end she knew him better than I did. I wished she was here right now, which was unusual, I'll admit. The opening bars from the Oscar-winning "Falling Slowly" rang sweetly: "*I don't know you but I want you all the more for that . . .*"

John took my hand and slid the diamond onto my wedding finger.

"*Take this sinking boat and point it home . . .*"

We held each other so tightly it hurt.

"Will you have me, Beth?" he whispered into my ear.

"I'll have you, John. I will have you forever if you don't mind, thank you very much!" We laughed and then kissed hard and then harder until our mouths really stung. I stopped only to look into his eyes and occasionally down at my ring. Somewhere up there I knew Dan was looking down on us.

By finally letting John go I'd got him back. For good.

Chapter Twenty-seven

"I officially declare Beth's Bitz open!" Tara Tomelay stood on South William Street in the freezing cold and cut the red ribbon across the door of my new jewellery shop.

Christmas was only days away and we'd worked so hard to open the shop before the big day.

I had changed my opinion on her radically since we'd met and we had become good friends. She was a very, very hardworking and clever woman. She had been brought up in Cleveland Ohio, named after Tara the plantation *in Gone with the Wind* by her single mother. Tara had left school at fifteen to take care of her mother, who had developed MS, working in the local Around the Corner Saloon on Detroit Avenue. In her pink uniform with pink hat, white apron, white ankle socks and white trainers, she worked double shifts five days a week. She saved and saved and saved until she eventually made enough money to buy a battered old Ford Transit. She put their furniture from 1477 River Side Drive, Lakewood, into storage. Then, at eighteen years old, she hauled her mother across

America to Los Angeles. They rented a room long-term at the cheap, but clean, Hollywood Palms Inns and Suites on Hollywood Boulevard. The place was exceptionally basic but location-wise it was a dream and it had a microwave, refrigerator and cable TV so her mother was happy. She couldn't afford gas so she parked up her transit in the car park and walked everywhere. It was exactly a fifteen-minute walk to the Hollywood Walk of Fame.

Within a week Tara started work as a waitress in Dillon's Irish Pub on the Boulevard and she fell in love with Irish people.

She took acting classes at night. She fought hard, tooth and nail, and blagged herself into any auditions she heard about. She couldn't land a role. She kept going and going and never gave up on her dream.

Tara knocked on the door of every actors' agent in LA and was always told the same things: either "My books are full, honey" or "Come back to me when you have a show reel, honey." A show reel? Surely she needed an acting job before she could get a show reel?

They hadn't got a spare penny. She didn't have long to make this dream happen. If it didn't work out she had to go back to night school, get her high-school diploma and go to college. She often thought about being a kindergarten teacher. But the movies were her one true love. Everything about them. She could sit in a dark cinema on her own for hours and hours and disappear into another world. The idea of becoming another person was deeply fascinating to her. She adored actresses like Jessica Chastain and Charlize Theron who had struggled to do this work too.

The acting classes she took were incredible. She lived

319

every second of them. One evening, when she was behind on her instalments, Margie her tutor called her outside. The stifling Los Angeles air stuck in her throat. Was Margie going to tell her to forget it, to move on, that she didn't have what it took?

Quite the opposite.

"You're really good, Tara, really good. I don't say this often or to many people but do not give up."

The sunnier climate in LA suited her mother and it wasn't long before she was able to do a few more bits for herself. Tara used to take her every Saturday night to Bubba Gump's Shrimp Diner on Santa Monica Pier. It was cheap yet the seafood was incredible. They ordered the exact same meal deal every Saturday night. It was twenty dollars for a big bowl of shellfish. You never knew what you would get in it but it was always fresh. Tara would let her mother eat the most of it, claiming she'd eaten in work, and she would drink a diet lemon and scour the trade magazines and circle with her faithful red pen any suitable auditions for the coming week.

She had managed to get a dodgy photographer to take headshots of her on condition she posed for a nude life painting. She'd agreed. They had done the headshots in his seedy loft apartment above an Adult Movie store and when it was over he'd begun to set up his easel and paints. She could see him becoming fidgety and tense. Excited.

"So can I like grab these on a disk too, Doug?" she casually asked him as she started to unbutton her black shirt.

He grunted and fiddled around on his computer, burning images before handing her the disk.

"Everything off," he coughed then, his head bowed.

"Every last bit. Please leave your panties on the table here." He'd pointed a visibly shaking finger to a small brown table laden with panties.

Some poor unfortunate girls had actually gone ahead with this. She felt sick to her stomach. She started to button her shirt back up, sliding the disk down the back of her jeans into her safe-as-houses panties.

"Doug," she backed toward the loft door as he was moving the various panties into a semi-circle, "there are three policemen downstairs waiting to arrest you right now. All I need to do is press this panic button in my jeans." She tapped the CD disk hard. "We have been surveying you for some months now. This has to stop or you will go to prison. You are violating these women. It is wrong. We will continue to monitor you for another six months and then some. Take this as your only warning."

She backed out and fled, her disk cutting into her bottom as she ran. She knew it had been an incredibly stupid risk but sometimes you just had to take them. She could never have afforded professional shots and without them she simply couldn't call herself an actress: they were her main tool.

Anyway, that night in Bubba Gump's she showed her mother her newly printed glossy headshots. Even if she said so herself, she looked amazing. The black shirt open at the neck and her side profile turned to camera was striking. Those eyes. Her mother's eyes and her grandmother's before her. Captivating. She had imagined the camera had just insulted her, just said the worst things imaginable to her, and it came across in the photography. Her eyes just told a story. She could take a good picture and she was more than relieved about that.

"What if I don't look good on camera?" she had wondered time and time again to her mother. Hundreds of girls were pretty but didn't translate to the lens.

"You couldn't look bad if you tried, sweetheart," her mother had said, smiling warmly at her.

Then, that very evening, Franco came into her life. Franco was the general dogsbody at Bubba Gump's – he cleared tables, washed the pots and pans and swept the floors. He had been clearing dishes from their table as Tara was showing her mother the photographs. He had lingered too long and she'd realised he was staring at the headshots.

"Do you mind?" he'd asked and she said "No, not at all, go ahead".

He wiped his hands down on his stained brown apron before lifting the photographs. He had stared long and hard at every shot. "These really aren't bad." He wasn't one for over-praising as she was soon to find out. "Let me start again, sorry. Hello, ladies, I am Franco. I am one of the best actors' agents here in Hollywood." He'd extended his hand.

Tara had laughed and her mother had given her a filthy look as she shook his hand warmly. "Hello, Franco – I'm Tara Tomelay. I'm one of the best actresses here in Hollywood."

They had locked eyes and it was the beginning of a beautiful relationship and one of the most successful business relationships in Hollywood. Franco didn't know how to take no for an answer. Like Tara he was living day to day, sleeping on a friend's floor, and he was trying to build up his own actors' agency.

He had given her his card, The Actors' Stable, and

asked her to call. She hadn't. The following Saturday night he handed her his card again. "Please call me." She hadn't. She just didn't have the time to waste: time was running out. Then one night he was drinking in Dillon's and he approached her behind the bar. Slightly drunk.

"Just give me a chance. I mean, what have you got to lose? You can't make it on your own. You need me. This is Hollywood, baby, and everyone needs each other. Take one day and come around with me, that's all I ask. I can do this. I will make The Actors' Stable into one of the biggest new agencies in town and you will rue the day you said no to me." He'd grinned and raised his bottle of Miller.

"One chance, Franco. If I say that's it, then that's it. I have my mother relying on me too. This isn't a game to me."

He straightened up tall. "There are no games, I promise."

He had meant it. He banged on every studio door with her by his side, never gaining entry until one night he'd had a brainwave.

"Okay . . . I have access to the diner after hours. I sweep up and scrub down. Why don't we rent some really good lights and a shit-hot RED camera and shoot a scene in here? No one has to know it's just us doing it – we put it on your show reel as the *only* piece and we sell it as a scene from an up-and-coming movie you're starring in."

They had spent the next three weeks writing and rewriting scenes. They wanted to showcase her every talent in the scene. Comedy. Dramatic. Emotional. She could do it all.

She hadn't been totally convinced it would work until

she'd arrived at one o'clock in the morning to Bubba's and the place looked like a film set. Franco had borrowed hundreds and hundreds of dollars from his friends and rented the best film equipment money could buy. He even employed a professional cameraman who had worked on Paramount's lot for twenty-five years, and a professional film and TV make-up artist.

"This is our big chance. I believe in you. I believe utterly and completely in you. Now let's go sell Tara Tomelay to the movie business."

They had written a wonderful scene where a girl and a guy are breaking up in a restaurant. The guy, Franco, is the one doing the breaking up. In the opening scene the girl, Tara, tells him she has just been diagnosed that morning with breast cancer and yet he still walks out on her. It was harrowing and hard to play until the very end of the nine-minute scene where he walks back in with a bunch of pink roses and they kiss. Franco had to be in it too as they couldn't afford to ask another actor in case word got out, even though they could have got anyone for free. She had given it everything. She had played that scene like her life depended on it. It had depended on it. She had cried method tears of sadness at her past life and kept the tears rolling as she imagined her life ahead. Her mother would soon need more medical care. They had no health insurance. She cried more and when Franco (who played a blinder in the scene) returned with the pink flowers she had kissed him for real and he had kissed her back for real and they had fallen in love. They were one of a kind. When Franco pulled away and yelled "Cut!" Tara looked around. The make-up artist was in floods of tears and, as Scott the cameraman started rolling up leads and wrapping up cable, she caught his eye and he'd winked at her and then given her the thumbs-up.

The show reel had been an instant success. Franco had taken it only to the biggest film producers and Scott Steller at Primer Pictures had loved it.

"I want her – she's great!" he had drawled, while lighting an enormous cigar in his mansion of an office on the famous lot.

Franco had elaborated on his bluff outside Steller's open office window, pretending to make various phone calls letting down other producers, making sure Steller could hear.

"You got yourself a deal, Mr Steller," he laughed when he returned.

Like all successful Hollywood producers, signing hot new talent that would make him millions of American dollars made Mr Stellar very happy.

How Tara had laughed when Franco had relayed this story. She had been signed up on the spot for a small fortune to star in Primer's new romantic comedy *Tears Are for Toddlers, Aren't They?* It was a massive box-office hit.

Just like that, Tara Tomelay was a movie star. And the Actors' Stable was one of the most sought-after agencies in Hollywood. Franco looked after all the up-and-coming actors and actresses and by all accounts he was an unbelievable dealmaker for them all.

Tara's mother was still very ill with MS but she was now so much better looked after. They had a house in the Hollywood Hills with an elevator for her mum's wheelchair and everything money could buy to make life for an MS sufferer just that little bit easier.

I looked at her now talking to Rory, shivering in a tiny LBD (she'd told me that the shorter the dress she wore, the longer the column inches Beth's Bitz would get). Yes, she was blessed with the looks that any man or woman would remove a big toe for. She had sent me a huge bouquet of flowers after the awards in Dublin and we had stayed in touch. She liked me. She trusted me. She said I reminded her of herself. She told me things she really shouldn't as she didn't know me all that well and I could have gone to the papers and made a fortune off her. I told her this all the time. She told me I would never make a fortune off her, that I just wasn't that type of person, that I was too much like her. I wasn't one hundred per cent sure she was right. Well, okay, I was. Then when John had to go to LA to meet with a new agent, about him directing his first feature *Clear Hats*, we'd all met out there for dinner. We had gone to Chateaux Marmont and I was in awe of the place. Its history of film was thrilling. Unfortunately for me, Franco was still a bit of a pain in the hole, but we'd clicked a little because of our similar relationship situations. Franco did indeed adore Tara and she adored him back. They had a Hollywood grounding that was very unusual. There was no element of 'Is she/is he with me for the right reasons?' It was a solid relationship built before the fame. Tara told me that was invaluable. She was down to earth and real.

John loved LA and so did I, but we agreed we could never live there. He knew lots of people there and I had been nervous about the stories I'd hear from this mates but they rarely shocked me. "So you are the famous

Beth?" the guys would say. "So you're the reason John wouldn't go on any dates?" the plastic dolls would say if they could move their inflated lips.

He showed me where he'd lived when he started, on a US soap that had been on air for twenty years – a lifetime in America. It was very therapeutic for me. I saw that he just worked and worked and studied and funnily enough he had met with Franco early on but Franco didn't think he was going to stick at it. Franco had been right. It was never acting, it was always directing John wanted. He brought me to all the places he loved in LA and then all the places he hated. He had missed me greatly, I sensed that, and it was perversely wonderfully comforting.

I held his hand tightly now outside my new shop as he thanked Tara and then lifted me up.

"John!" I was mortified as he carried me across the entrance. I had worn a bloody dress – a short one – I was not expecting to be lifted. I had worn the dreaded skin-coloured Spanx and now I was sure they could be seen by all halfway down my thighs.

Everyone was here – my mam and dad, David, Rory and Alice and Lucy, Louise and Brad, Suzie and other market friends, Mr and Mrs O' Toole and Mr and Mrs Callan.

John would leave in January to start directing his first film in Canada and we'd be apart for six weeks.

I was looking forward to it. He was wrecking my head. True love never runs smooth, I knew that, but, Jesus, I had forgotten how completely irritating he could be to live with. He was obsessed about the film. The cast, the crew, the storyboard, the rig, the lighting, the call sheets, the first AD, the second AD, the wardrobe people, the this and the that. It was endless. It was never, ever boring though. I had been asked to make jewellery for some of Hollywood's finest actresses and I barely mentioned it. I just wanted him to get the film started. After being with Rory I'd forgotten how intense John could be but I loved it. I loved how he could push my buttons and I'd still have that feeling of wonder and life when I was with him.

The shop was perfect. Yellow walls and yellow-and-white tiles. Tiny white flowers were hand-painted on the walls and cabinets with the initials BB twisting through them. My designs were housed in small glass cabinets with dark navy velvet around them. The media scrambled to get in to get shots of Tara and she was brilliant. For every shot she held up a piece: a necklace, some earrings, a bangle and my top sellers, my hair jewels. She was wearing a silver clip decorated in emerald stones with clear beads encrusted into it. I wouldn't be here without her now, I knew that much.

"Em, Beth," Alice waddled over, "I hate to do this to you but we have to go. Now. Right now." She coughed into a folded tissue in her hand. Her hair was in a swinging high pony-tail with one of my encrusted gold grips pushed through. Her face did look pretty swollen tonight though. Pretty but swollen.

"It's only opened – I haven't even popped the Moët!" I smiled over at Tara, very distracted.

No one was taking my picture and that made me even happier. The more the flashes went off on Tara, the more coverage Beth's Bitz would get in the papers and magazines. But I was no fool. I knew as soon as the press buzz died away I was on my own and my work needed to stand up for itself.

"Beth, baby," Alice whispered into my ear now.

I stared, wondering why she was calling me 'baby' – she never did.

"Are you okay, Alice?" I stood back and looked at her.

"The baby, Beth. I think I either peed myself on your brand-new showroom floor or my waters have broken – get me out of here now before I die of embarrassment!" Her face reddened as I had never seen it redden before.

"Sweet Lord above! *John! John!*"

He was chatting to a man with the longest beard I had ever seen and drinking from his hipflask again. Whiskey, I'd put anything on it.

He came over. "What? I'm in the middle of a conversation with Tuppi."

I waved at Tuppi whoever he was. "He'll have to wait! We need to get Alice to the hospital. Baby is coming. *Baby. Is. Coming.* She's pissed on the floor!"

"Ah, come on, lads, bit of respect please – who has spilt something on the floor already?" Rory was asking the crowd now before squatting down to examine the liquid.

I approached him. I knelt beside him and whispered, "Eh Rory . . . it's Alice's water."

"What's she like? I know she's clumsy right now and I told her not to wear those stupid high wedges. I bought her flat shoes in Penney's yesterday when we were buying Lucy's Christmas pyjamas – I told her to wear –"

"Dude!" John crouched down now. "That's like . . . womb water you're touching."

Rory looked like he'd been zapped with a metal prong. "Oh God!" He jumped up and rubbed his hands up and down his jeans.

"Dude . . ."

John really liked to call Rory 'dude' – he did it all the time. It was so irritating.

"Yeah?"

"We gotta get her to the hospital. Can you take Lucy home?"

"No! Oh, no way, John, dude, man, dude . . . we'll come . . . we'll wait in the area where people wait . . . dude." Rory was walking around in circles.

"Where is Lucy?" I asked.

"She's with Mrs O'Toole – look, over by the Christmas tree." Mrs O'Toole was looking over, having noticed the rumpus. I pointed and waved at Alice and mouthed, "It's okay, it's okay, it's okay!"

When we had gone to Cork to tell the O'Tooles about Dan's unborn child I swear I'd seen life pour back into Mrs O'Toole's face. She had a reason to live again. She was never off the phone to Alice and Lucy, and at least twice a week packages arrived by post – of baby accessories and tiny hand-knitted cream and yellow clothes and little pressies for Alice and Lucy. There was even talk of them relocating to Dublin once Mr O'Toole retired next year. Alice said she'd be delighted to have them nearby.

I tipped Tara. "I have to go – Alice is going into labour."

She was pretending to drink the champagne – Tara didn't really drink. "Oh go, go, I'll stay as long as it takes! I'll hold the fort."

"What's happening?" Franco was on it in a flash.

Tara explained.

"Well, we're due for dinner, darling, with Bono in The

Clarence in . . ." he rubbed the massive face on his gold Rolex, "precisely ten minutes actually." He smiled at me and put his hand at the base of Tara's back.

"Franco," she smiled that Oscar-winning smile at him, "Beth needs me here right now, and this is where I will be. Please give my apologies to the talented Mr Bono and I will get a cab just as soon as I lock up here."

"Don't be facetious, Tara – you can't stay here alone."

Beaming smile again as another camera went off in her face. *Flash. Flash. Flash.* Through her blinding white teeth she spoke again. "I can and I will. This is Ireland, Franco – remember I worked in Dillon's, the Irish bar? This is why I love it so much, this is why we will build a place here – for that very reason. I can stay here alone. Irish people have more intelligence – they ignore famous people – they actually go out of their way to pretend they don't know who we are just to annoy us and put us in our place, and I love it. Besides I have two ex-armed-forces bodyguards, don't I, darling? Now please, go – just go and I will follow . . ." Her eyes widened. "Oh my God, Beth, see what I did there? 'I Will Follow'? The U2 song"

"Oh yeah!" I laughed out loud, slapping her on the shoulder as Alice pinched me so hard on my arm my laugh turned to tears.

The O'Tooles took Lucy in their car back to Alice's house and we all piled into Rory's new navy jeep. Rory drove which astounded me as surely his light foot was not what the accelerator needed right now.

I panted for some reason and John drank whiskey. I had been to all the pregnancy yoga classes with Alice and to all the ultrasounds. I had watched this baby grow. It was a miracle seeing the little hands and feet on the grainy black-and-white screen. I had reminded Alice to take her Pregnacare every day. I had massaged her swollen ankles and fetched and carried for her. I had kept her stocked up in Bio oil and Gaviscon. I had framed all the scans we got (we chose not to find out the sex) and now I was nearly about to meet this big bump.

"Want some, sis?" John brought me back to the moment as he spoke to Alice in the back – he was on one of those seats that face the wrong way and flapped up and down because he kept standing.

"Seatbelt, John, please, and no, it's not the best time to offer me booze, bro." She breathed like an overworked racehorse through her nose.

"Surely it can only help?" John wiped his nose on his suit jacket sleeve as I watched brother and sister through the rear-view mirror. Genetically blessed. He didn't put on his seatbelt and I knew better than to ask him.

Alice was hit with a contraction and she doubled over.

"*Fffuuck!*" John glugged the hip flask.

I crossed my legs in the front.

"Hurry, Rory, it's getting worse," Alice puffed.

"Ah Jesus, we don't have the hospital bag!" Rory told her, slamming on the brakes.

John spat the whiskey all over poor Alice as he coughed and spluttered. She should smell good to the doctors and nurses now. "Dude, what the fuck with the brakes?"

"So what? What's in the bag that's so important?" I asked, turning in my seat trying to pat Alice down with my hand but I couldn't reach her, so it only served to look like I was having some type of fit.

"Who are you waving at, Beth?" Alice panted at me.

I ignored her and said to Rory, "Surely she doesn't need a bag to have a baby? Go!" Rory ever so slowly put the jeep into first gear, ever so slowly focused on the road and got ready to move off.

I'd had enough. Years of pent-up frustration with Rory's oh-so-slow driving collided in my head. "Move!" I wrestled him out of his seat belt. "Move! Out!"

"Beth!" He went back into neutral (fast) and clung onto the steering wheel.

"What are ye doing up there?" Alice screamed.

"No, Rory, enough is enough! I'm driving the rest of the way and I am driving fast!" I tugged at his brown duffel-coat collar and he tugged it back.

"You are not insured to drive my jeep!" He dropped his head onto the steering wheel, knuckles white.

I pulled the tufts of his newly grown-out hair.

"*Ouch!* Beth, what are you doing?" He rubbed his head.

"Lads, what the fuck?" John's head popped up behind the passenger seat. Reeking of whiskey. "Let her drive, dude, you know what she's like, she won't give in. We will end up delivering the baby in the back – yer seats'll be ruined – I've seen *Casualty*, I've seen the shit that comes out . . ."

Rory moved. Out of the jeep, around the back and into the passenger seat. I slipped into the driver's seat.

"I . . ." Alice lifted her head from between her legs.

I turned the key and jammed her into first and we were away! Second. Third. Fourth Fifth. Red light!

"I can't imagine that I am actually in this scenario. It's all so weird . . . *ooouuucchh! Ooohhhh! Ooohh!*" Alice panted. "I miss Dan so much but I want to say thanks, Rory, you have helped me . . . so much I can't explain . . .

you are just amazing . . . and *ooouucchh! Oooohhh!* Ride me, Granny Miley!" She panted low now, short bursts of breath.

Who the hell was Granny Miley?

"And shut up – no one interrupt me!" As if we'd dare. "As for you, Beth Burrows, you never gave up. I tried to make you, I didn't support you enough but you never gave up on love . . ." She stopped and her hand flew down between her legs. "It's fucking coming, the baby is coming! Oh please ring an ambulance! Where are we?"

Green light. I put my foot to the floor.

"Two minutes, Alice, hang on!" I drove in through the small wooden gates of the hospital and almost went through the glass doors at the entrance.

John jumped out of the jeep and fell right into the wishing-well fountain.

I gently moved Alice out of the jeep and we took tiny baby steps to the reception.

Rory ran past us into the hospital foyer, screeching now and waving his hands in the air like a madman on speed. "Help! Please help us! The head's coming out!"

Alice and I staggered in.

Rory's glasses fell off and he stood on them.

John came in, dripping wet, laughing his head off, and neither Alice nor I looked at him.

"It's all going to be fine," I told her.

As quick as lightning a team were down with a moving hospital bed and Alice was secured on.

"Who's the father here?" a very large man in a light-blue suit asked.

"Who's asking?" I shot back at him as the lift doors opened.

334

"I'm the obstetrician on call this evening."

I'd thought he was Robbie Coltrane visiting someone. It was a private maternity hospital after all and they had VIP patients.

"*He's dead!*" Alice shouted. "*She's* coming into the delivery ward with me!"

I was, wasn't I? I'd almost forgotten. I'd tried to forget. Would I get through this? Would I? I felt faint already.

"Rory, you and John stay here," I said as Rory tried to balance his broken glasses on his nose, his head tilted to the left.

We entered the lift and exited into the delivery ward. I was told to scrub my hands and handed a gown.

A friendly nurse, with thick brown hair and *Gráinne McGarrell* on her yellow name-tag, winked at me. "Just hold onto the gown – you're okay unless we need to go to theatre."

I hoped they weren't showing *Rosemary's Baby*.

Alice was being hooked up to all sort of drips and machines and I sat at her side on a padded brown chair. One nurse took blood (I looked away) and another set round black sticky pads onto Alice's massive tummy and set up some kind of machine. Suddenly the room was filled with a rhythmic thump-thumping.

"What on earth is that?" I grabbed Gráinne by the hand.

"It's okay, pet," she answered, detaching herself from me. "That's just the electronic fetal monitoring – we call it the EFM. Basically it's assessing the fetal heart rate of the baby during labour."

I grabbed her again, this time both of her hands. "Of course it is, sorry, I've heard it loads of times at our Gyny appointments, I'm just a bit jumpy, what with John falling into the fountain and Rory breaking his glasses. I know exactly what the fetal heart rate is. The fetal heart rate just gives us an indication of how the baby is tolerating labour and if he or she is receiving enough oxygen."

"I am aware of that but thank you anyway." She prised my hands off hers and asked Alice, "Do you know the sex of your baby?"

We both shook our heads and Grainne went about her busy business.

"Calm. Down. Beth." Alice spoke very slowly to me.

I flopped into the padded chair and shut my eyes while I caught my breath.

"I'm going to examine you now." The large doctor at the end of the bed raised a blue-gloved hand before it disappeared again and Alice groaned. I'd seen an episode of *Emmerdale* once when a cow was in labour and the sound Alice had just made was uncannily like that.

"Okay, well, you are still only at five centimetres, Alice – it wasn't the head you felt anyway – probably a bruised pelvic bone." He whipped off the glove, opened the white pedal-bin at the back of the room with his foot and dropped the glove in. It closed with a loud clatter. "I will leave you now in Gráinne's very capable hands and she can call me if you need me. I'm on until breakfast so hopefully you might have delivered by then."

I laughed on the soft brown chair. Then I stopped. He wasn't looking amused. He wasn't joking. Could it really take that long with the pain she was already in?

So we laboured. We moaned and we swore a lot. I read a *National Geographic* in between times.

Alice's plan was not to ask for an epidural, so knowing

Alice as well as I did I was surprised when I heard her raised voice say the words: "Epidural, if you please?"

I didn't dare say, 'But I thought . . .'

"Yeah, of course," Gráinne said. "I'll call the anaesthetist right away. Is it okay if I just examine you again before I go?" She fussed around Alice and fixed drips and pillows before going down to the end of the bed and feeling for those precious centimetres.

I was still in this really uncomfortable dress and shoes so I decided to change into the scrubs anyway. "I'll be back in two seconds, Alice," I told her.

I changed into the much more comfy blue scrubs and put the little blue plastic shoes on over my tights. I spotted John and Rory on a couch reading magazines and watching a portable TV at the same time. *Coronation Street* was on and both of these men in my life had denied ever watching it a day in their lives.

"Wow, love of my life, you are looking smurftastically beautiful!" John laughed.

"Well?" Rory jumped up. He'd obviously gone to the jeep and got his new glasses which he was keeping for special occasions. He always kept a spare of glasses for emergency driving situations in his jeep. These ones were just too trendy for Rory, I knew. Since John had broken his last pair (even though Rory had them repaired), he'd felt responsible and took Rory to buy new ones, on him. John had picked them out. They were very trendy with Marc Jacobs frames that appeared invisible at times and they were pretty damn cool.

"Yeah, well, she's nowhere near as advanced as we thought – they say she might not deliver until the morning."

"Deliver what?" John was looking at some hotty's huge cleavage behind the bar at the Rover's Return.

"Are you serious? The morning?" Rory tried to push the glasses up his nose but they were already in perfect position. He wasn't used to them obviously as they never moved. Basically he just slid his finger up and down his nose. It sort of looked like he was insulting you. "Can we see her?"

I shook my head. "No, Rory, I think we should just let her relax. I'll go sit with her – let's not get her up to ninety again. She's getting an epidural now."

"Here, I got you these from the little shop downstairs." Rory pulled a brown bag from under his chair.

I opened it. Apples, Kit Kats, Capri Suns and Snax crisps. "Thanks." I kissed him on the cheek. "Now go back to *Corrie* and I'll pop out again in a bit."

"We weren't watching it," they both protested as I smiled and squelched away on the parquet flooring.

I pushed open the door of the labour room and nearly fainted. Even though I had read up on every aspect of childbirth nothing had prepared me for the size of the needle I saw. There was my best friend hunched over, clutching a pillow, while a man in a turban stuck a needle the size of a Vienna roll into her back. Alice's eyes were shut tight but she wasn't screaming. Gráinne made a sign for me to stay still and I did.

"Nearly there, my dear," the man told her. Then he attached a tube to whatever was now sticking out of her back and, throwing his gloves in the bin, went to the door. "I will be back in a bit to check how well it has taken."

Alice sat back with the help of Gráinne. There were pads and pads under her bum and they were saturated now with some sort of fluid that was pouring out of her. Her dress was hitched up over her pregnant tummy. I guess she'd left her dignity at the door as we were all supposed to.

"Okay, that should kick in pretty soon," Gráinne said. "I can tell on this," she waved some paper that looked like a fax to me, "when you are contracting so we can tell how well the epidural is working. If you are still feeling pain I will get him back. I need to fit a catheter now, pet, okay?"

"Okay, thanks so much."

I approached Alice.

"Mother of God, Beth, what do you look like?"

Ha, she could talk! But I didn't say so. "I couldn't breathe in your dress." I rummaged around in the bag. "Here's a packet of Snax."

Gráinne stopped me. "Oh, no – no food during labour!"

"Did you not read your notes?" Alice asked me, both women glaring at me.

I did. I'd forgotten. In case there might be an emergency section, no food in labour.

"I mean for – for after the baby – you know – as a treat," I lied my way unconvincingly.

"*Oh oh oh!*" Alice gripped my hand and I burst the bag of Snax – they went flying up in the air, landing on the white bed sheets and the blue top sheet.

"*Ooops!*" I gathered them all up as soon as she let go. Their smell was overpowering.

I sat and stared at the floor as Gráinne fitted a catheter and cleaned Alice up again. She put fresh paper pads and sheets under her.

Alice had been quiet for a while I realised now as

Gráinne leaned over and said, "Okay, that's quite a big contraction – are you feeling that, pet?"

"No . . . oh, mercy!" Alice punched the air. "Whoever invented this thing should be given the Nobel Peace Prize! Holy shit, Beth, those contractions were not fun!"

"Describe them," I couldn't help but ask.

"Okay." She pulled herself up a bit in the bed now. She reminded me of that girl in the movie *Airplane* with the guitar and all the tubes hanging out of her. "Imagine someone lit a fire in your belly, then poked a huge boiling hot knife into that fire before adding acid, well, something like that."

"Is it okay if I examine you again, pet?" Gráinne was at the bottom end.

"Yes, of course." This time Alice wasn't in pain as Gráinne poked and prodded,

"Okay, still at six, I'm afraid, so I'm going to pop off now and go on my break – the best thing you can do is try and get some sleep."

I laughed out loud.

"What?" Gráinne smiled at me.

"Well, you're obviously joking, right? You can't sleep when a baby is about to pop out of you."

"No baby will be popping out any time soon, I can tell you that much, so yeah, I strongly suggests she sleeps."

Alice pulled the blue top cover up to her neck. "I will actually, Beth, if you don't mind. Why don't you pop up to the canteen with the boys and get something to eat? I'm getting cold and I want to snuggle down."

Her teeth were beginning to chatter so I kissed her on the forehead and went to the canteen with the boys.

We bought some food and drinks, settled down at a

table and tucked in.

"Tell me now, Rory," John said, black coffee to his lips, "like, are you and my sister going to continue living together after the baby is born? She'll be titty-feeding and all that."

Rory went puce.

"John!" I dropped my plastic fork into my chicken salad. "That's not appropriate conversation."

"Well, John," said Rory, "I would like that eventually one day down the line I may see a real tit in the flesh and sure it may as well be your sister's."

I couldn't believe it. "Guys, what are you two on? Stop. Think of Dan – this conversation isn't even funny."

They both looked suitably embarrassed and disgusted.

"We have discussed our futures, though – well, our immediate futures," Rory said then, taking a huge bite from his sausage sandwich.

"What?" I wanted to know more.

He chewed for what seemed like eternity, pointing to his mouth as he chewed.

"Yes, I know you are chewing, Rory – that's why I am waiting for you to swallow so you can finish what you were saying."

John spat a little of his coffee over the table and rubbed the brown liquid with his hand. "I just find it hilarious that you two thought you were compatible," he said.

"We were!" we both shouted at him now.

"Listen," said Rory then. "We have talked about being in each other's lives. I love being with Alice and Lucy and I want to be around all the time for New Bubble."

I'd never heard the expression 'New Bubble' before and it hurt a little. I thought it was called Bumpy.

"We just talked about being together, as friends, as companions, as . . . we get on so well . . . she says in a way I remind her of Dan. Well, I'm happy . . . I'm happy with that . . . *dude*!" He spat the word 'dude' at John, who had taken the rest of Rory's sausage sandwich and eaten it all while he was talking.

"She never told me any of this." I was kind of relieved though. I got a warm fuzzy feeling in my stomach. I knew Rory would look after her and Lucy and the new baby and I was also overwhelmingly relieved that he was happy.

"It's not a big deal. She sees it as a clever move and so do I . . . split bills, baby-sitter on tap . . . I'm still hungry now . . ."

There was no more to say on the subject.

"Can I borrow a phone? I need to call Tara," I said.

Rory obliged and I dialled her. She told me everything was perfect, that she was just locking up, that the RTÉ News had been down and she had given an interview and that now she was going to meet Bono. I rang off.

We had another round of coffees and John and Rory paced up and down the canteen.

"Okay, let's go back," I said.

We cleared off our table and the lads went back to sit in their seats and I went into the delivery room.

"You're ready to push. We need to get you into the labour room immediately," Gráinne was saying calmly but strictly to Alice as she began to push the bed towards the door.

"*Beth!*" Alice yelled at me.

"*Fffuucckk* . . . I thought you were going to sleep?" I did a jog on the spot before running my hands over and over through my short hair.

"She progressed really quickly, almost unheard of," said Gráinne. "I just examined her and she's ten centimetres now."

I clapped. I don't know why.

"Her epidural has worn off and she has asked me not to top it up," said Gráinne as we sped along. "She feels prepared now to feel her own contractions."

We entered the labour room.

"Oh! Oh! Here's one, Gráinne!" Alice sat bolt upright and squeezed her hands tightly together.

"Okay – if you can grab a leg," Gráinne told me, "and, Alice, can you grasp the other leg? Bend your knee and hold your leg tight from behind the knee, like this – and when you feel that next contraction, remember, chin down and eyes wide open, and when I say push, pet, you push."

I grabbed her leg and bent it, her foot pushing into my hand. I closed my legs together, pulled up that imaginary zip on my vagina.

Gráinne had her head up Alice's ass and in a muffled voice she said, "And, okay, let us know . . ."

Alice let out a tribal roar. "*Arghatatfhhathaaaallahhh eelllalllllaaaapooooopppppp!*" Her head fell back onto the pillow and she looked at me. She didn't need any words – her eyes said it all.

"Okay, pet, but I need you to keep those eyes open and push for a little bit longer, okay?"

We waited. It was like waiting for a bomb to go off.

"Okay, here we go again!" Gráinne said. "And *push*! Keep pushing, keep pushing, keep pushing, keep pushing, keep pushing, keep pushing, keep pushing, keep pushing . . ."

Alice, in fairness to her, was pushing.

Nothing. No cry. No baby.

We waited again.

"It's coming again! They're getting worse now!" Alice shouted.

"Push it! Push it real good!" I offered. I cringed.

"*Arrrrrrrrrrrrrrrrrgrthhhhhhhhhhhhhhh tits!*" Her head fell back. Her face was purple, the veins in her neck the size of thick udon noodles. I was steering clear of Wagamama for a while.

Gráinne went in again. "Okay, Alice, relax for a minute and don't push again until I tell you. Breathe though it, pet, breathe through it . . . The baby's head is there all right but I think we are going to need some help getting baby out. I'm going to have to call the doctor . . . I'll be right back."

She left and we looked at each other.

"Oh God, what does that mean? The head is what? Where? Why do we need the doctor?" Her face was purple and wet with sweat. She who never sweated, or 'perspired' as she would always correct me: 'Women do not sweat, they perspire.'

Well, Alice, you are sweating now, love, sweating like a pig! I didn't say this.

The doctor entered with Gráinne. He headed to a silver trolley and picked up a contraption. It looked like a massive rubber sink stopper.

"This is a suction cup, all right? I'm going to attach it to baby's head and I will pull and guide and you push – we need to get Baby out now. You can't get it out yourself." Suddenly I was really scared. I didn't like the sound of his tone. I looked up at Gráinne – she wasn't smiling now either.

"Alice, listen to me now – when the next contraction –"

He didn't get to finish. Alice was roaring and pushing and going an even darker shade of purple and he was doing a sidewards jog with his rubber partner down the bottom.

I was useless. Again. Lately in Alice's life all I was was useless. But then it hit me as I gripped her hand: I was there. I was here. I was always here or there for her. Always. I didn't have to have the answers. I just had to be present.

Alice yelped. She pushed and pushed and I encouraged and encouraged until Gráinne put her finger on her lips and told me to shush: I had been making more noise than the labouring woman.

"Listen to me, Alice," said the doctor, "stop pushing – lie back a minute and relax – take some deep breaths – good girl – on the next push we can do this so I need you to give me the longest push of your life, okay? It's the hardest pooh you have ever had to get out!"

Alice lay back, eyes blazing. Linda Blair in *The Exorcist* hadn't a patch on her. Serena Williams would have been proud of the noise that came out of her mouth next. "*Hhhhhhhhhhhhhhhhhhhhhhhhhhhhhhhhhhhhhhhhahhhh hhhhhhhhhhhhhhhhhhhhhhhhhhhhhhhnnnnnnnnnnnnnnnnn nnnnnnnnnnnnnnnhhhhhhhhhhhhhhhhhhhhhhhhhhhhhhh hhhhhhhhnnnnnnnnnnnnnnnnnnnnnhhhhhhhhhhhhhhhhhhh hhhhhhhhhhhhhhhhhhhhhhhhhhhhhhhhhhhhhhhhhhhhhh hhhhhhhhhhhhhhhhhhhhhhhhhhhhhhhhhhhhhh!*"

The doctor stood up. Nurses ran. The paediatrician had entered too: I guessed that was what he was as he had pink-and-blue teddy bears down the middle of his cap.

Something blue and floppy was whisked to the corner

and a group of people huddled around it.

"Is it okay? Is my baby okay?" Alice cried now.

I grabbed her hand. "Of course Baby's okay! They have to check everything out, remember, like we watched. Clear the air path and all that? Are you okay? What a job? You are totally amazing! I love you, Alice Callan!"

Still no cry. I needed to keep talking.

"Did it hurt much then? It didn't seem too bad to me now."

She looked at me now with her big wet eyes and then, joy of all joy, a roar from over yonder and voices were heard again.

Gráinne turned to us. "Congratulations, Alice, you have a beautiful baby boy!" She placed a purplish, whitish, wriggling creature all wrapped up tightly in a blue towel on Alice's chest.

"Cut this, can you?" Alice beseeched the nurse as she tugged at her party TK Max maternity dress. The nurse cut the pink material away.

I don't think Alice had been as prepared as she'd thought. It was impossible to be prepared for labour, I realised, as it was an area no one knew how to handle. No one.

Alice placed the baby on her bare flesh and held him close. I stared at him as he tried to open his tiny eyes. He snuffled his little nose and his mouth opened slightly. I saw his pure pink tongue slip out and then back in. He smelled his mammy. He was beautiful. Oh so beautiful. With tiny tufts of bright red hair.

"He is perfect – nine pounds exactly," said Gráinne, "so well done you! I'm going to make you a nice cuppa tea and some toast."

"Thank you, no sugar," I answered, never taking my

eyes off the baby. His head was cut from where he'd literally been sucked out. Like someone had carved a semi-circle into his head.

The doctor was still down Alice's end, awaiting the arrival of the placenta, I knew. I drew the line at the placenta. Even the word made me gag. God knows what else he was doing. I tried to put it out of my mind as Alice winced and covered her mouth with her hand.

"Okay," I squeezed it, "you're nearly there – look what you have, oh Alice, look what you have!"

She put her index finger into his tiny palm and he held it tight. He smelled wonderful. I breathed him in deep. It was a smell I'd never smelt before. I knew John would tell me I was smelling Alice's insides so I vowed never to tell him of my infatuation with this new smell.

"Will you feed him yourself or give him formula?" Gráinne asked.

"I'm going to do a bit of both, please. I'll try him now on the breast but I'm going to give him formula at night. Rory's offered to share some night feeds with me." She looked up. "And thanks, thanks so much, Gráinne – you were amazing!" She lay her head back down. "Oh, thank God that's over!" She smiled at me.

"Congratulations, Mammy," I said and I kissed her forehead.

The doctor was pressing on her tummy now, still awaiting the placenta, and needed to take more blood, so Alice held up her right arm. No veins left. They went to her left.

"Oh Beth, that was indescribable! I can't say what it was – I felt every inch of him come out through my body – it was so painful it got to a stage where it wasn't sore any more – I was becoming immune. It was the pushing I found hardest – it was utterly exhausting and I had a really quick labour! You hear of women who actually labour for days! I will never look at any mother in the same light again. How do we do it? Have I put you off for life?"

It was almost time for her first feed and she gritted her teeth now as the doctor sewed some tears. I felt she needed some privacy.

"On the contrary, Alice – for the first time really in my entire life, I think . . . I really, really want a baby! And I don't know how to say this, but . . . but . . . all I could think of when I saw him being lowered into your arms was . . . I can't wait to go Converse-shopping for him!"

Chapter Twenty-eight

It's bitterly cold as I look out at the Paris Christmas street lights twinkling back at me. We are in The Ritz. I know. I can't believe it either. We both had business meetings here. I have been asked to design the wedding jewellery for an aristocratic Parisian family for a June wedding here at the Ritz next year. John is meeting a famous French actor he wants to star in his new movie. I saw the two having coffee in the hotel's Le Petit Jardin under the enormous indoor chestnut tree this morning. I'd popped out to buy an extra hot latte and a chocolate croissant. I had to stop and stare at the pair of them, just like every other woman in the hotel. We were all just standing there, staring at these two unbelievably sexy men. I had leaned against the tree and sipped my coffee while I stared. John saw me but just smiled and kept on talking. He had scripts and pens and yellow notelets splayed all over the table.

Earlier this morning John Callan had handed me a box. All wrapped in shiny gold paper. I opened the box slowly. It was my charm bracelet. I had taken it off the morning of the wedding and I hadn't been able to find it since. Well, to be honest, we'd all been so occupied I'd presumed it was in the house somewhere so I wasn't overly worried. I was secure in the knowledge it wasn't the type of bracelet anyone would want to steal. Well, it hadn't been until now. Anyway, I'd looked at it for a few minutes before I saw what he had done. He'd had it fixed. The broken dog, the broken lady, the broken glitter ball all as good as new. But it was the fourth charm that really got me. My broken heart. A metal charm in the shape of a heart that had cracked with age and wear and tear right down the middle. He'd had it fixed. It had been welded back together, probably some metal added to it, and he'd had our names engraved onto it in tiny, tiny letters: John on the top and Beth on the bottom. *John loves Beth*. I held it tightly up to my squinting eyes. I looked closer. You couldn't tell where they had once been old and forgotten and tarnished. Now they were gleaming and polished and fixed. Just like me.

I was lost for words so I did what I did best with John. I had sex with him. Right there, right then.

I'm wearing my bracelet now. John is sprawled out on the bed, topless in just his black Gap jeans and bare feet. He got his hair cut this morning – it's short and sort of spiky – it really suits him (surprise surprise). He looks happy and contented. He is drinking a whiskey and Coke.

We are soon to leave for the airport for our flight home. I stare back at the lights and light a cigarette. My last packet. We are both giving up on New Year's Day. I mean it this time. I inhale deeply and hold the smoke for too long at the thought of parting with this old friend for good. We made a lot of plans last night over dinner.

I think about our date now. It was all John's idea.

"Let's go out on a date, meet in a restaurant somewhere. Let's get dressed up?" He looked like a sixteen-year-old boy. He was excited by the idea of going on a date with me.

"What? Like in me wear a dress?" I asked, appalled.

He laughed. I melted.

"Yeah, darling, a dress. You did bring a dress, to Paris, the fashion capital of the world, didn't you?"

I nodded.

I lied. I ran to the shops when he was observing people for an hour in reception and bought one.

He got ready first while I dried my hair. He made me close my eyes as he left the room. I don't know why but I found it really sexy. He put an address on a piece of torn-off hotel stationary paper in my hand. "Meet me there in an hour." Then he felt my bottom and left.

I did my make-up and tried to copy the make-up artist's look on the wedding morning. I thought about Dan. Big Dan not Baby Dan. Although I do think about Baby Dan all the time too. Baby Dan O'Toole is the most beautiful baby in the world. I am his godmother. John and I are his godparents. Rory and Alice seem very relaxed around each other. I know that one day it will turn into a romance and so do they but it's a long way down the line. Alice's heart will never love the same way again. She's been saved in lots of ways by the baby and having Lucy but she's still rather empty. Rory is the perfect filler. We go to Dan's grave all the time. All of us.

She's been running Beth's Bitz like a professional. Like she's been at it all her life. The shop is doing incredibly well. It looks fantastic and I have been finding it really easy to design pieces for it. On the yellow walls we have pictures of all the famous people who have worn my jewellery and pictures of non-famous people who have worn it. My favourites are the pictures of the schoolgirls wearing The Individuals and brides wearing my pieces. These comfort me somehow.

I'm not all that religious, but I have belief, my belief, and sometimes I don't share because I don't want to be judged. But I can't help thinking that Dan was behind all of this success of mine. It's just a deep deep gut feeling.

Tara continues to promote my work all over the world and sometimes the phone rings and I nearly collapse when I hear the famous name on the end of the line who she recommended me to. She's a great friend and an inspiration.

Louise, who was home with Brad to pack up the last of her belongings, had come in to see the shop last week. She and Brad had bought a small farm holding in Arizona and they were hoping to both work at The Meadows while raising cattle. She looked brilliant. She'd put on a lot of weight but it really suited her. She smiled all the time. She had written some of the most beautiful letters I have ever seen to Lucy. She and Brad and Lucy had gone to see the latest Disney movie. I'd asked her about Frame and designing again but she'd shook her head. She has no desire to own a store like me. "I still make things, for the patients mostly as good-luck parting gifts – that's enough for me."

I'd had to ask her about Paula Mak. Her mother had tried to woo her back, she told us. When she'd gone to visit her on the last trip Paula had been all "Oh how I've missed you, darling, I'm so glad you are back, here's a bottle of vodka, now go up to your room and design, we are way behind on new pieces."

Her father had sat on a chrome chair and said nothing.

Louise hadn't spoken either. She had simply tottered over the huge marble floor and up the massive winding staircase and pulled her rucksack from under her bed.

"What on earth are you doing now?" her mother had asked, raising her voice at her.

"I am leaving, Mother. I am moving to Arizona and I want to close Frame."

"Over my dead body, you stupid, stupid girl!" Paula had begun shouting.

Her father had appeared at the bedroom door. "Let her go, Paula, it's time, let her go." And she had.

And Louise had never spoken to either of them since. She'd bought a few pieces in the shop, although I tried and tried to get her to just take them.

"You never know, I might be needing a fancy white piece soon," she'd winked at me and Brad had laughed.

"Will you ever speak to them again?" I'd asked her as we hugged at the door.

"I guess I will, Beth, someday. Brad wants me to. I'm just not there yet."

Louise was another great friend and another inspiration. I was blessed with wonderful friends.

I thought I did a good job on my make-up. Eyes dark and kohl-lined. Light foundation and clear-glossed lips (not too glossy as John didn't like kissing sticky lips).

I took the dress out of the bag. It had been bloody expensive. It was white. A wonderful blinding white. Like the first fall of snow onto rooftops. It was above the knee (just) which is so short for me I can't even tell you. It was sleeveless and backless. I wondered if I had made a huge mistake and would have to put my jeans back on.

I slipped it over my head and I didn't look in the mirror.

353

I had no tights. I was no longer tanned. I lost my tan in a few days once I was back home in Ireland. I was white but I thought that was okay as I am a white person. I shoved my feet into the black high heels Alice gave me with the red-painted soles and heels. I only brought them to wear around the bedroom as I know John loves them.

I stood. I wobbled. I turned to the mirror and I smiled. Motherfucker, I looked sexy as hell. The dress clung in all the right places and my arms were toned from carrying stock to and from the car for so long at the market. I had also been carrying Baby Dan a lot lately.

I stared at myself again. My hair was letting me down as it had grown out somewhat and I needed it cut again. John liked it. He did say one night he preferred it long and straight but I'm sticking to my short cut. I love it. It's so handy. I went to my bag and fished out a red flower grip. I had made it before we came away. The flower – a little rose – was made of deep red velvet. I slid it into the side of my hair and it grasped the overgrown fringe. I was done.

I grabbed my coat and I headed to reception where they called me a cab. The Ritz is pretty good at stuff like that. The taxi drove fast and Paris whizzed past my window, like one of those movies where the lights blur into one. The restaurant was down a dark alley (wouldn't you know) and it was called La Maison Beath. I got it. I paid the taxi and pushed the marble-looking door open. The smells were divine: garlic mixed with coriander and the sweet smell of sauces (my appetite arrived back the second John and I got engaged . . . with a vengeance . . . wouldn't you know . . .) I very carefully held the banister as I trailed down the stone steps. I removed my coat.

And there was my date. My fiancé. At the bar. He was

in a black suit, a crisp white shirt and skinny black tie, shoes polished. He looked better than any dish they could serve me in here. He smiled and then stood and then smiled wider and then sat and stood again. He ate me up in the dress.

He laughed and spat the pip of an olive into a tissue on the bar beside his drink.

"Christ on a bike, you look amazing. God, you are amazing! Sit." He pulled out a stool and I wriggled up.

"Champagne, madame?" he offered.

"No, you know I hate champagne. I'll have a nice glass of cold white wine though." I pulled at the skirt, convinced everyone was seeing my green Monday, days-of-the-week-themed Penney's knickers.

He ordered the bottle of wine and I stared at his hands as he held the money in them. I was so lucky that they were the hands that I can hold. I reached out and touched his hand. I still had that fear of the time in the Globe bar when he pulled it away from me. But not any more.

I need to let it go.

The wine came and he poured and we clinked glasses.

"Hot date?" he role-played.

"Well, I was seeing this guy, ya know, for years – he dumped me so, ya know, I'm on the prowl now." I pursed my lips together, probably a bit more like Mick Jagger than Marilyn Monroe.

He nodded. "What an asshole he must have been!"

"Yeah, he was a bit, I suppose," I said a little quieter than I meant to and we locked eyes.

"I bet he'd be really fucking sorry if he could see you now?" John looked away and swirled his wine around his frosted glass.

"You think?" I grinned.

"Oh yeah . . . I know that for a fact." He drank a long drink and held the wine in his mouth for a few seconds before swallowing.

"He said he loved me too much . . . that's why he left me."

John nodded and put his wineglass down, picked up the whiskey glass and sipped it. On occasion John liked to have two different drinks. "I'd imagine, deep down he always thought you were too good for him, yeah?" he said, finally revealing a card.

"I don't know why he'd ever have thought that. I always thought we were very equal," I whispered to him.

"I don't know the guy but I imagine he thought you could do better than him," he whispered back and looked down at the sawdust on the floor.

"No . . . never could, impossible . . . my heart rules, you see, and in fact he's the greatest guy I've ever met. In every way. He's so clever and interesting and sexy and kind and he's my soul mate."

John took my hands and pressed them to his lips. His lips were warm. "You never gave up on me, Beth. You never thought I was a waster dodging around being mental, did you?"

"No." I shook my head and my rose came loose. I needed to rethink the grip on these. Extra rubber maybe?

John fixed it. "It was me who thought that about myself," he said. Then he took a deep breath that seemed to come from his heart. "I think I left you also because I thought you wanted me to change, Beth, and I didn't know that I could. That day . . . the same day you said about the actors . . . you said . . ." He laughed now and shook his head. "Unreal. I can't even remember what you said, but anyway you slagged off the profession. I just thought: she doesn't get me. Added to the fact I was sitting in a restaurant again with you paying and I had not a brass penny in my wallet. It's not good for a man's ego. I thought: I'm never going to be who she wants me to be. She deserves a guy who can protect her, who has a steady job and a normal frame of mind, not me." He paused. "I did love you too much. I loved you too much to see you ending up with a loser like me. I wanted the world for you, Beth, I wanted it all."

I shushed him. "It's okay – you've told me all this before."

"Last time, I promise. I just want to get the rest out," he sighed. "It's because you are perfect. I never so much as looked at another woman in all the time we were together. Then when I got to the States and got that job so quickly it kind of took over my life. I struggled so much to learn the bloody lines every night that my entire day and night from the second I walked off that set was spent learning lines. It was a frighteningly quick turnover on set – no rehearsing just bang, bang, bang. I hadn't learned anything in years. I struggled. I had no time to think and it was great and, yes, whenever I rang Alice I asked about you and she always told me you were brilliant, that you had moved on, and that it was the right time for us to split. She told me you had found yourself, that you were finally able to go back to college and become a designer, that I had stopped you from achieving that, that you wanted to settle down and have a family. She basically told me I wasn't good enough for you, Beth. Alice said some incredibly harsh things to me . . ."

I swallowed hard. It still hurt. How could she have done that to me?

He went on when he saw my face. "But now I understand what she was doing. She was pushing me, pushing me hard to see if I really loved you. To see what would I do for you."

"But she knew I was hurting so bad," I whispered.

"Yeah, she did, and just before the wedding she told me that you still loved me, that you would always love me. She warned me not to play with you and I got so uncomfortable and excited that I told her I was playing with everyone – don't ask me why I said something so idiotic. Anyway, she told me what she thought of me and left. The next time I see her I am on the ground comforting her after her husband-to-be dies."

We both took a moment. I drank. He refilled.

"Anyway, that's why when you knocked on my hotel door I didn't tell you to go back to Rory. I think I knew we were going to be okay."

"She told you I loved you *before* we'd slept together?" I asked now, my mouth wide open.

"Yeah, she did, just before you knocked on my door actually."

So that's why she'd been so cross in Bruxelles as she bit her nails hard! She had given him the information, told him I still loved him, put my life in his hands and he'd said something so stupid like he "was playing with everyone". Typical John. That must have driven Alice up the wall.

The waiter approached us to tell us our table was ready. We picked up our drinks and followed him down more concrete steps, John linking me.

The dining area was in fact a wine cellar and it was

superb. Yes, the Eiffel Tower was out there and the Champs-Elysées and the Louvre Museum and Sacre Coeur but this was one of the most special, untouristy places in Paris I had ever been to. We sat and the waiter shook beautiful blinding-white linen napkins across our knees.

I looked at John over the red candle in the wine bottle, the old wax creating a wonderful design on its neck, like valleys of small rivers. I picked at it a little bit.

He was pulling at his tie.

"Take it off." I leant over and undid it.

"Christ, that's sexy, Beth," he groaned.

"Really, is it?" I folded the tie up carefully and put it in my bag. I've always loved carrying things for John in my bag. His keys. His phone. His wallet. His naggins on occasion. I'd happily carry it all.

He undid the top three buttons on the white shirt and his tanned skin appeared. "So it's not like I can't explain and it's not like I ever stopped loving you. I just got caught out, got caught up and the soap took over and when Alice told me about the dude I did try and date another actress. The first time I kissed her I felt my mouth was too big and her tongue was horrific – well, I guess what I felt, Beth, was that she wasn't you."

I leant back.

"But you slept with other women, right?"

He leant back now and allowed the waited pour our wine. "No. Never."

I was gobsmacked. Literally my mouth was dangling open.

"That night in the hotel, in The Shelbourne was the first night I had sex since I walked away from you."

No wonder it was so bloody good. "Come on, that is not true, John Callan!"

"Cross my heart, Beth, it is." He shut his eyes tight and crossed his heart with his left hand. "I can't think of you and the dude doing it, I really can't."

"Stop!" I raised my hand and he raised his to pull mine down and then I see it. He is wearing the promise ring I made him.

He saw me spot it and he twisted it off and handed it to me. "I wore it every day on every show I filmed and you never noticed? Did you never watch? I mean, were you never curious about whether I was any good?"

"No, sure we don't get it here." I stared hard at the ring.

"But I sent copies to Alice all the time."

I shook my head and let a slow low breath out. "She never told me."

He nodded slowly. "Wow, she really didn't want us to be together, did she?"

I digested the information. "She loves you, John. She loves me. I think she thought we were too different. I don't think she ever watched the tapes herself – you know Alice, she hates soaps. Alice isn't mean – it's just not in her nature to be so – so I guess she did what she thought was right. She saw how bad I was when you left me – she was scared. I really scared her and my family. I scared myself. I was completely devastated and out of control. The thought of walking the rest of my life and not having you by my side was too much for me to bear. Alice minded me, she took care of me. She was and is an amazing friend. I don't know where I'd be in my life without my Alice."

Our soups arrived and the waiter crunched out lots of black pepper as we sat back and watched. When he left John leaned over the small square table and took my face in his hands. He kissed me then, hard and lingering, and I tasted the inside of his mouth, the wine and the whiskey, our tongues wildly caressing each other. Then I slipped his promise ring back onto his wedding finger before he sat back, leaving me breathless as usual.

"So just one other thing I have to ask. Were you really going to marry the dude?"

I thought about his question for a few seconds. "I honestly don't know, John," I replied truthfully.

"Did you love him that much?" He shook his head.

I just wanted to kiss him again and again. "It's like this, John – he was, he is, a great, kind, easygoing guy and we fell into each other's lives by chance. I was just rolling along, gathering momentum, trying desperately to get over you. No one wanted to hear about you any more – but he did . . . he listened . . . we were okay, really . . . it wasn't *Casablanca* but it wasn't *The Mirror Has Two Faces* either. I . . . didn't want this again." I thrust my spoon at his beauty. "I think I just wanted simplicity – but then you came back and I didn't know what to do – so, me being me, I hastily moved in with him. I really hurt him, John . . . I still hate myself for it."

John flicked his index finger through the candle flame now at speed.

"Okay, one thing I have to ask you then too," I said. "That time you came home, you were auditioning for something and you stayed with some mad film director in Killiney. I went everywhere looking for you, to all your old haunts, I even stole a fruit bowl from my parents' house and called to your parents with it, pretending I was returning it. Why did you never come and see me? Why did you never try and contact me?"

He nodded. "I didn't come home for an audition at all

– I just said that. I came home to say goodbye to one of my Lifers – to spend his last few days with him."

I stared at him questioningly.

He sniffed. "He didn't have anyone left and I'd always promised him," he answered as though explaining himself to me. "Old Lar Kilroy – he was such an incredible man. Brave. A gentleman through and through. He was alive during the 1916 rising, you know. One day when all hell was breaking loose down at the GPO he ran into town with the looters. He saw them breaking the window of Kathleen's, a shop on O'Connell Street, and he ran over. People were taking everything. He fought his little scrappy way in and he stole a massive box of biscuits out of the window. Grown men tried to prise it from his dirty fingers but he held his ground. He ran all the way home in his bare feet, never stopping for a second, all down O'Connell Street, into D'Olier Street, down Townsend Street and over Ringsend Bridge into his room in a house in Irishtown. Up the stairs he went and shut the door tight behind him, putting his back to it. He slid his hands over the metallic box. He remembered the cover of the lid so vividly: brown and red. It was a round box with a painting of a little boy sitting on a red biscuit tin holding a chocolate biscuit up in the air in his right hand. He was wearing a dark brown waistcoat with a light brown shirt underneath, brown shorts and white knee-length socks with brown strap-over shoes. The boy was smiling. Slowly, with saliva forming in his mouth, Lar licked his lips and opened the lid. Now remember, Beth, he hadn't had food, never mind a fucking biscuit, in weeks – scraps was all he got – and when he opened the lid, wasn't it only a display box! He'd robbed the display box! It was filled with pebbles."

"Noooo!" I almost shouted. I was devastated for Lar. "Oh, you are not serious? Oh, no, that's absolutely awful!" I shook my head.

"Yeah, 'fraid so – anyway he was such an amazing man, so I always checked in with the home – Sir Patrick Duns – where he lived the last few years and we even got to speak a few times on the phone, so when I got the call from Eileen Kilkenny in there to say Lar was dying I flew home straight away. I told work it was my own grandfather. I sat by his bedside for three days and nights holding his old frail hand until he took his last breath. I never left him for a second. He knew I was there. I know he did."

My body shook with a huge sob but he grabbed my hand.

"No, come on, it's okay – Lar was happy to go. He had tremendous faith and he was looking forward to seeing all the people he once loved – he missed them all – he had been alone for too long – it was time." He sighed. "So basically I was in big trouble with the job for taking so long off – soaps wait for no man!" He laughed now – to mask his own sadness, I could tell. "I flew straight back the day he passed over but not before I went to Brown Thomas and I bought the most expensive box of biscuits the store had. I went back to Patrick Duns and I told Eileen, 'I want these biscuits to go in with him, you understand?' She did and she promised me. I didn't get to stay for his funeral but I wrote a poem and Eileen read it for me. He left me his brown waistcoat. He'd saved up for years and bought it in Switzer's when he got his first job in the ESB. A fantastic dark-brown suede waistcoat that I treasure. Just like the boy on the biscuit tin, he told me. I thought about you more during those days than I had in months . . . you consumed my thoughts, Beth."

I nodded at him and composed myself.

"Okay, your soup is going well cold, so come on. Happy eating date, girl, and congratulations on your kickass business – I'm so proud of you." He drew my hand slowly down his face, then let it go, before adding, "Thanks for taking me back, Beth Burrows."

His dark eyes darted in his head and I knew he was nervous about me and nervous of ever hurting me again. I knew right then he never would.

I blew on the spoonful of soup – it was still hot – then sipped a little. Potage Bonne Femme, it was called, and the words looked so fancy on the menu but really it was just vegetable soup. He had gone for the Chilled Asparagus and Lemongrass soup with Grilled Sea Scallops and Tangerine Essence, wouldn't you know. I wished I had. I might the next time. My spoon dangled mid-air.

"You were never fake, John, you were always you. You have always been true to yourself. You may have doubted yourself but you were always who you are. I've been fake because I pretended I could live happily without you and I couldn't. I existed but without you I never felt really, properly alive. I couldn't get over you no matter how hard I tried but I pretended, because I didn't want people to judge me, to think I was nuts. I was fake, simple as that. But you never cared what people thought of you and that's why I loved you and that's why I love you still. You can always be you and now I can always be me and we can live happily ever after."

We laughed.

I ate my soup. He tore apart a warm crusty roll and dipped it in his and sucked the soupy bread.

So now my life is firmly back on track. I still can't quite believe I am standing on the balcony in my room at The Ritz in Paris with John Callan's ring on my finger. Did I mention the ring was his grandmother's? It's beautiful and unique.

I look out at the lights. Paris at Christmas is something special. There isn't an ounce of tackiness about it. The bare trees on both sides of the road are glittering with white fairy lights entwined in the branches. The cold wind is almost visible. John and I haven't discussed wedding plans and I know we won't for many years if indeed ever. I am happy with that.

I think of the year about to close on us, of all that has happened. Of Dan being killed, of Louise, of my parents moving away, of hurting Rory, of Alice getting custody of Lucy, of the arrival of Baby Dan, of the massive success of Beth's Bitz, of my beautiful, incredible new store waiting for me in Dublin.

I lean against the silver railings. It's been such a whirlwind of emotions. I welcome the cold air as I turn around and look at John again. Still sprawled out on the bed, drinking his whiskey. Picture perfect. And finally I allow myself to think of us. I got him back. I entwine my fingers together and squeeze them tight. He's running his hands though his new short hair and he catches me staring at him. He winks at me and hops off the bed, our matching white Converse at the base, and he stands at the open balcony door.

I close my eyes and a salty tear trickles out of my left eye down my face. I stick out my tongue to catch it and I lick it away. He rubs the dampness it has left behind. Relief floods through my veins again.

I got him back.

I got me back.

If you enjoyed
I Always Knew by Caroline Grace-Cassidy,
why not try an exclusive chapter of her forthcoming
title *Already Taken* being published in 2015.

Already Taken – Chapter One

Kate Walsh

It was an unusual job, yes, I will freely admit that. I wasn't innovative in its creation – it had been done before but I never knew anyone with the job so it was new to me. I felt like I had created my own version of it. I felt like Zuckerberg and his Facebook. I didn't have a name or a title for this job of mine. I invented my own rules and regulations. Yes, agreed, it was a risky job. Yes, agreed, it was probably kind of stupid to advertise my services on the big wide scary tinterweb, but I was sick of being me. Sick of it all. Sick of being in shit form because of my shit job.

I'm not one to moan, well, rarely – I am a loner so there's no one there to listen to me really. Here's the thing though: I am a contented loner which I am surprisingly proud to admit. I love life, don't get me wrong – it's just I like my own company and sometimes I will admit it would be nice if life loved me back. Anyway, I was more than ready for a taste of life's widely reported adventures.

I was so fed-up I was close to the running-away-and-joining-the-circus state of mind. Basically, I was truly bored with the banality of my daily existence. Of getting up every morning and feeling like gluten-laden brown bread. Truly sick and tired of knowing where every solitary penny I earned was going. A rainy day would be very, very wet for me – the type of rain people say soaks you to the bone.

I had never known what I wanted to do for a living, granted, but I had always known just what I didn't want to do which was exactly what I *was* doing. I always thought something better was out there for me but, like so many of us, I thought it would just land in my lap. If it was for me it wouldn't go past me. I didn't think I had the power to make the changes. I'm not getting all 'The Secret' on you now – it's just in the end that's what happened: I did it for myself. (I haven't read *The Secret* but it does keep my couch level because one of the mini-wheels fell off it and the book sits in its place, so technically it is keeping me upright. It was a birthday present from my sister Ciara – she loves it. I choose to listen to her hyping of it but make no comment when she informs me of the asking-the-universe theory. She needs to believe it. God knows she needs to believe it.)

My life had been mostly pretty normal and predictable and then suddenly it went tits up. But before the boobies pointed upwards I'd always known what I didn't want to do and that was to be stuffed into the rat-race suitcase, the zips pulled together and then fitted with one of those tiny useless gold suitcase locks. Shit happens. I had no choice. I went to work to earn money. That was exactly how I had felt before the new job. Part of the rat race.

My alarm sickened my ears at seven every morning, I

smacked it a box then I trudged (some ladies may say padded, but I never padded anywhere unless it was my time of the month) to the loo, showered, put on my brown skirt, brown shirt, brown tights, brown shoes and yellow tie. I ate a bowl of Crunchy Nut Corn*fakes*. I could never afford the original brand of anything. I washed my bowl. I got my keys and I got my bag and I took my exact change in bus fare from the glass hall table and I walked the ten minutes to the overly crowded bus stop. I tried to shove my way on the bus. Sometimes I was successful, other times I used incredibly bad language when I was not successful. Then I got off the bus at the end of Suffolk Street and went up the battered stairs to the small office that I worked in.

Photocopiers Services. Yes. It did exactly what it said on the small plaque on the navy door. We serviced photocopiers. We sold photocopiers. I sat in between Jane and Lisa under the small window with the peeling white paint and the constant bird poo. Jane was the most boring girl I had ever met in my entire life. She quite literally had nothing to say. She wore her long thin black hair down around her face and applied bright pink lipstick throughout the day. Jane also ate those Bombay Mixes from nine to five, all day long. Crunch – crunch – crunch. She didn't sell the photocopiers – she did the very small accounts and fucked Mr Granger the owner every Friday night after their Bridge club. They were both in their forties. Lisa was okay actually – it was just that I had no interest in seeing people I had to see every day again at night or on weekends. She did try, in fairness to her, to get me out for a piss-up but I always declined. Lisa was from Tipperary, an only child, and she supported her mother who was caught for pension fraud and had her pension

368

revoked. Lisa was small, wore bright electric-blue framed glasses and had tiny plaits in her hair. She sold a fair amount of photocopiers. She did better with the country people than I did. Honestly, in Tipp she had sold photocopiers to farmers and old age pensioners, she sold to people who simply had no use for them just because she told the story of her poor pensionless swollen-ankled mother.

Anyway, to say I can't look at the colour brown any more is an understatement but back to my new job – this job had kinda fallen into my lap by accident. My friend Amy from dance classes was chasing some girl she worked with. She wanted me to sit in the beer garden of O'Donoghue's and make this girl – well, I said 'jealous', she said 'interested'. "Just sit with me and laugh a lot – that's all I need you to do," she begged of me. I did. She bought me two pints of Coors Light in return. I couldn't believe it but it worked. They are still going out together, believe it or not. Now, Alison, that's her, just thinks we are a couple of sickos – which we are, I suppose. So it just sort of snowballed from there. Word of mouth from Amy firstly and I make a few possible girlfriends jealous but then it took off with the lads. I started getting texts to help them out. Innocent stuff just like with Amy – sitting in a beer garden or asking them to dance in a club. It was starting to get really crazy so that's when I decided to charge for my services.

First paying job was to stop a guy called Kevin. We had arranged our timing to perfection. I had to 'bump' into him at the top of Grafton Street and make out like I was an ex-girlfriend. I had to tell him that I wanted him back, that I had never stopped loving him – while the new girlfriend looked on horrified. I charged €50 for that. It was a bit cringey. However, I only came out with €200 after tax in the brown job. This took me fifteen minutes.

The second job I did after Kevin I charged double. Dan. Dan wanted to take me to his brother's wedding. Grand, I thought – it was only by the airport and it was essentially a free meal and some free booze. I borrowed a dress from one of the girls in the studio. I went. Dan was a perfect gentleman. He had emailed me a list of how we met etc the few days before and he collected me in a taxi the morning of the wedding and paid for my taxi home. Dan was wheelchair-bound and the nicest fella you could ever imagine. I wouldn't have minded kissing him but I think he imagined it was a bit of a *Pretty Woman* situation, and really I was no hooker. This was my business, plus I'd never had enough interest or, if I'm honest, pleasure from sex. I charged Dan €150. Dan has another wedding actually at the end of the month and I'm going along with him again. He's becoming more adventurous though – he wants me to say I have changed jobs from the last time and I'm now modelling for Assets.

Now bless Dan, but I'm no model. I'm not exactly model thin. I was once, but it never bothers me in the slightest that I am not now. I associate thinning with ill-health, hunger, dissatisfaction and unhappiness. I am a happy Size 14, which I consider by the way to be a normal size. Ciara tells me that a 10 is a normal size. Ciara is probably a Size 6. My stomach is pudgy, I will admit that – it rolls over my waistband and therefore I don't wear tight tops so I don't subject others to it. It's not like a baker's dough rolled out before it transforms into a crispy delicious loaf – it's just a bit of extra flesh. It is most likely due to the amount of wine and pints I drink. I have a rule: no drink during the week until Friday night but then I go hell for leather and find when Monday comes I'm more than thankful I don't have to look at a drink for five days.

I might as well describe the rest of me now. My hair is light brown and wavy to my shoulders. No problem to maintain. I rarely straighten it. I have a pretty enough face and I am always complimented on my full lips, recipients of torturous insults as a teenager but now all worthwhile. If I was to tell you who I have been compared to you might take it as gospel, but believe me it's not. I have a very, very, very faint look of Kate Winslet when she is at her 'normal' size, a Size 14. I wear comfortable clothes that suit my shape. I usually wear baggy boy jeans and white vest tops with loose cardigans over them. I love coloured cardigans. Someday I want a red cashmere cardigan. There was one in Avoca opposite where I used to sell the photocopiers. I used to go in on my lunch break and just stroke it. Like a child in a petting zoo.

Did I mention yet I also have a very strong Dublin accent? A *hard* accent, I'm told, as though it's not a good thing. I happen to like my accent. I am who I am. Ciara, the aforementioned sister, practises her vowels. She sounds like Eliza Doolittle up in her bedroom drawling on about the Rain in Spain. She sounds ridiculous and you might say to me 'That's not fair – isn't she trying to better herself?' But why? Her accent is perfect. How is she bettering herself by the sounds leaving her mouth differently? She is still saying the exact same things. I loved Imelda May – I kept leaving articles on her lying around for Ciara to read. She didn't have to better herself. She was the best. I have been told on occasions at various interviews that my accent is difficult to understand. It really isn't.

I hadn't moved too far from home when I eventually

was able to move out, from the *flats* in Ringsend over the bridge to the *apartments* in Ringsend. A six-minute walk but worlds apart. I loved Ringsend but, as I said, I am a bit of a loner and you can't be a loner in Ringsend. Everyone knows you. Everyone knows your ma and your da, your granny and yer granddad, yer first-second-third-fourth cousins once removed, what you bought in the chemist yesterday. And they stop and talk. They natter. I could have got a flat in our block when Mrs Heaney in Number 142A died but I didn't want it. I wanted to live around the area yet still be a stranger. The apartments were perfect. The blow-ins, as they were referred to locally, all lived there. The day I moved in I cried. I cried a lot. Bucket-loads. I couldn't believe I had it. It was mine. It didn't smell of his shit.

I had one other thing about me I should probably tell you now: I kind of see flashbacks. A lot. It's become normal to me now but it might seem slightly strange to you. Whenever something happens to me, or I just see something good or bad, I see Jennifer Beals in the movie *Flashdance*. If it's bad I see the image of her falling down at the audition, if it's good I see her moving like a goddess and pointing those dancing fingers at the judges. I don't think it's weird – it's just me. You see, I love dance. I love it like Oprah loves books. It happened to me completely out of the blue the first time I saw *Flashdance* in the Classic cinema in Harold's Cross when I was fifteen years old and feeling hopeless. It blew me away. If you are not familiar with the film it's about this girl with no family connections, a Pittsburgh girl with two jobs, one as a welder and one as an exotic dancer. She had a dream to get into the prestigious Pittsburgh Conservatory of Dance. Now don't get me wrong, I don't want to be a professional dancer – God forbid, and I'm not that delusional! I just want to dance. For me. For no one else. I never want to dance in front of other people.

I do dance now. I still can't believe I am doing it when I do it. It's private. I never tell anyone about it. It's mine. Personal. Precious. I took the plunge after Mam left – not straight away – I had too much responsibility minding Ciara and him. But when Ciara was old enough I went into an internet cafe and Googled dance classes. There were a lot. Then I Googled '**What type of dancing is the dancing in Flashdance**'. My answer appeared and I read it slowly on the screen: '**Flash dancing began in the 1920's and 30's as a combination of dancing and acrobatics.**'

I loved that it was a bit of a mix-match. It wasn't classical in its origins. It had evolved. I found a small school, above a bar in Townsend Street that offered classes in 'Modern Dance, Hip Hop, Ballet'. It was run by a very flamboyant gay man called Phillip Speed. Phillip was extraordinary and I loved him from the word go. This was quite unlike me – I never usually trusted people until I got to know them really, really well. Like me, he wasn't from the type of background that saw him having a career in dance. He was originally from Salford, in a rougher part of Manchester, and was bullied for his sexuality most of his life – even ending up in hospital once when they cut his short shorts off him with a Stanley knife and managed to give him a six-inch cut up his leg to his groin in the process which resulted in his losing one of his balls. (I suppose when I tell that story I should say 'testicles'?) He will show you the scar if you ever meet him. He was always draped head to toe in Pineapple Dance Studio clothes. Yellow mainly. He loved teaching and he was brilliant at it. Never, ever, ever does Phillip lose his patience teaching a step or a movement. Never does he give you the impression you simply aren't good enough or you just can't do it. He is encouraging and accepting and fabulous. He comes back with me on a Friday night after classes most weeks and we open a few bottles of wine and watch 1980's movies, like *The Breakfast Club* and *Pretty in Pink*.

The first day I crept into the back of the studio my face burned red (it is a function room with a wooden floor but Phillip insists we call it 'the studio') I was mortified. I saw a few people warming up and I went to run for the door. What was I doing here? I couldn't dance! I was such a freak! As I put my hand on the tarnished gold doorknob I felt a hand on my shoulder.

"Hey, chuck, why don't you just sit this one out and watch?" Phillip gave me a huge smile and I shook my head.

"Ah no . . . thanks but I think it's a waste of time, I – I have – I have never danced." Jesus, why was my face so red? I could feel it burning.

"Oh, you have, chuck!" He raised his hand very slowly and isolated his index finger from the rest of his fingers. Then he brought it to the front of his head and tapped it every so lightly about twenty times before simply saying: "In here."

I sat.